I0686198

Of Kings and Dragons

Book One

The Emerald Throne

© 2025 Aiden Kortjohn

All rights reserved.

No part of this book may be reproduced, distributed, or transmitted in any form or by any means,

including photocopying, recording, or other electronic or mechanical methods,

without the prior written permission of the author, except in the case of brief quotations

embodied in critical reviews and certain other noncommercial uses permitted by copyright law.

Of Kings and Dragons is a work of fiction. Names, characters, places, and incidents are either

the product of the author's imagination or are used fictitiously. Any resemblance to actual

persons, living or dead, or actual events is purely coincidental.

ISBN 979-8-9936416-0-7

ISBN 979-8-9936416-1-4

Cover Design © MadliArt

The Kingdom of Lungalea

The Barren North

The Home of the Elders

Barra

Balora

The Last Palace

Mt. Morta

Bukatta

The Golden Desert

Lungala

Contents

Prologue

I

At the end of the reign of Arturus III, the Kingdom of Lungalea went to war.

II

It was a golden day throughout the Emerald Kingdom; one of celebration that would be remembered as one of great tragedy. On the day the land began to burn, King Arturus III was celebrating his twin children, Roserené and Davit, on their thirteenth birthday. The king had invited the entirety of his capital city, Lungala, into his brilliant marble palace to partake in the festivities. The city was alive and flowing with energy in a way it had not been in years. Carts and games were put up outside of the palace so that even those who could not fit inside the grand halls could still participate in the joyous occasion. Thousands of citizens flowed through the palace gates, excited to see the ceremony where the royal twins would take the Vows of the Throne before the gathered masses. The celebrations began before the sun rose, and they continued long into the day as the sun climbed high into the sky.

As the blue sky began to turn gold, a single cloaked figure quickly made their way into the royal palace. This figure was not going through the large, open doors that the rest of the city had gone through, but rather a small, hidden path at the back of the palace. They did not want to be seen as they snuck in.

With their knowledge of pathways unknown to most in the kingdom, the cloaked figure quickly crawled into the palace through a small, open window at ground level. The window led to a small stone cellar that, unfortunately for the cloaked intruder, had its floor well below the ground level outside, causing the mysterious figure to drop six feet onto the cold stone floor, losing any subtlety their entrance had. Quickly recovering, the figure sprang back to their feet, brushing any dirt off themselves and removing their cloak, tossing it to the side of the cellar. Clad in the royal green garments of the kingdom and with a freckled face topped with red-brown hair, the young Prince Davit quickly stepped outside of the small, cramped room.

Davit looked around his surroundings as he exited. The massive halls of the royal palace were devoid of any other people. Davit knew this was either a very good sign or a very bad one for his chances of success. He decided that it was a good one. Davit briskly made his way through the palace halls towards the throne room. He thanked himself for deciding to head out of the palace that morning already dressed in his royal garb. So what if he had lost track of time while he was out in the city, playing games and trying food he had never even heard of from all types of assembled stands? Davit knew the Ceremony of the Vows should be bogged down by literal hours of formality. As long as he was quick, he could still make it to the throne room in time for his comparatively small part in it all.

All had been going according to Davit's plan, until the young prince rounded a corner and was instantly filled with dread. At the opposite end of the hall stood his older brother and the heir to the kingdom: Percival. His back was turned, but judging by his blond hair, his similarly royal clothes, and the general way he was standing, Davit knew it was him. Momentarily panicking, the younger prince stopped dead in his tracks. The sound of the halting footsteps on the floor caused Percival's head to snap around. Davit silently cursed himself.

He knew his brother had always been able to hear from fifty feet away what a regular man wouldn't be able to hear from ten. It was a part of his abilities, one Davit found especially annoying.

Percival glared at his younger brother from across the hall, quickly walking towards him. Thinking on his feet, Davit stretched his arms back wide, yawning loudly. "Oh wow, I slept *late* this morning!" he said dramatically, putting all the confidence he could behind the lie.

"Come off it," Percival snapped, walking close to his brother. "We had guards check your room hours ago. You were in the city all day, weren't you?"

Davit did his best to hide his surprise and panic, but the accusation of doing exactly what he actually *had* been doing made the young boy's internal voice scream in terror. Admitting defeat, Davit decided it was best to try to limit his losses. "So, I may have been exploring some stands," he began, holding his arms up defensively. "*Shouldn't* we be exploring the culture of our people?"

Percival rubbed his eyes, not in the mood to deal with his brother's cockiness. "Do you have any idea what time it is?" he asked angrily.

"Actually, I do," Davit retorted, stepping past his older brother. "There is just enough time for us to make it there before the Vows, but not if you keep holding me up."

Percival stayed put. "The ceremony is over, Davit," he called behind his brother, frustrated.

Davit paused, suddenly feeling unwell. *That couldn't be right*, he thought, turning. "What?" Yes, he had stayed in the city longer than he should have, but he rushed back as quickly as he could. There still should have been time!

The heir to the throne narrowed his eyes at his brother. "You really think you get to have everything, don't you?" He scoffed at Davit's entitlement. "Half of the honorees were missing. The ceremony ended hours ago. I bet your day of fun didn't account for that, did it? Only *one* of you took the Vows of the Throne."

"Rose," Davit said under his breath, thinking of his twin sister. The consequence of his actions was only beginning to dawn on him. He thought of his sister having to go through the hours of ceremony in front of hundreds of people by herself, all while he was enjoying himself in the city. He felt awful.

Percival had his arms crossed. "You left her there. It was a duty to be shared by the both of you, but you didn't care. You abandoned her." His voice was laced with anger.

Davit became defensive. The young boy furrowed his brow. "Don't say I don't care about our sister," he objected.

The crown prince made a sound almost like a laugh. "Why not?" he asked. "You certainly don't act like it." Davit clenched his fists at his side, angered.

Before anything more could escalate between the two brothers, a dark-skinned man rounded a nearby corner. "There you two are," the man said to the children. He was wearing the emerald-green armor that immediately distinguished him as a knight of the Crown's Circle. The boys knew this man well. He was Pevincy, their father's closest advisor and friend. "The king has summoned both of you."

Both princes had a different reaction. The pit within Davit's stomach grew exponentially deeper. He knew no matter how bad the confrontation with Percival over his absence had been, the discussion he was about to have with the king would be much worse. Percival, recognizing this fact as well, glared with satisfied anger at his younger brother. "Well, Pevincy," the older of the two siblings said, without taking his gaze off Davit, "we had better not keep our father waiting."

After what felt to Davit an eternity of walking through the marble halls, the three of them arrived at a massive pair of aged wooden doors carved with scenes from the kingdom's history. With Pevincy between the two boys, the aged knight heaved open the heavy doors, and the three of them entered the throne room.

Room did not do justice in describing the extent of the area they had just stepped into. The throne room of Lungalea was closer in size to a grand hall, built entirely out of smooth marble. Stained glass windows lined the extent of the regal chamber, similarly depicting scenes from history and stories the kingdom held dear. At the far end of the room was the largest display of them all, taking up the entire far side room showing the six divine Elder Dragons who had created everything on the continent.

There was no furniture within most of the room. There was only one seat: the emerald throne; a massive column of the precious gem that reached from floor to ceiling. Occupants would have to stand for whatever occasion was being held, basking in the splendor of the throne as it reflected the glimmering sunlight. This made the throne room a wide-open chamber, and as Davit walked, his steps bounced back across the walls, making the young boy feel even smaller. He wrapped his arms around his chest. The throne room was often much colder than the rest of the palace by default, and it did not help that Davit was on edge before he even entered.

Pevincy stopped short behind the two boys. "I shall leave you two here while I attend to other matters," the guard said. "I believe your father would want privacy for this." He nodded his head forward. The two boys looked in the same direction.

At the far end of the throne room stood a flock of five knights, similarly clad in the same green armor as Pevincy. As Percival and Davit approached, the Knights of the Crown's

Circle made way for their arrival, revealing a raised central platform where the Emerald Throne was positioned and where two familiar people were now gathered. Standing on the platform was the boys' sister, the princess Rose. Her hair, the same color as Davit's, covered one of her eyes, as it always did, and her twin brother noticed her fidgeting hands underneath her royal regalia as he approached. Davit flashed his sister a playful smile, but she turned away from his gaze, wearing a look of equal scorn and hurt. Davit's face went flat, his unease over the entire situation worsening. And he had good reason to be nervous, for standing next to his sister on the throne platform was King Arturus III of Lungalea himself.

The good king resembled Percival far more than his other two children, with his stoney features and mane of golden hair. But the noble lord still held the same caring, ocean-blue eyes that connected him to all three of his children. Arturus looked down at his two sons from his raised platform as they approached. "Percival," he said in a regal voice, looking at his eldest. The king's head turned. "Davit."

"Father," Davit said weakly, the king's piercing gaze drilling right through him. The two brothers knelt to one knee in the presence of the king. Even Davit, who usually always had a quip, did the action as a reflex, silently. He knew remembering his manners was the best chance he had at getting out of this situation.

Arturus continued to look at his two boys. "You may rise, Percival," said the king in his strong, flat tone.

"Thank you, my lord father," the heir said as he arose. Davit cursed his brother silently for remembering the formal way for the children to address the king, making his own half-startled greeting look even worse by comparison. The young boy was under no false impression about his grim fate with his father, particularly because he noticed he was the only one *not* given permission to stand.

Arturus waved a hand at the five green knights surrounding him. "Some privacy, good sirs, if you would please." At the command, each of the men and women of the Circle saluted their king by crossing their chest with an arm. Then, the five knights marched in unison to the door of the grand hall, giving the four royals enough space to speak without being overheard in the grand room.

Davit's eyes were glued to the floor. In the top half of his vision, he saw his father calmly step towards him. "Today was the day you were supposed to recite the Vows that welcome you into royalty, Davit," the king began. "Instead, you ran, shaming your family in front of the assembled kingdom. But more than that, you abandoned nearly three thousand years of tradition to go gallivanting in the city. I want to know why."

The king's eyes were a storm in the middle of the ocean, and Davit could feel the turmoil. The young prince felt like he could throw up at any moment. He wanted to be anywhere else in the world but there, in front of his father. But Davit was too nervous to think of a lie. His tongue was a desert. So, he had no choice but to tell his father the truth.

"Father, I don't *want* any of this," the prince said, still kneeling. He looked up to meet the king's gaze. "I love you, and I love our family," Davit said sincerely. "But I did not ask to be born with a thousand-year history already laid out for me to inherit, and I don't *want* it! Out in the city is when I am not weighed down by centuries of tradition. It is where I get to be myself." Davit had never told his father what he was saying now, or anyone else besides Rose for that matter, but as he continued speaking, he realized he couldn't stop. "I'm sorry." Davit met his father's eyes, seemingly pleading. "You are meant to rule. You and Percival." He glanced at his brother. The crown prince was watching silently with a look of scorn towards his brother, but deep down the seeds of longing subtly influenced his expression. "But me?" Davit shook his head. "I'm not."

Arturus looked silently at his youngest child. His face was torturously unreadable to Davit. It was something the king prided himself on, always thinking through his decisions, never leading with emotion. Finally, surprisingly, Arturus' face softened, and the king began to chuckle. This unnerved Davit even more. Out of all the reactions his father could have shown, he wasn't expecting this. The king looked at his son with a half-smile, wrinkles at the edges of his eyes. "I understand," he said softly. "I see more of your mother in you every day."

The king brought Davit to his feet, his arm on his shoulder. Davit was stunned. He was expecting shouting for doing something so foolish, or at the very least a quick and decisive punishment. But instead, his father was *smiling*. Arturus looked his son in the eye and sighed. "Davit, no matter what path you choose in life, be that the crown…" The king paused. "Or something else, you will *always* be met with challenges. You cannot run from everything." Arturus wrapped an arm around Davit's shoulders. "I was hoping today would be a grand day for all three of you." He motioned a hand at Percival, and then Rose. "Your siblings have passed their challenges. They are ready for the responsibility I am about to give them. But you, my son…" Arturus looked back at his boy, a warm smile still on the king's face. "You need more time. You are not yet ready."

The comment burned Davit, but he couldn't quite say why. He couldn't fight against it; his father was correct. Yet hearing the confirmation from the king's mouth made Davit's failure more real to the young boy. It made it more personal. Hurt, Davit did what he always did when he felt attacked: he defended himself.

The young prince pulled away from his father's embrace. "Maybe I will *never* be ready, then," he said bitterly. His brow furrowed. "Maybe I never *want* to be ready." He pointed hotly at his two siblings, standing on the platform in front of him. "If their responsibilities chain them closer to the crown, good on them." Davit shook his head. "But not for me." With that, the young prince turned sharply and walked toward the throne room doors.

"Davit," King Arturus called after his son, but it did no good. The young boy was too frustrated to hear or think clearly. He stormed past the group of knights by the doors and slammed them shut behind him, sending a reverberation throughout the entire chamber. Davit's heart was racing outside the throne room. Within seconds, he found himself blinking back tears. This only made the prince angrier, cursing himself for crying when he couldn't even say why. With a huff, he once again made his way through the palace halls.

Back in the throne room, King Arturus sighed, looking at the space in front of the doors where his son had been just seconds ago. Percival walked to the king's side. "I apologize for him, my lord father," the crown prince said, looking bitterly at the same spot as the king.

"No, Percival," Arturus corrected. "Davit has not found yet how he fits into the Divines' grander scheme. But he will one day. He just needs to grow." With another pained sigh, the king turned to face his two children. His face turned, once again adopting a warm smile. "But you two have already proven yourselves ready." He walked up to his daughter on the raised platform. "Roserené, you did very well today. I could not be prouder."

Rose smiled from ear to ear at the compliment. "Thank you, Father," she said humbly, still in her exaggerated royal clothes from the Ceremony of the Vows.

Arturus turned his gaze to his son. "And you, Percival." He placed a hand on the prince's shoulder, meeting his eye. "Every day I look at you and see a better king than I could ever hope to be."

Percival lowered his head to the ground in recognition. "You honor me, my lord," he said.

The king looked on with a happy smile for a moment longer. Then he turned his gaze back to his daughter. "Rose, could you bring me the satchel I gave you earlier?"

Without hesitation, the princess nodded. Taking a large brown bag from behind the large emerald pillar that was a throne, Rose made her way towards her father and brother. Her progress was strained, however, as she had to carry the satchel with two hands, still just barely holding it above the ground. Finally, Rose placed the bag gently between the three of them. "Whatever is in there is heavy," she huffed.

Arturus laughed softly. "Yes, I imagine they would be." The king knelt and undid the straps that held the satchel closed. "Your mother wanted you to have these when you three were ready," Arturus went on as he worked. "I had hoped to give them to you all at once, but…" He sighed. "Davit will get his when he is ready." Rose and Percival glanced at each other. Their mother had died from illness years ago when they were both very young. They each wondered what she could have left them that was so important.

Suddenly, there was a commotion on the other side of the throne room. A sound like muted thunder filled the hall as the wooden doors were thrown open once again. The knights of the Circle drew their weapons. The king and his children turned their attention to the noise.

At the entrance, a man in a hooded black cloak stood in the circle of emerald-green knights. The distance was too great for the three royals to make out any details about the figure; he appeared to just be silently standing in the open doorway. "Identify yourself!" one of the Crown knights barked at the mysterious intruder. They did not reply.

"State your business!" another ordered.

The cloaked figure waved a single hand in the air. On command, a bright column of orange flame lit the space around them. Flames so intense the three royals could feel the heat on the other end of the room knocked each of the Crown knights backwards multiple feet. Within a few seconds, the intruder stood on an unopposed path to the king and his children. Each knight writhed slowly on the ground, alive but dazed.

Arturus felt panic grip him, and his instincts engaged. In one swift motion, the king grabbed his hidden weapon from behind his throne, a lesson he'd kept with him from his days as a soldier. A six-foot-long, polished bronze spear now in his hands, Arturus stepped in front of his children, shielding them from the aggressive intruder slowly approaching.

Percival sidestepped the king. "Father, let me help you!" The crown prince was wearing what was trying to be a determined expression, but the fifteen-year-old royal was failing to hide his sudden fear. Still, his fists were clenched at his sides. Small arcs of faint blue electricity sputtered to life, running up and down the length of his arm.

"No, Percival!" the king snapped in a dire tone. His eyes flashed from the approaching figure to his son multiple times a second. "Stay behind me!"

"But!" Percival pleaded.

"I command you!" Arturus roared. He would not take any risks to endanger his children. Especially when he knew so little about the enemy in front of him. As soon as Percival returned behind the king, he turned his attention back to the cloaked figure who could control fire. The king pointed the tip of his weapon at the man, who was now just barely twice the weapon's length away. "I do not know who you are, but this need not end in violence." Unlike his son, Arturus' voice was loud and steady without a hint of fear.

The cloaked man stopped. "Have you forgotten me?" a strong, cold voice from the darkness of the hood asked the king. "I don't blame you. The years have been long…" The intruder raised their hands and brought down their hood from around their head. In front of the three royals now was a middle-aged man with a thin, boney face. His straw-blond hair was cut just above his black eyes. "Brother."

III

As Davit walked the halls, audibly cursing as the tears blurred his vision, he suddenly heard an ear-splitting ringing within his own skull. The hair on the back of his neck stood straight, and it felt like there were bells clanging in his head. He clamped his hands to his ears, but that did not diminish the harsh noise. He shut his eyes tight, but then a pit deeper than anything he had ever felt created itself in his stomach. He thought back to the throne room he had just left. His father. His sister and his brother. They were all in danger. He didn't know how or why, but he was certain of it.

Before he even had time to think, Davit found himself running back. The young boy who was not ready for the responsibility of life was now running faster than he ever had toward what he knew, somehow, was terrible danger. He rushed past a man who may have called out his name, asking him to stop, what was wrong. But Davit was not sure of this; he couldn't even remember the man's face. All that mattered was the throne room.

IV

King Arturus had a horrible realization. He tightened his grip around his weapon, still pointed at the man in front of him, the man who had called him brother. The man who he had begun to recognize, despite the progress of time. The intruder wore a blank expression, unfazed.

"Brother?" Percival almost gasped at the word. He looked at Rose, who had shrunk behind their father. She wore a face warped with confusion. Then Percival turned back to the king. "Father, you told us your brother died years ago."

Arturus gripped his spear tightly, slowly moving towards the strange man in front of them. "He did," he confirmed. The king glared at the man. "My brother, Ahaax, died at the hands of a madman twenty-five years ago." Arturus glared; he and the man had locked eyes, ocean blue and dark brown. "He died in my arms."

The mysterious man cocked his head ever so slightly at the king, as if he were a curiosity to be examined. "Look at me, Arturus," he began. Walking slowly, the man extended a single hand and opened his palm. Amazingly, a small flame was dancing in the space he had created. "How else could you explain this? It is me, brother." His voice was soft, almost familiar. But the two children standing behind their father could detect something deeply wrong with the man. Their heads would not stop buzzing since his arrival.

Arturus shook his head as he looked at the impossible flame the man had conjured. "It's not possible," he said. "Ahaax would never have done that." Neither of the two children understood what their father and the man were talking about, but they both could tell based on the king's expression: he was unsure. His spear dropped just slightly. He began to doubt himself. The man was just steps away from him now, as if Arturus were too preoccupied to notice.

Ahaax nodded, his face unnaturally even. Finally close enough, he was able to rest a hand lightly on the king's shoulder. He leaned in and whispered something into his ear. Something the children couldn't hear. Arturus' spear lowered to the floor.

The king pulled back just enough for his children to see his face. He was wearing a mix of shock and fear. "Brother?" he asked.

It was over in less than a second. There was a knife in Ahaax's hand. Thrust into the side of the king. Arturus gasped, a breath of air escaping his punctured lung. Ahaax clasped his hand tightly onto his brother's shoulder, looking him directly in his deep blue eyes. He pulled out his knife, letting the red-stained blade fall to the floor, his mission accomplished. The king staggered backwards and fell against a wall, blood coming to his lips, trying to find words and trying harder to speak them. His spear clattered to the ground.

Rose gasped; Percival was stunned. Both were in a state of shock, and neither could move. They couldn't process what they had just witnessed. Their father would get back up any moment and strike down this imposter with his mighty weapon. But the king did not.

Ahaax sighed as he watched his brother fall slowly against a pillar. The intruding man turned his gaze to the two children. His face hardened, and the man made his way towards them. Meanwhile, each child was able to see what was happening in front of them, but they were still rooted in place.

There was a pained cry at the far end of the hall. "No!" All eyes turned to Davit as he panted in the open doorway. The young boy looked around. He saw his two siblings with tears running down their faces. His eyes turned to the strange man in the black cloak whom he had never seen before. Finally, Davit's eyes rested on a huddled mass propped against a wall. His father. He was too late.

His brother's scream offered Percival enough of a chance to break free from his stupor. Acting on instinct, the crown prince raised his hand towards Ahaax. Immediately a bolt of blue-white lightning shot forth from Percival's open palm and made direct contact with the intruder's chest. The cloaked man was flung across the room. Sliding across the marble floor, he came to a rest when he collided with a pillar on the opposite side of the room, momentarily dazed. Percival fell to the ground, still conscious but drained of his energy.

Rose dropped to her brother's side, shaking his arm, trying to get him to stand, tears streaming down her face. She was barely able to breathe. Percival groaned.

Davit ran across the hall, tripping over himself multiple times. He slid on his knees towards his father. What he saw frightened him more than anything the young boy had ever experienced. The once powerful face of the king was now almost paper white. Davit looked down at his father's robes. They were marked by a dark red stain that was frighteningly large. Davit placed his hands over the red, trying desperately to stop the bleeding, but more and more kept flowing, onto the robes and his hands.

"Father!" the boy sobbed, panicked. He was now trying to see through a swell of tears; he was practically blind. He looked frantically around the room, but his only allies were his barely conscious brother and his sister trying desperately to revive him. "Help!" Davit shouted around the hall. "Someone! Someone please help!" He turned his attention back to the dying king. "Father. I'm so sorry. I'm so sorry."

Arturus turned his head towards his son weakly. He opened his mouth and tried to offer reassurance. Everything would be alright. But he was cut off.

With a sound that quickly became as loud as thunder, multiple pairs of boots rushed into the hall. A line of palace guards clad in silver armor stood in the wide entrance, crossbows at the ready. At their head was a single man adorned in green plate. Pevincy had brought his finest men. The head guard scoured the room with his sharp eyes, absorbing every detail, looking at Percival and Rose on the raised platform, then to Davit and the dying king. Finally his gaze landed on the black lump in the corner that was Ahaax. Frighteningly, the man who had attacked the king was rising shakily to his feet. Hunched over, Ahaax looked at the line of palace guards now in front of him. Pevincy returned the glare. The old guard looked at his men. "Nock!" he shouted at them, raising a gloved hand. All of the soldiers loaded their arrows into the crossbows.

Ahaax watched weakly as all this happened. He did not move. His eyes turned for one final time towards the dying king, and Davit. The young prince would never forget the face he saw: one of ruthless determination. Ahaax brought his gaze back to the palace guards. Pevincy brought down his hand. "Loose!"

In a swift motion, Ahaax flung his back cape around himself and was instantly engulfed by a fireball that reached the ceiling. When the flames cleared, the intruder was gone, and the stained glass window he had been standing in front of was broken. Pevincy rushed over and looked down. "Damn!" the guard shouted. "He's gone!" He rushed back to his men, shouting, "I want every soldier we have stationed at every possible siege tunnel, inside the palace and out. Now, now!"

On the raised throne platform, Percival slowly opened his eyes more fully. Rose sobbed out of a mix of shock and relief that her brother was fully conscious. With great effort, the two stood as a pair, Percival's arm over his sister. The two limped to their fallen father, quietly sobbing as they walked. Arturus smiled weakly as his son and daughter collapsed at his side. Each of the royal children was bawling. The buzzing in their heads was slowly fading, Ahaax was no longer in sight, and the danger seemed to have passed. But now they were left with a far worse reality. Each of the children looked down at their pale father.

Pevincy quickly dismissed his line of men and rushed to the four. He fell to his knees and looked around, almost frantic at the three children surrounding him. "Are you injured?" he asked no one in particular. He was met with only sobs. The old guard's eyes fell reluctantly to the pale face of the king. "Arturus, hold on. We will get your healers at once. If we hurry we can…"

The king shook his head, tired. With what little strength he had left, he lifted a finger to point past Pevincy. The head of the guard looked to where he was pointing: a brown spot on the ground lying a few feet away. "The satchel, what…?" he asked curiously.

Arturus nodded weakly.

Pevincy bowed his head. "Of course." One last instruction. He stood and quickly retrieved the heavy satchel, making sure he used what little time he had left wisely.

The lead guard gently rested the bag at the king's side. Arturus smiled, his eyes shimmering like the ocean they reflected. He struggled to raise his hand to open the satchel. "Let me, old friend," Pevincy said. A single tear slid from the guard's eye. The king did not object. Pevincy grabbed the satchel and opened its top. He looked inside, and the royal children saw the remaining hope leave his eyes. He looked back at the king. "Arturus," Pevincy pleaded. But the king gave him one final look, a plea of his own. Pevincy sighed and emptied the bag of its contents one by one.

He reached in and brought out a yellow, oval-shaped object with a gray mist swirling inside of it. He gently set the object on the ground, then reached back into the satchel, bringing out a similar object, except this one colored dark brown, with veins of leafy green running all along its side. After setting this down, Pevincy reached into the bag a final time, bringing out an oval like the first two, but this one a solid shade of blue, the color of the deepest oceans. With all the objects on the ground, Pevincy arranged them side by side next to the king.

The children all furrowed their brows, confused. "Eggs?" Rose sniveled.

Pevincy nodded grimly. "Dragon eggs."

"Dragon eggs?" Percival asked through a sob. He looked at the king. "Father... what..."

Arturus held up a finger, silencing his son. Weakly, he pointed from Percival slowly to the yellow, fog-filled egg lying on the ground. Percival looked to the egg, confused. He turned his attention back to Arturus. "Father..."

Arturus did not listen. He moved his finger to Rose, who was sobbing quietly. The king pointed at her, then slowly to the brown egg, flush with green, on the floor. "Father, please..." Rose whispered.

Arturus refused to listen. He felt weaker by the second. Finally, he pointed at Davit.

Davit grabbed his father's hand. "Father, please," the boy sobbed. "I'm so sorry. Please don't leave. Please." He could barely see his father's smile with all the tears in his eyes. Arturus softly positioned his hand on his son's face. He used his thumb to wipe away his tears.

Then, slowly, the king's hand fell to the ground. His face went blank. "Father?" Davit asked. He squeezed the king's hand tighter than he ever had before. It was so cold. It didn't squeeze back. Davit let the air out of his lungs. There was no life behind the king's eyes.

Pevincy took a shaky breath. Cautiously, he held out a hand in front of him. Hesitating, he rested it softly on the king's eyelids, closing them one final time. He dropped his head. "The king... is dead," he whispered, barely audible.

Each child wailed. Pevincy grabbed all of them, wrapping them in his embrace as he held back tears of his own. King Arturus of Lungalea had been murdered, and the world turned darker.

The sobbing continued for an amount of time that never seemed to end. Pevincy held each of the children in his arms, consoling them the best he could. He had become a second parent to them after the death of their mother, and now they were orphans.

Eventually, Percival found he physically had no tears left to shed. The crown prince's eyes landed onto a glowing yellow object behind Pevincy: the dragon egg his father directed him towards in his last seconds alive. The mythical object almost appeared to sparkle in the golden sunlight filtering through the windows.

Without realizing, Percival found that he was walking towards the egg, almost in a trance. It was a move based purely on instinct, almost as if he wasn't the one moving his legs. Suddenly, his hand felt like it was burning. He was startled. He did the first thing that came to his mind, another instinctual reaction. He placed his hand on the dragon's egg.

As soon as he rested his hand on it, the burning sensation Percival had felt vanished, as if plunging his hand in ice water. Where Percival had touched the egg, a large crack emerged, then another, and then another, until the egg was completely covered in cracks and split in half. What Percival saw next made his jaw drop. His siblings and Pevincy turned their attention to him.

There was a small creature lying in the shattered eggshells, about the length of a forearm. It raised its spikey, fist-sized head towards Percival and chirped. The prince's eyes widened, and something happened in the back of his mind. Looking at the creature, it was like he discovered a new aspect of himself in an instant. The baby dragon was golden yellow and had electric blue eyes. Surprisingly, it didn't have scales on the vast majority of its body, but feathers the color of the sun. The little thing only had two rear legs. Shakily it stood, using its two wings near its front to balance it. The small dragon sat on its hind legs and weakly stretched out its feathered wings while it made another small squeaking sound. Percival slowly extended his hand. The dragon looked at it for a second, tilting its head. Then it peacefully shut its eyes and pressed its head into the boy's palm, nuzzling his hand. "Gods be good," Percival whispered in disbelief.

Rose was watching all this happen silently. Slowly, she shifted her gaze to her own brown egg that her father had pointed out. She shuffled quietly towards the brown oval lying on the floor. Cautiously, she kneeled and outstretched her hand. She began to feel the same burning Percival had moments before. She touched the egg, getting relief for the sensation. This egg also formed many cracks and split in half at her touch, but the dragon inside was much different than Percival's.

The dragon was the same size as the one that had hatched from Percival's yellow egg, maybe slightly bigger, but that was where the similarities ended. Rose's dragon was a light brown, with big green eyes and a head shaped like a box. The only spikes it had were two small white nubs behind its square head. This dragon had four legs, each thick and sturdy like small tree trunks. Its wings, while it did have two situated on its back, seemed relatively small in regards to the rest of its body. The dragon looked up at the girl who had just hatched it, who herself was staring back at the little creature in awe. The dragon puffed a light plume of smoke from its nostrils and began to circle Rose's ankles, nuzzling its head on her legs. Despite everything that had happened to her, Rose couldn't help but giggle slightly at the odd sensation.

The two hatchling dragons soon caught sight of each other. Stretching their freshly hatched legs, they slowly made their way over to the other. Percival's dragon chirped while Rose's made a deep humming sound. Rose's dragon nudged

Percival's with its head, and in response the yellow dragon playfully batted at the brown with its wing.

Rose, Percival, and Pevincy were all watching this scene with utter fascination and awe. No one had seen a dragon for centuries. Davit was still kneeling close to his father, resting his forehead on his, his eyes closed. Percival and Rose turned away from their dragons and looked at their brother. Immediately reality came back to both of them.

"Davit," Percival began lightly. His brother opened his eyes and looked at him. Percival motioned towards the deep blue egg lying on the floor. The only egg that had not hatched.

Davit got the message. He stood, shaking his head. He looked frightened. "No." He held back tears. "No, I can't. I *won't*."

Percival stepped towards his brother, hand outstretched. "Davit," he said softly.

Davit flinched away. "No, Percival," he insisted. He glanced at his father lying lifeless against the wall, but it hurt too much. Instead, he turned his gaze back to his brother. "He said I wasn't ready. And he was right. If I had been here, I could've done something."

Pevincy stepped forward. "Don't do that to yourself, Prince Davit," he begged. "You're a boy. There's nothing you could have done to prevent this." He placed a light hand on Davit's shoulder, looking into his blue eyes. "Don't go down this path, please. It has ruined too many people."

Davit shook his head, stepping out of his reach. He took a shaky breath in. He glanced at his father again but quickly turned his attention to the egg near his feet. He pointed at the deep blue object. "Pevincy, I want that egg destroyed. Do you understand?"

Pevincy strained his face. "Davit," he began.

"Do you understand?"

"I…" Pevincy began, but stopped. He was obligated to follow the orders of the royal family. He lowered his head. "I do, my prince."

"Good," Davit said. He looked around. The cold of the room was suddenly biting at his skin. "I need to get out of here." With that, the youngest of the royal children ran out of the throne room once again.

"Davit!" Rose called, but Percival took her hand and shook his head, looking pained.

"He won't change his mind," Percival said sadly. He knew this was true. They both did. Still, part of Percival wondered if he could have said something to Davit to convince him, and another part of him wondered why he didn't try. After a few seconds of looking at his own dragon in a numb state, Percival got up and walked over to Davit's blue dragon egg. Slowly he kneeled and put his hand on the egg, but nothing happened. He did not feel the same burning sensation and the egg did not crack; it was cold. Percival sighed. "It can only be him," he said sadly. He looked at Pevincy. "Do not destroy this egg," he said.

Pevincy walked over to the young boy and nodded. He rested a hand on his shoulder. "I know," he began grimly. "You're going to need him for what lies ahead. That was the last thing your father knew."

Percival bowed his head. He was right. He might not have realized it at the time, but he would soon understand the truth in everything the old guard had just said. With the death of the king, war would descend upon the land.

V

Weeks after the death of King Arturus, across Lungalea, on a red mountaintop under red skies, a small gray tent had been assembled. Inside the small fabric structure, Ahaax sat on a cot, looking forward absently. The man who had murdered a king, usurped a kingdom. At least, that was his plan. But his plan had failed. Ahaax crushed his hand into a fist. Being driven away by the palace guard was not his intention. He should be king by now. He *needed* to be king by now. But all of that would change soon, he knew. What he was about to do would change history forever.

Ahaax heard the light sound of footsteps approaching his tent. He looked up and was greeted by the sight of a stout man with half a head of gray hair and a bushy beard to match. Red tattoos drawing lines spanned the length of both his arms until they were covered by gray rags that had been thrown together to form a robe. "You look troubled, my friend," the old man said in a kind voice.

Ahaax remained emotionless. "I am troubled by our lack of progress, Abominus," he agreed. Turning his look to the man, he asked, "How goes your work?"

The little man nodded uneasily. "Nearly complete," he said with a hint of nervousness. "Come." Ahaax got up from his seat, and the two men walked farther along the mountainside until they reached the top, the edge of a massive crater twice as deep as it was wide. At the bottom was a maroon fog swirling, hiding the actual depth of the pit, making it appear potentially bottomless. Thunder would crackle occasionally in the mist. It was a swirling storm.

The two men looked down. "This is where the war ended," Abominus started. "If you believe the legends. Where the five victors banished Them for their crimes." He looked at Ahaax. "Finding the exact area took much research. Technically, there are remains of Them scattered through all the ground of the land, but I believe this is where they remain strongest."

Ahaax nodded, not looking up from the red haze of the crater. "Banished… until today."

Abominus tilted his head, grimacing. "Yes…" He paused. "Ahaax. This is very old magic. Something like this, it has never been tried before. This act marks the line over what man can even control. Even if we succeed… especially if we succeed, we must bear the consequences of our actions. If our gamble fails…"

Ahaax shook his head. "No, Abominus," he said, determined. "We cannot stop now. Tell me what I must do."

The old man sighed. "The spell is cast," he said. "I've used my magic to weaken Their bonds. Now you must only say the words I taught you." He paused, clearly troubled. "I recommend that we both show Them the proper reverence." With that, the stout man kneeled slowly, facing the chasm before him.

Ahaax nodded. "Of course," he lied. Like he could ever truly see even this *creature* as an equal to him. Then, the king slayer kneeled toward the crater as well. He breathed in deeply. His life, and the history of the entire kingdom, was about to be irreversibly changed. "I, Ahaax, son of Oriond, brother of Arturus," he began strongly. He paused, reflecting on the weight of his new titles. "Lord of Lungalea, King of the Lungaleans and High Sovereign of the Emerald Lands, free you, the great Elder Dragon Venerus, Harbinger of Death, Bane of Your Kin. May you rise from your prison and our fates be one and the same."

Abominus made a quick movement with his hands. The tattoos on his arms began to glow the same shade as the colored mist below the two men. Red light appeared and surrounded Ahaax, who made a sharp, pained gasp as it entered him, then just as quickly exited. Once the light was out of Ahaax, it had taken the shape of a man. The red light was still for a moment. Then it dove into the pit of the volcano. Ahaax fell from his knees and lay flat on the ground.

"Ahaax," Abominus asked, hesitantly reaching out a hand near him. "Ahaax, are you alright?"

The man on the ground snapped out of his daze. "What happened? Did it work?"

As he said this, the light in the crater of the volcano disappeared. From a cloud directly above the mountain, a magenta bolt of lightning came down and made continuous, unbroken contact with the bottom of the pit. The two men shielded their eyes from the blinding light. After a few seconds, the bolt of pure energy dissipated, and all was quiet except for the faint buzzing of electricity remaining. Then the ground shook violently. The two men had to hold their hands out to steady themselves. Abominus fell on his back, but Ahaax managed to stay upright with great effort. The rock at the bottom of the crater began to crack. Ahaax stepped backwards.

A deafening roar emanated from the crater. A massive, dark, and leathery wing tipped with a single red talon rose and grabbed the edge of the pit, and then another. A gigantic head slowly rose from the crater. It was slim, made of very visible bone with skin stretched tightly across it, dark as night. On top of the head were two horns as big as a human was tall, swept backwards. The eyes were red, the color of blood, with a slit of magenta in the center. The dragon's maw was lined with teeth, each as big as a grown man's hand, the same color as the eye, almost glowing.

Once the dragon was fully out of the crater, Ahaax was able to view all of it. They were larger than any dragon mankind had on record by far. They only had two legs, with Their two massive wings assisting Their walking. Their scales were pitch black, except for the veins of sickly pink running along Their wings and body, and They had spikes the same glowing red color running along Their head to Their tail. At the end of Their monstrous length, Their tail was ended with a barb like that of a scorpion. It took all the strength Ahaax had not to cower before the terrible creature. The mere sight of the Elder Dragon instilled in him a primal terror; every one of his natural instincts was screaming at him to run and hide, that staying in this being's presence was deeply wrong. But there he stood, rooted to the ground. Abominus was frozen in a combination of fear and awe.

After taking a long, shaky breath that sounded like the rattling of bones, the dragon opened Their mouth and began to speak. "**Sufass, aknar de sufass paluss,**" They uttered in a voice that shook the earth. They reared up on Their hind legs, opened Their mouth, and shot a bolt of pure, concentrated magenta lightning into the night sky. The Elder Dragon Venerus then emitted another powerful roar so strong that birds from the bottom of the mountain flew out of their trees. They had broken Their bonds. The Elder Dragon was free.

Venerus fell to Their wings. They looked around, finally noticing Ahaax and Abominus below Them with Their frightening red eyes. A piercing sensation clawed its way into the two men's heads like metal scraping on metal, sharp, vicious teeth gnashing in their brains. Venerus swished Their barbed tail. *You,* Their voice spoke in the two men's minds. *Your language. It is primitive: easy to learn.* Venereus brought Their pointed skull down mere feet from Ahaax. *Why have I been freed by man?*

Ahaax hesitated for a second, but only a second. It was enough for Venerus. Their face molded into a grin; They were getting pleasure from this fear. "Elder Venerus," Ahaax began strongly, making sure not to let the dragon get any more of a sense of his true terror. "I require your great strength to help me reforge this land. To guarantee my success in the quest that lies ahead."

Venerus's nostrils flared, enraged, insulted. They raised Their neck back. *I will not be used by a human! I am not your pawn. You are nothing. Tell me why I should not kill you and fly away right now.* They grinned once more. *I do so yearn to feel the wind beneath my wings once again, human.*

Ahaax picked up his stature. He rationalized there must be a reason Venerus had not killed him yet. They knew he must have a plan to get Them to his side. "I assume you would want revenge on the ones who imprisoned you here," he said.

Venerus tilted Their head. They brought Their piercing eyes close to Ahaax once again. *Explain yourself.* Ahaax's plan was working.

"If you help me in my goals," Ahaax continued, "I will help you in yours. I can help you get revenge on the Elder Dragons. You would not be my pawn, great Elder; you would be my partner."

Venerus seemed amused. As if the proposition were so outrageous to Them. An ant claiming to be equal to a man. They breathed steam through their nose. *My goals are beyond your understanding,* They began coldly. *Yet I could kill you now and accomplish them on my own,* the Elder Dragon said.

Ahaax nodded, conceding his point. "You could." This was what he had prepared for. The entire plan hinged on this aspect. He was terrified, but if he betrayed even a hint of that to the Elder, he knew he was dead. Ahaax looked into Venerus's eyes. His instincts were screaming at him. "But if you do that, then you die too."

Venerus snarled. *What are you saying, human?* Their claws scraped the red earth beneath Them, creating gashes a foot deep.

Ahaax looked smug, his fear lessening out of both confidence and arrogance. "Because of a spell my Magus cast right as you rose," he said, motioning a hand towards Abominus on the ground. Venerus glared at the old man as he slowly backed away. Ahaax continued, "Our lives are intertwined. This means if I die, you can die too, but if I live, you cannot die."

Venerus was clearly annoyed and angry. *You are ignorant, human,* They growled. *I cannot be killed by your means.*

Ahaax looked up to Them. "Under this spell," he said, "you are immune from the power of even an Elder. Nothing that is known shall be able to touch you."

Venerus stamped Their feet into the ground and uttered a deep growl. Clearly They didn't like being at the will of a human. But then They were quiet for a moment, seemingly considering the offer of true immortality. Eventually, They said to Ahaax, *I will keep you alive, and I will assist you in conquering this land, however long that shall take. A year? Ten? The lifetime of man is insignificant to me.* They growled menacingly at the two men, making sure they knew that the Elder Dragon would not be a junior partner in this alliance. *But when we are done, you will use your resources to help me achieve my goals. My...* They paused. *Revenge.*

A smile crept across Ahaax's face. He bowed his head, knowing he had just secured an insurmountable victory. "Elder Venerus, that is all I could ask for."

Venerus huffed, looking down at him literally and figuratively. *You are not like any human I have ever before encountered. Why would you turn against your own kind?*

Ahaax laughed slightly. He sighed. "This deal is not against my own kind, great Elder," he said. He remembered all the steps he had taken to get to this moment. How much he had lost. He was suddenly filled with a great resolve, a sense of duty. No, he decided, he could not, would not, turn back now. "For too long the greed of men has caused others to make deals against their own kind." He paused. "I seek to end it, whatever the cost."

A sneer appeared on Venerus' face. A look of detached disgust. They couldn't care less about the motives of the ant. What mattered was that They were free. Once again, the Elder Dragon raised Their head to the sky, roared a deafening roar, and shot a column of electric red lightning into the cold, dark air. For millennia They had been forced to wait. They would wait no longer.

Davit

A Beachside Retreat

VI

Gray. For the past six months that was all the world had been. Gray waves crashed onto colorless sand. Beyond the waves, the rough, gray ocean stretched for miles until it reached the gray, stormy sky. A single, soundless bolt of lightning flashed down from the clouds in the distance. A few quiet seconds passed. Thunder rumbled. I looked up at the clouds overhead. Overcast, but not dark, that storm was still miles away. I considered myself lucky.

I took a deep breath of the salty ocean air as I rose off of the rock I had been sitting on. I took in my surroundings. White sand covered the ground in all directions except to the ocean in front of me and the deciduous forest bed fifty feet behind me. The average branch or rock littered the ground, but otherwise, the beach was barren.

Ever since my father's death, I found myself coming to this secluded little spot more and more. The beach was perfect. I was right at the ocean, which was my favorite place to spend time, and it was a long walk from the palace, so I had privacy, but not too long to where I would be exhausted. I had stumbled upon an oasis that was solely my own. Whenever I needed time alone, I would go down there. I'd spent quite a lot of time there over the past six months.

I walked ankle-deep into the ocean. The water was cold as it rushed past me in waves, but I didn't mind it. I never had. Ever since I was a kid, whenever our parents would bring us on trips to the beach, I would always be the first one to rush into the ocean, not feeling the cold, as Percival and Rose were left behind me adjusting to the frigid temperatures. One of the benefits of my gift, as my mother would call it. I smiled softly. She always had a way of making me feel special.

I breathed in the bittersweet memory as my hand reached down to my side. Taking hold of the hilt at my belt, I unsheathed the old sword I had grown accustomed to practicing with. I held it with both hands in front of me. The sword was rusting and battered from many battles from before I was even born, but it would have to do for the time. When Percival would finally let me go fight the war in the east, I would get a new one.

I felt the sea water give my body strength as I began practicing the defensive stances I had learned. Being in water always energized me; it gave me strengths I otherwise lacked and a heightened sense of awareness, and the sword gilded through the air effortlessly. Everything should have been so easy.

But learning how to wield a sword from combat and learning from the pages of a book are two very different things. I had spent the past six months with my nose in every book I could get my hands on about swordsmanship. In theory, I should've been an expert. Yet the sword felt heavy and awkward in my hands. I misremembered multiple important steps that would've gotten me killed on the battlefield. I put my foot down for a proper stance but was caught off balance as the sand beneath me gave way, retreating into the ocean with an outgoing wave. I'd had it. I screamed and kicked the water.

It had been half a year since the beginning of the war, and Percival had personally sought to ensure that Rose and I would be nowhere near anything resembling combat. Meanwhile he rode off on his dragon for weeks on end, going on scouting expeditions and running the war in the east. He had even fought in several battles at that point. It wasn't fair. I deserved to be fighting this war. I needed to be fighting it. Ahaax destroyed my life just as much as he did Percival's, and

I was determined to make him pay. But Percival didn't trust me. It was ridiculous. Ever since he had become king, his inflated sense of power in our sibling dynamic had only grown. King Percival had so far ruled with a stubborn streak.

So, I would show my brother I could handle myself in combat. If I could handle myself well enough with a sword, I would be a better fighter than him or Rose on two feet while they soared in the sky. But I wasn't becoming a great fighter. I was tripping over myself and making mistakes. It was stupid. I needed to get better, so why wasn't I?

My thoughts were interrupted by an earth-shaking boom: thunder, right on top of me from the sound of things. My shoulders dropped. Was the storm already here? Would I have to go back to the palace already? I looked at the sky, but it was still as it had been. Overcast, the storm was still miles out at sea. So what caused…?

From the clouds above me, a giant yellow blur swooped down in an instant. It couldn't have been more than ten feet off the ground when it extended both of its massive wings in one fluid movement to cancel all of its velocity at once, sending out clouds of beach sand in all directions and knocking me on my butt. I spat out a couple of mouthfuls of sand. *It would be nice if he would not do that for once,* I thought.

I had to admit, though, the golden dragon that was now perched just feet away from me was a creature of unmatched beauty. It was rare for someone this far away from the Home of the Elders to ever see a dragon, even rarer to live to tell the tale. Yet I had seen this one every day for the past six months, and it still never got old.

Apolion (that was what Percival had named him, after a centuries-old king that I couldn't tell you anything about) was standing in the middle of a crater of sand his wings had created as he landed, crouched on his rear haunches. In the six months since he'd hatched, he had grown to the size of three adult griffs. A respectable size, and at an incredibly fast rate, and he would only grow bigger as he aged. The large dragon arched his feathered head down at me from atop his long golden neck. He was looking directly into my eyes with his own, the color of lightning. I shivered, but not out of fear. There was an instinct that told me the creature I was looking at was an ancient power. Not just Apolion; this was more than that. I looked at the dragon and knew that this power could start or end kingdoms on a whim.

Very quickly, my wonder subsided, and I remembered that if Apolion was here, Percival must be as well. Sure enough, the dragon lowered his neck, and there he was, seated in his saddle, my brother, the king. Percival had noticeably changed since the outbreak of war. He began to keep his golden hair closely cut so it wouldn't interfere with his armor; his face overall had lost much of the softness it used to have. He looked like a soldier; you wouldn't be able to tell he was only fifteen.

My brother rose from his saddle and hopped onto the beach sand. He looked around, taking in the scenery of the gray outcropping of beach he'd landed on. He raised an eyebrow. "Charming place," he said.

I sighed and stood, brushing off the sand from my fall. "It's secluded and peaceful," I said, shrugging. "What more could I need?"

Percival walked ankle-deep into the water, eyes fixed on the storming sky on the horizon with a boyish fascination. I walked to his side from behind him, wondering how this would end for me. He wouldn't come all this way for nothing.

"So," I began, attempting to break the ice, "where's the Circle? You can't step a foot outside the palace without them being on you."

"On their way," Percival responded curtly. "The brush on the path here slows them down, but Apolion..." He gestured back to his dragon, standing regally in the crater he made. "Nothing can match him in the sky." There was a hint of pride in his voice.

I nodded along with him. "Right."

"You wish to march to war," my brother started coldly, completely changing conversational topic so fast I nearly got whiplash. He turned his head towards me. "Why?" His face was hard. I knew I wasn't talking to my brother now; I was talking to the king. Much, much worse.

My stomach dropped. This was the conversation I'd been dreading. It had to come up at some point. I figured there was no point in lying. I looked Percival in the eye. "Justice," I said truthfully.

The young king furrowed his brow. "You mean vengeance."

I shrugged. "The two can both apply."

"Vengeance will make you reckless."

"Maybe some recklessness is what we need right now."

Percival rolled his eyes. "I don't know what I thought would be different." He turned around and began walking toward Apolion. I followed.

"Six months," I began, my voice raised slightly. I had rehearsed this pitch repeatedly. "Our father's killer has been waging war without any check and shows no sign of slowing. Something isn't working, Percival!"

"I won't hear this," he muttered, clearly getting annoyed.

I kept pushing. "Every day we do nothing, he only gets stronger! We have three soldiers who can control fundamental aspects of nature, and two full-size dragons. We should be able to match all of his forces on the land, sea and sky, yet we're still losing! Rose has control over one of the largest creatures we know of, something that can destroy entire fleets on his own, and you keep her on the damn island! Keep both of us there! If you let us go to battle…"

"No!" Percival stopped dead in his tracks. Thunder rumbled from the sky. I stopped too. The anger that had been fueling my speech was quickly replaced by twice as much dread. Since becoming king, my brother had rarely ever raised his voice (or showed emotion of any kind), but when he did, it never ended well for anyone involved.

Percival turned partly around, his hand holding a rein from Apolion's saddle. He took a deep breath, his voice softer. "You wish to have something that you can never have back once lost." He looked me in the eye, his face perfectly molded to not show any emotion. "You do not know what war is, Davit. There are battles. Sieges. In the past six months I have fought in both." He shook his head. "It's my wish that you never have to experience either." He sighed and turned, putting his foot in Apolion's stirrup as he climbed up to his seat.

I walked over to the dragon. I could tell Percival had let his guard down for this conversation, so I decided not to push my point using anger, but I was still determined. "We are at war with someone who seeks to destroy everything we have ever known, me, you, and Rose very much included," I said up to him. "It may be in the east now, but it's coming here, so I can either be prepared, or not."

Percival stared down at me from his seat. It looked like I had gotten through to him. For a second, I was hopeful. "Your dragon's egg was never destroyed," he said in one abrupt statement.

And just like that, things became so much worse. It felt like I was punched in the stomach. It took me a split second to process what he had even said. The egg. That stupid egg. Still causing problems. How could he not destroy it? I took a step back. "I ordered Pevincy to destroy that thing."

"And I ordered him not to," Percival said back. "It was a direction from the king, so he couldn't refuse. Don't be angry with him."

I shook my head. "Oh, I'm not. I'm angry with you!" I couldn't believe this. I couldn't stand still. "That was my egg to decide what to do with. You had no right…"

"I was not going to destroy one of our most powerful weapons moments after we had war declared upon us," Percival snapped in his kingly voice. "Father couldn't have anticipated the trials ahead of us, but if he could, he would want you protected. That's why he gave that egg to you in the first place."

I grimaced, remembering a painful memory. One Percival got incorrect. "In case you've forgotten," I said darkly, "I wasn't given an egg that day. He decided *not* to give it to me."

Percival nodded. "And why was that?" I stormed away from the dragon, exasperated. "Could it be that you were just thirteen years old? Unready for the royal duties of your status, much less prepared to march into war?"

"I will never be ready if you won't let me do anything!" I turned around and shouted back at him. Waves as tall as I was began to churn onto the beach all around us, but I was so angry I hardly even noticed. What he was doing wasn't fair. He couldn't get away with this. "You have no right to control me like this! You may be king now, but you're still my brother, which is what you will always be. You will *never* be a ruler like our father, no matter how desperately you want to, so just stop trying!"

I didn't know if I meant that or not. At the moment, though, I didn't care. I wanted it to hurt. I wanted him to know how betrayed I felt. I wanted *him* to hurt.

Either my words meant nothing to him, or he had perfected the art of controlling his face, because my brother showed no sign of guilt when I was done shouting. That made me even more furious. Did he even care? We both waited silently for a moment. Percival took a deep breath. "Hatch the egg or don't," he began. "It's your decision. But if you keep ignoring the challenge in front of you, you will never so much as see a battlefield. Children do not go to war."

That was it. That was the final straw. Something inside me snapped, and I saw only red. I stretched my arm towards the churning water. There was a tugging sensation deep in my gut as the waves grew larger. I threw my arm towards Percival sitting high on top of his dragon. A twenty-foot-tall geyser of water followed my motion, shooting directly towards the both of them.

Percival reacted instantly. With Apolion's reins in his hands, he brought the dragon several feet into the air, just barely avoiding getting drenched. Apolion roared in frustration and dropped back to the ground, once again sending a cloud of sand in all directions. Percival glared at me from his elevated position. I glared right back.

"That's enough, Sire," called a voice off to our sides. We both turned our heads. In a clearing was a group of six men and women clad in the same sets of emerald armor. With flowing green cloaks hanging from their shoulders and a specially forged sword at each of their waists, there was a power around them that let everyone know they were the six best warriors in the realm. The Circle of the Crown had arrived.

Each knight had come mounted on a griff, further symbols of their status. In the center of the group was a dark man whose black hair was just starting to show specks of gray. "There is enough discord among the royals without you two going for the other's throat," Pevincy continued.

Percival shot me one last nasty look, then shifted his attention towards his Justiciar. He took Apolion's reins in his hands and steered his large mount to the newly arrived group. The griffs all stamped their talons nervously as the dragon drew closer, probably worried (and not entirely unjustified) that they'd be his next meal.

Just like that, I thought. *I am once again an afterthought in the king's mind.* Percival addressed the lead knight. "You're right, Pevincy," he said. "I lost my temper." I could hear the barely hidden contempt in his voice from ten feet away.

Pevincy, along with the five other knights he brought with him, dismounted and kneeled for their king on the damp sand. "My lord," he began. "I come bringing dire news."

The king's face hardened. "Rise and speak it," he commanded.

The knights rose. Pevincy continued, "Refugees fleeing the eastern provinces have arrived at the city gates. There must be a thousand or more. The fear is they might try to storm for entry."

"Why deny them a safe harbor?" the king asked, confused.

"The regency council ordered it, I'm afraid," Pevincy responded. "They don't want any more mouths to feed than they already have."

The king cursed. "That insufferable council defies my will at every opportunity."

"They still see you as a child, especially now that they have less than a year left before they must give up their power and let your reign begin," the old guard explained. He sighed. "My vote on the council will always be with you, my king, but even as your Justiciar, my voice cannot overrule the rest."

King Percival nodded. "You need not reaffirm your loyalty to me, Pevincy," he said. "Your actions speak louder than you could know." He paused, seemingly lost in thought. After a few moments he began again. "Take the Circle to the city gates. I shall return on Apolion at once and meet you there.

These people have fled all this way; they deserve to hear from their king."

Pevincy bowed his head and placed his right fist on his breast in a salute. "As you command, my lord."

The king nodded. "Be on your way," he ordered. And with that, the knights of the Circle of the Crown mounted their griffs and galloped back on the path from which they came.

When the dust settled, Percival's head dropped. He muttered something, but I couldn't hear it with how far away I was. It was probably another curse, was my guess. I couldn't blame him. The small, rational side of me knew that as much as I hated him for it at times, it couldn't be easy having the responsibility of a kingdom thrown onto you in a day. Still, it couldn't hurt for him to be a little less of a twit.

My brother steered his dragon towards where we had been standing during our confrontation minutes ago. I crossed my arms as we made eye contact. "Seems as if you have a little crisis on your hands, Your Majesty," I said with bitterness still lingering in my voice.

Percival stopped Apolion alongside me. He nodded and sighed. "Yes," he began. "Which means I do not need one from you." He reached down and offered his hand to me. My eyes widened at what he was proposing. "You *do* want to return to the palace?" he asked.

"I, uh," I stammered. My gaze shifted slowly from my brother to the massive winged creature he was sitting atop. Apolion huffed. I swear against the Elders that dragon grinned. "Fly?"

"It's the quickest way." Percival shrugged. "By far," he added.

I gulped. My palms were suddenly sweating. But I couldn't refuse. Percival already thought I was too much of a child. *He knows what he's doing,* I thought. *Either I refuse to get on the dragon and look scared* and *like a child, or I ride back to the palace on dragonback a thousand feet in the air.* The idea wasn't thrilling. Sometimes I forgot just how clever my brother was. Still, I didn't have much of a choice.

With another gulp, I reached out and took his hand in mine, pulling myself into the saddle behind him. The leather was cold and hard and instantly uncomfortable. I didn't know how Percival could stand this being his main mode of transportation. "A piece of honest advice?" he said back to me. "Hang on to something."

"Hang on to something," I repeated, nodding. I was trying my best to hide the rapidly growing sense of dread I was feeling. "Right." Mustering what little control of my muscles I had left, I gripped tightly onto the edge of the large saddle.

Percival leaned closer to Apolion's head. He was grinning. Why was he grinning? "Take us home," he whispered to his dragon. Slowly, two massive golden wings began to unfurl.

I glanced to my side and caught a glint of light in the sand. I looked closer. My memory suddenly came back to me all at once. "Wait, I forgot my swo…"

What happened in the next few seconds still remains somewhat of a blur to me. It was literally a blur; the wind rushing in my eyes made me tear up. There was a lot of screaming, flashes of yellow, and I swear my body left the saddle and was in the air for at least ten seconds. The sheer amount of wind rushing past me was nearly enough to send me flying off the back of the dragon, not even to mention the rapid movement. Apolion had to have been covering at least one hundred feet per second on his ascent.

It was beginning to be too much to hold on, and I was starting to wonder if Percival would let me fall off or would even be able to prevent it. Then, Apolion began to level out, and the harsh wind pushing me backwards turned into a manageable gust. We broke through the cloud cover, a trail of white vapor following behind us.

I began to relax some of my muscles as Apolion took on a pattern of strong but rhythmic wing beats. The view around us was surreal. Below, the ground was completely hidden from view, covered entirely by a fluffy white veil. Above and around us was a clear evening sky of dark orange. To my right was the setting sun, looking ten times its usual size. I was astounded. This was a beauty I had never before experienced on the ground.

"Wow," was all I could manage to express my wonder. It was less of a word and more of a sound that escaped my open mouth.

Percival glanced back at me. He didn't say anything, but he visibly relaxed. He seemed more at ease a thousand feet in the air than he did with two feet on the ground. For the first time in my life, I was beginning to understand why.

We flew through the air in silence for the next few minutes. We must have been going even faster than I'd realized, because soon enough Apolion made a quick barking sound, and we began to descend through the cloud layer. As the clouds cleared, the outline of a city came into view. But this was no ordinary city. Settled on an island in the middle of two merging rivers, we had arrived at the capital of the kingdom, the seat of the royal crown of Lungalea for over a thousand years, the jewel of the realm: Lungala. My home.

The island was completely covered with buildings. It was a challenge to make out any patches of green grass that remained from before it was settled. Most of the buildings were single-story homes on either side of a stone street, with the occasional market or square scattered here and there. The reason for this mass overcrowding was rooted in centuries of complex tradition that even I, as a member of the royal family, couldn't quite understand, but I had been reassured many times there was a good reason.

The buildings got progressively bigger until they reached the center of the island, whereupon a circular stone wall rose, and inside it was the jewel itself, the royal palace. With its mazes of marble hallways and towers, the palace was the largest structure ever constructed on the continent. With a history too long to mention here (and even *this* palace was still the third in the line of castles the royals of the kingdom had ever built to live in) the palace remained a feat of engineering that brought a sense of wonder and awe to anyone who saw it.

The island itself where the city was built was connected to the mainland by four bridges on either side enclosed by a set of massive stone gates. It was at one of those gates where I first got a sense that something was wrong. From our position in the sky, there looked to be a black mass swirling around the entrance. As we descended, though, the view became more focused. There were people surrounding the gates. A lot of people. Men, women, and children were all huddled so close together it was difficult to tell them apart. The clothes they were wearing were rags, and they all looked just a few steps from collapsing. *This is what the regency council is afraid of?* I thought. These people weren't a threat. They needed help.

Percival pulled back on Apolion's reins and had us hover in the air. "This isn't good," he observed astutely. A little bit of an understatement, but I decided to remain silent. "There has to be five thousand of them down there. Maybe more."

"What are you going to do?"

He shook his head and sighed. "What I can," he responded. He turned back to me. "I'm going to drop you in the palace, but it's going to have to be quicker than you might like."

"What do you mea—" Before I had time to finish my sentence, Percival lashed Apolion's reins. The dragon tucked his wings close to his body, and we began to dive. While I had thought the ascent on a thirty-foot dragon was fast and uncontrollable, Percival brought us back to the ground like he was bordering on suicidal. We were shooting downwards at a ninety-degree angle; every cloud we passed through felt like little pebbles being thrown at my face. Percival had enough thought to get as low to his dragon as possible; meanwhile I was left being blown nearly entirely backwards by wind speeds that could rival a hurricane.

It was after about five seconds of this sick torture method that my brother used as transportation when Apolion shot his wings out in one lightning-fast motion. Nearly all our forward momentum was immediately canceled out, a cloud of dust exploded all around us, and it felt like all of my bones rearranged themselves in opposite directions within my body, but at least we landed softly on the ground. I sat up straight like a board, groaned, and then rolled off the saddle that I'd thought I would never leave. While I wouldn't describe the ten-foot fall to the ground I experienced as pleasant, it was far better than what I had just gone through. Solid ground had never felt so good. Or solid, I observed with a painful groan.

Mustering all the strength I had left in my exhausted muscles, I managed to push my upper half off the dirt-covered ground... and immediately fell back down, promptly vomiting up all of my stomach contents. Figuring I couldn't get any lower than I already was, after a few moments I once again forced myself to fully stand without falling over. After stumbling around for a minute, I got a sense of my surroundings.

We'd landed in a large open courtyard within the palace walls. There were some soldiers practicing their swordsmanship on some straw dummies in a corner, seemingly unfazed by the massive flying reptile that had just landed. To my right were the palace stables, where there were multiple griffs closed up in stalls stamping nervously. It was only upon seeing them that I momentarily forgot about my nausea and the taste of vomit in my mouth and remembered Percival.

I turned around, back towards my brother. The young king was sitting high on top of his golden dragon, looking completely unfazed by the same experience that had rearranged my inner organs. *Figures,* I thought. Nothing ever fazed him. Remembering the sight of the thousands of refugees we had seen just moments before, I decided to appeal their case to Percival. They needed King Percival right now, not a council. I knew, even if it was buried deep down under royal procedures, that my brother still cared about his people. Holding back another wave of flying induced vomit, I began, "Percival, I…"

I didn't get the chance to finish. "To the gates, Apolion," Percival commanded, reins in hand. With that, the dragon made a deep purring sound, stretched out his massive wings, and jumped into the sky, taking flight. Like clockwork, I was once again enveloped in a cloud of dust. I scrunched up my nose. That was something I never wanted to get used to.

I sighed, pointing a raised thumb at where he had flown off. "Yeah," I said. "Thanks." I was hoping the men in the courtyard couldn't hear how pathetic I sounded.

Cerulia

VII

I stood there looking at my brother and his dragon fly off until they were only a small golden dot. I kicked the grass I was standing in. The sight of the mass of desperate people wouldn't leave my head. Someone had to help them. I wished that this wasn't the first time this had happened. I wished that it would be the last. But I knew both of those wishes were foolish. As the war dragged on, the crowds of refugees would only become bigger and more frequent.

I became angry. Angry at Ahaax. My father's killer's face had been seared into my mind ever since that day six months ago. Somewhere off in the east he was waging war right now. It wasn't enough for him to ruin my life, but he had to uproot tens of thousands of innocent people who didn't even know who he was, people who couldn't even fight back. *I could fight back,* I thought. I knew that somehow, if I ever came into contact with Ahaax, it would be different from when I last saw him. It had to be.

But I couldn't fight back. I was being kept in a palace on the other side of the kingdom, powerless as my home was destroyed. My anger shifted towards Percival. I was being held back because of him. Those people at the gate needed all the help they could get, and they weren't getting it. I began to heat up. It wasn't fair. None of this was fair. I deserved to be helping them, to be fighting this war, to be fighting Ahaax. But I wasn't! I was being treated like a child!

It was at this time I noticed that my right hand was getting significantly warmer than the rest of my body. It was nearly burning. I furrowed my brow, looking down at it. This wasn't because of my anger, I thought. What was causing it? The realization hit me almost instantly, even if I didn't want to accept it. "Your dragon's egg was never destroyed," Percival had said. Something in the back of my head always knew that was the truth, my hand always burning more and more depending on where I went within the palace. A gut instinct had formed within me ever since I first saw that thing. I gritted my teeth. Standing there in the courtyard with my hand feeling like it was surrounded by an invisible fire, I knew I could no longer run from this choice. The sight of the desperate refugees at the gate once again flashed in my mind. If there was one way to prove to Percival I had changed enough to go to war, this was probably the surest way to do it. With that realization, I knew I had already made up my mind.

Taking my right hand in my left to alleviate some of the burning feeling, I sighed one last massive sigh and entered the large wooden doors of the courtyard into the royal palace. The long walk through the halls was constantly narrated by two opposing voices within my head. *You don't deserve this*, one voice said. *You haven't earned this. This is a mistake.*

I know, the opposing voice responded. *But this is the only way I will ever be useful in this war. This is the only way I can help!*

Help? What help could you ever be? The antagonistic voice countered. *You weren't any help the day he died, and you know it. You think doing this will redeem you in anyone's eyes? This is a disgrace to his memory.*

I stopped dead in my tracks. The voice was right. I didn't deserve this. I'd failed that day. This wouldn't change that. This wouldn't redeem me. *But no one else suffers.* With that, the two competing voices went silent. I brought my right hand close to my chest, the dull burning becoming more and more unbearable. With my jaw clenched and a single tear rolling down my cheek, I kept walking.

The interior of the royal palace resembled a maze of white marble. You could be forgiven for getting lost in it; many wise men of years past had. Living in the palace my whole life, I knew how to navigate the halls well enough, but even I had never seen the entire layout. Still, I walked the halls without any hesitation. It was like there was a compass inside me, guiding me to where I needed to go. I knew my destination. With every corner turned and every flight of stairs descended, the halls around me grew darker and darker until I could tell I was completely underground and the only light was from torches placed on the walls. The farther I went down, the air became colder and more and more damp.

Eventually, the marble steps I was on turned to stone ones, and after that, turned to just stones, rough outcroppings that were barely wide enough to stand on. The polished marble walls told a similar story, turning to old stone that became rougher as I walked. Off in the distance I could hear the faint, rhythmic dripping of water into a puddle. I had wandered into what was essentially a cave. With each step I took, my hand began to burn more. This wasn't just irritation anymore; this was pain. I knew I was getting close. Anxiety built within me.

Eventually the stairs and long hallways ended, and I had come to a pair of large wooden doors. Unlike many of the other doors in the palace, these had no intricate design telling a story. These were not meant to be seen. They looked as old as the palace itself. This was it.

With great effort, I used my body to push through the doors. On the other side was a room dark as night. A cold wind blew my hair back. Hesitantly, I took a torch off the wall and walked farther into the room. Each step I took echoed off the cold stone walls. Waving the torch around so I could better see where I was, I realized where my journey had taken me. On each side of the cavernous room were cells with no one in them. The gates to the cells were rusting from age. The palace dungeons. I shivered. Only the worst people the kingdom could produce were ever held here, and never for long. Using the compass within me, I took a deep breath and continued to walk forward.

I knew I had found what I was looking for as soon as I saw the glow. A faint, cerulean light was emanating from a cell to my side. This was it. I walked around the rusted metal wall and entered the open cell. It was completely empty, with the exception of hay strewn all around, covering the cold floor, and a foot-long blue oval with white veins running up and down its length. The sight of the egg filled me with a sense of dread I had only ever known once before. But there was also something else. In the back of my head was a positive feeling. Something that almost resembled a childish joy. I pushed that feeling back as hard as I could. This was not a good thing, I kept telling myself.

I approached the egg and kneeled. Setting my torch on the ground, I breathed out as steady of a breath as I could manage, able to see the mist from it in the air. "Father," I whispered. All of the emotions I was feeling were difficult to hold back, or even describe. I continued, struggling, "I know I do not deserve this. I know I failed you that day six months ago. But I no longer have a choice. I can't let the people of this kingdom suffer while I sit by doing nothing. Ahaax has been causing chaos unchecked for too long, and this may be the only way I can stop him. It's the only way I can avenge your death. I know this isn't enough for you to forgive me, but..."

I meant to say more, but I choked up, and words wouldn't come out. The guilt I was feeling just being down there was too much. I didn't know if I believed if my father could hear what I said or not. Honestly, I didn't know which option was worse.

The pain in my right hand began to be unbearable. It felt like the flesh was melting off, but it was completely undamaged. "Ah!" I gasped, gripping my wrist. I began to panic. The pain wasn't going away, and I didn't know what to do. The instinct within me took over, and I laid my eyes on the glowing blue egg in front of me. Without thinking, I threw my hand onto it.

There was a bright blue explosion. The force knocked me onto my back. My head was fuzzy, and I was seeing double. But the burning sensation in my hand was gone! Now I would just have bruises all over my body. "Ugh," I groaned in pain.

Groggily, I rose using my hands and looked toward the egg, but it was gone. There were blue shards scattered all over the cell, and at the spot I was looking, there was now something else entirely. A dragon.

She was a little creature lying on her side like she had just tripped. She was a she, first of all, something inside me knew. She couldn't have been more than a foot long, smaller than the other two dragons when they hatched, if I remembered right. Her body was a deep blue, similar to the color of her destroyed egg. She had four muscular legs, with webs between each of her four toes like they were made for swimming. Her head was smooth, and the scales that covered her entire body shimmered in the little light of the room. Unlike my siblings' dragons, she had no spikes at all, not on her head, not on her wings, nowhere. Her tail was unusual as well; it resembled a shark's more than it did the other two dragons'.

I sat there dumbfounded for a few minutes as the little dragon shakily stood on its freshly hatched set of legs and took its first hesitant steps, walking nowhere in particular. I did a sort of laughing gasp as the full realization of what I was looking at hit me. A dragon. I had hatched a dragon. A creature that could level cities and wipe out armies. As I watched the little thing fall over after trying to stretch, I found it strange that the two images were related.

She heard my sound and looked over, waddling towards me. "Hey, little one," I said softly, gently running a finger along her back, causing her to roll over and shake one of her back legs in what might have been the cutest thing I had ever seen. A thousand thoughts a minute were running through my head.

Remembering why I had gone down there in the first place, I centered that thought in my mind and stopped petting the dragon, enveloped by a sudden wave of fresh guilt. *You don't deserve this,* the familiar, distant voice whispered. It was right.

The dragon noticed my hesitation. She flopped into an upright position and made her way closer to me. With a chirping noise, she nuzzled her small head into the back of my hand. In that moment, a series of images flashed before my eyes. Well, they were less images, more than they were thoughts. They weren't *my* thoughts, though. I knew that for sure. All these thoughts wove together into one comprehensible thing.

"Cerulia," I said aloud. She looked up at me and chirped again, seemingly satisfied with her new name. Cerulia, having probably extended what little energy a new dragon hatchling had, began to purr and curled up in a tight little ball next to me, closing her eyes.

The wave of stinging guilt returned immediately, and I remembered my purpose. I gently pushed Cerulia a couple of feet away from me so that we were no longer touching. She lifted her head groggily. "Look," I began softly to the dragon. "You're a means to an end, okay?" I didn't mince my words. I wouldn't let myself become attached to this creature. Besides, she wasn't human; she probably couldn't even understand what I was saying, although as I looked into those giant, ocean-blue eyes, something inside me guessed that wasn't the case. "You'll allow me to go off to the east and finally start making a difference. That's all."

Cerulia cocked her head. What was I thinking? She was an animal, of course she couldn't understand what I was saying. Just as I thought that, the little dragon stood. She folded her two front legs and stretched her wings. It took me a second before I realized that she was bowing. My eyes widened. I didn't know what to believe anymore.

But it changed nothing. I got my father killed and helped start this war. I didn't deserve this little dragon named Cerulia, but I would use her to help fix what I'd caused. I deserved nothing more. However, as I looked at the ocean-blue dragon kneeling in reverence towards me, I was suddenly aware of just how real this war had become.

Rose

Those In Need

VIII

I pushed aside the wooden hatch with a hefty grunt and scrambled up from the tunnel in the ground. I looked around to get a sense of where I had come up. In front of me, there was ten feet of mud before, stretched out to fill the entire horizon, a massive flowing river sent itself over an unseen waterfall to my right. To my left, in the distance there was an aged structure made of cobbled stone that I recognized immediately as one of the gates to the city. *Perfect,* I thought. We'd come up exactly where I'd intended.

There was a full moon out, creating shimmers in the rippling river water. In the light, I looked down at my clothes. Sure enough, everything I was wearing, blouse, pants, and cloak I used to hide my face, were completely filthy. I grinned. *All the better.* I brushed my hair out of my eyes and walked towards the river. Hunched low, I took a handful of mud and rubbed it on my face.

"Should I even ask?" a man said, kneeling in the muck next to me. His red hair reached just above his eyes, and the amount of freckles on his face gave him a dark look in the little light. He was clad in a set of light leather armor, and a sword was hanging from his waist. Although he didn't look much older than Percival, his rank suggested that he was at least a few years the king's senior.

I made sure my entire face was covered with mud and dirt. "I'm the sister to the king, Kil," I began. "The heir to the throne. I'd prefer to do our business tonight unrecognized."

Kilian nodded. Chewing on his lip, his gaze turned to the muddy riverbed. With a sigh, he picked up a handful and began to rub it on his face like I had. I let out a sharp laugh of surprise.

"What?" Kil asked, furrowing his brow.

I looked down to avoid eye contact. Trying not to laugh again, I said, "Well, it's just that I'm the crown princess, so my face needs to be obscured. But you..." This was a delicate situation. "You could be any other soldier. So, you don't really need the mud." I flashed him a huge, smug grin and a thumbs-up.

The muddied soldier was silent for a few moments, staring at me blankly. When he seemingly realized what I said, his eyes widened, and he quickly brought his face down close to the water, furiously washing the river muck off and sputtering. I stood, laughing so hard I nearly fell.

"Ha ha," Kil deadpan feigned laughter, standing once his face was washed. "Thank you for reminding me I'm expected to fight and die in a war for people who won't even know my face or name. It really means a lot, Princess."

"Don't be like that," I said, playfully punching his arm. "You're not expected to die for people who won't know your name. You're expected to die for *my brother* who won't know your name. You know this."

Kil nodded. "Of course, Your Highness."

From behind the two of us, we heard voices rise from the tunnel. "Okay, now push! To the right! The rig... the other right!" A man's shrill voice was commanding.

"That's left, you idiot," a woman responded. "Why do we have to twist it anyway? We're in a straight tunnel!"

With that, and two large *huff*s, a chest was launched from the tunnel's exit and landed a few feet away on the ground. "Hey!" I shouted. "Careful!" I ran over to the crate to make sure nothing had come loose. It was on its side, but hadn't opened, luckily.

Kilian shook his head as he walked to the tunnel's exit, from which two people emerged. There was a man and a woman. Both looked to be in their fifties and wearing the same sort of armor as the younger soldier. The man was the same height as me, but probably more than double my weight and had a balding head of gray hair. The woman also had gray hair, but that was where visual similarities ended. She was a head taller than even Kilian, with well-defined muscles and a stone-cold face.

Kil walked up to the two of them. "The princess has asked us to do one thing." He gestured with his finger to form a *1* inches from their faces. "That is, get that crate safely delivered intact outside of the gates." He spoke in a direct, authoritative voice, reigning in his companions.

The round man nudged the woman's side with his elbow lightly. "Hey, Kilian." He gave a hearty chuckle. "Looks like you've got a little dirt on your face. Were you trying to make yourself look better?" He chuckled madly; he was clearly very satisfied with his own joke. Kil's face didn't move a muscle.

I grabbed the top of the chest as I tried to reposition it right-side up, but it was too heavy for me. I heaved with all my might, but it didn't move an inch. "Maybe I overpacked," I said lightly to myself, out of breath. With another burst of energy, I tried lifting the chest again, but I was met with the same result. The muscular woman standing beside the man and Kil took notice of my efforts. She left the two bickering soldiers and walked slowly to my side. Without making a sound, she leaned over and lifted the chest effortlessly. I was left standing there, looking up at her, faintly aware of how small I was. "Thank you, Julianna," I said with as much dignity as I had left.

"Of course, Princess," Jules responded, bowing her head respectfully.

The two men by the riverbank walked over to join us. "It's a noble goal, Princess," the round man said as he approached, scratching his head. He turned towards the river. "But it might be harder than you were expecting given the fact that we don't have a boat." Kil flicked the back of the man's ear. "What?" the stout man exclaimed.

I smiled and rolled my eyes. "You look, my dear Archibald," I said to the man. I walked farther along the shore to a tree so low its branches were stuck in the river mud Reaching out my arm, I felt a slight tightening sensation in my gut. At my prompting, the tree came alive, its leaves slowly shaking and rising until it was as straight as an arrow and its branches were no longer touching the mud, revealing a rowboat just big enough for the four of us to fit that I had placed there hours before. I smiled. The tree was as healthy as the day it sprouted.

"But you do not see," I finished, turning around to face my friends, grinning. Archie had scrunched up his face, but Jules and Kil were both looking impressed at my showing off. I had long since stopped trying to hide my satisfaction over my powers with this group. The looks on their faces after I manipulated a tree or brought the occasional precious gem up from the earth were too good.

"Hidden from view," Kil said, nodding approvingly. "Good thinking." I flashed a toothy smile and placed my hands on my hips, basking in the glory.

Archie shook his head. "Every time I think I've got her, she goes and uses magic. It's just not fair."

"Not magic," I objected, raising my index finger. "That's just pure talent." Archie rolled his eyes.

I clapped my hands together. "Right," I began. "Let's get this show on the road. My twin brother keeps trying to run away from his problems, so the palace guards are wise to the 'sneak out by putting a dummy in your bed' trick by now." I hopped into a bench on the rowboat, patting my knees and waiting for the rest of the group to join me.

Kil shook his head. "Your brother has rarely ever gotten past the palace gate. We can't have long before the king sends out search parties."

"Exactly, but they're searching for someone else," I said deviously. "They're running on bad information. They don't know the most important thing to help them with their search."

"What's that, Princess?" Jules asked in her calm voice.

I grinned madly at all of them. "I am *not* my brother."

The journey across the river was short. Within a couple of minutes, our had boat bumped softly into the muddy shore on the far side. We had crossed. I jumped out of the side of the boat onto the soft ground… sinking six inches almost instantly. I laughed in surprise. *Wasn't expecting that.*

The passengers of the rowboat looked over. Archie grimaced. "Do you need help, Princess?" Jules asked sincerely.

With great effort, I lifted one leg out of the muck. "Nope!" I heaved. I took one step forward, pulled my other leg out of the mud, and took another step: repeat. It took me a couple of minutes, but I managed to walk farther onto the shore, stopping after ten feet or so where a field of grass began. I bent over and put my hands on my knees, breathing hard. That took a lot of effort. Between pants, I realized that from my knees down it was essentially completely black from all the mud. I sighed. Really?

"I don't suppose you brought a change of clothes, Princess?" Archibald called to me.

I stood straight and looked towards the run-down boat. "Unnecessary," I breathed. Raising my right hand, I tensed my fingers. There was the same familiar tightening in my gut, but lighter than when I moved the tree. With a flick of my wrist, the mud covering my legs flew off, landing in the grass five feet away. Checking to see the quality of my work, I lifted my right leg. I moved it around and placed a finger on it. Completely dry. This was good even for me. I had never been able to get it completely dry before.

"Nicely done, Princess," Jules said. Kil nodded approvingly.

I set my leg back down. "Thanks," I said, regaining my breath. I tried to flip my hair behind my head, but I was still adjusting to the new ground and stumbled, causing it to fly right into my face. I had to spit out a lot of mud just then.

Archie looked over the side of the boat down at the mud. "I don't suppose you can do that for us too?" he asked, looking over at me.

I cocked my head, wondering what he meant. Then I realized that he and the others on that boat were probably very aware at that moment that they did not have the ability to manipulate mud.

It took about ten minutes for everyone to get out of the boat and over to where I was standing on the grass. I probably could've helped them by trying to create a path through the mud, but their struggling trying to stomp through the muck was fairly amusing, so I decided against it. Kil was making his way through well enough, but Archie was behind him, sweating as he dug a path through the muck for Juliana (who was carrying the chest we'd been moving all on her own), with a little trowel he'd pulled from a small bag he was carrying on his back.

As I waited for my friends to catch up, I started noticing my surroundings. We were in a large open clearing. The closest trees to us were over one hundred feet away, but they had to be at least twice that in height, not uncommon for the forests around the capital, but still awe-inducing. The full moon bathed everything in a silver glow. I closed my eyes and breathed in the crystal-clear air. I could smell the dirt and the dew on the grass. It was absolutely beautiful.

Kil and the others finally made their way to me, albeit out of breath. The red-haired soldier hunched over. "Awaiting your command, Princess," he managed to pant.

A light breeze passed through the clearing. As I felt the cool air on my face and admired my surroundings, I was overcome with a sudden wave of energy. "I've been cooped up on that cramped island for the past six months," I said to them. "Same dirt, same grass, same trees." I turned to face my three friends, beaming a bright, toothy smile. I couldn't contain it anymore! I grasped Kil's hands in mine. "I command you to dance with me, soldier!" What I did next was more swinging arms and hopping around than dancing, but I didn't care. I never wanted this feeling to go away.

Kil stood tiredly in place, only moving his arms because I was moving them for him. "Oh, Princess, do we have to?" he asked, not out of malice but sheer exhaustion.

I smirked. "That's an order!"

Kil flashed a glance at Archie and Jules standing off to the side, as if to say, *Get me out of this!* However, the two siblings were conveniently looking in different directions. I smirked again.

The soldier brought his attention back to me; meanwhile I was still dancing madly and laughing. Even tired, Kil flashed a smile that was warm enough to melt a glacier. I slowed down. Divines be good, was I blushing? He softly tightened his grip around my hands and began moving us throughout the field smoothly. We were dancing. Actually dancing. It felt wonderful, but also, I didn't know he knew how to actually dance. I wasn't prepared for this. Thinking on my feet, I once again put myself in control of both of our arms and began twirling the two of us in a circle wildly. As we started spinning faster and faster, I couldn't help but start laughing again. Killian, however, looked concerned that we were about to fall over any second. He had good reason. Abruptly, I let go of his hands, and we both went sprawling onto the damp grass, out of breath.

I was laughing madly. Kil brought his hands up to his face and wiped it. Even he started chuckling. His chuckle made me laugh even harder, which caused him to break into a real, genuine laugh. I didn't hear those from him often. It warmed my heart.

He looked at me, both of us still in the grass. His eyes were sparkling in the moonlight. "Never change, Princess," he said. "Never change."

I smiled at him. "Why would I change? I have you three." I turned my head, so I was now looking up at the twinkling stars. "I like things just how they are."

"Princess, you should come see this," Jules called. She sounded alarmed. She and Archie were both looking towards the city.

Kil and I frowned at each other and stood. We walked over to the others and saw what had raised the alarm. Across the river, there were little dots of light dancing along a city road. We all knew what they were immediately. "Guards," Kil said.

"They haven't crossed the river yet," I said defiantly. "We still have time."

Kil shook his head slightly. "We may need to cut this expedition short, Princess."

"No!" I said firmly, louder than I'd intended. The three of them turned their heads towards me. My eyes widened. I looked back at each of them. I didn't mean to shout, but I wouldn't let myself go home when so many people needed our help. Regaining my composure, I began again, "We've come this far; we just need to get started." With that, I put my hood over my dirt-covered face and began to walk farther inland away from the river. I turned my head towards the three soldiers. "Come," I told them. *That* was an order.

We didn't need to walk very far to find what we were looking for. Five minutes down a dirt path and we began to see the flickering orange lights of torches. As we got closer, each of us was shocked. We all knew there was a vast amount of refugees outside of the city gates, but I don't think any of us were prepared for just how many there were.

There was a small city of hastily assembled tents and structures spanning farther than we could see. From just our vantage point, we saw hundreds of people in tattered clothes moving about. I estimated there had to be at least a thousand more throughout the encampment. My stomach dropped. Suddenly my job had just gotten a lot larger.

Archie walked up next to me and sighed. "I think we're going to need a bigger crate."

"We help who we can," I said, brushing off his comment. It was true. We wouldn't be able to help everyone who needed it; that much was obvious. But if I could make this night easier for even one person, then I would consider this mission a success.

We began to walk into the camp when I felt something speak to me. It wasn't a voice—more a feeling or an instinct, communicating with me inside my mind. The feeling was wary of me entering the refugee camp without him. I knew where the feeling was coming from immediately. He had grown significantly more talkative in recent months as he grew older.

I can't have you come with me here, Redwood, I said to my dragon companion in my head. *I left you at the palace for a reason. You might scare these people.*

I could tell Redwood was very displeased with this information. He didn't care who he scared; he would protect me at any cost.

Stay at the palace, Redwood, I told him firmly. *Percival probably has you under watch right now anyways. If you leave, you'll bring him right to me. I'll be back soon.*

If something could grumble within someone's mind, Redwood had just done that. But finally, he relented and went quiet within my head. *Thank you, sweet boy,* I said to him. *I'll be home soon.* Another grumble. I grinned.

Kil must have seen me having this wholly mental conversation, but to him it must've looked like I'd stopped just at the border of the refugee camp and stared for a minute or two. It probably unnerved him. "Are you alright, Princess?" he asked me.

I did my best not to laugh. I must've looked very strange. I smiled. "Yes," I told him. "Just an overprotective friend."

The soldier smiled curiously. "Right," he said, no doubt very confused.

With that exchange, we walked into the camp. It was similar to walking through the streets of the capital, but far more distressing. Almost everyone we saw was either in tattered rags or bore some sort of injury, be it a broken arm, a gash somewhere on their body, or even a missing limb. It made my heart hurt.

We walked to the center of a makeshift plaza that had been hastily set up. We were surrounded by tents. Each one was designed to hold three or four people, but right now they looked like they were each holding three families. To my right was a stand set up that looked like it was providing the people with food, which relieved me somewhat, but I couldn't even tell what the soldier behind the stand was ladling out: it looked like gray soup.

I shook my head. This had to change. "Juliana, will you place the chest down in the center of the plaza? I'm going to make an announcement."

The muscular soldier nodded curtly and proceeded to gently set the container down. I walked over to it, running my hand along the embroidered lid. I brought my other hand up to my neck and removed the key I had been carrying on a string. It felt strange. It was heavy and cold. I put the key in the crate's heavy lock and turned it. It took more effort than I'd thought it would; I had to use both my hands, but finally it turned with a loud *chunk*. I had to use both my arms to lift the golden lid.

I was met with the sight and smell of a feast's worth of food. The chest was packed to the brim with loaves of bread, fruits and vegetables of all kinds, and even a few cuts of meat. Everything I could've taken from the palace kitchens without being noticed. The smell alone made my mouth water, but I held myself back. This wasn't for me.

I turned to face my soldier friends and the crowds of people around us. I was ready to shout as loud as I could to try to get as many people's attention as possible in this loud plaza and bring them good quality food. When I turned, I was surprised. The plaza had turned dead silent. Not one person made a sound. All of their eyes were glued to the chest of food. Just the smell of actual food wafting through the air was enough to bring this square of a hundred people to a complete silence.

My voice died. These people were desperate, more desperate than I had ever seen anyone in my life of luxury. That desperation was scary. The amount of suffering these people had to go through where they were reduced to a near animalistic hunger was unbearable. I closed my eyes, trying to find the right words. I wouldn't let myself be scared. Not when these people needed help.

"Greetings," I called to the crowd in the strongest, most confident voice I could muster. I adjusted the hood of my cloak, making sure my whole face was covered. I couldn't be sure of what would happen if this crowd knew I was the crown princess, but I was sure that everything would be easier if my identity remained hidden.

I grabbed a roll of bread and held it out to the crowd, continuing, "My friends and I bring you food to eat. There is no catch; there is no price." I walked along the edges of the crowd, observing the faces of the people who made it up. Most of them were a mix of confused and wary. I couldn't blame them. I didn't know exactly what they'd gone through, but I imagined it made it hard to trust.

My eyes landed on a girl standing in the front of the crowd. She couldn't have been more than eight, and she was wearing what looked like a potato sack and nothing else. Her hair was a tangled mess, and I could see the bones in her arms under the skin. She looked up at me with watery eyes too large for her head as I walked closer. Any fear I had about this crowd was instantly forgotten as I knelt in front of her. "Take it," I said, smiling, offering her the roll I had grabbed from the crate.

The little girl hesitated, clearly wary of accepting food from a stranger, no matter her hunger. I understood her caution. Gently, I brought up my opposite hand and moved my fingers around slightly. Slowly, a red rose began to sprout and grow upwards from the soil below us. The flower grew all the way to my waist in seconds, where I plucked it from its stem and offered it to the girl. Her eyes grew wide. With a smile of awe, she accepted both the flower and the roll from my hands. It warmed my heart.

I rose back to my feet and continued to address the crowd, walking back and forth. "All we ask," I began, trying to make eye contact with every person I saw, "is that you keep the peace. Come, fill your bellies, but do so with order and civility." I motioned to my friends, who had spent the entirety of my speech standing off to the side of the plaza. They were all wearing the same wary look as they scanned the crowd, even Archibald, who was usually cracking some sort of joke. Kil was resting his hand on his sword in its sheath. "My friends are here only to maintain peace," I said. "You need not be afraid of them, but they will use their weapons if necessary." I made one last scan of the crowd. No one stood out as a criminal or looked like they would cause trouble, but I couldn't be sure. I stopped walking. "Do you accept our terms?" I asked the crowd.

The answer was unanimous. One loud, collective, "Yes!" was all I needed. I stood aside and motioned a hand towards the open crate filled with more food than some of these people had ever seen at once in their lives.

"Then be full."

Things went better than I'd imagined at first. There was no violence or crime of any kind. Despite coming from a war zone with nothing left to their name, every person in the plaza lined up in front of the crate and patiently waited their turn. I couldn't help but smile, partially out of relief, but also out of genuine happiness. Archie and Jules were helping hand out food along the line while Kil stood next to me, looking for any sign of trouble with his hawkish eyes.

"Something worked," I said lightly. "I can't believe it. Something good actually worked." This was a nice feeling.

Kil narrowed his eyes. "Don't start celebrating yet," he said, still scanning every face in the food line. "I won't until I know for certain you are back safe in your bed, Princess."

A cold chill instantly ran down my spine; the hair on the back of my neck stood up. I widened my eyes at Kil. "Don't call me that here!" I snapped in a hushed tone. I looked around to see if anyone had heard, but luckily it seemed everyone was too focused on the possibility of receiving food. I pulled my hood lower all the same.

Kil's eyes widened. He'd caught his mistake almost instantly. He cursed himself under his breath. "Forgive me, ma'am."

"Ma'am?" I said playfully, letting my mouth hang open. "I'm thirteen! My name won't hurt you, you know."

"We'll have to agree to disagree then, ma'am," he replied, smirking slightly. "I'm a soldier, and you are technically my commander. It's a sign of respect."

I huffed, sensing I wasn't going to win this battle. *I'll get him to use my name one day*, I thought defiantly. I decided to change the subject. "Well then, *soldier*," I smirked back at him. "You did well tonight. You all did." I motioned towards Jules, who was handing out a basket of apples to a group of small children, and Archie, who was holding a large piece of bread. The short man took a long inhale, smelling the scent coming off from the baked good. He flashed his eyes to either side, thinking he wasn't being actively observed, and slowly began to move the bread into the sack on his back. Kil glared at him from across the plaza, which startled the man, who then began to whistle inconspicuously and walked farther down the line, resuming handing out food.

Kil sighed. "Well enough, I suppose," he responded. "But this was your idea. You planned this. You just asked us for help. The victory belongs to you."

I smiled. It was nice to be recognized and not overshadowed, for once. Then I remembered how many people we had seen on our approach to the camp. I remembered that however much good I did tonight, while I was proud of my work, it wouldn't be enough to help everyone. My smile dropped, and a sigh escaped.

Killian looked at me. "What's wrong?" he asked sincerely.

I opened my mouth to tell him. The words never even had time to form.

It felt like I was standing in the middle of a temple with all of its bells ringing at once. It wasn't an actual sound; it was in my head, banging against the inside of my skull. I cried out in surprise, doubling over and clasping my hands to my ears in a desperate but vain attempt to quiet the sound. The hair on my neck stood straight up. Kil lowered himself so he was face to face with me. He looked concerned, and I saw his lips move like he was saying something, but I couldn't concentrate enough to hear it. Something wrong was happening.

I felt my hood get tugged away from my head by someone behind me. I spun around in surprise, nearly falling over because of the disorientation. A bearded man with a sunken face was pointing at me repeatedly. He was talking to me; I could pick out a couple instances of *princess* by reading his lips, but everything else was just noise.

The man grabbed my arm, hard. I was too overstimulated to do anything. All I could do was stand there, helpless, as the man's eyes welled with tears. He was *pleading*. He was pleading to *me*.

Killian grabbed the pleading man's arm and shoved him away from me, shouting something I couldn't understand. The soldier drew his sword. I felt like I was about to vomit. Everything was collapsing so fast. I turned back to the center of the plaza. The people standing in the food line had heard the noise we were making. They were all looking at me. Archibald and Juliana exchanged nervous glances. My stomach dropped. *They all know who I am.*

As if someone had flipped a switch, the entire crowd changed. They all rushed forward, desperate to have the heir to the kingdom hear their pleas. Jules and Archie tried to hold the surging crowd back, but the amount of bodies made it nearly impossible. I held out my hands, trying to deescalate the situation, but all I could manage to get out to calm them was a weak "please." This peaceful crowd was quickly becoming a mob, and I was too distracted with whatever was going on in my head. All I could do was try to back away slowly from the advance. The pounding rain made it even harder to concentrate.

Wait, I had just enough coherence to think. *How long has it been raining? It wasn't raining before.* As if to answer my thought, I saw a white flash in the sky and felt the ground shake with the rumble of thunder.

Killian rushed over to me, or at least, he tried. He saw that I had backed towards the plaza's center and tried to run towards me. He had to push through all the bodies that were now between us, but he didn't get far. Each person in front of him kept trying to shove him back. I could only see his face in the thick mass of people.

Rose! I read from his lips. I could tell he was shouting, and he was scared. *Rose!*

"Killian!" I shouted back, hoping he could use my voice to navigate the crowd easier. I couldn't even hear myself shout.

Soon, I lost sight of him. Too many people were rushing towards me. I continued walking backwards until I tripped on a loose stone in the road. I fell on my behind, scraping my hands on the stones. Tears welled in my eyes. I didn't know what to do. My senses were so overstimulated, with the pounding in my head, I struggled to even process what was going on around me.

I crawled farther and farther back. *These people might kill me,* I thought, *and I can't even understand what they want.*

Suddenly, I felt the same familiar feeling in my mind. It was like a candle in the darkness, reaching out to me. He was frightened, but not for himself. He was frightened for me. He was confused as well. Of course he was; he was all the way back at the palace. His presence in my mind quieted the bells somewhat, enough to send a message.

"Redwood," I gasped aloud. "Redwood, please get here. Please find me. I need you." I could tell that was all that was required. He'd heard. I could feel him stamping his legs on the ground just as I could feel him extend his two massive wings. Something very large had just taken off into the night sky.

Suddenly, the entire crowd stopped moving at once. Judging by their lips, they'd stopped shouting too. I breathed a couple of hard, quick breaths, using the lull to regain some of myself. The bells had quieted to where I just felt my head buzzing, but it was still very distracting.

I looked nervously back at the crowd with warm tears still running down my face. They were all looking up at something behind me. *Looking up,* I thought. At that moment I realized I could no longer feel the heavy raindrops. I curiously patted my head just to make sure. Yes, my hair was drenched, but it was no longer being rained on. My fear from moments ago was replaced with a cautious curiosity. After all, ten feet in front of me I could *see* the rain still pelting down on the crowd.

Another flash of lightning. Two large shadows were illuminated against the dozens of people behind me. I recognized the shapes of the shadows almost instantly as I watched them slowly unfurl. I cautiously brought my head up to finally look at what had gotten the crowd's attention moments before I would've been swarmed. I was met by two giant, electric blue eyes gazing back down at me, cutting a light through the darkness. The dragon's head was so large he was literally blocking the rain from hitting me.

Apolion turned his massive head towards the crowd of onlookers, almost all of whose faces had gone pale, and one had fainted. The dragon shook his head, sending a movement of muscle all the way down his long, serpentine neck. I didn't need the ability to hear to *feel* what happened next. Apolion opened his jaw and roared a sound so powerful I felt the ground shake. The crowd backed up a dozen feet, all with their hands clasped over their ears. With the dragon's roar, the bells in my head died instantly. My senses had returned, and I was greeted with another explosive boom of thunder and the familiar hammering of rain. *What happened to me?* I could only wonder.

The arrival of Apolion meant the arrival of Percival. My brother slid off his dragon's wing to the ground, our father's bronze spear in hand. He didn't even glance my way as he walked in front of me, facing the crowd. Bolts of blue electricity were running up and down his weapon; he was ready to fight. Killian, Juliana and Archibald had been abandoned by the crowd when they moved back out of fear of Apolion. The three soldiers saw my brother and all knelt instantly like it was instinct.

"I am Percival," my brother shouted at the crowd in a strong voice, "son of the murdered King Arturus and the rightful Lord of all Lungalea! By royal proclamation, I pardon any of you involved in the assault on the crown princess, my sister, on the condition that you go now in peace. Stay, and I cannot guarantee your safety."

I had never heard Percival so tense before. He was hiding it well; I doubted the crowd could pick it up, but I knew the signs. For instance, under normal circumstances, Percival would never allow himself to brandish his weapon at civilians.

Murmurs went through the crowd over the proposed deal. Most seemed receptive to it, but one man raised a fist. "What kind of king would let a dragon loose on his own people?" he cried. I recognized his face. It was the same man who had exposed my identity to the crowd and separated me from Kil, starting the mob in the first place. I found myself in disbelief over how much of a problem this man was making himself. Just as fast, the crowd murmured in agreement with his question.

Percival glared straight through the man, electricity still crackling along his spear. "I wasn't referring to the dragon," he said in a low voice, followed by another rumble of thunder. "Leave. *Now*."

The ragged man glared back at Percival. For a few seconds, neither of them said a word. Finally, the man spat at the ground. "Behold, everyone," he said to the crowd, "your Boy King." With that, he stormed off, and I never saw that man again. The pacified crowd mumbled quietly in agreement before slowly dispersing, leaving me, my three friends, my brother, and his dragon alone in the plaza.

I saw Percival drop his shoulders ever so slightly. The electricity crackling along his arm and spear fizzled out and died as he sighed. He turned and walked towards me, kneeling once he was close. "Give me your hands," he told me. I did.

I grimaced at what I saw. My hands were bleeding. I must've scraped them when I was crawling away from the mob. I'd never even felt it until that moment, when a stinging sensation was getting increasingly painful.

Percival took my hands in his, narrowing his eyes to analyze my injury in the little light. "Surface level," he said. "Return to the palace and see Jocasta; she will give you bandages. You probably had more fear than injury."

I took my hands back from him. *Figures he'd see if I was okay and then send me straight back to the palace*, I thought.

The three soldiers rose cautiously from their kneeling positions behind us. "Your Majesty," Killian began to my brother, "I can give you a report of what happened if that is your wish."

Percival furrowed his brow, slowly turning to face my friends as he stood. "*What happened* is you took my sister into the middle of a volatile area full of desperate people carrying the only thing they wanted. What did you *think* would happen?" He walked closer to Kil's face, his voice lower. "I expect better judgment from you, Captain. Especially with who I have put under your care." Kil said nothing, bowing his head.

Being able to see how much trouble my friends would soon be in, I stood and told the truth. "I commanded them to come with me."

A wave of silence washed through the makeshift plaza. Percival turned his head back to me. "What?" he asked.

"Yeah," I said, unwilling to let Percival punish my friends for my decisions. "I'm of royal blood, making me a commander of the kingdom's armies second only to you. As a commander, I commanded them to come with me to distribute supplies. None of this was their idea; it was mine."

Percival glared daggers at me, then slowly turned his gaze back to the three soldiers. "Is she telling the truth?" he asked Killian.

The young captain glanced at me. He looked unsure. I made direct eye contact with him. I was hoping he could tell what I meant. *Don't lie for me, Kil.*

He said nothing, but finally the soldier nodded curtly. It looked like the action pained him. Percival sighed, rubbing his eyes with his thumb and index finger. He looked back at the soldiers. "If any of you three ever put my sister in danger again, your ranks will be stripped and you will be assigned palace cleaning duty for the rest of your days, am I understood?" He was talking to them, but I could tell that message was meant for me. My heart sank. The three all dropped their heads.

"Return to your posts, the three of you," Percival continued. He turned around, this time addressing me. "And you come with me."

Old Days

IX

After my friends were dismissed and on their way back to the palace, Percival took us on a private path through the woods by the camp (but not before ordering the remaining soldiers stationed there to make sure the food from the chest was handed out in an organized way, I noticed). He had Apolion follow a few hundred feet behind us so the dragon wouldn't disturb us with the noise of a creature that size just moving.

Neither of us said anything until we were out of earshot of the ramshackle community. The forest was alive with sounds in the warm night, from the crunching of foliage under our feet to the peaceful buzzing of chickbees somewhere in the distance. The full moon served as our only light, but Percival and I managed to walk just fine.

"You know you're supposed to stay within the city," my brother began. He didn't sound angry; he didn't sound very emotional in general. His voice was eerily flat.

"I'm not a prisoner, Percival," I responded. "You can't keep me trapped on that island when I've done nothing wrong." I shrugged. "Besides, we barely left the riverbank."

Percival shook his head. "It's not the distance that's my concern," he said. "It's your actions." For the first time in our conversation, he stopped looking ahead and turned his gaze to me. "You could've been seriously injured tonight. Or worse. I don't have you stay on the island to keep you prisoner. I do it to keep you safe."

For a moment I thought I heard slight emotion from him. "But how long do we prioritize my safety over the condition of our people?" I asked. It was a question I had been constantly pondering since the outbreak of war. "Father came to the throne after a long line of our tyrannical ancestors, and because of him our kingdom changed for the better. He had the courage to focus on his people instead of his family."

Percival looked deep in thought. "Father never fought a war as king," he said quietly.

"He didn't need to."

Percival was silent. Maybe that last comment was too harsh. I decided to change the topic. "How were you able to find me so fast?" I asked my brother. "Davit I understand, but *I* take care to cover my tracks."

The young king grinned ever so slightly. "You do," he admitted. "I had nothing to follow you except a low-stocked kitchen and five thousand hungry people just outside the gates."

Hearing it out loud, my plan sounded horrible. In an effort to make Percival think I wasn't *totally* helpless, I opened my mouth and said, "Well, I knew you'd find us, I just wanted to slow you down."

"Ah," Percival said. "Well, you certainly did that. The council has been in a fit since they found out about your disappearance."

I nodded. "I'm sure." As the heir to the throne, I usually attended meetings of the regency council that governed the realm in Percival's name until he turned sixteen. I always listened intently during the meetings, but I never cared for the council's members. I saw them as a bunch of old lords constantly bickering with each other instead of doing what they were actually supposed to do and rule. Out of its members, Pevincy was the only one on the council I liked to be around.

Percival shook his head slightly, probably thinking of the headache the council no doubt caused. "They were shouting for an hour," he said. "In the entire time I was there, they never even brought up the idea that you could've used the siege tunnels to escape."

"Truly the realm's greatest minds," I said, hopping on a fallen tree and stretching out my arms to balance as I walked.

"Once I was out of that mess and on Apolion," Percival continued, "finding you was easy."

I sighed. "That shows me for trying to hide from someone with the eyes of an eagle."

The young king stopped walking and leaned on the side of the fallen tree. "There's another reason I found you so fast," he said. "I was actively looking for you before I knew you snuck out."

I furrowed my brow. "What for?" I asked, hopping down from the tree. As heir, I held a great deal of symbolic value, but my royal duties were usually pretty restrained, and the opportunities to have anything to do were few and far between.

Percival looked me straight in the eye. Our eyes were so blue I had no trouble clearly seeing his, even in the low light. "Davit hatched his egg."

My brother paused, giving me a moment to absorb that information. It felt like a bucket of cold water was slowly dumped over me. Davit never wanted to talk about his dragon egg; as far as I knew, he didn't even know his order had been ignored and it wasn't destroyed. Whatever caused him to change his mind must've been big. "Because of the people at the gate?" I asked Percival warily. It was the only thing I could think of that would affect Davit enough to hatch his egg.

Percival nodded. "That's what he says," he confirmed. "But I have my doubts."

I cocked my head. "Doubts?"

My older brother sighed. "I don't know if it's concern for the people that motivated his decision," he said, looking over at me, "or his hate for Ahaax."

Just hearing the name sent a shiver down my spine. The face of the man who murdered my father forced its way into my mind. I tried concentrating on other things to get his image out of my head. That was a place he would never be allowed.

I thought of Davit hatching his egg. I wanted to imagine that his decision was based purely on his love for his people, but I couldn't be sure, and I hated that feeling. For our entire shared lives, my brother had been happy, funny, and kind. Ever since Father's death, though, he had changed. He was quieter, and whenever Ahaax was brought up there was only anger. In those moments it was like I was speaking to a stranger.

Percival noticed my silence. He must've been dealing with the same thoughts. "I've come to ask a favor of you," the young king admitted.

I cocked an eyebrow. "Oh?" It was a very rare instance where *I* held a position of power.

My older brother nodded. "Teach Davit how to fly with his dragon," he asked. He was still speaking in the way of the king, but something about his tone had softened, like he may let himself become my brother again. "Your bond with Redwood and mine with Apolion have been foundational to us. Maybe if Davit bonds with his…" Percival looked at the ground, deep in reflective thought. "Maybe he won't go down this path of blood and vengeance."

I crossed my arms, thinking of the task that had been given to me. "That could be pretty hard," I said, unsure. I remembered everything that Davit had ever told me concerning his egg. It usually all boiled down to one message. "He kind of hates that thing."

Percival sighed. "Will you do it?" he asked. "I don't have the time, with my duties running the war." The king looked at me with eyes resembling a young animal. He was *vulnerable*, I realized. The last time Percival was outwardly vulnerable was six months ago. My brother's expression tugged at my heart. I knew I would probably help him, especially if it would help Davit as well, but I also knew I was in a position to leverage the king.

I huffed. "I don't know, I'm very busy these days." I looked down at my nails nonchalantly.

Percival furrowed his brow. "No, you aren't," he retorted. "You haven't left Lungala in months."

My face took on an expression of mock surprise. "And whose fault is that?" I asked aloud.

The young king's face went flat at my snark. He knew to expect this attitude from Davit, but he often forgot that I was his twin. "What do you want?" Percival asked.

Now is my chance, I thought. I put my hands on my hips, determined. "I want you to promise that you will do everything in your power to help those refugees we just saw." It was a simple request, I thought. One well within the power of the king.

Percival looked confused. "Of course, I will try to help them, Rose…"

I shook my index finger. "That's not good enough." I was enjoying being the negotiator. "I want you to promise that you won't let the council stop you from getting those people the help they need."

This gave Percival pause. He was bound by tradition to obey his regency council, but there was no codified tool that allowed them to rule over the king. From my point of view, Percival needed to find his own way to rule, not to be constantly dragged around by his indifferent lords. With a sigh, the king acquiesced. "Alright," he said with a nod. "I promise to get those people all the help within my power." I could tell he meant it. At the end of the day, Percival was still a good person who cared for his people.

I beamed and hugged my brother in the warm night air. I couldn't remember the last time we had shared a personal moment like that between us. It felt nice, but at the same time it made my heart long for days gone by.

Percival returned my hug, smiling softly as well. "It's late. I should bring you back to the palace now."

I stepped away from him, still giddy with joy. "That's alright," I said. "My transportation should be here any moment." Sure enough, I felt the familiar comforting presence return to my head, signaling his arrival.

In front of me, the soil on the forest bed rose and formed a mound, growing larger and larger. As it grew and shifted, the dirt fell back to the ground, revealing the massive creature that was rising from the soil, or rather, was transforming *from* the soil. Slowly, Redwood clawed the upper half of his body above ground as his rear and tail gradually took solid form from the dirt it had been seconds before.

My dragon companion was easily the largest creature that I had ever seen. While Apolion and Redwood may have hatched around the same size, in the six months since, the latter had grown to about the size and a half of the former. His legs were short and thick as tree trunks, and even his footprints were four feet wide. His body was at least seventy feet long from his box-like head all the way down to the tips of his two separated tails, and his scales had darkened to a red the color of Lungalean tree bark, hence his name. His two wings looked disproportionately small; it was a wonder he was able to lift his enormous body off the ground.

Redwood made a low, deep rumble of pleasure upon seeing me. "Hello, sweet boy," I greeted him, smiling. The sight of him always made me happier than I had been. I climbed the rope netting draped around my dragon that allowed me to reach the saddle high on his back. I had never much enjoyed flying, but it was a short distance back to the palace, and my spirits were too high to let anything drag me down.

Percival looked up at me from his position on the ground. "Straight back to the palace now. I don't want you running off again," he said in a lighthearted but still serious tone.

I nodded, looking down on him. A wave of exhaustion swept over me all at once. It just occurred to me how much I had been through in such a short time. Before I left, I gave my brother a final goodbye. "Goodnight, Percival.".

The young king smiled softly. "Goodnight, Rose." And with that, my dragon took off into the warm night sky.

Percival

To Be King

X

I stood on the forest floor as I looked up, watching my sister and her dragon become an increasingly smaller dot against the black night. I was feeling a range of emotions. I felt pride for my sister. The determination she showed in going on her quest, and then from making a demand of *me,* was an aspect of Rose that I had always admired. But my pride was quickly overshadowed by worry and fear. It was that same determination that brought Rose into danger tonight in the first place—what brought her into that mob.

I shivered, suddenly feeling cold despite the warm night air. There were few times in my life when I had been more frightened than when I was between my sister and those hundreds of people. It wasn't fear for me, but for Rose. I sighed. No matter how I felt, that night had only served to confirm my instincts. I had kept my siblings confined to the capital city since the outbreak of war for the sole purpose of protecting them. I had already had to see more war in the past six months than I'd thought I would ever in my whole life, and I was determined not to let my siblings fall into the same fate. I would keep them safe, no matter how it made them feel. Or how it made me feel.

I sighed again, suddenly aware of a heavy weight on my back. Reaching around, I unhooked my father's spear from its notch behind me. The bronze felt heavy and cold in my hands. The weapon felt like it was someone else's. Turning the spear, I noticed my reflection in the polished metal of the tip, but it was my father's gaze that was looking back at me, the man who had forged the spear I had merely adopted. It was the only physical connection I had left to him that wasn't mired by the weight of the throne.

"What would you do?" I asked aloud. The only answer I received from anywhere was a soft breeze brushing past my ear. It was a foolish thing to do, confiding in my father's weapon. Yet I found myself doing it more and more as the war progressed.

The sound of rustling foliage and heavy footsteps alerted me to the arrival of Apolion behind me. With one last sigh, I placed the spear on my back and turned to face my dragon. Even in the low light, his massive frame seemed to glow from his golden feathers. Slowly my dragon lowered his large serpentine neck closer to the ground so I could scratch behind his head. He must've sensed my troubles in the same mysterious way he always did. The dragon made a series of chirping sounds closer to something a cat would make instead of a forty-foot-long flying reptile.

"I'm alright, friend," I reassured the dragon. "There are just a lot of thoughts on my mind." That appeared to do little to ease Apolion's concern. I looked up at the sky through the tree coverage. The moon was almost directly above us. "What say we head back to the palace now?" I turned my gaze down to my dragon's head.

Instantly, Apolion poked his head up, extending his long neck so that he was now the one looking down at me. He opened his mouth wide, exposing multiple rows of teeth in a sight that would likely have frightened the casual observer half to death. I only smiled, watching as my friend yawned groggily. I'd had to wake him in a hurry when I left the palace to get Rose. Climbing onto Apolion's saddle, I craned my neck up at the night sky full of glimmering stars. With my voiceless command, the dragon extended his vast wings and the two of us leapt strongly into the air.

What happened in the next few moments was some of the only joy I was able to regularly experience in the past six months. We were above the towering treetops within one second. It was a constant battle to stay in the saddle. At any point I could lose my hold and the wind would sweep me off and away, but I was never scared for a moment. It was part of the thrill of flying.

As the force of the wind blew my hair back from my face and made it hard to close my eyes just to blink, I couldn't help but smile. The sky was my domain. For however long me and Apolion were up there, I could ignore all my problems on the ground. As far as I could convince myself, I wasn't even the king: just a boy and his companion. It was the only time I had when I didn't feel like I was making decisions for an entire world.

Apolion lowered his back and evened out his flying, keeping us in the air with the rhythmic beats of his wings. As we flew, he would chomp his jaw at the occasional cloud or flock of birds. It made me smile. He had his own ways of keeping himself entertained, just as I did.

Below us, the full moon illuminated the rolling hills for miles around, turning the green grass into a beautiful shade of silver. From this high, even the grand city of Lungala only looked like one or two dots of light. Still, against the blackness of the night below, the city shone like a beacon. I couldn't look away, my eyes drawn to the capital.

With a sigh, I continued gliding above the city on Apolion, looking down. I knew I needed to return. At the very least, it was past midnight, and I would need to sleep eventually. But something within me resisted the urge to return to my home. I knew that as soon as I did, I would become the king again. I leaned flat against Apolion's back, looking up at the stars above us. Many things about the day my father had died six months ago stuck around in my head, but I would often find myself reflecting on one moment from the throne room in particular.

"I didn't *ask* for this!" Davit had said to our father in his outburst. I sighed. *Neither did I.* As I watched the stars above my head, I couldn't help but get lost in my thoughts.

It was a night filled with stars similar to this, years ago. I was probably half my age at the time. This was before I had truly begun my lessons in chivalry and rulership that would define my childhood. At that time, I didn't have a care in the world.

I remembered I had been playing with my best friend for as long as I could remember, a black-haired boy my age named Bryce. Bryce's father was the former head of the Crown's Circle before Pevincy. The head guard had carried over from the previous king, my grandfather, into service with my father, so I had known Bryce for my entire life, and at times our bond felt closer than even that of my biological siblings.

The two of us children were playfully sparring with wooden swords in the palace courtyard, although truthfully, we were swinging the swords wildly without any thought behind our movements. Our wooden blades locked together. I was using all my might to push against Bryce's stance, but with cat-like speed, the boy in front of me managed to swing his leg into mine, knocking me off balance and sending me to the ground bottom-first with an *oof.*

Bryce held out a hand to help me up, flashing a smile with a single tooth missing. "Got you again!" he boasted.

I grinned at the competition, taking my friend's hand. "I'll beat you one day," I vowed, rising.

Bryce laughed confidently. "Yeah, right!"

Someone cleared their throat politely behind us. I saw Bryce's eyes widen, looking past me. Turning, I was met by the sight of my father standing next to Bryce's, both looking down at us.

"Are you boys enjoying yourselves?" my father asked us kindly. He looked at me with a warm smile.

I nodded enthusiastically, completely disregarding any formalities in front of the king. "Uh huh!" I confirmed to my father. "We're going to be soldiers!" I held up my small wooden sword with immeasurable pride. The king chuckled.

Bryce's father grunted. "Not if this one can help it," he said gruffly, nodding at his son. The head of the Crown's Circle, Brane, shared a familial resemblance to his son, with his black hair and lean stature, but the elder man looked and acted far meaner. Even as a boy, I was wary of him. Bryce shrank away at his father's piercing stare.

Brane turned back to my father. "As I was saying, my lord, I truly believe…"

The king's face hardened. "I will hear no more of this, Sir Brane," he said decisively. I didn't know what the two adults were talking about, but I could tell it was making my father angry. "That will be all for now, thank you."

Bryce's father was visibly angered by the king's refusal. I could see his teeth clenched from where I was standing a couple feet away. "Yes, my lord," he strained. Turning, the head guard walked stiffly back into the palace. At the entryway, he half craned his head behind him. "Boy!" he called.

Bryce looked at me, then back at his father. "Bye, Percival," my friend said to me, then quickly ran to his father's side.

As I watched Bryce leave, my own father walked up and rested his hand softly on my shoulder. "Come," the king said. "There is something I want to show you."

A few minutes later, the two of us were standing on a large balcony on the far side of the palace, overlooking much of the city. Unusually, I had noticed that all of the lights in the buildings below had been dimmed or snuffed entirely. Yet, there were still hundreds, if not thousands, of glowing pinpricks of light down in the city. At this distance, they looked like glowing firebugs. The lights moved through the streets below in a coordinated fashion, as if they were putting on a show.

"Woah," I said, amazed at the spectacle I had never seen before. I stood on the tips of my toes to be able to see above the balcony's marble railing.

My father smiled. "The Festival of Lights," he said by my side. "Every ten years, cities across the kingdom come together to honor the Heavenly Gods above, a tradition we keep from our ancestors across the sea." He extended an arm above him. I looked up and was met with a black sky speckled end to end with countless glimmering stars. I had never seen so many at once before. My mouth hung open. The king noticed my expression. "It's beautiful, isn't it?" I could only nod silently. He smiled.

The two of us looked out into the dark city filled with dazzling light for so long I lost track of time. I only remembered when my father began speaking again. "One day, everything you see here will be yours to rule, son. As it is mine now." He looked down at me.

I looked back to my father. I had known that I was going to be king, but I had never quite realized what that had meant. I looked into the city. I would be in charge of everyone?

"How does that make you feel?" my father asked me genuinely.

I didn't know, and I said as much, shrugging. "That's a lot of people," was all I managed to comment.

My father smiled again, putting a hand around my shoulder. "Yes, it is," he acknowledged. He leaned closer to my level. "But they will all need you, Percival." He touched the center of my chest lightly. I cocked my head. My father went on. "A king," he said with a sigh, "lives a different life from everyone else. They must be like the rivers you see around this city." He motioned one hand to his left, and one hand to his right. "Strong, but always moving forward. Steady and sure… Alone, but they must always protect their people. The river is not swayed by emotional causes. It flows regardless of who needs to cross. That is the duty of a king. Does that make sense?"

My brow was furrowed. Truthfully, I was lost in my father's conversation relatively quickly. I did my best to summarize what I understood. "A king is supposed to be different from everyone else?" I asked.

My father nodded. "Yes," he confirmed. There was a strange look on his face. One I didn't understand at the time. "That is the burden of the crown. But in carrying that weight, you will lead our people greater than anyone has before. I know that you will one day become a far better king than I could ever be." He tightened his hug around my shoulder. I reached an arm around his back, although I couldn't even make it across his entire body due to my size. Together, the two of us looked on at the scene of dazzling lights and shimmering stars.

As I looked up at the night sky, resting on the back of Apolion still flying through the air, my mind was replaying that night over and over in my head. My father's lessons in kingship had stuck with me over the past six months, and it all began that night. I would never get to live a normal life. That was not a king's place. But still, as I dreaded returning to the royal palace, it was difficult not to long for a life that could never be.

The Huntress

XI

Suddenly, I heard a series of strange noises from the woods below us. The unusual sound caught my attention immediately. I sat straight up. No normal person would've been able to pick out the sounds from the noise of the rushing wind blowing past my ears as Apolion flew, but due to what I could only attribute to my abilities over air, I was able to hear something that sounded out of place.

"Ho," I said as I pulled back lightly on Apolion's reins. My dragon came to a standstill in the air and stayed aloft with powerful rhythmic beats of his wings. Had I not been used to flying by now, the forward momentum from that quick of a stop would have sent me forward off his back.

I closed my eyes as I tried to concentrate on the strange noises below me. It was difficult trying to hear past the buzzing of chickbees and the rustling of wind through the forest bed, but eventually something stood out. It was slow at first, like someone winding up a clock. Then the noise stopped, and there was a quick *thwick,* followed by a *thump,* gurgling, and what sounded like a struggle.

My eyes widened. That was all I needed to hear. The woods this far outside of the capital occasionally had problems with bandits. Someone could've been getting attacked below me; at the very least the sounds told me that someone was injured. I had to help.

Down, Apolion. Quick and quiet, I thought. We flew silently to an open clearing in the woods. Our landing was not the only aspect of the scene that was silent. As I dismounted Apolion, I realized I couldn't hear anything. The previous buzzing of insects and rustling of wind was gone, and the only sounds were my steps. It was unnerving.

I lightly took my spear off of the dragon's saddle, being extra cautious now that I knew a single sound could alert whoever or whatever was making those noises. *Return to the sky, Apolion,* I said to him through my mind.

Apolion, in turn, looked down at me with big, hurt eyes.

I'm sorry, but you're too big. You'll alert whatever's down here! Apolion offered a slight *coo* in defiance.

I shook my head, holding my ground. *No. I can handle myself. If I need you, you'll be just overhead. Now go. This isn't up for debate. Someone could be hurt and we're wasting time.*

Apolion huffed out of his nose, clearly displeased, but ultimately he extended his wings and leapt into the night sky without making a sound. I grinned slightly. He may object from time to time, but he would always be there for me when I needed.

Spear in hand, I turned around to observe the clearing. There didn't look to be any immediate threats; I seemed to be the only living thing around. Closing my eyes, I once again tried to listen for the alarming sounds that had caught my attention. It wasn't nearly as hard this time as when I was trying to listen on the back of a flying dragon. Almost instantly I could hear the rustling of leaves and a slow, burdened breathing. I didn't have much time left. I walked up to the edge of the clearing and, with a deep breath, took my first step into the dark woods.

Finding what I was looking for wasn't hard, surprisingly. The trees in the woods were so tall and close together that almost no moonlight made it through to the ground, but that didn't seem to matter. I moved through the forest like I was designed for it. The little light didn't make a difference. I hopped over fallen trees and jumped over ditches with a speed that rivaled running, but I didn't make a single sound. I knew I didn't have much time; that someone was in danger.

As I got closer to the sounds of struggling, I started to hear a new sound, louder than the previous one. It was a voice, a woman's from the sound of it, but I couldn't hear what she was saying from my distance.

Soon I came upon another clearing, although this one was smaller than the one Apolion and I had landed in. I could tell both the woman and whatever the original struggling sounds were coming from were both in the clearing together. I slowed my pace as I drew closer to the opening, finally crouching behind a large rock just by its entrance so I wouldn't be spotted by anyone; that way the element of surprise would remain mine. There were few trees in the circular clearing, so moonlight shone down on the small meadow, and as I leaned out slightly from behind my rock, I was finally able to get a clear look at the situation.

There *was* a woman, but she was at an angle from me so I couldn't see her face. She didn't have a very large frame, and her voice sounded young—my age, even. She had a long flowing curtain of full raven-colored hair that shimmered in the moonlight. She was hunched over something, but she wasn't doing anything to it. Her hands were clenched and still. As my eyes moved down her form, I saw that she had a bow slung around her shoulder, and as my eyes went even lower it became clear why.

"A deer?" I whispered, my jaw dropping. The woman was kneeling over the body of a deer, freshly killed most likely. I threw myself behind the rock and slapped my forehead, wondering how I could be so stupid. "She's a hunter," I whispered softly to myself. *These woods might have bandits in them.* Or they had hunters chasing deer! I cursed myself, embarrassed for my lapse in thinking but ultimately happy no one was being attacked.

Satisfied that there was no danger, I picked myself up from behind the rock, ready to leave, turning around one last time to see if I would be able to get a clear look at the woman. That was a mistake.

An arrowhead was held in suspension inches from my face. The woman in the clearing must have heard the sounds I was making, because she was now standing over me, her bow readied.

"Woah!" I cried, falling backwards on my palms. I raised my hands into the air. "Peace!" I called, mustering all the confidence I could with a readied bow inches from my face. "I mean you no harm."

The woman narrowed her amber-colored eyes at me. "Then why do you 'ave a spear?" she asked in a beautiful voice with a slight hint of a Westerland accent. She pointed her weapon towards mine, which was lying a few inches away from me in the grass.

I cursed myself silently. I had forgotten I was even holding my spear as I ran through the woods. "That," I began, unsure of what I would say, "doesn't look good," I admitted, "but I promise I'm not here to hurt you."

The woman scoffed, her bow still aimed at me. "So why *are* you here then? You stalk me on a hunt in the dead of night, *carrying* a spear, and you say you're not here to hurt me? I don't even know who you are."

I opened my mouth, ready to clear up the misunderstanding instantly. "I'm Perc..." *Wait,* I thought quickly. *She doesn't know who I am?* "I'm Percy," I played off my hesitation as naturally as I could.

The huntress scowled. "Percy?" She raised an eyebrow.

I nodded enthusiastically. "Yup!" I lied. My thoughts were racing. It made sense that this girl wouldn't know what I looked like. The kings of Lungalea ruled through decrees; they didn't advertise their face in every city. She probably knew of King Percival, but she didn't know he was the lanky, golden-haired boy on the ground before her. *So, if she doesn't know I'm the king,* I thought. My mind went back to the conflict I had within myself while I was flying Apolion. Something within me felt dangerously excited. This was possibly the first person I had ever met who didn't immediately know that I was the king. For the first time in my life, I could act like a normal human being. I wouldn't have to be king, I could just be my genuine self, not caring whom my actions affected or how this would shape my kingdom. Even if it was just a short conversation with this woman, the burdens of war had been stacking on top of me endlessly. I was desperate for any chance I had to break away, even momentarily. Something inside me ignored my brain saying what I was about to do was a bad idea.

The woman in front of me narrowed her eyes. "You seem out of your element here, Percy." She looked me up and down. I realized I was still wearing the elegant green and gold clothes of a royal. It wasn't as fancy as some of my kingly garbs, but it definitely wasn't common fashion either.

"I… my parents are nobles within the city," I thought quickly. It was just enough of a lie to be believable while still concealing my true identity.

"Noble, eh?" the huntress huffed. "And what brings a little lord all the way out into the woods at night?"

I thought through my answer. "Clearing my mind?" I offered, not technically untrue.

The woman scowled. "And the spear?"

"It's dangerous at night," I said, holding up my hands defensively and getting slightly annoyed at all the questions with an arrow still inches from my nose.

The hunter was silent for a moment, probably deciding whether to believe my story or not. But I could tell by her eyes that she was unsure holding her bow. She didn't want to shoot me. Finally, she sighed and lowered her weapon. "Well, you're definitely not telling me *something*, Percy," she began. She shrugged. "But you look like a good person. I hope I won't regret this." She offered me her hand to help me up from the ground. I froze. It was only with her bow lowered that I was able to clearly see the woman in front of me.

She was gorgeous. I knew instantly when I saw her face that she was the most beautiful girl I'd ever seen. She was wearing traditional hunter garbs, so I could guess that this wasn't her first night out on a hunt. My guess based on her voice appeared to be correct. She looked almost exactly the same age as me, maybe a year younger or older. Her caramel skin shone in the moonlight and looked as soft as a newborn babe's. But the thing that caught my attention the most was her eyes. Those beautiful eyes. Two amber gemstones shining in the darkness. I couldn't look away.

"Are you alright, Percy?" the woman asked, her arm still outstretched. "You look like you've just seen a ghost."

"I," I stammered, trying to not stupidly get caught up on my own tongue. "Yes," I finally managed to get out, "yes, I'm alright." I took her hand in mine and stood. She was stronger than I was expecting, so I stood pretty fast and nearly ran into her. I steadied myself by holding onto her shoulders; she held onto my arms. We locked eyes. I could feel her warm breath on my lips. It only lasted a moment, but I didn't want it to end.

"You know my name," I managed to say in a near whisper. "But I don't know yours."

The woman's eyes widened. She stepped away from me. "Oh," she said. Even in the little light, I thought I could almost make out a blush on her face. She looked back at me and flashed a smile that melted my heart. "Delilah," she said. "My name is Delilah."

"Delilah," I said, smiling. "That's beautiful."

Delilah shrugged modestly. This time she was definitely blushing. "Thank you," she said. "'Twas my mother's idea. She always had a way with the finer things."

"Had?" I asked.

Delilah dropped her eyes. "Sickness took her last winter," she said quietly.

I immediately felt terrible. "Oh, I'm so sorry," I said. "I didn't know."

"Don't be," Delilah said, shaking her head. She didn't say anything else. The only sounds were the buzzing of insects that had returned to the clearing. Her entire stature shifted. I could now see that the girl in front of me was hiding a battle she was fighting with a great sadness. It looked familiar.

"I lost my father last winter," I told her softly. I didn't think about saying it; the words just slipped out of my mouth. I hadn't talked about Father's death with anyone, not Pevincy or even Rose or Davit. Being the king wouldn't allow it. But watching Delilah in front of me, I couldn't leave her there alone.

She turned her big eyes up to me. "I'm sorry too," she said. "It's a terrible loss. Like you lose a piece of yourself when they go."

I nodded solemnly. I didn't feel nice, but it almost felt good, knowing that there was someone else who knew what I felt.

Delilah turned her head up to the sky, looking at the moon. "I've been out longer than I should; it's late." She turned her copper gaze back to me. It took all my effort not to blush myself. "You should come with me back to my home, Percy. You can ride back to Lungala with my father in the morning, and he can get ya back home."

I had grown so complacent talking to this beautiful girl in front of me that I had completely forgotten about my other life. My *real* life. My eyes widened, but I tried my best not to let Delilah see my surprise. "Oh, I don't think that'll be necessary," I said, trying to sound normal. There would be no way that I would allow myself to not return to the palace. I could only imagine the hell that would break loose throughout the council, not to even imagine Pevincy, if I wasn't there in the morning.

Delilah shook her head. "No, s'more than ten miles back to the city, and it's pitch black out. There's all kinds of things in these woods like bandits, an' I don't want to offend you, but that spear you brought would look more like a toothpick to an angry rockbear. You have to come; it's not safe."

I appreciated her concern, and I couldn't tell her that I had a dragon flying just out of sight that could get me back to the palace in less than ten *minutes* and make any threat in these woods obsolete, so I sighed and gave in, telling myself that I would find some way to slip out undetected later in the night. "Alright, I'll come with you. Thank you, Delilah."

The girl in front of me smiled and put her hands on her hips, satisfied with her victory. "Of course," she said. She turned her attention back to the deer she had hunted, the reason she had come out all this way. The two of us walked farther into the clearing together.

Suddenly, Delilah stopped. She turned, putting her hand on my chest. "Oh," she said, as if remembering something. "Wait here a moment." With that, she quickly skipped the few remaining feet between her and the deer and knelt, clasping her hands again like she had when I first saw her. She bowed her head. "Grant this life a restful sleep, an' grant me forgiveness for taking it," Delilah began. She was praying, I realized. She continued, "For from life comes death, and from death springs forth life. Bless this cycle that has always been and will always be. Grant me speed, strength and caution, Reyanna, an' may we hunt together someday, in this world or the next."

Slowly, Delilah stood and brushed the damp grass from her knees. "Reyanna," I said from behind her, recognizing the name. "Goddess of the hunt."

Delilah turned, still wearing her now-familiar slight smile. She nodded. "She's always been with me, watching over me ever since I was a babe. She's my patron, y'know? My mother would always help the temple in the closest town to us.

'Twas like her second home, it was." Delilah laughed sadly at the memory. "But anyway, she taught me the importance of honoring the Divines, both the Elders and the gods." Delilah turned back to the deer and leaned down.

I held out my hand in front of her. "You're opening your home to me for the night," I began. I put my spear back into its resting position in its harness on my back and knelt and wrapped my hands around the deer carcass, hefting it onto my shoulder. I found a slight humor in the situation. Six months before, the closest I'd been to a carcass was when Father would take his court out on hunts, but even then I would never be in direct contact with the animals. Now, though? After everything I'd seen… I found it a relief that it was just a deer. I stood, and the muscle I'd built up in the past months made the once no doubt difficult task relatively easy. I looked back at Delilah and continued, "Please, this is the least I can do."

Delilah smirked softly. "Alright," she said. "I'll allow it." She walked towards the entrance of the clearing. Turning to face me, she said, "Come, follow me. My house isn't far."

Delilah moved through the dark woods with the silence and grace of a big cat. She wasn't slowed by anything in her path, not even the darkness. It was clear that she was used to being out at night. We were only walking, but I still struggled to keep up with her. She would be ten feet in front of me, would stop, turn around and see I was lagging behind, apologize, and then come back and join me, only to naturally pull ahead again a few minutes later. I found it charming.

It was after one of those times, as this new girl that I had found in the woods was walking back towards me, that I finally opened my mouth and asked the question that had been lingering on my mind. "What are you doing out here, Delilah?" It didn't make sense to me that someone as sweet, and especially as young, as her would be the sole hunter of her house.

Delilah's face dropped. She understood the deeper meaning of my question. "Father stays home to watch the children," she said.

"Your siblings?" I asked.

Delilah nodded. "Five, in all, not including me. It used to be Mother's job, and Father used to do all the hunting but, well. The youngest, Erin, she's just a babe of a few months. It was shortly after delivering 'er that mother…" She stopped herself. She didn't need to go on. I understood.

"I'm so sorry," I began, trying to comfort her. "You've had to grow up faster than anyone should."

At that moment I had a realization. Delilah was me. She presented a perfectly crafted persona to the world as a shield to protect her true self, but the whole time she was hiding her reality. The reality that she was just a fifteen-year-old girl thrust into the world without any guidance. My heart broke for her, but there was another feeling. A quiet relief over the fact that for the first time there was *someone* who knew exactly what I felt. I couldn't abandon Delilah. I was a moth to a flame. I had only met her that night, but I felt like I had known her all my life.

"Thank you, Percy," Delilah said. "Really. Come, my house is just through those trees."

All at once the beautiful portrait I'd mentally painted of Delilah and my relationship had jarringly tilted. *Percy,* she had said. Any relationship that I might develop with Delilah would ultimately be one based on a lie. *So much about knowing every aspect of each other,* I thought bitterly. But that was the only way this could possibly work. If she found out who I really was, she probably would never want to see me again.

Can you blame her? You lied since the moment you met her. She doesn't know who you are, a small voice in the back of my head whispered. I pushed it away.

Delilah took my hand in hers and walked me through the remaining trees in our path. Instantly I forgot all about the moral dilemma I was debating within my head. My heart raced. She took my hand so easily, without any hesitation. And her hand! It was as soft as a light breeze, with a hint of new callouses beginning to form from her work with her bow. I felt my face heat up and scolded myself silently. *A king does not blush.*

Before I could even stop myself, I felt a numb tingling in my arm. There was a faint buzzing in the air. It was too late. I could only watch helplessly as a small arc of blue electricity ran down my arm and right onto Delilah's hand, shocking her. *Damn it. Control yourself, Percival!* I chastised myself.

Delilah pulled her hand away with a surprised gasp. She looked back at me. "What was that?" she asked, rubbing her hand.

Unwilling to let Delilah discover my true identity so soon after our relationship had just begun, I had to think quickly. "I don't know," I said, sounding as confused as I could. "I heard the buzzing, but I couldn't see anything. It must've been a bug. Very strange. Is your hand alright?"

Delilah furrowed her brow, rubbing where she had been shocked. "Yeah." She shrugged it off, seemingly no worse for wear. "You get used to bug bites living in the woods. Come along." I let out a silent sigh of relief. I was still learning the extent of my powers and didn't want to accidentally end up hurting her.

The two of us emerged from the trees into another clearing, but this one was occupied. A small wooden cottage was sitting in the center under the pale moonlight. The windows were lit with the orange glow of flames, and smoke was billowing out of its stone chimney. There was a small garden of flowers by its front porch, but that was the only decoration around the small house. It was a large change of pace from my home in the royal palace, but that made the sight of the small, warm house even better.

"Welcome to my home," Delilah said modestly, stepping onto the porch. "It may not be much compared to your lordliness, but it's served us just fine my whole life, it has."

"Nonsense, I love it," I said honestly. "It's cozy."

Delilah smiled. She turned, raising her hand to open the door.

The door swung inwards forcefully. A giant man was now standing in the doorway, his thick arms positioned on his waist. He must've been at least six and a half feet tall. His limbs more resembled small tree trunks than arms and legs, both in color and size. He had a head of close-cropped black hair, and a thick, bushy beard covered his lower face, which was beaming at me and Delilah with a mouth full of white teeth. His eyes were the same color as Delilah's, who I now assumed was his daughter.

"Lilah, you're back!" the man boomed in a deep and gregarious voice. Unlike Delilah's, his accent was so thick I had trouble understanding him at times. He stretched his neck over his daughter, now looking directly at me. "An' you've brought a friend! Wonderful! Whose this then?"

"Pa, this is Percy, he's from the city," Delilah began, gesturing to me.

"Sir," I said curtly. I didn't know what to say. I had never been introduced to someone whose titles I wasn't supposed to have memorized. It was a strange feeling, acting normal.

Delilah continued. "He got out inta the woods later than he shoulda, and wound up bumping into me right after my hunt. He carried the deer the whole way back an' I offered him a bed for the night, seeing as you're going to the city come morn'."

The man shrugged. "Might as well." He turned his gaze towards me, still wearing his large smile. "Well, boy, any frienda Lilah's a frienda the whole family! Lemme take that off ya, must be heavy for ya, all skin an' bones, ha!" He wrapped his arm around the deer carcass still slung around my shoulder and lifted it singlehandedly without any effort, resting it on his shoulder. He turned and walked through the doorway into the house, calling behind him, "You two come inside now, don't ya. You'll freeze yer whiskers off out there, ha!"

I slowly stepped through the door, with Delilah shutting it behind me. The interior of the house was just as minimalist as the exterior. There was only one room, which contained a table in the center, a few seats positioned randomly, and a pot over a small fire situated in the corner to my left next to what looked like a butcher's table. The far side of the room contained three doors, probably to bedrooms. "So," Delilah began, "that's my pa."

"I like that man very much," I said genuinely, as I watched him mount the deer carcass onto the table next to the pot and begin dressing it with a butcher's knife. He was a man who wasn't held back by any royal procedure, someone who wasn't afraid to be himself, no matter who saw. I admired it.

Delilah grinned. "Yeah, we bear with him." She looked around. "Ah, you're lucky, Percy, it looks like the little ones are already off to bed. It'll spare you wantin' to tear your own ears off."

Delilah's father chuckled heartily as he worked. "Yeah, I senta chillins' off to sleep. Did they whine, I tell ya! Wantin' to be up fer their big sister's return. But I say, 'No. You've had yer sup, now quit yer bellyaching or else yer sister'll never wanta come back! Ha! Did that do the trick!"

I laughed. I couldn't help it. This man just seemed so genuine, and for the first time in my life I felt like I was surrounded by people who weren't held back from acting how they wanted because they were nobility. I was happy. The giant of a man chuckled with me.

Delilah's father waved his hand. "Look at me, talkin' yer ears off. I'm sure you two're exhausted. Lilah, why don't ya get Percy set up there and put 'im up in our open room?"

Standing next to me, Delilah nodded. "Sure, Pa," she said. Gesturing for me to follow, Delilah walked the two of us into the door on the far-left side of the opposite wall.

It was a very small room, but that didn't seem to matter, as there was only two pieces of furniture in the entire thing: a wooden bed frame in the corner, and a small end table positioned on the wall opposite me. On the table were two things: a candle to give the room light, and a small piece of parchment.

I walked over to get a better look at what the parchment contained, and a pang of sadness went through my body. It was a painting, or more accurately, half of one. A beautiful woman was looking at me through the portrait; her face was painted but her clothes were still only outlines. A heartwarming smile covered her face and wrinkled her eyes. I recognized from the similarities that this must've been Delilah's mother.

The huntress girl was busy smoothing out a bedroll on the mattress. She looked up, noticing I was distracted. "Ah," she said. I turned around. Her eyes were fixed on the painting in my hands. "That was her last one," she said. "She never finished."

"She looked very kind," I said, trying to be comforting.

"She was," Delilah confirmed. "And talented." She walked closer to me, getting a better look at the painting. She turned her gaze around the room. "Ma loved to paint. She'd always place her art supplies at the top of her list for when Pa went to the city, before food even." She laughed sadly. I smiled with her. "She would keep all her paintings in this room," Delilah continued.

"What happened to the others?" I asked.

Delilah hesitated. "When Ma…" She paused. I let her have her time. It was the least I could do. The huntress took a breath and went on. "Well, Pa couldn't bear to look at her paintings. It hurt him too much. So he buried them with her. All but this one." Delilah brought her eyes back to the painting we were now holding in both of our hands. "I suppose to him an even worse thought than constantly seeing her paintings would be throwing away his last look at her."

Tears rolled down Delilah's cheeks. "I'm sorry," she said, looking away, wiping her eye.

Without thinking I embraced her in a hug. She gasped at the sudden move, but then she wrapped her own arms around me, sniffling. "You have nothing to be sorry for," I said, looking into her shimmering amber eyes. I felt as if I had no one to confide in. In that moment I swore that Delilah would never feel the same way.

Delilah and I stood there in embrace for a few moments longer, saying nothing. Nothing needed to be said. Eventually, she pulled back slightly, still sniffling, but her tears had largely stopped. "Thank you," she said.

"Of course."

Delilah took a deep breath and gently took the portrait from my hands. She walked around me and lightly returned it to the spot where I'd found it on the end table. With that, she turned to face me. She offered a slight smile, but I could tell she was trying her hardest to force it.

"Thank you, Delilah," I said, looking into her eyes, "for everything you've done for me tonight."

The raven-haired girl in front of me rubbed her nose, sniffing one last time. "Ah, well," she started. "It's not every day you meet a spear-wielding lordling in the woods." She took my hand softly in both of hers. "Specially not one like you, Percy."

I smiled, but it was bittersweet. How good could I be if I never told her the truth about who I was? It was as good as her talking to a stranger.

"I'll let you get some sleep," Delilah continued, gently letting my hand drop. With that she turned and headed toward the room's only door.

"I'll see you soon," I said as she stepped into the doorframe. I wouldn't be able to stay the night in her house, as she and her father had graciously offered, but I wasn't willing to let this new relationship end after only one night. Somehow, I would see her again.

Delilah, no doubt confused by my statement, raised an eyebrow at me from halfway behind the door. "You sure will," she said with a smirk, and then the door closed softly, and I was alone in the room that had once been full of paintings.

I stayed still for a moment, breathing out a satisfied sigh at the evening's turn of events. But then my other life beckoned to me from the sky. There was a presence in my mind, telling me to come outside the house and return to him. After all, I had been gone long enough already. "Alright, Apolion, quiet down," I whispered aloud. "I'm coming."

A climb out the window and a brisk walk through the woods later and I came upon the same clearing Apolion and I had initially landed in. The dragon was already there, and he greeted me with a series of quick chirps, his golden feathers shimmering in the moonlight as his body moved. "Calm yourself, Apolion," I said, waving my hand at him. "There is no law saying the king cannot befriend his own subjects."

Apolion barked a response.

"Because if I told her I was the king," I replied, "she would treat me differently or refuse to see me at all. I need this to be genuine. I need someone, a friend. I need…" I paused, remembering my first interaction with Delilah: how we nearly ran into each other as she pulled me to my feet, her warm breath on my lips, the softness of her skin, the sparkling pools of copper that lay in her eyes. "I need her," I said.

Apolion let out a low moan. He looked down at me with a sympathetic face. He didn't approve, but he understood. I smiled as I lightly rubbed the bridge of his nose, feeling his emotions as much as he was feeling mine. There was uncertainty, fear, and worry, but also hope. Hope was the message Apolion wanted me to receive. "Thank you, my friend," I said to him.

I don't remember the flight back to the royal palace; I was too preoccupied with my thoughts. I lay on Apolion's saddle as he glided through the night sky, lost in plans for how I would see Delilah again. There were many options I could take to develop the relationship I had formed. All of them would be difficult, but that didn't matter. So long as I could return to that small cottage in the woods, and return to her, it would be worth it. For the first time in the past six months, I couldn't stop smiling.

Davit

A Rude Awakening

XII

I was awoken by a sudden knocking at my door. So sudden, as a matter of fact, that I rolled off the side of my bed out of surprise. If the abrupt noise didn't fully wake me, falling onto the cold stone floor of my bedroom certainly did. I groaned as I opened one of my eyes, content to stay on the floor in a state of groggy helplessness. Alas, there was another series of knocks.

"Coming," I said, slowly rising to my feet. *The world had better be ending*, I thought, slightly annoyed at the awakening, as I shuffled towards the sound. With a tug, I yanked open the thick wooden door to my chambers.

"Ah, Prince Davit," one of Percival's messengers greeted me from just outside my doorframe. Eadward, I thought his name was. Or maybe he was Eathan? I couldn't be sure. Percival had so many, their faces occasionally blended together, not to mention that they all wore the same puffy brown tunics and waist-long capes. "I hope I didn't disturb you?" Eadward Eathan said.

"Nothing can be done now," I said, defeated, as I felt my last chance of getting back to sleep slip away and my brain began to wake up. I scratched the back of my head lazily. "What is it?"

Eadward Eathan clasped his hands together. "His Grace has called a meeting of the council and thought you would like to attend."

I thought it over for a moment. Percival never thought about asking me to all his other council meetings. This one must've been important. An exciting thought came into my mind. Maybe there was news about the war! Surely that must be it; what other reason would I be involved in? Grain trading routes? Unlikely.

I perked up. Now the bland man in front of me had my attention. "Sure," I said. "Let's go."

Eadward Eathan sucked in air through his teeth. "King Percival usually enjoys a certain…" He looked me up and down. "Formality, at meetings of his royal council."

My face went slack. "Thanks," I said unenthusiastically, getting his message. With that I closed the door, a little harder than I would normally, hoping Eadward Eathan heard. I shuffled to a wash basin resting in a carved, waist-high marble pillar situated against the far wall of my room. There was a mirror hanging above the basin, and I *did* look a mess. Half of my hair was plastered to the side of my face I landed on the ground with, and there was even a faint line of drool going in the same direction. "Egh," I let out, wiping the line away with my hand. Eadward Eathan was right; I could use some freshening up.

I washed my face and hair with the scented rose water in the basin. Once cleaned, I changed out of my pajamas and donned a pair of brown pants and an emerald tunic lined with silver thread: fancy enough to be respectable, but not so fancy that I would need someone else's help to get out of it. Satisfied that Eadward Eathan would let me leave, I once again opened the door to my room.

"Ah, much better, Prince Davit," the messenger said.

"Let's get going then," I responded.

The walk from the tower that held my bedroom to the council chambers was a long and winding one, although to me all the paths through the palace were long and winding. Eventually, after I had lost count of the flights of stairs Eadward Eathan and I had descended, we walked through a pair of massive wooden doors into a sunlit courtyard. The courtyard marked the separation between the more personal side and the business wings of the palace and was lined with emerald-green grass and flower bushes that were every color of the rainbow. This courtyard was also the only place in the palace large enough to serve as the dragons' stables.

As the royal messenger and I walked under a covered pathway to the side of the courtyard, I turned my head and saw Rose's dragon, Redwood, lying on his back lazily soaking up the sun. It was still incredible to me just how *big* that dragon was. His wingspan was probably just short of the width of the courtyard, which was even more mind-boggling to me when I realized that his wings were actually *smaller* in relation to his body than Apolion's were. By all rights he should've been too big to even get off the ground, yet somehow Rose took him flying on the rare occasion when she was granted leave from the palace.

Redwood's pre-afternoon nap was disturbed when Cerulia leapt from the shadows of a nearby tree right onto his belly, wanting to play. The much larger dragon let out a plume of smoke from his nostrils and slowly rolled to one side, his back now to Cerulia, wanting to ignore this new nuisance.

Cerulia, despite having only hatched a week earlier, was now roughly the size of a dog. She seemed to be developing at a much quicker pace than the other two dragons, the reason for which I (and the much smarter minds Percival had trusted to oversee the dragons) could only guess at. She was beginning to test out her wings, running through the courtyard and being able to glide if she got fast enough, when it had taken Apolion and Redwood both a month after hatching to get that far.

I stopped walking for a moment and leaned on the marble railing of the path, watching the two dragons interact. Cerulia didn't let Redwood's lack of interest stop her from getting her entertainment. The little blue dragon scampered to Redwood's head and put her two front legs on his snout, trying to get some sort of reaction. The older dragon responded by nipping at her, not in any way that would hurt, but giving her just enough of a spook so that she left his snout and ran a few feet away, where she then proceeded to chase after a butterfly that had found its way into the courtyard.

I laughed slightly. The young dragon never seemed to run out of energy. She reminded me of myself in more ways than one: young, reckless, occasionally stupid. I stopped smiling and sighed. I *wanted* to like her. In fact, it was hard not to like the little creature. But every time I looked at her, I saw the light leave my father's eyes, felt his cold hand fall slowly from my face. The friendly feelings I had towards Cerulia conflicted with the fact that I hadn't been there to defend my father those months ago, and now he was dead. I didn't deserve his gift.

"Prince Davit?" Eadward Eathan asked. I snapped out of my trance and looked towards the messenger. I must've stopped for longer than I'd thought. "Are you coming along now?" Eadward Eathan continued, sounding slightly annoyed, as though he didn't have enough time for my detour.

I scoffed. "Well, don't let *me* ruin your day," I said, standing from the railing and continuing on our path. With one final look towards the little blue dragon rolling around in the grass, the two of us walked through another set of heavy wooden doors, this time entering the royal business wing of the palace.

After another ten minutes of walking (no palace needed to be *that* big) Eadward Eathan and I came upon a simple wooden door that I recognized as the entrance to the king's council chambers from when my father would hold his meetings. The royal messenger stepped in front of me and opened the door, but I could tell from the look on his face that it was purely out of royal courtesy and not out of a strong passion for me.

As I stepped into the chambers and looked around, I noticed that the room had hardly changed since my father's reign. The council chamber itself was essentially just a smaller version of the palace's grand hall, with tan polished stone making up the walls, ceiling, and floor, and with marble pillars acting as supports. Various tapestries lined the walls between the pillars and torches that lit the room. What was unusual about this was that, if I was remembering correctly, *none* of the tapestries were different from when my father would meet in the same room. It was traditional that every new king would install different decorations around the palace when they began their reign. Percival didn't do this. Maybe he was too busy to worry about changing decorations, or maybe it hurt too much to take them down. Either way, I couldn't blame him.

There was a large wooden table in the center of the chamber carved in the shape of the kingdom. Situated around the table was every member of the king's council. I was the last to arrive, but maybe they wouldn't notice. Sitting at the table's north end was Lord Carrington, a grizzled, bald man with a sharp goatee who oversaw the provinces of the kingdom's north. Next to Carrington was Lady Aemelia, who oversaw the southern peninsula. With her waist-length glossy black hair and graceful makeup, the lady was often the most beautiful person in the room, and she would always be the first to acknowledge it, but she ruled effectively.

Across the table from the pair of them sat the siblings Lords Finnian and Florian, who ruled over the rest of the south and the west respectively. Looking nearly identical with their dirty blond heads of hair and chubby faces, each sibling often did their best work when they were disadvantaging the other. Finally, seated at the side of the table with his back to me was Lord Alaric, who oversaw the kingdom's eastern provinces. Alaric had lost just about half of his territory when Ahaax declared rebellion, and since then he had fled to the capital and his health had taken a turn for the worse, lately more resembling a skeleton than a lord. Already a cautious man before the war, nowadays Alaric rarely wanted to leave his chambers, let alone rule.

Seated at the side of the table facing me was Pevincy, the sixth and final member of the king's council, and the only one to not officially hold any land, wearing an emerald breastplate fitting the head of the Circle of the Crown. Rose was also there, dressed in a dark red blouse that matched our hair color. She looked up and made eye contact with me when I stepped into the room. Seated between the two of them was King Percival.

Percival sat upon his large emerald throne, which was to be expected of the king. Smaller than the true Emerald Throne in the throne room, this seat was still carved from a large green block that must have weighed a ton. A heavy royal crown, centuries old, rested on top of his hair, although it looked just slightly too big for his head. Percival looked in rough shape. He was slumped in his throne and had dark circles under his eyes. Suddenly I was uneasy about this meeting.

Eadward Eathan closed the door and stepped into the room as well. "Prince Davit has arrived, Your Grace," he declared in a loud voice he had definitely practiced repeatedly.

All the heads of the council turned to face me. I felt my stomach drop. There would be no chance of slipping in quietly now. I glared at the royal messenger, wishing looks could kill.

Percival rubbed his eyes. "Thank you, Eadgar. Please fetch our guest now, if you would?" he said.

Eadgar, damn, I was close at least, I thought, happy I was able to get even one letter of the name of one of hundreds of royal messengers right.

Eadgar (apparently) bowed his head and once again left the chambers to do as he was asked. I wondered what guest Percival had in mind.

I speed-walked towards the raised platform the council's table was on, painfully aware that I was the target of gazes from no less than sixteen eyes. Finally I was at the table, and… there was no open seat. I looked around, willing to settle for a rotten stool just so it could mean I could have the attention taken off me, but no luck.

Percival, his reaction speed probably delayed by exhaustion, realized I was looking around stupidly. "I'm sorry, Davit," he said blankly. "I forgot to set out a chair for you."

I waved my hand, dismissing him. "That's alright," I said, taking my position standing next to Rose. *Maybe if I was invited to more of these things, you would've remembered,* I thought, but I pushed it down.

Rose sat up straight discreetly. "Where were you?" she whispered out of the corner of her mouth.

"Taking in the scenery," I whispered. She scrunched her brow in confusion. I winked. I figured it was easier than telling her I was in my bed sound asleep when this meeting began. More fun too.

Percival sat up in his throne. "Thank you all for coming," he began in the best kingly voice he could currently manage. He looked around to each of his council members. "I have been up through the night hearing reports from the leaders and citizens of Balora, and…"

"The destroyed village?" Lady Aemelia asked, half paying attention, looking down at her painted nails. I frowned. Did she even care? Lord Alaric put his head in his hands and moaned when he heard of another village in his former territory that Ahaax had made a ruin.

Percival looked blankly at the lady. "Yes," he confirmed. He went on, "And the reports they brought me would be enough to make any sane man lose sleep."

"The only thing causing me to lose sleep," Lord Carrington declared boisterously, laying a hand on the table, "is the fact that we have overwhelming numbers against our enemy, and we are still losing! If I had the army, I would march to Ahaax's black stronghold and win this war within the fortnight."

"The armies of the kingdom cannot be organized without the consent of the king," Pevincy said calmly, his arms folded. "The king cannot organize the armies without the consent of his lords." The head guard of the Circle looked at the belligerent lord. "That decision is up to you, Cedric."

Carrington glared at the man across from him. "Entrust my soldiers to a child?" He glanced at Percival seated in his throne. "Please."

Pevincy tensed. "Watch your tone, *Cedric*," he cautioned. "He is still your king."

Percival held up a hand to his Justiciar. "That's alright, Pevincy," he said, defusing the tension in the room ever so slightly. The young king turned his attention to the rest of his lords. "The fact is, I cannot win this war without your support, my lords. You have seen as much from the past months of conflict. We are losing. Ahaax is able to form an efficient offensive; meanwhile we are left scrambling and disorganized."

Carrington crossed his arms. "Leading an army requires trust," he said to my brother plainly. "And put simply, you don't have any."

The attitude of all the entitled lords in the chamber pushed me past my breaking point. Couldn't they see the suffering people outside the city? They needed to act. The comment caused me to laugh. I couldn't help it. All the eyes in the room once again turned to me. Rose tugged on my sleeve from her chair. "Don't," she urged. I didn't listen.

Carrington stared daggers at me. "What is it, boy?" he demanded.

I grinned. "Oh, I'm sorry, it's just..." I began. "That talk about trust? That's all a bunch of nonsense, right?" I looked around the lords of the table to support my point. They all looked at me as though I had some kind of disease. Unfazed, I continued talking to Carrington. "You don't care about *trust*. He's the king! You're supposed to be at his service. I think the heart of it is you just don't want to risk the chance that you might lose power to a child. But hey, what do I know, right?"

Percival sat straight up in his throne, glaring at me. "Davit!" he scolded. I looked back over to him, surprised. *Why are you mad at me? I'm defending you!* I thought.

Carrington slammed his hands on the table. "I will not be disrespected by you, boy!" he bellowed.

"My lord, please," Percival began, raising a hand and trying to calm the angered ruler.

"But you have no problem disrespecting your king?" I asked him smugly. I couldn't stop now; I was on a roll.

Carrington rose fiercely from his chair, which fell to the floor behind him. He moved towards me. Pevincy placed a hand on the pommel of his sword.

Before things could escalate, the wooden door at the front of the room creaked open loudly. Everyone froze and turned their attention to the new noise. Standing in the open doorway were three figures, each wearing the same shocked and confused expression after witnessing the mayhem from seconds before.

Eadgar the messenger had returned. To his right was a very round man with a heavy gold ring on each of his sausage fingers and a blond mustache hanging down nearly to his waist. His hair was tied back in a single braid that was almost as long, and he was out of breath from the walk from whatever room he had been waiting in. I realized that he must've been the guest Percival was talking about, but I didn't recognize the portly man.

I *did*, however, recognize the man standing to Eadgar's left: Bryce, Percival's oldest friend and the son of the last head of the Circle before Pevincy. With his wavy black hair, pale skin, and scar across his left cheek, Bryce looked like the ghost of a teenage soldier, but he was always kind enough, if a little distant. I couldn't blame him though. The reason his father was the *former* head of the Circle was because he'd tried to assassinate my father. It all happened when I was very young, and Bryce certainly wasn't going to share any details, if his father told him any at all, so I didn't know much about the event. What I did know was what happened in the aftermath. Pevincy, who was only a member of the Circle at the time, uncovered the plot and stopped it. In return, my father promoted his longtime friend to the head position after Bryce's father had died in his coup attempt. Bryce, now orphaned, was taken in by my father as something of a third son, and since then he had been Pevincy's apprentice, being groomed to one day take the old guard's position.

The council chamber was silent, with the three new arrivals staring in shock at the frozen scene of conflict in front of them. Bryce cleared his throat and nudged Eadgar with his elbow.

"Oh, r-right," the messenger stammered. "Earl Ferrant Westerling of Balora, Your Grace."

The rotund man took a step forward and did his best at a bow, although with his body it was mostly just his head turning down. "Your Majesty," he said in a squeaky voice.

Percival stood. "Welcome, Earl," he said. He turned his eyes towards his messenger. "Thank you, Eadgar. That will be all."

Eadgar bowed low. "Your Grace," he said. With that he turned and left the room.

The rest of us at the council table looked at Lord Carrington, who looked pretty stupid standing frozen in a half lunge position towards me. The lord turned his eyes to each of us individually, then huffed and picked his chair off the ground. He sat back down, his moment having passed. I made sure he was looking at me when I flashed him an expression that said *try it again*. His face turned red with rage, but he stayed in his seat.

The two men at the door began walking towards the table. "Bryce," Percival greeted his friend in his kingly voice, "what brings you here?"

Pevincy spoke up. "I asked him here, my lord," he said. "I figured it's a good learning opportunity for the lad."

"Unless you object, my lord," Bryce said, bowing before the king.

"Of course not." Percival smiled softly, looking slightly relieved. He sat back down on his throne. "Now, the reason I called you all here. Earl Ferrant, would you please tell everyone what you told me."

The stout earl waddled forward, jingling from his jewelry with every step. He clasped his hands together and wore a look on his face that suggested that he really did not want to retell this story. "Yes, Your Grace," he said hesitantly. "It all began a few weeks ago. Food and wine were plentiful and life was good in Balora, until *he* came." No one in the room needed to ask who *he* was.

Ahaax, I thought bitterly. The memory of that day six months before flashed into my head once again. I remembered my father's killer's expressionless face. He had escaped by jumping through a window in the throne room. I had hoped it had killed him, but a few weeks later, when word came of villages being stormed in the east, I knew that hope was a fool's dream.

Earl Ferrant continued. "Ahaax marched to my village with a force of about one thousand or so, my scouts estimated. The strange thing was, he left his men just outside the village boundary. He walked to my mansion accompanied only by a small guard."

"He's arrogant," Carrington muttered. "He thinks he's invincible."

"You haven't seen the power Ahaax now possess," Pevincy said darkly. Percival, Rose, and I all silently agreed, remembering how Ahaax was able to bend fire to his whim. In any story our father had ever told about his brother, he had never been able to do that.

Rose leaned forward in her chair. "You said he came to your mansion," she said. "What did he want?"

The earl looked at my sister. "He came with an ultimatum, Princess: join his rebellion against King Percival, or he promised he would burn every building in Balora until there was nothing left." The fat man stopped.

"You refused him?" Pevincy asked.

Earl Ferrant nodded, looking towards Percival. "It's because of the reign of King Arturus that I was able to grow this fat!" He laughed softly, as if remembering a fond memory. "The kingdom has always been good to me," he continued. "Ahaax must've realized that I wouldn't submit when we never sent a messenger to his army's camp. We thought he would attack, so we prepared defenses, but instead he dismantled his tents, and his army rode off over the horizon."

"He just left?" Lord Finnian asked in disbelief.

Lord Florian shook his head. "Just like that?"

The round earl closed his eyes in pain, or maybe fear. "Yes, my lords," he began. "But the next morning, the sun never rose. Storm clouds spanned the sky in its vast entirety.

Then, suddenly, without any warning or notice, bolts of lightning in the hundreds rained down at once on my village. It was horrible: red bolts of death striking every building, houses and streets on fire. People were running. They realized they weren't safe in their homes, so they ran outside, but they were struck there too. It was as if the sky itself was screaming. A horrible, horrible sound."

The council chambers were silent for a moment. Partly out of mourning, partly out of shock. "Red lightning?" I asked, raising an eyebrow. "What could've caused a storm violent enough to destroy an entire village? And red?" None of it added up.

"My lightning is blue," Percival admitted, rationalizing the bizarre phenomena. "There can be different colors."

Carrington shook his head. "Are you saying Ahaax has the ability to control lightning now? As well as fire?" There was more than a hint of mocking disbelief in his voice.

Percival ignored him. He gestured towards the earl in front of him. "Please, continue, my lord."

Earl Ferrant shook his head, as if snapping out of a daze. He continued, "The lightning wasn't controlled by Ahaax, my lords. I believe he merely… summoned it." A deep breath. "While fleeing Balora, I came across a patch of woods. It was in those woods that I re-encountered Ahaax, although he didn't spot me before I was able to hide. He was talking, but I couldn't hear any voice that he could've been talking to. It was only when I adjusted myself that I saw… I saw…"

"Spit it out," Carrington said gruffly.

The fat earl looked at everyone in the room, his eyes watering, as if stalling for time before he had to say what he was dreading. Finally, "Ahaax, he was talking to a great dragon."

The council chambers erupted with a series of questions from every lord seated around the table. "Why did it have to be a dragon?" I singled out hearing Lord Alaric shout to the sky in front of me.

In the confusion and overstimulation of the many shouting voices around me, I noticed Rose sit up straight as an arrow. Her face had turned a ghostly shade of white. Slowly, the voices in the room died and everyone turned their gazes towards her, as if also taking notice of her change of posture.

"Red lightning," she said, barely above a whisper. "Total devastation. Dragon. *The Coming Dark.*" Those last words were whispers. No one in the kingdom dared to say them any louder. We all understood what she meant. Every child born in Lungalea was told stories of a horror man couldn't hope to fight.

Rose looked at Earl Ferrant for confirmation, her hands gripping the rests of her chair so hard they resembled bone. One by one we all looked at the earl as well. It was all he could do to nod his head and say one word, the word we had all been dreading, the word we all knew was coming. "Venerus."

If word of a dragon sent the council into a fit, now it went downright hysterical. I heard none of their words. I only heard a faint but persistent buzzing. My entire body went numb, and I felt lightheaded. The hairs on the back of my neck stood straight up. Just hearing that name opened a chasm inside me that was deeper and darker than anything I had ever felt before. The word itself felt wrong.

The council's incoherent ramblings were growing louder and louder. It was all too much. I started to sway; my palms were sweaty, my mouth dry. What was that buzzing?

"Order!" Pevincy shouted to the bickering lords, rising from his chair. That did it. All of the lords of the council went silent and looked at the head of the Circle of the Crown. I came back to reality as well. The quiet helped, and the buzzing inside my skull slowly faded as I regained feeling throughout my limbs.

Pevincy sat back down. No one spoke; it was like each person was daring someone else to be the one to break the silence. "That," Lord Carrington began, noticeably shaken. "That's not possible. The other five Elders sealed Venerus away nearly three thousand years ago. There's no way They could've gotten free."

Everyone around the table seemed to nod in silent agreement. Afterall, we all knew the stories, didn't we? *There's no way in heaven or earth that Ahaax could've undone the work of the Elders*, I told myself, but there was something instinctual in me that was unconvinced. My palms were still sweating.

"Your Grace," a voice spoke up. It was Bryce, standing next to Pevincy. "If I may?" he asked.

Percival looked at his friend. "Yes, of course," he said, waving a hand towards Earl Ferrant, allowing Bryce to ask his question.

Bryce continued. "Earl," he began, "was anyone else with you when you spotted Ahaax?"

The earl's eyes widened, as if he was only just realizing how important it would be to have a witness to back up his story. He clasped his hands together. "Er, no."

Rose raised an eyebrow. "No one? In the entire village you were evacuating?"

Earl Ferrant began to stammer, trying to explain, but he never answered for himself. "That's because he didn't evacuate with the rest of his village, Princess. Did you, Westerling?" Pevincy said coldly. "He fled for himself, abandoning his rule."

"No! I, I—they said it was better that way, I swear!" the earl said in his defense, but it was too late. I could tell the entire council had quickly soured on the round man before us, as did I. Instead of a fearful man who barely escaped death, I now saw a coward who grew fat from his people and abandoned them the second there was danger. It made me angry.

Lord Carrington glared at the earl. "If what you say is true, how did Ahaax not kill you, you fat fool?"

"I..." Ferrant began. Then he sighed, turning his gaze to the floor. "I played dead." I groaned unintentionally, causing a few heads to turn my way. The earl continued, "I must've made some noise, because Elder Venerus' head snapped towards me. Elders Eternal, it was like They were looking right at me. Then I heard a terrible sound from *inside* my head, like that of scraping steel. I didn't know what else to do, so I collapsed, doing my best to stay still."

"Go on," Percival said without a hint of emotion.

The Earl looked ashamed. *As if that makes what he did okay*, I thought bitterly, *or rather, what he didn't do*. Ferrant continued, "Ahaax said he would investigate, but I still didn't hear who he was talking to. And then he..." A brief pause. "...came over to me. Gods, I felt the heat of his weapon against my head. I thought I was going to die. But then, he just said 'I agree,' and left, just like that. Clearly whoever he was talking to thought I *was* dead. Some god must be looking after me," he chuckled morbidly.

Rose and I glanced at each other, both equally unconvinced that was what Ahaax thought. *After all, if Ahaax wanted him dead, he would make sure*. My father's cold hands crept back into my mind.

The room was silent. "And?" Lady Aemelia asked, more invested than I had ever heard her, although still somehow detached.

Earl Ferrant looked at her. "That's it, my lords," he said. "Once I was sure Ahaax and Elder Venerus were gone, I began my journey here."

Percival sighed and leaned back in his throne, seemingly disappointed there were no new revelations after already having heard this story. "Bryce," he asked, "you asked if the earl had a witness. Why?"

Pevincy was watching his apprentice closely. Bryce stood as straight as a board. "I believe Balora was raised, Your Grace, and I believe it was Ahaax who did it." The young man paused. "But, as Lord Carrington said, Venerus has been trapped under Mount Morta for thousands of years, and despite the new power he somehow possesses, I don't believe even Ahaax would ever be able to break an Elder's power."

The earl's face dropped as members of the council one by one lost faith in his story. "What do you believe happened then?" Pevincy asked his student.

Bryce sighed. "Of that I'm less sure, Master. Likely Ahaax's forces assaulted the village, and in the mass panic and trauma that followed, perhaps the blasts of mortars could be confused as the rumble of thunder? It could explain the red lightning."

Pevincy smiled, clearly pleased with his student. "Well done," he said. He turned his attention to Percival. "I agree, Your Grace, that *does* seem more likely than Ahaax somehow managing to free an Elder Dragon."

Earl Ferrant was not smiling. He shook his head desperately, "No, no, my lords, Your Grace." He looked up at Percival seated on his raised throne. "I know what I saw. I didn't hear the cracks of mortars. I *saw* a *dragon*. You need to believe me! Devastation is coming! Something we haven't prepared for, something…"

Percival raised a hand, silencing the man. It was a strange feeling realizing my brother had that kind of power. "That's enough, Earl Westerling," he said in the emotionless tone of King Percival. "My council will discuss what you have told us. You are dismissed."

The fat earl looked at each member of the council one by one, desperately hoping that someone would support him. No one did. Once he realized his cause was lost, Earl Ferrant dropped his head and turned towards the door, leaving without another word and even forgetting the customary bow. The man disgusted me—a ruler who would abandon the people who he was supposed to protect. And yet, I felt sorry for him. Despite that, I didn't think he was lying. I just hoped desperately that he was mistaken.

The council chambers were silent as the heavy wooden door slammed shut, echoing throughout the stone room. Percival sighed again, then turned his attention to Rose and me. "You two are dismissed as well," he said flatly. "These are the most concrete reports we have had about Ahaax's presence in months. I thought you would like to hear them."

Just like that, it felt like a bucket of ice-cold water was poured over my head. "That's why you asked me here?" I asked my brother. "To give us an update?" It felt like a slap in the face. I thought Percival had actually started to care about including me. I thought hatching Cerulia had finally made him change his mind. But apparently I was wrong. My face turned red from anger.

King Percival shot me a look that said, *Don't make a scene, Davit.*

I hated that look. "You won't even let me in on the *discussions*? I can help, Percival! I've been studying! This is my war too!" I had raised my voice before I'd even realized it.

Percival raised a hand. "Enough, Davit," he began.

I cut him off. "That trick might work on your stooges, but it won't work on me." I felt my face heat up. *The nerve he has*, I thought.

"What of the people outside the city?" Rose interrupted, furrowing her brow. "The people of Balora who are living in tents and living off gruel, what of them?"

Percival leaned back, rubbing his eyes, clearly annoyed at this battle now on two fronts. "I told you, Rose, I'm doing the best I can."

Rose stood, visibly angered. It was an unusual look for someone who was usually so refined. "This is your best, Percival?" she demanded. I noticed she didn't say Your Grace, or king. I never cared about the proper titles, but Rose did. I shrank back a little, shocked that I wasn't the angriest person in the room. "It's been a week and you keep putting off even speaking about it!" Rose continued.

Percival straightened his back. A dark look washed over his face. "You are dismissed," he said, glaring at us. "Now."

I stood beside Rose. "You can't just throw us out of this! It isn't right!" He needed to understand that this was our war as much as it was his.

Percival didn't say anything. He didn't need to. All around the table, the members of the council were muttering to each other.

"They think they're the ones in power," Lord Carrington said, amused.

"What do you expect?" Lady Aemelia replied. "They're only children."

I snapped my head towards the two of them. I opened my mouth, ready to shout and scream at the lords, at stupid King Percival, at anyone who was in front of me. I wasn't just a child! I was more powerful than any lord at that table! I could kill Ahaax myself, since clearly none of them were strong enough to do it!

"Davit," a soft voice said from the other side of the table. It was Pevincy. "Rose." He looked at the two of us with sorry eyes. He didn't say anything more. His eyes said enough. *Please don't do this.*

Looking at the old guard's face, I lost any bluster that I had. I couldn't bring myself to shout at Pevincy, a man who had treated me like a son he never had when I lost my father. Rose seemingly had the same thought process. She stayed silent, her hands still clenched into tight balls. There was no winning now. I knew I was powerless.

With a final look of pure disgust at Percival in his golden throne, I stomped around the council table. Rose followed me. I looked straight ahead as I walked towards the door, not letting myself catch the eye of anyone in the room. I felt my face redden as I exited the chambers, a scorned child being sent away when the adults talked business. I let Rose exit the chamber before me, then slammed the heavy door as hard as I could, hoping everyone in that stupid room could feel the rattle.

A Look to the Past

XIII

"Damn him!" Rose shouted in the courtyard as angry tears formed in her eyes. She slammed a fist into the grand evergreen in the center of the clearing. "Damn that entire council!" Another fist into the trunk of the tree. "Do they even care about the people they rule? Any of them?" She struck the tree a third time.

I walked up slowly behind her. "Rose, stop," I said, defeated. I could see her hands already turning red. She hit the tree again. "Stop!" I grabbed her hands lightly. "You're just going to hurt yourself."

Rose turned and looked at me. She sighed as she slid to the ground, her back propped against the tree she was just furiously beating. I sat next to her. Together the two of us sat there in silence, furious but just as powerless.

"I just…" My sister sniffled lightly beside me, regaining her composure. "What is a king supposed to do if not serve his people?"

I was silent. I didn't have a good answer.

I could sense there was a third presence listening to our conversation now. From behind the tree waddled Cerulia. Her wings were flapping and her tail was wagging. I could tell she wanted attention, or wanted to give me attention. Either option worked for her. She nuzzled her snout into the back of my hand. "No thank you," I said, guiding her head away from me and adjusting her path to where she went around me and was now walking towards Rose. The young dragon still wandered happily, seemingly completely unfazed by my rejection.

Rose giggled as Cerulia lay down, putting her head in my sister's lap. "I miss when Redwood was as little as you," she said as she began to pet the dragon. Slowly Rose smiled, and the tears left her eyes.

Rose turned her attention to me. "Percival's having me teach you how to fly when she's big enough, you know," she said.

I huffed, crossing my arms. "That'll be interesting."

My sister scrunched her brow the way she always did when she was frustrated. "You want to fight this war, right, Davit?" Rose asked me plainly. "You will be killed by the first soldier you fight if you keep refusing to acknowledge your bond with this creature."

Realizing my arms were already crossed, I scoffed. I never liked talking about this. I could explain my reasons until I was blue in the face, but that wouldn't make Rose or Percival understand them.

"I mean," Rose continued despite my signals. "When I hatched Redwood, from that instant, the second he was born, my entire outlook was changed. It was like I had just opened my eyes! Suddenly there was a new part of me, external from my body. And after what happened to Father…" Rose paused, then sighed. She looked me in the eyes. "As soon as Redwood hatched, I knew I wasn't alone. Surely you *must* feel the same thing towards Cerulia."

I looked away from her, straight ahead of me. "Sure I feel it, Rose," I said, acknowledging the seemingly instinctual pull that kept drawing me towards the dragon. Even then I was intentionally not looking at Cerulia lying in Rose's lap. I could feel the young dragon's gaze still focused on me, though, looking straight into my mind. I shrugged it off. "I just choose to ignore it. Simple as that."

Rose sighed from exhaustion. "How do you do that?" she asked genuinely. "How do you ignore something every instinct you have is telling you is right?"

"Right?" I snapped. I was getting annoyed. "Maybe you and I have a different memory of that day, Rose. You *earned* Redwood. Father *wanted* you to have him. I *failed* him. The only reason I was given that egg was because Father had no other choice. Tell me how it's right that I have to try every second of every hour to ignore the pull of something that no one in the history of the kingdom has ever experienced before, when even Father knew I wouldn't be able to handle it."

Rose was silent. I hated how she was looking at me: not angry, but sad. She opened her mouth, then closed it again, as if trying to find the right response. "Davit," she finally mustered softly. "I'm sorry."

"Stop," I told her. Something I had said caught my attention. *Something that no one in the history of the kingdom has experienced before.* Suddenly I had an idea.

"No, Davit…"

"Rose, stop." I stood from our seated position on the grass.

"What is it?" Rose asked.

I looked at her and grinned. "King Percival may stop us from leaving the city, but he can't control what we do inside it, and I'm tired of just sitting around. Come on, we're going to make ourselves useful."

In the center of the royal palace was the Grand Library. There was never a more appropriate label. The library could easily fit a large mansion inside of it (or two average-size mansions, I suppose) and every wall was lined with shelves packed with books from floor to ceiling on and on up through the library's ten floors. Between the bookshelves were tables the size of the ones in the feast hall, except these were packed with scholars from all over the kingdom soaking in all the knowledge they could get their hands on. The roof was capped with a massive dome made of stone and glass that allowed the natural sunlight to reach every corner so no one would be unable to read. Architectural minds would appreciate the library for the engineering marvel it was; to me it was always just a very large, slightly cold room, but it had its uses.

Rose followed me through the thick wooden double doors. She looked around. "What are we doing here, Davit? This is the library."

I turned to face her with an expression of mock shock. I looked around, bewildered, then put my hands on my hips. "Well would you look at that," I guffawed.

Rose punched my arm playfully.

I nudged my head in one direction. "Follow me."

We walked up multiple flights of stairs and through a winding path before eventually coming to a stop at a raised platform in a hidden spot on the fifth floor. There was a sheet hanging from a line that sectioned off the rest of the platform behind it. Undoing one edge of the sheet, I pulled it to the side, revealing a space the size of a small room with cushions and books strewn everywhere. The little area was given a warm glow by a single candle sitting on a shelf in the back.

I turned to face Rose, ushering her inside. "Welcome to my private study. No one ever comes to this section so it's all mine," I said, picking up book after book to see if it was what I was looking for. "Have a seat anywhere, we're not fancy."

Rose walked in behind me, taking in the limited scenery. "Wow, Davit, you set up a nice little corner all to yourself?" she asked. She picked a book off the ground. "I didn't know you read."

"Well, you didn't think I was illiterate, right?" I asked, still rifling through books. *Where was it?*

No answer.

I stopped rifling. "Rose!"

Rose raised her hands defensively. "Sometimes I wondered," she said.

Finally, something caught my eye under a pillow in a far corner of the room. *Ah, that explains it,* I thought, *it probably put me to sleep reading it.*

Rose was seated on a cushion with a different book now. She looked at it curiously. "Davit, all of these are about war."

I dropped the large cracked leather-bound book I'd been looking for straight in front of Rose. The book was so big it slammed the floor on impact, causing Rose to drop her book out of surprise. "Don't look at that," I said quickly. I sat across from her and pointed at the brick in front of us. "Look at this instead."

"Gods," Rose exclaimed, startled. "That thing has to weigh as much as me."

"I wouldn't be surprised."

Rose looked at the title. "*A Complete History of the Kingdom of Lungalea: From the Settlement of King Maggelle I to the Beginning of the Shattered Age,*" she read. Her eyes looked up at me blankly. "Doesn't exactly roll off the tongue, does it?"

"Maybe not," I said. "But if you ever can't get to sleep..." I clicked my tongue at the book.

"Why did you bring me here?" Rose asked.

"Right," I said, getting back on track. I flipped open the book's jewel-encrusted cover to the first page. "Well, I got thinking," I started. "At the council meeting. What if we *do* end up marching to war against a power we don't even have anything to compare to? An Elder Dragon." I paused, working up the courage. "Venerus."

Rose shivered.

I pointed my finger at her madly. "You felt it too!" I exclaimed. Even just saying that name felt wrong.

Rose brushed it off. "I don't know what I felt at the meeting," she said. "It was loud and chaotic. Easy to get disoriented." She shook her head. "Besides, there's no way They even got free. Ahaax can't be that powerful."

"Yeah, I know," I agreed, truly. *And yet.* I looked into Rose's dark blue eyes. "But don't tell me you haven't been thinking of Venerus ever since that meeting. Tell me something inside you hasn't been pulling you towards answers."

Rose and I wouldn't break eye contact. She stared at me fiercely, biting her lip, desperate to prove me wrong. Then, just for an instant, her eyes flicked towards the page. I clapped my hands. "Got you!"

Rose sighed, defeated. "What answers, then?"

"No idea," I said, shaking my head. This was where my wisdom ran out. Every story told about the Elder Dragon Venerus always differed slightly. The War between the Elders was three thousand years ago. Even historical details became unreliable in that amount of time. "But we've never lived with the Elders. There once were people who did." I tapped the page of the open book. "If anyone knows how to understand them, what to expect from them..."

Rose's eyes widened. "Of course," she said softly. She looked at the old book and began to read aloud:

*The Elder Dragons were here long before us. No one knows when the six Earthly Divines first came to Lungalea, but we do know that by the time of our first king Maggelle I's landing on her shores, this was **their** land, and beasts unseen the world over roamed the ground, land and sky.*

"Explains the dragons," I said, matter-of-factly. Rose looked up at me, annoyed at the interruption. "Sorry."

Rose continued:

After the destruction of the Imperial Fleet and our kingdom's separation from the Old Lands Across the Sea, it is said King Maggelle began to commune with the Elders. As the relationship between Man and Elder deepened, the kingdom was able to expand more and more from a near symbiotic relationship with the life of the continent.

Five of the Great Elders nurtured this young relationship. But Elder Venerus—Rose tensed—*despised Man. As the early kingdom grew, so too did Venerus' hatred. With cunning and trickery, Venerus swayed the Elder Glacius to join Them, and the two Great Dragons attacked the Kingdom of Man.*

Rose and I were both silent for a moment. The thought of living a normal life one moment, and then watching as an Elder Dragon swooped down from the clouds to destroy your entire civilization… I shivered. Any normal person would be terrified of that! My thoughts flashed back to the story of Balora. *Red bolts of death raining down.* The familiar pit in my stomach returned.

The remaining four Elders, Rose began again, *Terrus, Nebulus, Lara'sumus and Fyrnus, defended life. When Venerus the Black descended from the sky, the four Defenders would rise to face Them. Their clashes would shake the earth and change night to day.*

Elder Glacius would not attack Their fellow kin, and for reasons the Elders have never described, after a year of cataclysm, with the

Kingdom of Man on the very edge of destruction, They returned to the Defenders, to the side of life.

With the five Elders united, they pushed Venerus to the summit of Mount Morta. The battle lasted six days, but every time Venerus would defeat one Elder, another would take their place, until finally the Terrible Elder was vulnerable. The Great Elders, with power they possessed older than time, sealed one of Their own under the great mountain until this very day.

Rose had reached the end of the page. She carefully turned to the next, being sure not to damage the ancient paper. What we saw on the second page gave both of us chills. It was an illustration of Venerus. Their fangs were bared, and the two massive, black wings were unfurled above Them. Their eyes were two red gemstones. It felt like the paper dragon was staring straight through me.

Under the illustration was a final message which Rose read:

Under Morta Venerus has slumbered. It is said when the earth breaks Venerus shall be free once again, and take Their place as The Coming Dark. In this way, many scholars believe that should Venerus ever return from the earth, that shall be the first harbinger of The Final Night. Pray we are wrong, reader, for if Venerus returns to the Kingdom of Man, there will be nothing in our small power to stop Them.

Rose and I just sat there, speechless. The pit in my stomach was now a chasm. *Well, you wanted to learn about Venerus,* I thought. *You learned there's nothing we can do to stop Them!* My palms were sweaty. Rose's face had turned pale. She said she didn't believe Venerus was back, but I could tell she had the exact same train of thought as I did.

"Well," I said, forcing a smile. "Look at us being useful."

Rose

Through the Clouds

XIV

Flying was never my favorite thing to do. Unlike Percival, I was never able to appreciate the beauty above the clouds. Half the time I was hunched in Redwood's large saddle with my head down, trying to stay as stable as I could despite my dragon's gentle rocking with the air. When I was brave enough, I would open my eyes; however, I would usually regret this mistake almost immediately after looking down.

Redwood would always try his best to alleviate my anxieties by gliding as long and as smoothly as he could between the thunderous beats of his wings. Despite this, my hands would always be pale and sore after our flights from the stress of holding onto his saddle, and being away from stable ground would make me dizzy. No, I did not like flying.

I found myself caught up on this train of thought once again as we ascended through the golden cloud top. Shaking slightly from both the cold and my nerves, I tried to steady my breathing so that it was in time with Redwood's. This helped slow my beating heart, but the fear still remained. Instinctually, I knew Redwood would never let me fall (in fact, I would probably have to *try* to fall off of him, he was so large) but that did little to help.

Summoning my courage, I opened my eyes and looked around. The setting sun was almost blinding as we flew towards it, speckling the white clouds with golden crystals. Besides this, though, the view was almost entirely featureless. A completely level cloud top spanned the entirety below me, stretching to meet the deep purple sky on the horizon. I looked down at the clouds, waiting to see movement.

To our side, the smooth layer began to break. Slowly, very slowly, I watched as Davit's head, then his entire body, rose. Beneath Davit, Cerulia was flying them both into the air steadily and cautiously. This was their first flight.

In just over a month since her hatching, the wisest minds Percival assigned to her care declared Cerulia to be fully grown, despite the closest things to her siblings, Redwood and Apolion, still growing. Because of Cerulia's seemingly stunted growth, she would only ever be able to carry one person on her back and still be able to fly, but as a result this made her very fast. Not quite as fast as Apolion, but she would still handily beat Redwood in a race, and she was much faster than any griff.

Taking her reins, Davit carefully steered Cerulia closer to Redwood and me. Even with my limited vision, I could see the uncertainty on Davit's face as he drifted through the air. The reins looked heavy in his hands, and he was constantly shifting slightly in his saddle. His anxiousness was rubbing off on Cerulia, who, for her part, was doing surprisingly well for being so young, but her large eyes would constantly flick back to the boy flying on her, checking on him.

Taking a deep breath, I patted Redwood's rough, bumpy hide with my right hand. Understanding what I meant, the large dragon tilted ever so slightly to his side, giving me a more direct line of sight to my brother without being interrupted by his large intermittent wing flaps.

"You're doing a good job!" I shouted at Davit over the wind, trying to sound as supportive as I could. The wind and having to spit my hair out of my mouth didn't make conversations easy on dragonback. It made me thankful Redwood could understand my thoughts. "How do you feel?"

Davit shifted in his saddle. "Been better," he shouted back. "Does that feeling of your stomach lifting *up* ever go away?"

I laughed. "You get used to it!" That was mostly true.

The two of us hit a rough patch of air. The sudden turbulence had me duck down into Redwood's saddle abruptly, the limited confidence I had built up immediately vanishing. Redwood was an experienced flier, though, and he flew through it without any trouble.

I looked at the pair of dragon and rider beside us. Davit was struggling to stay on, and Cerulia was trying her best to both keep him stable and manage the rough air.

"You need to stop fighting her!" I shouted to Davit. "Quiet your mind! Listen to her. She'll tell you how she wants to fly."

"If she could want to *not* throw me off, that would be pretty great," Davit shouted, wrestling with the reins. Cerulia let out a quick bark as she flew. "Well, try harder!" Davit retorted down at her.

Without warning, a fierce gust of wind rushed past the four of us. Redwood braced himself, but it caught Davit and Cerulia off guard. The wind picked my brother off his dragon's back and practically threw him backwards. Before I could even process what happened, Davit was screaming as he plummeted through the cloud layer.

"Gods!" I exclaimed in shock. "Davit!" I couldn't let myself panic. I had to think quickly; every second I wasted, Davit fell another hundred feet. I sank low into the saddle. *Dive, Redwood!* I thought. *Dive!*

Redwood let out a powerful roar. The tips of his wings angled up, and we began a rapid sharp incline. Knowing what was about to happen, I slipped both my legs into the tightly secured stirrups. Time seemed to slow as Redwood looped upside down through the sky. It felt like every organ in my body swapped places, and I could feel myself pull away from the saddle, but because of the stirrups it was only by a few inches.

Time accelerated again as Redwood, at the peak of his loop, tucked in his wings and began a trajectory straight down. The wind was deafening as we plummeted, first above the clouds, then through them, and emerging again below all in the same second.

I could barely keep my eyes open, and the tears from the wind made seeing even more difficult. The green hills below were becoming larger and larger with each second. We had Davit in our line of sight as he tumbled through the air, screaming muted screams. We were gaining ground on him, but the hills were gaining faster. I sat lower in the saddle. We *had* to reach him.

A blue blur rushed past in my peripheral vision. Cerulia, with her wings pulled in similar to Redwood, had closed the gap between her and Davit in no time flat. Davit couldn't have been more than one hundred feet from the treetops as his dragon grabbed his arms with her two front legs and extended the width of her wings, rapidly slowing their momentum.

Relying on instinct alone, I pulled Redwood's reins as hard as they would allow. With something resembling more of a screech than a roar, Redwood similarly unfurled his wings. The wind generated from the massive dragon made a noticeable indent on the trees below. Another second and we would have been going too fast to avoid crashing into them.

The two dragons glided softly for a few moments before landing in a nearby clearing. Redwood touched down softly with an immense *thud*. However, I stayed still in the saddle for a few moments longer, my heart nearly beating out of my chest. I lay my face down on the cold leather as I regained control of my breathing. *Davit is safe,* I reassured myself, eyes clamped shut. *Everyone is safe.*

Cerulia slowed herself for landing with repeated flaps of her wings, setting Davit on the ground lightly on his feet. Davit immediately collapsed, his arms outstretched to either side like he was hugging the earth. He let out a long and continuous groan, but other than that, he seemed unharmed. Cerulia sat down a few feet away from him, her head tilted curiously.

I slowly slid off of Redwood's saddle. My legs buckled as I hit the ground. As I walked they felt like jelly, only slowly regaining feeling. However, just being on solid ground again was comforting. I walked up to Redwood's head. His eyes were only half open in the sleepy gaze he always wore. "Thank you, my sweet boy," I said. I scratched under his chin where he loved. "That was excellent flying. Well done." The large dragon rumbled deeply, pleased with the praise. A steady plume of light smoke came from his nostrils.

I smiled at his happiness. With one last pat on his head, I turned and walked towards my brother, who was still lying flat on the ground. "Will you survive?" I asked Davit sarcastically, crossing my arms.

The only part of Davit to move were his eyes, which turned up to look at me. "I'm alive?" he asked.

I rolled my eyes. "You're so dramatic."

Davit pushed himself onto his back. Looking straight up at the sky, he said, "I just fell like a thousand feet, Rose. I think I've earned it."

"You didn't hit the ground," I countered. I looked at Cerulia. "Don't you think someone deserves a thank you, Davit?"

Davit ran his hands over his face. "You're right," he said. He turned his gaze to his dragon. "Thanks for dropping me."

Cerulia's curious expression went slack. She made a sound between a grumble and a huff. *Don't hurt yourself,* it seemed to say.

"Davit!" I scolded him. How could he be this thick-headed? "You wouldn't have fallen if you just flew *with* Cerulia instead of against her."

"Oh, I'm sorry," my brother said sarcastically, standing up. He brushed dirt off his knees. "She physically cannot plummet to her certain death." He jerked a thumb at Cerulia. "I'm the victim here."

I groaned. "You're impossible sometimes, Davit. You really are." I turned away from him and started pacing, working off my annoyance. My twin had the occasional ability to infuriate anyone with just his face. "I can only teach you so much," I began. "But I can't form the bond between you and Cerulia. Only you can do that."

Davit extended his arms outwards at the elbows. "I'm not asking you to do that, Rose," he said. "And neither is Percival. I just need you to teach me how to fly. I'm not looking for a friend."

I rubbed my temples. "You don't get it, that's just not how it works." I sighed. "Have you ever wondered why no one has ever been able to ride a dragon before us? People have tried, you've heard the stories."

"Poor King Bail the Burnt." Davit chuckled slightly, remembering his favorite example.

I continued. "No one before us has had a bond with a dragon seemingly tailor-made for them. Percival has Apolion, I have Redwood, and you..." The two of us turned towards Cerulia, who was now lying peacefully in the grassy bed. "You have her."

Davit furrowed his brow. Multiple thoughts were clearly going through his mind at once, but I couldn't understand any of them. I could only hope what I said got through to him.

A golden ray of sunlight caught my eyes through the trees. The adrenaline from Davit's fall had worn off, and I was just realizing how low in the sky the sun had gotten. I sighed. "It's getting late. We should get back to the palace before dark. The rockbears have been more active in this part of the forest lately."

Davit stayed silent. He was still looking at Cerulia, unmoving. "Fly back?" I offered.

Davit shook his head, as if snapping out of a trance. "No, um," he began. "I think I've had enough of flying today, actually."

"Davit."

"I know my way back," he said. He walked towards the trees at the edge of the clearing. The matter was settled. "I'll see you back at the palace." Without another word, Davit began his walk through the trees.

Cerulia perked her head up from her resting position. She stood and stretched out her wings, taking to the sky once again. I could see that she was following Davit from above, circling his position above the trees.

I sighed, frustrated from Davit's lack of progress, but also out of a general sadness for my brother. In the short time he had been around, Redwood had become my best friend. If I ever needed someone to really understand me, he was there, despite being a completely different species. After my father died, I cried so much so often I thought my eyes might fall out, but he was with me every time, even when he got too big to sleep in my room. I wished Davit would let himself know that support.

Redwood shuffled up slowly from behind me. I smiled softly. He always had perfect timing. I placed my hand gently on one of his armor-like plates. "Let's go home, sweet boy."

. . .

"And so I said to him, 'Now look, I may be short, and fat, *and* balding,'" Archie, mouth full of sausage stew, exclaimed. He waved his spoon with each word for emphasis. "'But I always pay my debts when I lose a game of cards, unlike you. Also unlike you, friend, my mother was *not* a sow!'"

"Wow," Killian said with mock admiration. His head was resting in one hand propped on the table by his elbow. "Big words. Did you fight him?"

Archie's mouth fell open, half full with stew. "Are you kidding?" he asked. "I'm short, fat, and balding!"

Kil turned his head to his side and looked up at Julianna, who was sitting next to him. "I got him his coin back," she confirmed curtly, taking a sip of her own stew.

Killian couldn't help himself. He let a chuckle slip out. This got a response from the other two, and soon all three of them were laughing at the story.

The dining hall was one long room made of the same polished, tan stone as the rest of the royal palace, with two notable differences. The first was the size. The hall was much bigger than most other rooms, only beaten out in size by the King's hall, where the ruler was crowned and conducted public business. The second difference was the furniture. Twenty long dining tables lined the walls, with a window separating them from each other. A single bench served as the seat for everyone at the tables. The only chairs in the entire hall were at the front of the room, where, on a raised platform, a single, similarly large dining table sat facing the rest of the hall. This table was exclusively for members of the royal family and other lords.

I almost never sat there. The only other royals were Percival and Davit, and the three of us were never in the hall at the same time, and the only other people at the table were nobles decades older than me. Sitting up at the front of the hall was at once very noticeable and very lonely.

Because of this, I always sat at one of the benches reserved for everyone else: soldiers, scholars, servants, and many others. It was one night sitting like this that I'd met the three palace guards I was sitting with now. Archibald noticed the girl sitting and eating alone, and before he even realized I was the princess, he invited me to join the three of them.

"Something the matter, Princess?" Archie turned his head towards me. "My tales could always get a smile from you."

I snapped myself out of my train of thought. I had been looking down at my bowl of stew for the last few minutes, only half listening to my friends. I looked up, trying to play it off. "Oh," I began, "just a lot on my mind, that's all."

"Something you can share?" Kil asked from the other side of the table, raising an eyebrow. He wouldn't pry if he knew I didn't want him to.

Davit's lack of progress had troubled me more than I'd thought it would. Seeing my brother have the option to bond with Cerulia yet still refusing to do so just felt unnatural. Combining my brother's near-death encounter with the story of Venerus we'd read earlier in the day, I was unsettled in some way or another as I carried on.

"Oh, just royal duties," I said. "Nothing to worry about." I hoped I was convincing enough.

"Royal duties, eh?" Archie replied, buying my excuse. "You know, Princess, I know a thing or two about royal duties."

The round soldier's sister scoffed. "You do not," Julianna said.

"I do too," Archie defended himself. "You know, back when we were in our training days, I was pretty popular myself. King of the Barracks, they called me. I could tell all those boys looked up to me. Believe me, it was a lot of pressure. My every move was analyzed. It was very stressful, so I understand, Princess."

"That's exactly it, Archie." I smiled. "Right as always."

Archie grinned. "There's that pretty smile."

The four of us looked at each other, happy to be with the company. We continued our meal. I brought a spoonful of stew up to my mouth but nearly spit it back into my bowl. "Oh," I said, my face souring in surprise. "That's cold."

"I'll take it." Archie didn't miss a beat. He slid the cold bowl out from under my spoon over to him. Not fazed by the seemingly below-room-temperature stew, the soldier dug in.

The remaining three of us looked at him. Archie looked back at us individually. "What?" he asked with a mouthful. "This is good food."

"Selfless as always," said Kil.

I smiled again and patted Archie on the back. "Enjoy it," I said. I turned to address all three of them, standing up. "I'll go get another bowl."

I turned away from the table and walked towards the center of the hall, where an iron pot ten feet in diameter and filled with stew was hanging by a chain from the ceiling above a fire. When I took a bowl from the stack next to the cauldron, I heard the giant doors to the hall open on the far end of the room.

"All rise for Percival, the first of his name, Lord of all Lungalea, King of the Lungaleans, High Sovereign of the Emerald Lands and the Seventy-Fifth Heir to Maggelle!" the powerful voice of a royal messenger called.

The sound of all the benches in the hall being pushed back at once as their occupants stood was nearly deafening. Everybody in the room stopped what they were doing at once, either eating or talking, and stood up straight, as if it were second nature. Turning to face the open doors, I was met with the sight of Percival walking towards me. He was wearing the leather gloves and slim clothes he wore when flying Apolion as opposed to his traditional royal clothing, and his spear was in its notch on his back. He was either coming from or off to someplace, I thought.

I walked across the floor to my brother and met him halfway. "Your Grace." I curtsied out of respect for tradition.

Percival looked down at me from his extra head of height. "Saddle Redwood," he said in the voice of the king. "You, me, and Davit will be flying to Bukarra within the hour."

I nearly dropped the bowl in my hands. What did he just say? "Huh?" was the best I could manage. Bukarra was on the complete other side of the kingdom.

Percival leaned closer to me, as if he were worried someone would overhear. "Scouts have spotted Ahaax in the region. His troops are moving. Bukarra is the largest settlement in the Golden Desert. The three of us will fly there and coordinate a response, attempt to cut off whatever he's planning." Percival paused, as if thinking over what he would say next. "After that, you and Davit will fly back home. It should only be a couple of weeks for you two."

I was still processing the fact that I had just been given an official mission in the war. My mind was moving a mile a minute, but my mouth couldn't keep up. "Wh—I," I stammered. "Why now? Why us?" I finally managed to get out. It had been seven months of war; why was Percival just involving Davit and me now?

Percival shook his head lightly. "Not enough time. To organize and then march troops to Bukarra? No time, at least not from here."

"Okay," I said slowly, processing. "But why Davit and me? You've been determined to keep us in the city for the whole war until now. What changed?"

"Now all of us have dragons capable of flight," Percival replied. "And three is always better than one." The young king stopped and looked into my eyes for a moment. "Will you be with me on this?"

I was frozen. Not a lot caught me off guard, but I was completely lost for a response. *The first time I leave this island in seven months*, I thought, *and it's to go to a war zone*. I thought of the war, the stories of destruction I had heard. I could hear the screams of terrified people fleeing their burning homes. I could see their faces. The faces of people outside the city gates at that very moment.

"No," I whispered.

Percival's eyes widened. "What?" He lowered his voice again in the strange way he'd been speaking. "Rose," he snapped in a whisper, leaning closer. I could tell he was aware of the dozens of people still standing silently around us.

"I won't help you," I dug in, even though the tips of my limbs were numb. "Not unless you swear to help those poor people outside our gates the instant you return."

"Rose," Percival stressed. "I told you I'm trying. If you want me to swear to do more than I can, I…"

I shook my head. "Not you." I hadn't stood up to Percival like this since my first council meeting when I'd shouted at him to do more. It had been almost two months since then, and nothing had been done. It went against every tradition and conduct I was taught, but somehow I found myself dictating terms. "Swear on our parents. Swear on their souls that you will help those people outside."

For a split second, the king in front of me vanished. In his place was the brother I had grown up with, had run in the yard with, had cried with. His eyes were the color of the ocean crashing against the shore, and they looked wounded.

But it was only for a second. The young boy retreated, and Percival the king had returned. He was silent for a moment; his face had grown hard. Then he nodded shortly, breathing in. "I swear on the souls of our father and mother that I will do all in my power as king to help those people outside come my return."

I looked him up and down. "Okay then." It wasn't that I didn't believe Percival. My problem was with the king's council. Just because Percival wasn't technically of age yet didn't mean he had no power at all. He needed to realize that he was the king, and he needed to show the council that, no matter what they thought.

Percival motioned his head behind him. "Come," he said. "To the courtyard."

I had begun walking with Percival when I noticed something out of the corner of my eye. In all the excitement of learning I was going on a mission, I couldn't believe I'd nearly forgotten about them. "Wait," I said to Percival, stopping. The king turned. "Let me say goodbye to my friends." I motioned to the table I had just been sitting at, where Archie, Julianna, and Killian were all standing at attention. I could tell they were all trying to look over at us as subtly as they could. "Please."

Percival looked unsure. He thought it over. "Quickly," he relented. He leaned close one final time. "Tell them nothing of what you're doing." With that, my older brother turned and walked out of the dining hall, and the great mass of people who had been standing sat back down and resumed their meals. Why had Percival been acting so strange?

I walked back to the table in a daze. I set my empty bowl down where I had been sitting. My friends looked at me expectantly. They could sense the air from the conversation I'd just come from. "I..." I began, hyper-aware of every word I said. "I have to go now." None of them said anything. "For a couple of weeks," I continued. "But then I should be back."

"Royal duties?" Killian asked. I nodded. He didn't ask anything more.

All at once, my three friends stood and walked over to me, embracing me in a hug in the center of all of them. The warmth of their bodies felt comforting, and feeling slowly came back to my limbs, but something within me still felt unusually cold.

"Whatever you're off to, we'll be waiting here for your return," Kil said, looking down at me. He smiled. I smiled back, feeling my face heat up.

"Come back with some good stories," Archie piped in. "It's not fair that I'm always the one that has to keep you three entertained." I giggled.

Julianna towered over all of us. "We already know you're strong, Princess," she said. "But be safe as well, for us." I nodded, hoping to put their fears to rest as well as my own.

I stood in the middle of them for a few moments longer, not wanting to leave. I knew it couldn't last. Eventually I left my friends' embrace and walked to the doors of the hall. I turned, taking one last look at the three of them. They had all sat back down but were still looking at me. I waved goodbye, putting a smile on my face I didn't believe in. I didn't know why I was feeling so much dread. All I was doing was flying to a city and then flying back. I wouldn't be in any danger. Yet I couldn't shake the feeling that things were about to change forever.

Into the Dark

XVI

Redwood was not pleased at being woken in the middle of the night. The large dragon was sleeping soundly in his section of hollow wall within the palace courtyard, only stirring when I approached.

I tried to break the news to him as easily as I could. I walked up to his head and kneeled so we were eye level. I petted his hide lightly. "Time to get up, sweet boy," I said to him softly. "We have places that need us."

The dragon rumbled deeply, unmoved. *I don't want to.*

I walked to the wall where his saddle was hanging. "Come now, Redwood," I said. "Please? For me."

He still wasn't happy about it, but Redwood slowly lifted himself with his four powerful legs, allowing me to slide the straps for his saddle underneath his body. I rubbed his belly as I emerged from beneath him. "Thank you." He huffed again.

Redwood tucked in his wing and fell to his side. I climbed on top of him and adjusted the saddle to the right position at the top of his back. Then I hopped to the ground and connected the saddle straps from the top of him to the ones underneath his belly. It was a very intensive effort, and by the end I was breathing heavily.

"Well, I dare say we're getting good at this, huh?" I heaved out to my friend. "That might have been the fastest we've ever done."

Redwood shuffled slowly out of his hideaway into the larger yard. He grumbled again as he stepped into the silver moonlight.

I put my hands on my hips. "Oh come on," I said. "Are you going to be in a sour mood for the entire flight?"

The dragon turned his large head back to me. Two puffs of smoke left his nostrils. *If I want.*

I shook my head at him. Walking into the courtyard, I could look into a similarly hollow portion of wall situated next to where Redwood slept. This cubby was occupied by Cerulia and likewise Davit as he worked to secure his own saddle onto his dragon.

Davit was unusually quiet as he worked. He looked to be adjusting the saddle exactly as I'd taught him, but I could tell he was tense and agitated. I walked up to the two of them. "How are you coming along?" I asked.

"Fine," Davit replied curtly, not looking up from his work.

That was a conversational dead end. "How are you feeling about flying again?"

"Fine," Davit said again.

I scrunched my brow, once more placing my hands on my hips. "You know," I began. "We're twins, Davit. I can tell how you feel almost as well as I can about Redwood."

Davit tightened his saddle around Cerulia, finished. He ushered his dragon into the courtyard. He turned to me and sighed. "It's stupid, Rose. Percival leaves us out of the war since it began, and even when we're finally useful to him, he doesn't let us actually do anything meaningful." Davit huffed. "We're just his backup." He paused, as if thinking it over. "Not even us. The dragons are his backup. He won't even give us weapons!"

"It's not like we need weapons," I said. "We're going on a support mission. Do you want a sword? Do you want to go rushing into battle?" Davit didn't answer. "Right," I said, my face falling flat. "Stupid question."

Davit crossed his arms. The two of us stood together silently for a moment. We looked across the courtyard. On the other side, Percival was talking to Pevincy and Bryce. The three of them were shrouded in shadows. Because of the distance, we couldn't hear what they were discussing.

"You can contribute to the war without going into battle," I tried to reconcile with Davit. "We can help people."

Davit laughed dryly. He looked over at me. "Do you really believe we're helping anyone right now, Rose?" he asked. "Really?"

I didn't respond. I thought of the people outside the gates. People I was flying away from.

Across the courtyard, Pevincy bowed his head and walked away from the group. Percival turned to face Bryce. The two continued talking for a moment longer, probably about the running of the palace in Percival's absence, if I had to guess. The conversation ended with a shared hug between the two young men, patting each other's backs. With one last word, Percival turned from his friend and walked towards Davit and me.

"Are you two prepared?" our older brother asked, looking at us. "It's a good few hours of flight before our first stop."

I nodded, confident in my and Redwood's ability to fly. Whether I would make myself sick or not was a different question, but I kept it to myself. I knew Redwood would try his best.

Percival turned his look to Davit, having heard of his last attempt to fly. Davit still had his arms crossed. "I'll manage," he said, not trying all that hard to hide the anger in his voice.

Percival acknowledged his snark with nothing more than a nod. "Come then," he said. The young king placed two fingers in his mouth and whistled. The air behind him grew wavy, as if a section of it was moving out of time from the rest of the air around it. The air began to glimmer and slowly turn gold as the shape of Apolion materialized, literally out of thin air.

Percival climbed onto his dragon's saddle. Without another word to Davit or me on the ground, the two of them took off into the night sky, completely silent despite Apolion's size.

"Don't wait up!" Davit called after them. He rolled his eyes. The two of us walked to our respective dragons on the other end of the courtyard. Davit climbed into Cerulia's saddle cautiously, as if he were worried every move he made would send him flying.

"Remember what I said," I tried to reassure him, climbing onto Redwood. "Fly *with* her."

"Yeah, yeah," Davit acknowledged. With that, Cerulia flapped her wings, taking to the air after Apolion.

I sat in Redwood's saddle. I breathed deeply. Redwood, still annoyed at being awake, could sense my anxiety. He would try to make it an easy flight.

"Thank you," I said, already nervous as we lifted slowly into the cold, dark sky.

The next week was mostly a blur. We would spend most of the days flying, only stopping at midday for a brief meal and rest for the dragons. We would spend the nights in the castles of various local lords, bringing excitement to whatever town or city we landed in. Crowds of joyous people would always flock around us, never having seen royalty, let alone dragons before. I enjoyed that part of the journey. It was nice to see people from all over the kingdom.

The last night of our trip was the only significant difference. We had entered the Golden Desert: a vast expanse of sparsely populated sand dunes completely alien to the green forests of the western coast. Because of its lack of significant population, the desert didn't have any castles we could conveniently stay at on our way to Bukarra on the other side, so the three of us made camp under the stars among the dunes.

Davit and I ate a small meal of dried sausage and hard bread around a campfire produced by Redwood as Percival told us the plan for the next day. We would fly to Bukarra to meet with the governor of the city, where we would discuss any and all movement from Ahaax and possibilities for intercepting his army. Percival said Davit and I could sit in on the talks, saying it would be good experience.

Davit rolled his eyes discreetly so only I could see. *The king deigns to let us sit in*, the look said.

The three of us opted to get to sleep early that night so we could be up early for the flight to Bukarra the next morning. I could tell by the snores that the boys had managed to fall asleep quickly, including Redwood, whose rumbling shook my body lightly as I lay on top of him, looking at the stars.

I listened to the peaceful crackling of the campfire. I was the only one awake for miles around. Just me and the stars. It was difficult for me to fall asleep. My stomach was twisting itself into knots. The dread I had felt when I left my friends at the palace had been growing steadily with each passing day. Now we would be in Bukarra the next day, and I couldn't shake it.

Eventually, despite my body's stubbornness, my exhaustion lured me into a restless sleep.

I was walking against a crowd of fleeing people. Elders be good, there must have been thousands of swiftly moving bodies, at least. I couldn't stop though; I had to push through. They needed me. I couldn't fail them. Something about the crowd seemed off, but I couldn't place it. They seemed familiar, but at the same time I didn't know any of the people rushing past me.

I emerged from the other side of the crowd. We were surrounded by mountains. *That's right*, I thought, we were in the mountains. The people we were protecting were making their way through a skinny mountain pass. From my vantage I could see a thin line snake from where we were to a few miles down the mountain. That was everyone who was left.

I was standing on the edge of the mountain next to a man a few years younger than me. He had dark red hair tied back in a ponytail. He was looking past our people. There was a rumbling cloud of dust getting closer and closer to where we were.

The man shook his head. He turned his head to me. His eyes were a deep violet. Those eyes, so familiar. "We're out of time," the man said. "We don't stand a chance against them all."

I knew he was right. We had been running for so long. Running and running and running and running. But we couldn't stop. We could either run or we would die. "Go," I told the man. "I can buy you some time, but you need to get everyone away from here."

The man's face turned down. He knew what I meant, what needed to be done. "No," he said stubbornly. He was always so stubborn. "Not without you."

I grabbed his shoulders firmly, looking deep into those violet orbs. "Be the leader I know you can be," I said to him. This was it; it was now or never. He had my faith. "Save our people."

The man had tears bead up in his eyes at this point. I was fighting back my own. I was never good at goodbyes. He placed his hand lightly on one of my own. "Find peace with the Elders," he managed to get out.

I smiled, then sent him on his way, towards the front of the crowd of familiar strangers. I took a long, shaky breath and then turned around, facing the cloud of dust that had grown bigger over the short conversation.

Elders give us strength, I thought as I raised my hands. I closed my eyes, giving my entire concentration. My stomach pulled every which way. I gritted my teeth as the entire earth shook.

I opened my eyes with a feeling of weightlessness. The dunes of the Golden Desert were collapsing all around me. I realized I could no longer feel Redwood's familiar rumbling against my back. I was falling.

Percival

The Sand Snake

XVII

I couldn't have been asleep long when I was woken by the sound of screaming. My eyes snapped open. To the east, the sun was just starting to emerge over the horizon. Davit ran past me, Cerulia right on his heels. I heard him scream, "Rose!"

Rose? I thought. *Was she in danger?* Blinking the grogginess from my eyes, I jumped to my feet and took off after Davit. The loose sand beneath my feet caused me to lose my footing and stumble, but I continued running.

Davit was standing completely still. He was looking down into a giant sinkhole at least thirty feet deep. Dread creeped into my stomach. I ran up beside him. He turned his head to me. "She's down there, Percival," he said, panicked. He looked into the hole and again shouted Rose's name.

"What happened?" I asked. I scanned the sand for any sign of our sister, but there was nothing. Everything was still. Panic rose within me.

Davit put his hands on the back of his head. "I… I don't know," he stammered. I looked at him. "Everything was normal. Then there was a loud rumbling, but after a few seconds it went away. Then…" He waved his arms at the sinkhole. "That!"

This confused me even more. What could have caused this? I didn't have time to worry about that now, though. We had to find Rose. I shouted her name into the pit, but there was still no response. I had to do something.

"I'm going down there," I said, having made up my mind.

"What?" Davit's jaw dropped. "No. Percival, it's a thirty-foot fall."

"I think I can use the winds to slow me down." I looked at him, projecting as much confidence with my voice as I could.

He shook his head, baffled. "You *think*? Have you ever actually done this before?"

"No."

"You're not even sure it'll work?"

"No."

"What the h—" Davit smacked his forehead, completely exasperated.

I grabbed my younger brother's shoulders. "You need to calm down, Davit," I said forcefully. I couldn't let emotions get the better of either of us. Not when the stakes were this high. "If this doesn't work and I get stuck down there too, I need you to bring the dragons down there." I motioned my head to Apolion and Cerulia, who were sitting a few feet away watching our conversation. "You will be our last hope. Breathe. Can you do that?"

Davit took a few gulping breaths like a fish out of water. Eventually he managed to get some sense of control. With one long, shaky breath, he nodded.

I nodded back, giving him my trust. I stepped closer to the edge of the pit. Looking down within was daunting as the sinkhole had seemingly grown deeper. I told myself this couldn't be true, but the task was already plenty intimidating. An uncontrolled fall from this height would almost certainly break both my legs, maybe kill me. I breathed in deeply, bracing myself both mentally and physically. Rose couldn't afford for me to be afraid.

Below us, the sand in the bottom of the hole shifted. Davit and I both froze. A large object slowly rose from the earth, streams of sand flowing off its ridges. Through the sand I could make out a big, green eye on what I determined was a head. The creature looked up at us and puffed a plume of smoke out of its nostrils. "Redwood," Davit sighed in relief.

Rose's dragon was almost completely buried beneath the sand. All we could see of the large creature was his head and half of his short neck; the rest was below ground. The dragon craned his neck around slowly and then yawned as if he had woken from a nap. Despite having fallen into the earth, he didn't even look fazed.

"Redwood," Davit continued, "is Rose down there with you? Is she safe?" The dragon looked at him with an aloof expression. His eyes were only half open. "Rose," Davit reiterated. Redwood made a harsh growl in response, as if to say *I heard you the first time.* The dragon looked to his side, and the ground began to shift again. This time a massive wing rose from the sand. Because of the wing's size, it acted like a big shovel. When it rose, it scooped most of the sand off of Redwood and Davit, and I could see his whole body. He had fallen on his side in the collapse, landing on his left wing but seemingly unharmed. Lying near his stomach, in a spot where his wing kept out the most sand, was Rose.

Immediately I felt an immense relief. I could see her, and she didn't look hurt. She was safe. I let out a long sigh. Davit did the same next to me. He bent and put his hands on his knees. "Thank the Divines," he breathed. "Gods and Elders, what the heck."

"Rose!" I called to her. "Are you alright?"

Our sister sat upright. Rubbing the back of her head, she began, "Yeah, I think so. A little shaken and bruised, but I'll live." She turned her head to Redwood and rubbed his stomach. "Thanks to your protection, my sweet boy," she laughed. The dragon kicked his back leg like a dog and made a deep purring sound. Clearly he enjoyed the affection. Rose ran her other hand through her dark red hair, making a face at the amount of sand that came out.

"Rose, did you do this?" Davit called. I was about to ask the same thing. "Like, in your sleep?"

Rose opened her mouth, offended at the accusation. She was about to say something but stopped herself. Her mouth closed, and she looked like she was trying to remember something. She shook her head, driving whatever she was thinking away. "No, Davit," she said, still sounding slightly offended. "Have you ever summoned a tsunami in your sleep?"

Davit scrunched his face. "Well, no."

Rose continued. "We have to be conscious to use our powers, as best we can tell." She stood, brushing the excess sand off her clothes. She shook her head again. "No, something else had to have caused this." She turned, looking at the size of the pit. "I don't think I could even do this awake."

"So what could?" I wondered aloud. I tried to recall everything I'd been taught about the Golden Desert that could explain the phenomena. Weather patterns, shifting dunes. I stopped, a pit forming in my stomach. *Burrowing.*

Rose placed her hands on her hips. "I dunno," she started, raising her shoulders. Suddenly, her face went slack. She dropped to her knees, placing her hand on the sand.

"Rose?" Davit asked. "What is it?"

Rose's face was pale. "Something's coming," she said. "It's big."

Davit furrowed his brow. "What? How can you tell?"

"It's underground." Rose looked up at us. "It's getting closer, fast."

My blood ran ice-cold. *How could I be so stupid?* I screamed at myself internally. A low buzzing filled my head as the tips of my limbs began to tingle. "Davit." I snapped my head towards my brother beside me. "Get on Cerulia and get into the air. *Now.*" I cupped my hands around my mouth and shouted into the pit. "Rose! Get on Redwood and get out of there!"

"What?" Davit asked. "What's going on?"

As he finished speaking, the ground began to shake. Davit and I were both caught off guard. I had to stumble backwards to prevent myself from falling into the sinkhole. Davit extended his arms to try to balance himself. The buzzing within my head was growing steadily louder. It was becoming more focused, though. What had been a slight buzzing all around me seconds before was now an intense sensation concentrated in one direction, right below Davit standing in front of me. Without thinking, I snatched his outstretched arm and jerked him towards me. Davit fell to the ground behind me, but the sand where he had been standing immediately collapsed. If I had been a fraction of a second slower, Davit would have fallen into the pit.

"Wow." Davit looked up at me. "How did you know to do that?"

I brushed off his question, instead helping him to his feet. "I put us all in danger. You two need to get out of here. I'll be right behind you." Before Davit could stammer any sort of response, I grabbed his hand and ran with him towards our dragons. Apolion and Cerulia both looked extremely anxious. They were barking quick sounds, conversing with each other, and stamping the ground as if they couldn't get away fast enough.

I practically threw Davit onto Cerulia's saddle. All that mattered was to get him high, away from the ground. My next message wasn't to him, but to his dragon. "Get him out of here," I said to Cerulia, looking into the young dragon's large eyes.

Cerulia let out a quick roar and reared onto her hind legs. Davit would've fallen off were he not already holding her reins. As both the dragon and her rider took to the sky, the last thing I heard from Davit was a shouted "What the hell?" get progressively quieter as they flew a few dozen feet off the ground.

I spun so fast I nearly threw myself to the ground. *Rose*, I thought. She was my next priority. I started running towards the sinkhole. I had to see if she and Redwood were able to make it out. The buzzing kept me alert and once again concentrated in a single spot, right below me.

An explosion of sand sent me flying backwards, spiraling through the air. I landed on my back, hard, in a nearby dune. Stars covered half my vision. I groaned from the wave of aching pain sweeping through my body. I could sense Apolion land beside me. He made a series of quick chirps and barks, concerned. I sat straight up, shaking myself out of my daze. *Rose*, I thought again. *Nothing else matters.* I had to get to her. A task that was just made significantly harder.

I was dozens of feet away from the sinkhole, but that was the least of my worries. Between me and the pit, rising from the explosion of sand its breaching to the surface had caused, was a massive snake. The creature had to be one hundred feet long, at least, just judging by the size of its body above the sand. Its limbless body was segmented and covered in slanted, blood-red and spike-like scales. There was no noticeable point where its head turned into its body, but the head itself narrowed to a point divided into three sections, and it lacked any eyes I could see.

The gigantic wyrm wiggled in an *S* motion in the air before the three sections of its head split open, revealing an interior lined with razor-sharp black teeth going as far down its throat as the light would reach. Its mouth was giant, probably capable of swallowing me whole. As I got my bearings, I thought it was strange that was the first thought my mind went to. I scrambled to my feet beside Apolion, who was hunched low and growled ferociously at the creature, his fangs bared.

The wyrm's head snapped towards us, and I looked straight into the blackness of its maw. It uttered a monstrous roar so loud I had to cover my ears and felt my bones shake. Not letting myself take my eyes off the creature, I could see in my peripheral vision Cerulia flying in circles about a hundred feet behind it. Davit shouted a curse. "What is *that* thing?"

"Dune wyrm," I muttered, even though there was no way he could hear me. The largest predator in the Golden Desert. Driven by instinct alone, I removed my spear from its notch on my back. I summoned a current of electricity to run through my arm, charging the weapon with high voltage. Small arcs of electric blue lighting ran the length of the weapon. Ultimately, it didn't matter how big the beast in front of me was. It was between me and Rose, and I had to get through it.

The dune wyrm sprang towards me and my dragon. It was fast, almost impossibly fast for something of its size. So fast that my eyes could barely process its attack, let alone counter it. In a blur of yellow, Apolion lunged to meet the wyrm. He crashed into its body, sending himself and the creature into the sand beside me, missing me by only a few feet. Apolion had the body of the wyrm in his jaw, and he was trying to use his two legs to keep it pinned to the ground, ferociously flapping his wings for whatever help they could provide. The beast let out another ear-splitting roar.

I ran towards the two clashing creatures. Apolion was big, but the wyrm was bigger, and my dragon was quickly losing control of his pin. I raised my spear above my head. My stomach tugged as I channeled a wave of lightning into the weapon. My spear was nothing compared to the size of the wyrm, but if I could get one good hit in, enough to puncture its hide, maybe that could make a difference.

Suddenly, the dune wyrm spun its body ferociously. The angle of its red scales flung sand in all directions. The wyrm thrashed wildly, and finally Apolion lost his hold. The massive wyrm raised its body and threw my dragon off, causing him to crash violently into a nearby dune, leaving a cloud of sand in his wake.

My stomach dropped. "Apolion!" I shouted. He had never been hit by something comparable in size to him before. In my second of inaction, the wyrm flung its body again, this time striking me. A flash of searing pain went through the length of my left arm where I was hit. Once again I was sent through the air. I was conscious that my spear flew out of my grip as I tumbled, but not much else.

I landed in the sand next to Apolion, who was picking himself up slowly. He looked dazed but otherwise unhurt. My dragon brought his head close to me protectively. I felt lightheaded. My vision was once again taken over by black splotches. I placed my right hand on my left arm, applying pressure. I gritted my teeth. When I took my hand away, it was covered in blood.

The dune wyrm slithered grotesquely across the sand towards us. It reared back and roared once more. Apolion tensed, ready to defend us. I was still on the ground, and I didn't even have my spear. I raised my unbloodied arm at the creature, little bolts of lightning running up and down. My body buzzed as I charged enough electricity to shoot at the wyrm, but the exertion was causing the rest of my vision to go dark.

A column of smokey flames engulfed the wyrm from behind, causing it to shriek in pain. I blinked hard, lowering my arm. *Did I overdo it to the point of hallucinating?* I could tell the attack wasn't a hallucination when I saw Redwood fly over the writhing creature, with Rose on his back. *She made it out of the pit,* I thought, relieved. That relief quickly vanished when Rose turned Redwood around and made another pass at the wyrm, again blanketing it in orange flames.

I stood slowly. *She needs to get out of here*, I thought. *They both need to get out of here. They're in danger.* Sure enough, the furious dune wyrm slithered away from me and towards Rose and Davit and their flying dragons. The wyrm snapped its sectioned jaws at my siblings in the air. The dragons did well enough avoiding the attacks by flying in eccentric circles, but I knew it couldn't last long.

I could feel a wave of new adrenaline rush through me. I wouldn't let them get hurt. I waved my arms around in the air. "Hey!" I shouted at the wyrm, trying to get its attention. "Hey!" Apolion beside me caught on. He planted his feet and wings firmly in the sand and unleashed a roar loud enough to rival the dune wyrm's.

None of this noise was working. The wyrm was still snapping at Cerulia and Redwood. One close call with Cerulia nearly caused Davit to fall off. I had to do something more. I raised my right arm back up at the wyrm and felt the electricity surge through my body. From the top of my head to the bottom of my feet I felt lightning move through me, channeled through my arm as one concentrated bolt of blue energy shot from my extended hand with a thunderous *vwoom*. Every hair on my body stood straight, and I stumbled, feeling suddenly faint.

The bolt of lightning hit the wyrm just under its head. There was a small explosion on contact, followed by a larger, crackling black cloud. The wyrm cried out its loudest roar yet. Then it turned its head back towards me and Apolion. I stood there in disbelief, panting from the exertion. I was really counting on that bringing the wyrm down. I didn't know if I would be able to do that again.

The dune wyrm roared again, then dove its head straight into the sand. It was burrowing. Judging by the direction of the clouds of sand being tossed up in its wake, it was burrowing right for Apolion and me.

"Percival!" my siblings screamed faintly from atop their dragons.

I waved my arm away forcefully. "Get out of here!" I shouted. "Fly towards the sun!" If Davit and Rose flew east long enough, they would eventually reach Bukarra. *And then they'll both be safe.* I looked at the rapidly approaching dust cloud. I had to think quickly. Even with my siblings safe, that didn't mean I wasn't going to let the wyrm have me without a fight.

I turned on my heel and ran as fast as I could up a nearby sand dune, thinking frantically. Despite the constant buzzing in my head from the direction of the approaching wyrm and the feeling of more electricity building within my body, I formed the beginning of a plan. It just required a good vantage point.

I reached the top of the dune and spun around, desperately searching the sand below me. Finally a glimmer in a nearby dune caught my eye. *My spear.* I extended my arm towards its position. Feeling a swift breeze through my hair, I called my weapon back to my hand with the wind: the vibrations running through my arm from when it made contact. Luckily that was less energy-intensive than summoning lightning. I was hoping my luck would last. If it didn't, I would probably die in this desert.

Apolion landed on the dune beside me. He chirped urgently, gesturing with his head to the rapidly approaching wyrm beneath the sand. I placed my free hand on my dragon's muzzle. "Go to Rose and Davit, Apolion," I said. "If this doesn't work, make sure they get to safety."

Apolion made a harsh sound. *Don't say it won't work.*

I shook my head. "There's no time for this, friend. I hope to meet with you all soon." He made another harsh sound, reluctant to go. "Grant me this," I pleaded with him.

Apolion shifted on his feet. Then, reluctantly, he flew into the air, towards Davit and Rose. I could hear them screaming softly, asking why I wasn't with my dragon. *To keep you safe*, I thought. I looked back at the approaching cloud. *Hopefully this works.*

I could tell the dune wyrm was getting closer and closer. The concentrated buzzing in my head was getting louder and more focused with each passing second. I couldn't stay still; I was bouncing on my feet, both from the amount of energy passing through me and nerves.

"Five," I said aloud, giving myself a countdown.

In that moment, I didn't think of my possible death, or about being king. My mind went back to that night two months ago, when I first met Delilah.

"Four."

She was beautiful, the way the moonlight caught her hair. She had said a prayer after her hunt.

"Three." The wyrm was at the foot of my sand dune.

Rayanna, goddess of the hunt. Let my aim be true. Let me strike swift.

"Two."

Grant me speed, strength, and courage, Rayanna. So that I may see her again.

"One." The buzzing was like a hammer in my head; the wyrm was right below me. I threw myself backwards, using the wind to give my leap a few extra feet. The sand below me exploded again as the dune wyrm rose. I landed in a backwards roll, my spear arm arched. I screamed as I threw the weapon with all my might directly at the center of the wyrm. I summoned the wind from behind me to speed up the spear on its trajectory.

The weapon pierced the wyrm true. Green blood gushed out of the fresh wound. Another piercing roar. I brought up both my hands. The energy within me had reached its peak. Lightning was shooting in all directions from my outstretched arms. The buzzing throughout my body got so strong I couldn't tell if I felt anything as two great bolts of bright blue lightning shot from my arms at the spear embedded in the body of the dune wyrm. The earth shook, and then everything was white, and then black.

I felt as if I were floating in an ocean of ink. I could hear faint voices calling out in the distance. "Not you too!" cried the voice of a girl somewhere I couldn't see. "Not you too!" There was another voice, a boy's. "Percival," the boy shouted. "Percival, wake up!"

Percival, I thought. *That's my name.* Slowly, thought began to come back to me. My name was Percival. I was the king of Lungalea, and I wasn't in an endless black ocean. I was in the Golden Desert.

I let out a long groan. Feeling was coming back to my body, and none of it felt good. Every joint ached, and I felt uncomfortably hot. I cracked my eyes open slightly. There were two blurry masses inches from my face, looking down at me.

"Rose," one of the blurs said. "Rose, hey, look." The face of my brother slowly came into focus.

The other blur gasped in relief. Rose wrapped her arms around my torso, lifting me in a tight hug. I gasped reflexively at the sudden pressure on my aching limbs.

Rose loosened her hold. "Sorry," she said sheepishly.

"It's alright," I said, strained. My vision was coming back. Rose had tears still running down her face. I looked at Davit, who was wiping away his own.

"You really had us worried there, Percival," Davit said, covering up any sign of his vulnerability.

I craned my neck around, rediscovering the extent of my motion. All three of our dragons, Apolion, Redwood, and Cerulia, were sitting in a row behind us. I made eye contact with Apolion, who was the closest of the dragons and whose long neck was extended so his head was nearly directly above me. He rumbled deeply, welcoming me back. I grinned.

I turned my attention back to my worried siblings. "What happened?" I asked. Everything before my blackout was still hazy in my mind. I remembered a sense of danger.

Rose shook her head, still shaken from the experience. "You were unconscious for a long time," she said.

Davit nodded in agreement. "Five minutes, at least. Maybe closer to ten by the time we got to you."

Rose took in a shaky breath. "You weren't responding to anything," she said. "You had a heartbeat, but there was no other sign to see if you..." She stopped, not wanting to give voice to the thought.

"I'm alright," I reassured them. I brought them in with an arm for a hug of my own. I could be king in a minute; for now, it was just nice to have my family.

A green wrapping around my left arm caught my attention. What was once emerald-green fabric had grown a darker shade of brown serving as a bandage. It was then that I noticed that Rose had one of the sleeves of her blouse torn off. I raised an eyebrow. "Your work?" I asked.

Rose shrugged. "There was a lot of blood, and it wouldn't stop. I did what I could."

I placed a hand on the bandage. Tenderly, I applied pressure. It still hurt, a lot, but when I pulled my hand away, there wasn't any blood. "I'd say it worked. Good job." Suddenly I remembered what had caused the wound. I looked at Rose and Davit. "What about the dune wyrm? What happened to it? Did it leave?"

Davit sucked in air through his teeth. Rose's face went flat. "What?" I asked.

Davit rubbed the back of his head. "Well," he began. "In a way, you can say it left." I furrowed my brow, confused. "Come on," he said.

My two siblings each took one of my arms and lifted me. I would have fallen right back down if they hadn't been supporting me. The three of us slowly walked up the sand dune, the two of them patiently waiting for me to catch up as feeling came back to my numb legs. As we reached the top, I could see a thin curl of smoke rising from the other side. When I looked down, my stomach dropped.

The fully exposed carcass of the once ferocious dune wyrm was lying on the sand. Smoke was still rising from its singed black body, as if it had just emerged from a fire. There wasn't any blood anywhere; it had all been cauterized. In the center of the long corpse was my spear, still embedded within the creature. It was covered in a thick layer of ash, making it almost completely black instead of its natural bronze.

I was able to stand without the help of my siblings, and I slowly walked down the dune to the carcass. I felt numb, but this time it wasn't because of my aching joints. I limped to my spear. As I reached out, I could feel the heat still radiating off the weapon. I was able to grab it without burning myself, and it might have been my imagination, but I felt I could still feel a faint buzzing.

I removed the spear. It wasn't easy. I had to put my foot on the still hot wyrm to give myself leverage to pull it out. I looked at the weapon, lost in thought. There was black blood stained on the tip. I tried to find my reflection in the metal, but the ash covered any sign of the noble weapon I'd started this journey with. "I…" I began, turning to Davit and Rose. I was trying to find words to convey what I was thinking. "I did this?" I asked, seeking to confirm what I already knew.

Rose broke the silence. "How much do we actually know about our powers?" she asked quietly.

Among The Ashes

XVIII

The remaining flight to Bukarra still took multiple hours, and I was troubled for all of it. Flying with Apolion was usually able to distract me from my troubles, but this time I had too many to be distracted. At first I sat thinking about the extent of my abilities and how I was able to kill the dune wyrm. It was unnerving. *What gave me the right to wield all this power?*

Then I thought about how I had already failed twice on this journey, both as a king and a brother. I cursed myself repeatedly for letting the three of us spend a night in the sand dunes, where I should have known dune wyrms hunt. A king would have prepared for that and planned another alternative, and a brother wouldn't have put his siblings in danger so carelessly. I was in such a rush to get to our destination that I threw away all the values I should possess.

This led me to think about our mission: the journey to Bukarra. I thought back to the night the three of us had left the royal palace. I had convened a meeting of the council as soon as I had heard Ahaax was spotted moving in the region. The six lords all approved of my plan to have us fly to Bukarra and lead a response from there. Though, truth be told, the lords often agreed with whatever plan didn't directly inconvenience their ability to gain power.

The only people in the room were the seven of us. Pevincy had suggested the meeting be held in complete secrecy, and as I began to dismiss the council he explained why. "I think we must start functioning under the assumption, Your Grace," he said, "that there is a traitor in our ranks."

Treason was nothing new in this war. After Ahaax had killed my father, a number of counts and dukes swore fealty to him, which was how he'd managed to gain control of everything east of the Black Mountains seemingly overnight. But a traitor for his side still working *inside* the palace was something I hadn't expected. The rest of the council didn't like the idea either. Lord Carrington at first suggested that Pevincy was looking for an excuse for why we were losing the war. But as Pevincy explained, it was the only possible reason why Ahaax was able to beat us at every step despite being under-manned and under-resourced.

The idea of a traitor within our ranks was deeply unsettling, and it added a sense of urgency to everything that was already going on. I had so little experience. I didn't know how to manage a kingdom at war, and now I didn't even know who I could trust. I had grabbed Davit and Rose immediately after disbanding the council and told them we'd be leaving before I even expected. I was determined not to give the traitor any more time to relay our plans to Ahaax.

I was stuck on this train of thought as the three of us flew through the sky on our dragons. The wind that blew through my hair was loud in my ears, but I wasn't processing any of it. I was only looking down at Apolion's yellow feathers and scales, lost in thought.

"Look!" I picked out Rose's voice from the wind rushing past. I looked back at her. She was in Redwood's saddle, pointing in front of her with a worried look on her face. I looked at where she was pointing, and my stomach dropped.

A thick plume of inky smoke was rising on the horizon, growing larger and larger as we approached and changing the mountains in the distance to a shade that reflected their name. The sand below us gradually turned black, scorched. In some places it had turned to glass. I looked down, feeling panic build within me. Everything was black; there weren't even any buildings, just piles of smoking rubble. We had reached our destination, but Bukarra was no longer there.

A blue blur rushed past my eyes and towards the ruined city. *Cerulia.* "Davit, wait!" I called after my brother's dragon. *Ahaax could be down there!* Davit wasn't thinking, I could tell. I needed to get after him, fast. I lashed Apolion's reins, bracing for a swift descent.

My dragon tucked his wings close to his body and dove. Everything around me became a blur of yellow and black as the wind reached deafening volumes. I could feel my stomach being pushed back as my vision seemed to stretch. Then, just as fast as the descent, we evened out seconds before hitting the ground, and Apolion slowed himself with heavy wing flaps as we landed on the charred sand.

I looked around anxiously as I dismounted. I scanned our surroundings, looking for anywhere Ahaax or his army could be hiding. But Ahaax wasn't here, and there was certainly no army. It was as if the largest settlement in the Golden Desert had spontaneously erupted into flames. I was left only with a mix of confusion and horror. *This wasn't supposed to happen*, I thought desperately. *We were supposed to come here to* save *Bukarra! How could this have happened?* I spun in a circle, seemingly hoping that when I turned around the city would be back and functioning. Of course, this didn't happen.

Behind me there was an enormous *thud* as Redwood landed beside Apolion. Rose slowly stepped down from the large saddle. The look on her face was one of pure terror. "Percival," she said softly, glancing wide-eyed around at the burnt carnage. "What… happened?"

I opened my mouth to respond, but no sound came out. I didn't know what to say. *This wasn't supposed to happen.* The reports said Ahaax was in the region, but they didn't say anything about something that could result in this much destruction. I had seen ruined cities in the past seven months of war. I had seen what Ahaax's army was capable of. But here, there wasn't even a single structure still standing, only burnt piles of wood and stone. Something about this was *wrong*.

I turned back to Apolion, feeling numb. Whatever I wished the situation to be, however many times I thought *This shouldn't have happened*, it had, and a king had to handle himself in crisis. "Apolion," I said to the large dragon. "Take the others and search the area from the air. Look for any signs of enemy troops. They have to be close by. Look for any..." I was going to say anything strange, but nothing about this situation was normal. "Be on guard," I decided to say.

I sensed something different about Apolion. He was... afraid. I had never seen him afraid before. His body was hunched low to the ground, and the claws from the tips of his wings were scraping nervously at the sand. I looked at Redwood curiously. Cerulia had moved next to him, and the two other dragons were similarly on edge. Something about just being among these ruins was sending three of the most fearsome creatures I'd ever seen into a panic.

Apolion seemed not to hear me. "Apolion," I began again. He was definitely afraid of something. The dragon rumbled quietly. He wasn't being defiant, I realized. He didn't want to leave me alone. "We'll be alright, friend," I said, trying to ease his concern. "Scout the area and come back quickly."

Apolion shifted reluctantly. Finally he barked at Cerulia and Redwood, and the three dragons took off into the air, each going a separate direction. As I watched Apolion fly away, I could feel his conflicting feelings. He was happy to be away from the burnt heap, but he also didn't want to leave us. I brought my attention back to the ground and looked around. I could understand why he was so uneasy. My head had been buzzing ever since we landed. There was something strange about these ruins, something wrong. It felt almost instinctual.

I turned my gaze to my siblings. Rose was crouched near a pile of burnt wood, holding a black plank in her hands.

She looked at the wood intensely, as if she was trying to imagine how it could have ever been a part of something besides a ruin. She was holding back tears.

Davit had been standing in the same place ever since the three of us landed. His back was to Rose and me. I could tell his fists were clenched, and they might have even been shaking, although with the distance between us I couldn't be sure. He was whispering to himself, but his voice carried across the air, and I could hear him as clearly as if I were standing right next to him.

"I'll kill him myself," my brother whispered angrily. I could hear the tension in his voice. "The next time I see him, I swear by the Elders I'll kill him myself."

I took a step towards him. He wasn't thinking clearly. "Davit," I began. I didn't know how to comfort him, as king or brother. I didn't know if I'd be able to do either.

Davit spun around and looked at me. I was taken aback. Angry tears were running down his face, and his eyes were filled with fury. The boy in front of me now was a far cry from my younger brother, who was usually always so carefree and happy. "I'll kill him, Percival," he spat. "He can't keep getting away with this! He's evil! And he needs to pay! I swear I'll kill him myself!"

"Davit." Rose had walked up next to me. She choked back a sob.

"There will be no need for that, Prince Davit," a disturbingly familiar voice from nowhere said calmly.

Behind Davit, a patch of air turned orange. Suddenly, a column of flames erupted into existence. Rose and I were both frozen, our eyes locked on the burning cyclone. Davit noticed us and no doubt felt the heat, turning around, where he too immediately tensed. There was only one thing this could be.

Rose gasped. She quickly positioned herself behind me. Instinctually I held my arm out to protect her. I gasped as well, panic quickly building within me. "Davit, get behind me," I said urgently. Davit remained frozen.

As quickly as they had appeared, the flames crackled out of existence. Left standing in their wake were two men. One was short and fat with gray hair in similarly gray robes who I didn't recognize. But the other man was lean and tall, adorned in black armor lined with red the color of blood. His dirty blond hair was swept to one side, and his black eyes pierced through me the same way they did in every nightmare I'd had for the past seven months. Except this wasn't a nightmare. Ahaax was standing in front of us once again.

"There needn't be any violence," Ahaax continued in an even tone. The murderer looked at each of us individually, first Davit, then Rose peeking out behind my back, and finally landing on me. "Hello again, children," he said with a voice completely devoid of emotion. "It's been quite some time."

I could feel Rose's breathing pick up behind me. In front of the two of us, Davit spoke with a mix of shock, anger, and fear. "You," he said quietly.

"Davit, get behind me now!" I shouted, not careful enough to prevent my own fear slipping into my voice. I was the only one with a weapon. I needed to get him out of there.

Davit didn't listen to me. His breathing had gotten faster. In one swift motion, he bent and pulled something from one of his boots. It was a dagger. I should have known he wouldn't listen to me when I told him he wasn't to carry a weapon. But none of that mattered now. That small blade wouldn't change anything with Ahaax.

Before I could do anything, Davit let out a scream of pure anger and charged the warlord in front of him. Ahaax sighed as if this were more of an annoyance than a threat. He looked at the short man standing next to him. "Abominus, could you please?" he said.

The older man with the gray hair, Abominus, nodded. He took a step forward and raised one of his arms. For the first time, I noticed both of the man's stubby arms were covered from wrist to shoulder in dark red tattoos. As he lifted his arm, the tattoos glowed a brighter shade of magenta. Without warning, a semi-translucent beam of the same color shot from his palm.

As Davit got within feet of Ahaax, the strange attack hit my brother squarely in the chest. Davit was sent flying through the air, his knife tumbling from his hands. He landed a few dozen feet away from the rest of us in a pile of burnt wood. There was blood on his head, and he looked unconscious. I gasped.

"Davit!" Rose screamed behind me. She ran out from behind my back towards Davit's limp body in the rubble, desperately checking over him.

My head went back and forth between my siblings and the two men in front of us. Panic was overwhelming me, and I was beginning to freeze up. I had been in battles since the start of the war, but I hadn't seen Ahaax since that day seven months ago. And now Davit was hurt, or worse. I didn't know what to do.

Ahaax lazily turned his attention from the unconscious Davit back to me. "Now that the more emotional factors have been dealt with, perhaps the more reasonable actors can have a conversation, eh, Percival?"

In that moment, my panic vanished, and it was replaced with a burning anger. How dare he have the audacity to speak so calmly, so casually. With one swift movement of my arm, I unhooked my father's spear from its notch. I willed lightning to charge through the weapon and took an aggressive stance, slowly maneuvering myself between the two men and my siblings. There was only one way this would end. "Tell me about reason, murderer," I growled at Ahaax.

I had to keep him talking. I wouldn't let him hurt Davit or Rose. No more than he already had. *Apolion, get the others and come back,* now, I called across the sky. Somewhere in the distance I could tell my call was heard. If I could distract him for long enough to get my siblings out of here, I would consider it one success after my repeated failures.

Ahaax held out his hands. "I meant what I said, Percival. I mean you three no harm." Ahaax shook his head. "It's of no use to me for the situation we're in."

I shook my head, gritting my teeth. "You know nothing but harm," I said. I was now between the two separate groups. Rose was still over Davit. I had to believe that he was just unconscious. I couldn't be distracted. "You murder whoever stands in your way, and you destroyed this entire settlement. You have no right to claim the role of a pacifist."

Ahaax *tsk*ed. "Now, that's where you're mistaken," he said. "*I* did not destroy this settlement." He paused. I could tell his beady eyes were analyzing my every move. "But something tells me you know what did." A slight grin appeared on his face. "*Who.*"

The subtle buzzing amplified in my head. A slight breeze blew through the ruined town, but it felt off, alien in some way. I shook my head again, refusing to fall into his trap. "Enough mind games." I did my best to speak in the voice of the king: flat, not letting him know how deeply he was getting to me. "You abandoned the element of surprise when you appeared to us. Why? What is it you want?" I was walking slightly towards him. If this was to end in a fight, I would need every advantage I could get, all too aware of the large sword hanging from Ahaax's back.

The armor-clad warlord lifted his shoulders. "A conversation," he said. "That's all. You three will come with me, and we will have a conversation. With that, this war can be over. No more harm will come to you unless you resist."

What was he getting at? I wondered. There was no way a man who had murdered his brother would want to end this war with a diplomatic discussion. I tried to search his face for clues but got nothing. He was both emotionless and unsettlingly at ease all at once. "How can I trust that you'll deal fairly?" I asked, just stalling for any more time I could get without genuinely considering his offer. "You began this war with deception."

Ahaax sighed. "Fair," he admitted. "But you have very few options left to you." He motioned to the burnt rubble. He was right; we were the only ones for miles around. "And frankly," he continued, "I'm not very inclined to trust you either, Percival. For the same reason I know you've only been having this conversation to stall while your dragons come back." The warlord's face hardened. "And for the same reason I know you've been slowly getting closer to me for the chance to strike first."

I lunged forward with everything I had. I extended my electrified spear right at Ahaax's chest. He anticipated my move, sidestepping the attack with uncanny speed. I missed him entirely, and my spear's head was sent deep into the black sand on the ground, discharging a shock. Buzzing from my head concentrated behind me, and with a *click*, Ahaax had taken a black great sword from his back. A column of flames went up the blade of his weapon with a *fwoosh*. I pulled my spear from the ground and swung back around to face him. Our weapons clashed between us, unleashing a flash of sparks.

Ahaax was strong. Stronger than I had anticipated. He was only holding his sword with one hand, but even with that he was able to slowly force his blade closer and closer to me. The only thing between his weapon and my heart was the thin shaft of metal of my spear. I had to get out of his hold. "I recognize that stance," Ahaax said. His eyes were moving constantly at my slightest shift, analyzing my every action

With a burst of strength, I threw his sword off and spun around backwards, putting some distance between me and him. *That was too close*, I thought, panting ever so slightly.

Ahaax continued observing me in that same analytical way. "The old man's been teaching you, hasn't he?" he said, taking a step closer to me. Our weapons clashed again a few times in rapid succession, sending a fresh wave of sparks each time they met.

I backed up again, regaining my footing. *The old man?* I wondered. Then my stomach dropped. *Pevincy*. Ahaax had grown up with my father and Pevincy. He had trained with them, fought with them. Of course he would recognize Pevincy was the one who taught me how to use a spear.

He can see my every move before I make it. Panic slowly regained its control over me. *I have to do something he can't have prepared for.* Suddenly an idea came into my head. It was my best chance, but it was risky. I glanced at my siblings. Rose was still over Davit, and he still looked unresponsive, but now that old man, Abominus, was with them. He was doing something to Davit's head, but I didn't have enough time to get a good look. What was he doing? Were they in danger?

I decided my choice was between the risky option of dealing with Ahaax with a chance of success, or certain doom for all three of us. It wasn't much of a choice at all. I turned my gaze back to Ahaax, who was stepping closer to me, his sword ready to strike. It was now or never.

With a shout of exertion, I brought my spear above my head with both hands and charged the warlord. I rapidly brought my weapon towards him in a concentrated thrust. Ahaax anticipated this attack. Casually, he sidestepped the point of my spear. With cat-like reflexes, his empty hand shot out and grabbed one of my arms. He threw me to the ground.

Exactly what I need, I thought. My spear fell out of my grip, but I didn't need it anymore. As soon as I hit the ground, I rolled to my back. I brought my free arm up and pointed it at Ahaax. In a split second, I willed all the lightning I could muster from my body into that hand, ready to blast Ahaax with all my might. *Now you fall into* my *trap,* I thought.

Small arcs of blue energy crawled up and down my arm. Ahaax realized he was caught. For a split second, I thought I could see fear in his calculating face. I willed the electricity to shoot from my palm.

The blue lightning crackled and then fizzled out. Suddenly I was lightheaded, and there were black splotches in my vision. No bolt of lightning came forth. It was suddenly as much energy as I had just to hold up my hand. In that moment my mind went back to my battle with the dune wyrm, and the two great bolts of lightning I had blasted at it. My energy was drained, I realized with a sick feeling. I couldn't use my lightning.

The fear that had been there for only a moment left Ahaax's face. He reclaimed his flat expression as he angled his flaming sword at my chest. "You are beaten," he said coldly. "Yield." I sat there on the ground, looking up at him, panting. I didn't know what to do. My spear was on the ground out of reach, and I doubted I had any energy left to use it if I could somehow close the gap.

A strange glint rose behind Ahaax's back. I squinted, trying to make out what the new object was. *A knife.* It quickly plunged into Ahaax's shoulder, slipping between a gap in his armor.

The warlord howled in a mix of pain and surprise. He turned to his side, and it was then that I saw Rose standing behind him, holding the knife Davit had snuck past me, now bloodied. Rose hunched, ready to push the attack, but Ahaax threw her to the ground with a blow from his good arm. Rose dropped the knife, and Ahaax turned his sword on her. His mask of calm was gone, and for the first time he was showing pure rage.

"Stop," I rasped weakly, raising my arm in my sister's defense. Rose was on her back, it looked like the blow had knocked the wind out of her.

Ahaax turned his furious eyes back to me, but his sword was still hanging above Rose. "Last chance, Percival," he growled. "Submit, or they both die right here. I only *need* the one who calls himself king."

I breathed heavily from exhaustion and despair. My eyes looked at Rose, who was glaring at Ahaax, angry but defenseless. Then I looked behind them to Davit, who was being tended to by Abominus in the rubble, still unconscious. I was truly out of options. *Apolion*, I thought desperately. *Please.* In my exhaustion, I felt like I heard a very soft roar far in the distance.

"You're a monster," I managed in little more than a whisper. I felt like a prisoner in my own body. I was so angry and frightened, but I couldn't do anything.

Ahaax straightened. "Maybe," he said coldly. "But I will remake this land, Percival. And if it takes a monster to do that…" He turned his gaze to Rose, who his weapon was still pointing towards. "So be it." There wasn't an ounce of hesitation in his voice. I could tell he was prepared to make good on his threat.

"I…" I began weakly. "For the sake of my royal siblings, I yield." It took all of my energy just to finish the sentence. Ahaax was right. I was beaten. We all were. The three of us never stood a chance.

Ahaax turned back to me. The fire along his weapon retreated to the handle, and it was out. Ahaax returned the sword to its sheath. He put a hand on his injured shoulder.

"Get up," he said, devoid of emotion. He turned and began walking towards Abominus.

At that moment, any small remainder of energy I had in my body left. My head fell to the black, sandy ground. Rose scrambled over to me. "Percival," she said, concerned.

"I…" I tried to say something, but I didn't have it in me. Rose put my arm over her shoulder and stood us up. The little exertion that took made my vision go almost completely black. Still, I tried to look at my sister's face. There was nothing but fear in her eyes. I could only hope I wasn't wearing the same expression. "It will be alright," I croaked at her. I didn't know if it was her brother or the king talking, but it was a lie. That I knew.

The two of us hobbled over to Ahaax and Abominus, who were discussing something quietly among themselves. Ahaax saw the two of us approach and turned his attention back to the fat man. "It's time for us to leave," he told him.

Abominus nodded. He took a few steps away from us. With another wave of his hands, his tattoos once again began to glow. In front of us, a hole the same magenta color appeared out of thin air. Then, on the other side of the hole, a room formed, completely separate from the area we were in. Rose and I both gasped. *Magic*, I thought. It had to be.

Abominus turned his attention back to Davit. He had a frighteningly large open gash at the top of his head, just above his eye, but it was no longer bleeding. It was an injury he must have gotten in his fall. Abominus waved his arms again. This time, magenta clouds appeared underneath Davit, lifting him into the air at about waist height. My brother groaned. At least he was alive.

With that, Abominus stepped through the hole in space he'd created, and just like that he was in a room however many miles away. He made a *come here* motion with his hands, and the clouds carrying Davit followed him through.

Rose and I watched all of this happen in silence, unable to muster anything else. I realized I had lost sight of Ahaax. I looked around, and the pit in my stomach grew even more. Ahaax was about a dozen feet away from us, leaning down. When he stood, he had my father's spear in his hand. "I remember you," he said softly.

The warlord walked back to us at the magical gateway. He looked at Rose and me individually. "Time to leave, children," he said in his same flat tone.

Rose scowled. "You won't win," she said defiantly.

Ahaax looked at her, not deigning to reply.

Then, an ear-splittingly loud roar was heard from ahead of us, then another, and another. I looked past Ahaax. Far behind him, three shapes were becoming clear in the distance, and they were approaching fast. The dragons! They'd arrived!

We're saved! I thought, excited for the first time that day. *We can get out of here!* I looked at Rose, and she appeared to be having the exact same thoughts as me. A big smile had grown on her face. I could begin to make out the yellow shape of Apolion; he would be here in only a matter of seconds.

Ahaax looked at the rapidly approaching dragons. "No!" he shouted. *It's over. You're finished now.* A smirk appeared on my face. With my spear still in his hand, he ran towards the portal we had all gone through. Behind him, Apolion had landed hard on the ground, sending dirt into the air. *How does it feel to have your plan fail right in front of you?* Ahaax was only feet from the portal now. "Close it, Abominus!" he shouted. Apolion roared once again. It was so loud it seemed to shake the ground. Ahaax reached the portal. He turned. *Wait.* My smirk was gone. Apolion reared his long neck back and charged the warlord. Ahaax lifted his arm towards my dragon's head. He shouted an almost animal sound as a column of pure white flames shot from his palm. He jumped backwards through the portal… and the doorway shut.

Where there was once my dragon coming to save us all just a second before, there was now only cold, rough stone. I couldn't believe my eyes. I had to blink several times to make sure I was seeing right. The doorway, our dragons, our escape. They were all gone. We were trapped. Ahaax had taken us. He won. The hope I had before was a spark snuffed out.

"No."

Davit

The Dungeon

XIX

It felt like a dozen hammers were banging on temple bells within my head. My entire body was aching. I could feel that there was some sort of cloth wrapped around my head. What was it? How did it get there? I couldn't focus. My entire head was foggy. My arms were held above my head. I couldn't move them, though at the moment I didn't have the energy to even try.

I let out a shaky breath. A fresh wave of stinging pain shot through my whole body. My eyes opened quickly in shock. What a wake up. I sucked air through my teeth, grimacing through the pain. Now abruptly awake, I tried to look around the room.

There wasn't much difference from when my eyes were closed; the room was so dark, and it didn't help that my left eye was covered by the rag I'd felt earlier. There was only one small torch on the wall opposite me to light the dungeon. And the room was clearly a dungeon, there was no mistaking that. The walls were made out of black, rough rock, as if the whole room were underground. I wouldn't have been surprised if it were. The entire room smelled like damp earth. I could hear the rhythmic dripping of water into a puddle from somewhere in the distance, along with the light squeaking of rats. The only entrance or exit to the room I could find was a large, heavy-looking wooden door just opposite me.

All around the walls of the room were rusted chains. Some were hanging from the ceiling. Shackles. I looked up at my hands. Sure enough, they too were chained to the ceiling in a pair of iron manacles. I tugged at the chains, but it did no good; my hands weren't going anywhere. I looked to my right, and a new feeling of dread emerged within me. "Rose?" I shook my head, my heart sinking.

To my side, my sister was chained to the ceiling the same way I was. Her long hair, which had been tied back this morning, was now hanging loose over her head, rough and tangled. Her eyes were closed tight, and she appeared to be muttering something under her breath, but I couldn't make any of it out. "Rose," I said, again trying to get her attention, only managing slightly above a whisper.

My sister's eyes opened slowly, as if she were unsure of what she was hearing. She turned her head to face me and immediately beamed. Her bright smile had always been infectious, and even now, in this unfamiliar, hostile dungeon, I felt myself ease, if only slightly.

"Davit, you're awake! Thank the Elders!" Rose let out a half sigh, half laugh of relief. "You were knocked out for so long, we were starting to…" She paused, her face flattening. She sighed again. "It's good to have you back."

I smiled back at her through my aching. "Good to be back," I said. I looked around at our surrounding sharp, dark walls and cold chains. "Well, maybe not that great, actually," I corrected myself. "How long was I out?"

Rose shrugged despite her bound hands above her. "Well, it's not really possible to tell time down here, but judging by the number of meals we've been brought, a couple of days?"

"Days!" I exclaimed in shock. Instantly a fresh wave of pain shot through my body. I would have doubled over if I weren't being held up by chains. I let out a long, pained groan, mentally cursing myself for something so stupid when it hurt just to breathe. *Well*, I thought. *If I was unconscious for multiple days, at least this pain means I'm definitely still alive.* I figured you couldn't feel pain if you were dead, and being alive was better than being dead, so that was a positive. I guess.

Once I regained the most composure I figured I'd be able to reach in the situation, I turned back to my sister. My mind was cloudy, and I couldn't remember how any of us got into this situation. "Rose," I breathed through my teeth. "What is this place? Where are we? What the hell happened?"

It was a different voice that responded. "We were attacked," said a male's voice. One I recognized. Despite the limited movement from being chained up, I leaned as far forward as I could, looking past Rose to her right.

"I led us right into a trap," Percival said. He was bound the same way Rose and I were, except our brother had the distinction of his hands being encased in what looked like a large, ornate metal box. I found this detail odd but assumed it must have been an extra security precaution. "I failed us all." His voice was quiet and lacking its usual prestige. His gaze was locked on the ground at his feet, refusing to look anywhere else.

"Were you just standing there in silence this whole time?" I asked.

Percival was silent for a moment. "I *am* relieved you're alright, Davit," he said, continuing to look at the floor. "But I still brought you here, brought you both here. Right into Ahaax's hands." He went silent again. "We're still trapped with no way out. I'm so sorry."

My eyes were beginning to adjust to the little light within the dungeon, and I was able to get a better view of Percival now. What I saw made my heart sink. He looked exhausted, like he hadn't slept in days, and his expression was hard, like he was clenching his jaw from pain, as if he'd come from a fight. There was more than that though. There was an air around Percival. More than just being beaten physically, it looked like his very spirit had been shattered too. It wasn't something I had ever seen before—not in the seven months of him being king, and not even before that when he acted like a human. I didn't know how to respond. It was frightening. It made me angry, angry that someone could do this to my family and get away with it.

"It wasn't your fault, Percival," Rose tried to comfort him. "You couldn't have known what would happen. Our intelligence was wrong. You couldn't have prepared for that; no one could have. And you saved Davit and me. You're the reason we're both still alive." She spoke with a type of compassion that almost seemed to plead with him not to blame himself. I got the sense that this was a conversation the two had had before, during the time I was unconscious.

Percival continued looking at the ground with the same mix of defeat and buried anger. "For what good that did," he said bitterly and quietly. Then, even quieter, "*I* should have known."

I turned away from my siblings, troubled. What Percival had said before was lingering in my mind. Specifically one part. "Ahaax," I said softly to myself. I brought my attention to the torch on the wall across from me, looking deep into its dancing flame. *Fire.* My memories of what happened before I was put in this dungeon were still cloudy, but they were beginning to come into focus. Fire. The burnt, ruined heap of Bukarra.

I remembered seeing Ahaax's face. As soon as I glimpsed the warlord, I only felt a white-hot anger. *That* I did remember. Anger. No, more than that. Rage. Hatred. In front of me was the man who had murdered my father and thrown my home into war, the man who had destroyed my life. In that moment I only cared about one thing. I wanted to hurt Ahaax. I wanted to tear him apart. I remember feeling almost *happy* that I'd slipped a dagger into my boot before we left the palace, in spite of what Percival wanted. I just needed to get close enough to him.

As I hung chained from the ceiling, feeling like I was breathing through a tunnel of shattered glass, I was able to recognize that charging the skilled fighter with only a six-inch blade probably wasn't the smartest thing I'd ever done. But I got close, though. *So close*, I thought regretfully.

But I remembered that before I was able to do anything to Ahaax, I'd felt a strong burning force right in the center of my chest. In my last few seconds of consciousness as I was flying through the air, I was able to see that it was from some sort of weird beam that the man standing next to Ahaax had shot from his hand. *That's right*, I remembered. *Ahaax wasn't alone. There was a man with him.* I thought for a moment about the man I didn't recognize. *What was his problem?*

I continued to gaze at the flame coming from the torch in front of me. Slowly, as my memory came back, the anger within me rose again. I shifted my gaze back to my beaten brother. "I will make him pay for what he did to you, Percival," I promised. "For what he did to both of you."

Percival didn't raise his eyes from the ground, but Rose looked at me. "Davit," she started softly. "That didn't work out so well last time, did it?"

Ouch. I looked into my sister's eyes. Eyes so blue they were distinguishable in what little light we had. I had to think of something to say that would make her go along with a plan to escape from this dungeon and get back at Ahaax. "This time will be different," I told her confidently. Rose's face went flat, unconvinced. *Damn.*

I didn't wait for Rose to come around. Something had to be done. I tugged hard at the chains holding me to the ceiling. I looked at the ring holding my chains in place above me. It was brown with rust. I grinned, struck with an idea.

I kicked my legs back onto the wall behind me, using my strength to keep me held up in the air with the support of the chain and the wall. With great effort, and more pain, I took one step up the wall. In one quick motion, I picked my foot up and put it back down behind me. It worked. I had inched up the wall—slowly, but it worked.

"Davit?" Rose asked. She raised an eyebrow. "What is it you think you're trying to do?"

"I don't think, Rose. It only slows me down," I grunted as I continued to inch up the wall.

"That's clear," she retorted.

I decided to ignore her comment. Step by slow step I inched closer to the ring holding the shackles in place. Soon I had made my way to the point where I couldn't go up the wall any farther. My legs were starting to shake just from the work of holding myself in the air, but it was worth it. Now was time for the fun part.

"Davit, what are you doing?" Rose asked. "Please don't. You're going to hurt yourself more than you already are."

I shook my head and flashed her a grin from my elevated position. "This thing is completely rusted over. It can give out at any second." I motioned my head toward the rusty chain. "All it would take is for something sufficiently heavy to bring down on it…"

With that I kicked off from my spot on the wall. I yanked my hands downward on the chain as hard as I could as I swung through the air. There was a lot of loud clanging, but I thought I heard a *pop*. Maybe something came loose or broke?

The wooden door to the room slowly opened as I was swinging… right towards it. A man, a soldier from the look of him, given the leather armor he was wearing, walked into the room. He was looking down as he was putting a ring of keys back onto his belt, which was probably why he didn't react to my feet flying right towards his face. My boots collided with his nose with a solid and very painful-sounding *smack*. The blow sent the man stumbling back several feet, dazed. His hand went to his face, and he let out a sharp, "Ah!"

I swung back to my original starting point beside Rose. My eyes widened and my stomach dropped. I gritted my teeth and cringed as I felt the man's pain. Next to me, Rose's jaw had dropped, and I noticed even Percival had brought his eyes from the ground in a concerned expression. "Uh," I started nervously, fully aware that my hands were still shackled above my head and just noticing how big a sword the soldier had on his belt.

The man grunted in pain. He turned his gaze towards me. His eyes had fire in them. "Why, you—" he growled. He unsheathed his weapon and quickly approached me. I looked around the room rapidly for anything that could help me, a way out, a weapon, anything, but there was nothing. With my hands bound, I was in an even more vulnerable state. With nothing else to do, I started to furiously shake the chains. They had to be close to breaking. No luck. I could only watch as the enraged soldier marched toward me aggressively. With his free hand he grabbed the collar of my shirt, bringing me close enough to him that I could smell his breath, which was rancid. I gulped. This wouldn't end well.

"Still yourself, Calivar!" an elderly voice snapped from behind the man. The man, Calivar I assumed, stopped moving, although his sword was still worryingly close to my face and my shirt was still in his grip. By the expression he had on, I could see he was running the calculations over what would happen if he ignored the order he'd just been given. For my sake, I hoped he wasn't a risk taker.

In the doorway at the head of the dungeon stood the man from Bukarra, Abominus. Was his name Abominus? I couldn't be sure, since it was one of the last things I'd heard before being knocked out. He certainly didn't *look* very abominable. The old man was a few inches shorter than Rose, and he had a well-fed physique that made it look like it had been years since he had even held a weapon, let alone used one. The man's features made him resemble someone's kind grandfather rather than a traitor to his kingdom, from his balding head to his bushy gray beard. Strangest of all were his eyes, big, sparkling green orbs. They looked sincere, which was definitely something I wasn't expecting from one of Ahaax's men.

It was really strange to think how a man like this found himself in the ranks of a warlord. Almost strange enough to make me forget that he was the same man who had nearly killed me in Bukarra. Almost.

"I don't know, Abominus," Calivar said, fury seeping from his voice, still focused on me. The man sounded and looked like a talking crysnake. His inky black hair covered half his face, but the half I was able to see was pale, veiny, and cold. His eyes were a light shade of yellow, making him look more animal than human. "I don't think he'd mind if I took a finger from him. He's got nine others, after all."

"Um, I beg to differ," I objected, alarmed. "I'm quite attached to all ten of them actually." My heartbeat picked up.

"Stand down, Calivar," Abominus ordered with a power in his voice that betrayed his stature.

"You don't control me, old man," the angry soldier snapped back. "We're equals on the council, remember?"

"Indeed," Abominus confirmed. "But would you defy your king?" he asked.

Calivar was silent. He turned his sickly gaze back to me. He looked like a volcano minutes away from erupting. However, with a shove he let go of my shirt and took a few steps backward, sheathing his weapon. "Of course not," he said with a hint of bitterness.

Abominus nodded. "That's what I thought," he said. He took a few steps into the room from the doorway. "Wait for us outside, if you would," he continued to Calivar. "You won't be needed at the moment."

"Now wait a minute," Calivar began. Abominus flashed him a stern look that said *you won't win this*. Calivar paused, then breathed out through his nose. "Whatever," the angry man said. With that, he walked briskly past Abominus and slammed the door to the cell behind him as he left.

Abominus sighed, turning to face the three of us chained to the ceiling. "I apologize for him, children," the old man said genuinely. "Captain Calivar is nothing more than a brute in my eyes, but the king sees his uses, and he *is* loyal, for all his many faults."

I couldn't help but scoff. Abominus turned his gleaming eyes to me. "The only king that should have his loyalty is chained in this cell," I said. "Yours too, for that matter." I looked at Percival, who remained silent.

The short, round man frowned slightly. "Yes," Abominus started, "well, let's hope that is one of many disagreements that can be resolved today." Before I could decipher what he meant by that, Abominus continued, "How are you feeling, Prince Davit?"

This took me by surprise. How was I feeling? What did he care? I looked the man in front of me up and down, trying to see what he was getting at. "Fine," I lied slightly through the dull aching in my head, unwilling to give him any more information.

Abominus clasped his hands together, smiling. "Ah, good." He took a few steps closer and reached towards the rag over my left eye.

I flinched instinctively against the wall. "Hey now," I said defensively, reluctant to let him get any closer. Abominus stopped moving.

"It's okay, Davit." I was surprised it was Rose who said this. "At least, I think he's okay," she continued. "He's the one who healed you in Bukarra."

This surprised me even more. I looked down at the old man. "Really?" I said, eyes wide. "You're the one who patched me up? Why?"

Abominus shrugged. "It's the kind thing to do." I couldn't detect any hint of dishonesty in his voice.

My jaw dropped. I couldn't help it. "You're joking."

Abominus smiled softly and once again reached for the bandage over my eye. Hesitantly, I let the stout man remove it. As he untied the bandage behind my head, he sighed softly and said, "Not everyone here hates you and your siblings like Calivar, Prince Davit. Some of us see your situation for what it is."

I narrowed my good eye at him. "And what's that?" I said low.

Abominus sighed again. "You are three children who hadn't even come of age before you were orphaned for a war you didn't start over a crown you would never wear." The old man's wrinkled green eyes bore uncomfortably deep into mine. "Am I close to the mark?"

I was speechless. I didn't even know what I *could* say in response. Of all the things I was expecting to see as a prisoner of Ahaax since I had woken up, *sympathy* from my enemy wasn't one of them. Something in the thought caught me. *My enemy.* It was almost funny. Eight months ago, my enemies were spoiled children of nobles I didn't get along with. Now I was hanging in a dungeon facing almost certain doom. How quickly things could change.

I could feel Abominus pull the bandage away from my head. My view didn't change all that much due to the low light in the room, but it was still nice to have both of my eyes back.

"Ahh," Abominus said, looking at where the bandage had been. "You'll have a noticeable scar, I'm afraid, but otherwise you've completely healed over." There was a curiosity in his voice, as if he were looking at an experiment that fascinated him.

"Yeah," I said curtly. "We heal fast." It was true. My siblings and I had always recovered from injuries much faster than any other kids our age. I had never thought much of it. It was far from the strangest thing in my life.

"Indeed," Abominus said softly with that same hint of fascination. The portly man looked me over and then turned away and walked back to the center of the room. He turned again to address us. "The king has requested an audience with the three of you."

A hole formed inside me. Ahaax wanted to see us, and we were his prisoners. The reality of the situation was finally starting to settle in with me for the first time since I awoke. We were in real danger, and as far as I could see, there wasn't anything we could do.

"What is it Ahaax wants?" Rose asked Abominus in the middle of Percival and me. There was a clear answer to her question in my mind: *us dead*, but I tried my best to push it back.

Abominus clasped his hands again. "That's really more for the king to say than me, Princess. Calivar and I were just sent to retrieve you." He shook his head reassuringly. "But I am cautiously hopeful. Should everything go well, I believe this war might be over today."

"When has anything gone well these past seven months?" I said under my breath. My eyes widened as I realized one surefire way to end the war would be to kill the three of us. Panic swelled within me, but I tried my best to control it. I was praying I was wrong. Abominus didn't seem like the type to be hopeful about the deaths of three children, but he also didn't seem like the type to be able to launch me halfway across a village, so what really did I know?

Abominus made a small movement with his hands in front of him. Three clouds of magenta-colored mist materialized around each of the chains holding me and my siblings to the ceiling. With a sweeping motion of Abominus' foot across the floor, each of the chains snapped where the clouds had covered. With the chains broken, we now had a greater degree of freedom to walk around, although Rose's and my hands were still in shackles and Percival still had to deal with that strange box.

I looked back at the limp, hanging half-chain that had been holding me. At first I wondered how close *I* had been to breaking the chain if Abominus was able to do it so easily. Then a more important thought quickly pushed that one aside. *Wait, was that magic?* I wondered. So that was what Abominus did to me! He hit me with magic! *Woah*, I thought, taken aback. *I was attacked by magic. And I survived!* Despite my dire situation, it was still a cool thought. Who was the last person in the kingdom to be attacked by magic?

Now able to walk freely, Rose, Percival, and I huddled closely. We would have hugged if any of us had greater use of our arms. "Are you two alright?" Percival asked in a hushed tone, concerned.

Rose nodded. "Yes. A little sore, but nothing I can't get over."

Percival looked at me. I would be lying if I said I was only *a little* sore, with my entire body still aching, but I nodded. "Yeah, same here. For the most part." Percival sighed, relieved. I could see him grimace slightly in pain. He still looked like the most worn out of all of us. "What about you?" I asked.

Percival was silent for a moment. "I'll live," he said, although I could see he was dealing with more than just physical pain.

"What should we do?" Rose asked. She looked up. Across the room Abominus was standing next to the wooden door, looking at us innocently, his hands folded.

Percival thought it over. "We have little choice," he concluded. "We follow him. See what Ahaax wants." We all recognized how desperate the current plan was. "Just," Percival began again, "you two stay close to me at all times." We nodded, both recognizing that as our safest bet.

Abominus cleared his throat politely. The three of us looked at him, ready as we would ever be. The old man made a swooping motion with one of his arms. Another small magenta cloud appeared around the wooden door's iron handle. With ease, the heavy door swung open, revealing a brown hallway lit with torches that seemed to go on forever. "Now," Abominus said with a kind smile, "if you three would please follow me."

In the Heart of the Beast

XX

The hallway outside had a less intimidating atmosphere than the room we'd just emerged from, but considering we had just come from a *literal* dungeon, that wasn't saying much. The rock walls were dirt brown instead of soulless black, and there was a torch along the wall every ten feet or so, making the cramped space relatively well lit. Compared to our cell, it was almost homey.

The man who'd nearly skewered me minutes before, Captain Calivar, was waiting outside for us as we walked out, his arms crossed. "Took you long enough," he grunted at Abominus. Pale, veiny skin seemed to stretch tight across the soldier's face as he spoke. Everything about him unnerved me. If Abominus seemed like a kind man in the wrong place, Calivar seemed to fit in perfectly.

"Hush, Calivar," Abominus told the guard. He ushered my siblings and me into the hallway. I had to squint for a moment to adjust to the light. Abominus continued to Calivar, "Lock the door behind us, would you?"

The old man didn't wait for a response. Ushering us down the hall, Abominus took the lead of our small group. Percival, Rose, and I huddled together in the middle, with Calivar grumbling a good distance behind us in the rear.

The silence in the stone hall was deafening. The only sound was our footsteps echoing off the walls. The tension was so thick in the air it almost felt like a physical barrier preventing me from moving forward. With each step, the fear inside me grew. I knew there was only one place this path ended.

Percival was the first to break the silence. "You're a Magus, aren't you?" he asked Abominus in front of us, sounding like he had been sitting on the question for a while.

Abominus, in turn, smiled softly and looked back at my brother as we kept walking. "Indeed, Prince Percival. You study well."

"As do you," Percival returned the compliment, seemingly not noticing the slight to his title. He was speaking in the kingly way our father's diplomats had trained him in for years. "Magic has been outlawed in the kingdom for one thousand years. How is it that you've become so skilled in an illegal art?"

The old man chuckled. "Kings are not immune from arrogance," he continued. "Indeed, it is the height of arrogance for one man to think he can outlaw what is beyond his control." Abominus shook his head. "No, Prince. One cannot outlaw magic any more than one can outlaw fire. It is nature. Man cannot hope to dominate it; we can only hope that we can use it. Some more successfully than others."

I looked at Percival. I could recognize the look on his face. He was thinking hard, absorbing this information. "I see," he said after a moment. "Then, naturally, there must be more Magi than the kingdom is aware of. That's how you were taught, isn't it?"

For the first time, Abominus tensed noticeably. He walked in silence for a few moments more, seemingly reluctant to answer. "There was," Abominus said. Another silence, then, "Not anymore."

Rose was the one to break the tense silence this time. "What happened?" she asked.

"The arrogance of Man, Princess," Abominus repeated, his voice tinged with sadness. "It's true, Prince Percival. For centuries after Dalmar the Depraved, the Magi survived in secret. There were attacks on us in the early years of the Restrictions, ranging in their destruction, but as the decades passed, the kingdom eventually moved on to other things, and we remained alive. For ages, we survived in the shadows, never letting our groups grow too large lest we be discovered. This is how we survived, and this is how I was trained."

Abominus continued, "It is Magi tradition to seek out their own disciples, typically at a very young age. When I was six years old, my coven descended from the mountains around my village and took me into their teaching for the rest of my life."

"They took you from your family?" Rose asked. "That's horrible!"

"Not so, Princess," Abominus said, not unkindly. "My village was very poor, and my family was very hungry. When the coven came and offered to take away one of the mouths they had to feed, my family could hardly refuse. In fact, they believed that they were sending me away to a better life."

"Were they right?" Percival inquired.

Abominus made a pained smile. "I suppose so," he said. "I never saw them again, but instead the coven gave me a full belly and something no one from my small village had had for many years: a future."

As our group was walking, I wasn't paying much attention to Abominus' story. I wasn't really interested in understanding his past, and instead I began to realize that our surroundings were shifting ever so slightly. The hall we had been walking through had become wider, and if it wasn't my mind playing tricks on me, I could feel a slight airflow coming from somewhere far off. The walls were still brown rock and the only light still came from torches, but it was clear that wherever we were was a very large and vast complex.

Our group passed a hall to our right that was pitch black without any torches lighting a path. Something made me stop moving. It was a strange sensation; a tingling on the right side of my head, as if something had just brushed past it, but nothing was there. There was something down that hallway, I knew. Something important. I strained to see down the hall as far as I could. There was a rusted iron cage at the far end. I couldn't see any farther through the shadows, until, suddenly, a pale, skinny clawed hand shot from between the bars. I jumped backwards instinctually.

Suddenly, I was shoved forward, hard. "Keep moving," Calivar snarled behind me. I glared back at the guard but ultimately did what he said. With one last look down the hall, I put the strange experience behind me. After all, I had bigger concerns where I was going.

As I caught up to my siblings, Abominus was still talking. "For years before, our contact with other covens throughout Lungalea had been dwindling. As the years progressed, one by one, they were snuffed out on orders from the king himself. By the time I was twenty, we were the only ones left."

I perked up for the first time listening to his story. "Hold on," I interjected hotly. "You expect us to believe that our father would hunt down and kill his own people, and then cover it all up? What kind of… he would never!"

Abominus chuckled in his soft way once again. "Ah, but your father wasn't always king, was he, boy? *His* father came before him. It was Oriond the Old who destroyed the Magi." He paused, like just saying the name held power. "You never met your grandsire, isn't that right, Prince Davit?"

"I…" I opened my mouth, trying to defend my family from this man. The words caught in my throat. I was never told much about my grandfather, but what he was saying couldn't be true.

Mercifully, Percival answered for me. "No. He disappeared two years before I was born."

"Ah, well, I never met him either, but I *knew* Oriond the Old," Abominus replied. "He was a man who loved power above all else. He knew the Magi posed the largest threat to the power of a king, and so he put a price on the head of all Magi, every last one. Coven by coven we were exterminated by mercenaries, thieves… criminals." There was pain in the old man's voice. He continued, "Eventually, the number of Magi in the entire kingdom dwindled down to single digits. It was then that we were betrayed."

"Betrayed?" Rose asked, intrigued. "By one of your own?"

Abominus nodded. "Someone I had considered my brother sold out his family for a couple pieces of silver." There was a great amount of pain in the old man's voice. Even I, who couldn't care less about the Magus in front of us, could tell how hard it was for him to relive this experience.

"You truly are the last Magus, then," Percival confirmed. His brow furrowed as we continued walking. "What ever happened to this traitor? Did he survive?"

The old man was quiet for a moment. "Ahaax killed him," he answered finally. With that explanation, the story of how this kind old man had been recruited into the service of a warlord was made much clearer.

Finally, our group came to a halt in front of a set of rusted iron doors. Thin bands of red metal wove around the frame, creating intricate pictures. Unlike the decorations back at the royal palace, these images conveyed scenes of violence and suffering. Centrally located on the door was the largest metalwork of all, depicting thousands of miniature people surrounded by a sickly red cloud. Above them, a red-crowned figure watched on in joy. With a sick feeling, I realized the scene was depicting a mass sacrifice. "What is that?" I asked, disturbed.

Abominus looked at the door, a grim expression on his face. He didn't answer, instead breathing in deeply. "You three can head inside." He motioned towards the door. Neither I nor my siblings moved. Why would the hen willingly go to the slaughterhouse? With another motion by Abominus (and an angry grunt behind him from Calivar) we realized we didn't have an option. Together, the three of us pushed open the cold metal door and stepped into the new room.

It might have just been my imagination, but the room felt about ten degrees colder than the outside hall. The first thing I looked for in my new environment was water of any kind. Unfortunately for me, there was a severe lack of puddles, and so I quickly realized that any fight I would get into would have to be fought with my hands. *My chained hands.* Not off to a great start. The pit in my stomach grew larger.

Our new setting was a small, cramped room with walls of the same brown rock as everywhere else in these catacombs. The room was lightly furnished, with only a desk in the far corner, an old bookshelf to the left of us by the door, and in the center a giant wooden slab of a table carved in a rectangle. Despite its size, the room was well-lit with torches, and as I looked around more, I began to understand why.

There were maps of parts of the kingdom laid out all over the room. There was one on a writing desk in the corner, multiple pinned to the walls, and hanging on the far wall opposite the three of us was the largest of them all. This was a map of the whole kingdom, except it was different from the ones I was used to back home. This map had a significant portion shaded in, from everything east of the Black Mountains and stretching far into the Golden Desert, as well as significant distances north and south. With a sinking feeling I realized that everything shaded was the territory Ahaax had conquered. It was frightening to see just how much he had taken in so little time.

As my eyes drifted from the large map, my body went numb from a mix of fear and anger. There, standing at the other end of the room with his back to us, was the warlord himself: Ahaax.

There was a presence around him. He knew we were there without needing to turn around, his gaze seemingly locked on the map before him. Every feeling I had in Bukarra came rushing back to me all at once. My entire body tensed.

The heavy door closed behind us with a loud *thud*. With that, Ahaax turned. He was out of the armor he had worn in the ruins. Now he was clad in the traditional clothes of royalty, green robes wrapped around his body, and he wore an undershirt dyed deep red. However, his cold, dark eyes were unchanged from what I remembered, and as he looked at us, he had the nerve to *smile*.

"Children," he said with his arms outstretched towards the three chairs on our side of the kingdom table. "Please, sit."

Instantly I was enraged. *Children? I'll show him a child when I tear his...* Without realizing, I had taken a step forward.

Percival stopped me going any farther by putting his arms out in front of me subtly. "Let me handle this," he whispered. Still angry, I realized he was right. I took my eyes off Ahaax and looked at my brother, nodding.

Percival nodded back, and the three of us walked farther into the room. The young king spoke for us all when he asked, "Why have you brought us here? You could have killed the three of us easily in Bukarra."

Ahaax sat in the chair on the opposite side of the table. "I do not wish to kill any of you, Percival," he said. "It would complicate my claim to the throne greatly. Now, sit." He said the last part as a command, no longer a request.

As the three of us reluctantly did as he said, it was Rose who spoke next. "You have no claim to the throne," she said curtly. "Our father was king and his claim passed to his heir, Percival. As the second son of Oriond, you—"

Ahaax raised a hand, cutting her off mid-sentence. "Do not lecture me on what is commonly known, Princess," he said with a controlled, subtle anger. He looked at my sister as if his vision were boring holes into her. My anger rose as well.

Ahaax continued. "The crown law of this kingdom goes back three thousand years. It has served many people well, but its usefulness has become worn and irrelevant. I seek to do away with the old laws and traditions, to completely reforge this land."

Ahaax's tone infuriated me. I hated how he had the nerve to act like he was so enlightened. "By killing your own brother?" I cut *him* off this time. My teeth were clenched together so hard I thought they might break.

Ahaax turned his gaze to me. He was wearing a look of barely hidden contempt. Whatever training Percival had gone through to control his emotions, it looked like Ahaax had been through as well. Throughout the entire conversation, his face held the same flat expression, the only hints of emotion he gave off coming from his voice. That made me even angrier, how controlled he was. My hands were clenched fists under the table getting whiter by the second. The warlord looked right through me with his black eyes. "If that is what it requires," he said without a hint of compassion.

The man on the opposite side of the table looked patiently at each of us. "What do you three know of the Eastern Uprising?"

We were all silent for a moment. Eventually, Percival spoke up, humoring our captor. "It was a revolt by a disgruntled farmer twenty-five years ago. Our father led the armies of the kingdom... along with you," Percival noted. "You were believed to have died in that conflict."

Ahaax nodded, as much to himself as to us. "Funny thing, death," he said lightly. He looked at Percival. "Why did the uprising begin?"

Surprisingly, not even Percival seemed to have an answer. His expression shifted to slight surprise at his confusion. When there was no answer, Ahaax replied for us. "Food." He glanced at us again. "For centuries the royal tradition had seen the majority of crop harvests funneled to allies of the throne, whether they needed it or not. Twenty-five years ago, there was a particularly bad winter, and the people of the eastern provinces had had enough."

Rose had furrowed her brow. "So, you expect us believe that you are on a righteous crusade to feed the hungry?" Her voice was laced with bile.

Ahaax turned to my sister. "During my time in the east, I began to realize that those who we were fighting were right. The kingdom is broken, children. Any institution that has been around for thousands of years will start to crumble and crack; it is inevitable. By the time of the uprising, the rot had finally reached surface level."

Percival shook his head. "Even so, your problems were with King Oriond, not with our father. He was *helping* people!"

Ahaax glared at the young king. He shook his head. "My problem is with the entire disease that has become the Crown of Maggelle." He paused. "Arturus was just the latest symptom."

I slammed my closed fists on the table, unable to control myself. "Bastard!" I shouted. Somehow, I managed to keep myself in my chair.

Ahaax didn't even pay me any attention, instead keeping his eyes on Percival in front of him. With the same maddeningly calm tone, he continued. "As far as most of the realm is concerned, there are currently two kings, both claiming to be legitimate. *That* is what is tearing this realm apart. *That* is what is causing this war. You and I have both seen it, Percival: there can be only one."

Rose shook her head lightly, putting together what Ahaax was saying faster than I was. "You need Percival to stop claiming to be king, but you can't kill him; otherwise everyone who supports him would never swear their loyalty to you." She paused, her face going pale. "That means…"

"Abdication," Percival answered for her. His voice was low. It was by hearing his tone that I realized Percival knew where this conversation was going before he even sat down. He continued, "If I renounce my claim to the throne, then there will be only one king, and this war will be over."

Ahaax leaned back slightly in his chair, completely in control. He nodded. "Renounce the throne, and all the death, the carnage and violence, it can end today." He looked deep into Percival's eyes, giving no hint that would betray what he was saying. He went on, "Of course, you couldn't stay here. If you did, your supporters would always have a claim to the throne. It would have to be exile, but as king I will let you choose where you want to begin your new life. Somewhere in the Thousand Isles, perhaps? Or if you wish, we could send you to the Old Lands Across the Sea. I promise you would never want for a thing." He was speaking of sending my brother to faraway lands like they were ten miles away, not thousands. I couldn't believe what I was hearing.

Ahaax leaned forward, never breaking eye contact with Percival. "But your siblings could stay. They could even remain in the royal palace if they so wished. Think of it, Percival. All of this could end so easily."

I scoffed. This entire conversation was ludicrous. Ahaax would never get what he wanted, and he *definitely* would never have us give it to him. But as I turned to Percival, my stomach dropped. I could tell by my brother's face. He was considering the offer. He was going to let his stupid concern for his people cause Ahaax to win!

Percival opened his mouth to respond. Rose stood angrily, putting her hands on the desk. "We will *never* go along with anything you would have us do!" she said to Ahaax defiantly. Percival snapped his gaze to Rose, wearing a mix of surprise and fear.

I stood as well, glad to finally be able to indulge in the anger I had been keeping bottled up since we entered the room. "You will have to kill us if you try to send away our brother, murderer!" I spat at the man.

Percival looked at me now. "No!" he cried. "Don't do this for me! You two can be safe!"

Rose and I both completely ignored our older brother. Honestly, I didn't care what he wanted. I kept my eyes fixed on Ahaax, trying my best to drill a hole through his head. Percival's will did not matter. I would rather die than have the same man who killed my father take my brother as well. By the look on her face, I could tell Rose shared the exact same thought.

Ahaax sighed, looking at my sister and me. "That's a shame," he said, not sounding all that sincere. "This cannot work if you do not accept me as king." He sighed again, sort of like an *oh well.* "And to think, you children fight this hard when your own allies are working against you."

Great, I thought, *he's playing mind games now.* I narrowed my eyes, but Rose couldn't help herself. "What do you mean?" she huffed angrily.

Ahaax cocked an eyebrow. He laughed. "Why, Roserené, one of your closest allies already works for me." He leaned back in his chair again.

I automatically assumed everything that came out of Ahaax's mouth was a lie, so I didn't put much stock into his claim. But Rose shook her head, confused. "You lie."

The warlord clasped his hands. "You should be thankful for them," he began. "It was their insistence that saved your lives. They would only provide me information on the condition that I left you alive." He shrugged. "I will have to hope they see the reason of my broader plan."

"Go to hell," I spat at Ahaax. This time I literally spat at him from across the table, and it landed on his face. The warlord wiped his head with barely a second glance. He looked at me. Instantly I felt frozen where I was. Something about his unnatural gaze. "Pity," he tsked. "If only you fought for your father this hard."

That was my breaking point. I lunged across the table, my chained hands outstretched for Ahaax's throat. In a blur of motion, I felt his own hand wrap around my windpipe. For a fraction of a second, I couldn't breathe, but it was soon resolved. Unfortunately, that was because Ahaax threw me into the wooden writing desk that was pushed into the corner of the room. The blow of the impact sent waves of pain through my sore body. My head hit the ground hard... and suddenly I was seeing through a different set of eyes.

I was standing in the snowy mountains. Something about my eye level made me feel closer to the ground. I looked to my left. To my side were both of my siblings' dragons. The yellow and brown forms of Apolion and Redwood were unmistakable. Seeing the two dragons, the realization instantly dawned. I was seeing *through Cerulia's eyes*.

Barely realizing, I knew this was possibly my last chance at survival. "Find us," I called out to my dragon. And with that, my vision returned to the dark cellar in Ahaax's keep. My two siblings were huddled around me on the floor, observing me nervously.

Ahaax was glaring at me, standing behind his desk. "'Find us,'" he quoted. He looked down at me ferociously. "What does that mean?" he demanded.

Playing dumb, I rubbed the back of my head, sounding dazed. "What?"

The metal door to the room opened once again. Abominus, with a worried expression, rushed in, along with two guards standing behind him.

"My lord, is everything alright?" the Magus asked Ahaax. He looked down at the three of us on the ground. His expression was concerned, but his eyes quickly went back to his liege.

Ahaax was breathing heavily, calming himself from his burst of anger. "Yes," he said gradually. He never took his gaze off my siblings and me on the floor. "Unfortunately, the children refuse to have peace. Abominus, begin preparations for our second plan."

Rose

The Arena

XXI

The guards walked the three of us through the rock tunnels to an open doorway that led into a small room completely devoid of light. Percival, Davit, and I stood outside for a moment in a line, reluctant to go in. One of the guards shoved the butt of his spear into Percival's back harder than he needed to. "Move," he grunted.

The three of us looked back, but there was no choice here. We slowly shuffled into the dark room. The door we had come through was closed and locked with a heavy *clang*, and we were alone in pitch blackness. It was impossible to ignore the sound around us. What had begun as a slight buzzing had grown louder and louder as we walked until it was clear that just outside of the room were hundreds of cheering people. We were about to be put on display.

"Why did you two do that?" It was Percival. His voice was quiet. There was so little light that I couldn't see my brother standing right next to me. He continued, "You could have gotten out of here. You could have…"

"Oh *shut up*, Percival," Davit said. I didn't need to see him to tell he was rolling his eyes. The annoyed tone stopped Percival in his tracks. "We were never going to leave you."

I could feel Percival's eyes turn towards me, looking for confirmation. It was true. Davit and I always thought the same way. Either all three of us would leave Ahaax's imprisonment, or none of us would. I wanted to hold my older brother's hand, but the metal box still sealed around his fists prevented any movement, so instead I rested my head on his shoulder. He was shaking.

"I wish you did," Percival said with barely a whisper.

With a loud, repeated clunking, the wall in front of us began to lower. Beams of bright light squeezed through the widening gap of the drawbridge, causing the three of us to shield our eyes to avoid being blinded. The cheering masses opposite us were now deafening. When our eyes adjusted to the new light, we were finally able to see why.

The small stone room the guards had placed us in was only an entryway. A large door opposite us was now completely lowered over a moat filled with running water, and on the other side was a massive arena. Seeing no other option, the three of us walked over the bridge into the open.

The arena truly was *ginormous*. It had to be at least twice the size of the royal palace courtyard. The ceiling was open to the glimmering starlight of the night above us. A circular bed of sand filled the interior, with scattered standing torches placed about randomly. Red mudbrick walls twelve feet high lined the exterior. *Impossible to climb*, I thought. Behind the walls were stands of benches layered one after another until they reached high into the sky. What I saw then turned my stomach to knots: the stands were packed with thousands of screaming people.

"Elders eternal," I said, somehow more frightened than I had been just moments before. "He has an army."

Percival turned around in a slow circle. He looked sick. "All these people…" the young king said softly.

Davit had his attention focused on the rim of the arena. There was a concentrated look on his face, and then a slight grin as an idea hit him. "Guys," he said to Percival and me. He turned his head in the direction of the moat surrounding us. It wasn't anything spectacular: just a ten-foot-wide strip of lightly flowing water.

I paused, understanding. "*Water.*"

Davit nodded. "Ahaax only saw Percival's powers that day. He never saw mine or Rose's." He chuckled, raising his shackled hands to eye level. "He probably doesn't even know! The idiot."

From the other end of the arena came a familiar, booming voice, ending our conversation. "Before you, citizens of the enlightened kingdom: a gift!" The three of us turned to find the voice.

In a large, raised dais on the arena wall were three men: Calivar was standing towards the front, addressing the crowd, Abominus was seated behind him, looking uneasy, and finally Ahaax seated next to him, his face completely expressionless.

Calivar continued. As he spoke, he would turn to various parts of the crowd, like throwing meat to wild animals. He was enjoying the showmanship. "Your glorious king, Ahaax the Strong, gives to you the last traitors of Lungalea! And with their deaths an end to this war!" By the end of his last sentence, Calivar was spitting every word. The crowd loved it, rising in thunderous cheers.

Davit raised a disbelieving eyebrow. "Are you serious?" he asked. He turned his gaze back to the three men in the dais and shouted, "You're the traitors!" He turned in a circle to address the entire stands. "All of you!" The anger of my thirteen-year-old brother only did more to rile the crowd up. Some jeered at him; others laughed louder.

Calivar chuckled, satisfied, as he looked down at us. "Mighty Ahaax won the Emerald Throne by right of single combat, going back one thousand years!" He turned his attention back to the crowd of people in the stands above us. "Only by refusing to honor tradition does the boy ruler in front of you all prolong this war." The crowd booed in unison.

A fire burned in my belly, momentarily replacing my fear. None of this was true! How dare Ahaax murder our father in cold blood and then claim it gave him legitimacy.

Percival walked past Davit and me, taking the lead. "Liar!" he shouted at the three men. His voice was filled with rage, any fear he'd had before gone. It was a side of him I rarely ever heard.

Percival opened his mouth again, but he was cut off by Ahaax standing abruptly. On the other side of the arena was another loud clunking. Another drawbridge, similar to the one from which we had entered, was lowering over the moat. It exposed a black chasm behind it. Then, a pair of glowing red orbs appeared from the darkness, then another.

"I, Ahaax, son of Oriond and the rightful Lord of Lungalea, condemn you to death for your crimes against the crown of Maggelle," the warlord said in a booming voice of his own, yet still eerily flat. Ahaax paused, as if contemplating, as he looked down at the three of us. "May the gods welcome you swift."

As soon as he finished speaking, the two pairs of orbs from the shadows behind the drawbridge leapt forth into the light. The two creatures looked like large, hairless cats with incredibly long bodies. They had three long claws on each of their four large paws. The frightening monsters were hunched low to the ground as they prowled slowly towards us, their knife-like teeth gnashing. I noticed with a slight sense of something almost like humor that they had the strong hind legs and, more noticeably, large pointed ears of a bluffit. However, as they approached threateningly, growling and gnashing, any cute thought was pushed from my mind. Their eyes shone like red beams piercing through flesh, pointed directly at the three of us standing defenseless.

The crowd of ravenous fans went wild at the sight of the creatures. Calivar addressed them once again. "These hookclaws were captured from the badlands outside our walls. Not much food out there, is there, men? Do you think they're hungry?" The crowd screamed in approval.

The hookclaws were circling us now. The three of us had our backs pressed to each other, eyes darting at the slightest movement. My hands were sweaty in the cramped box they had been closed in. I couldn't open my balled fists. Even if I could, what could I possibly do to get us out of this?

Percival was glaring at the dais from our lower position. "Look at us, Ahaax!" he shouted, manipulating the air to make his voice carry over the deafening noise of the crowd. His tone was packed with indignant frustration. If we were about to die, it wouldn't be quiet. "Is this your reforged paradise?" he spat. Ahaax looked down at us silently. He had retaken his seat on the throne besides Abominus.

The hookclaw on the side closer to me and Davit growled and snapped impatiently. I flinched instinctively, not allowing myself any more movement. I knew if I gave away even a slight hint of the fear I felt, it would be over.

"Yeah, that's enough," Davit squeaked in a mix of fear and his usual snark. In one fluid movement, he brought his chained hands up to his chest. A spout of water ten feet high rose from the moat near us. With another flick of his hands, Davit sent a concentrated spout of the water crashing into the approaching hookclaw. The blast was so strong it sent the hairless creature sprawling a dozen feet away from us, clearly dazed.

The entire arena went silent immediately. Even the other hookclaw opposite us stopped its pacing. There were some shocked gasps. I turned my attention briefly towards the dais. Calivar looked infuriated. Abominus looked surprised. But Ahaax was standing straight as an arrow. Even from my position below, I could see how wide the warlord's eyes were. He was wearing an expression I had never seen on him before: shock. But it was gone in an instant. Quickly looking around in a way that would never be noticed if you weren't already looking at him, Ahaax wiped his face clean with his familiar static expression. Slowly, uneasily, he sat back down in his seat.

The crowd in the stands came back alive with noise. Quietly at first, but it soon picked up to their original volume. They were laughing. I turned to see what got their attention, and my stomach dropped.

Roughly ten feet away from us, the hookclaw that Davit had just blasted with a fountain of water was shakily getting back on its feet. It shook its body all over, getting the excess water off. It stumbled a little, but other than that it looked completely unharmed. The creature turned its red-eyed gaze back to us, looking angrier than ever. The two hookclaws resumed their advance, getting closer and closer.

Davit's shoulders dropped. "Well," he began, "that's about all I've got." The hookclaw in front of him growled louder than before. It hunched lower to the ground, preparing to leap. Every muscle in my body tensed. Davit was ten feet away from me; I could never get to him in time.

"Davit!" Percival called out beside me, his voice filled with panic.

My twin brother turned back to us. Time seemed to slow down. I couldn't hear anything besides the blood pumping in my ears. I could only tell Davit said something by watching his lips, but I couldn't tell what. The hookclaw lunged. I forced myself to close my eyes; I couldn't watch.

I kept my eyes clamped shut, awaiting the inevitable. Then five seconds passed, and I was still alive. Then ten seconds. *Surely they would have gotten us by now?* I thought. Hesitantly, I opened my eyes, afraid of what I was about to see. I could never have expected what would be in front of me.

Standing over the motionless body of the hookclaw that was seconds away from killing him was my brother Davit. And he was holding a sword the color of ice.

Davit's eyes were massive orbs. He stared at the sword he was clutching in his hands, slack-jawed. Then, for some reason, he began to *laugh*. Crazily. My brother doubled over laughing, still holding the sword he had somehow managed to obtain. Then he stood and turned to face the stands of shocked onlookers. "Yeah! That's right! I have a sword now! Is that all you've got! Huh?!"

As I watched Davit brag in front of thousands of speechless spectators, flaunting an impossible weapon, I could only come to one conclusion. *I'm dead*, I thought. *The hookclaws got us, and I'm actually dead. This is just some sort of... after death?*

Then Percival broke the silence. "Davit," he said softly, taking a step towards our brother. "How... How did you do that?" *Percival is seeing it too? Is it possible that we aren't dead?*

Davit looked away from the crowd and back to the two of us, a mad smile still on his face. "I don't actually know," he said, leaning in close. Percival and I both furrowed our brows. *What?*

The shock and excitement of what had just happened was beginning to wear off of those around us. The still-living hookclaw looked at its slain companion on the ground a dozen feet away and shifted its gaze to Davit, enraged.

"Uh oh," my brother said as the furious animal launched itself off its powerful legs. With a speed I didn't think was possible, Davit brought his new sword up and swiftly back down across the underside of the airborne animal, drawing red. The hookclaw fell to the ground. It didn't get back up.

The thousands of onlookers who had gathered to watch our deaths stared on in silence. The atmosphere in the arena was so quiet I could hear the sound of Davit's heavy breathing from a dozen feet away. It was as if everyone silently agreed not to move a muscle.

Above us, Calivar was gripping the railing of the dais. His face was as red as blood. Abominus was wearing an inquisitive expression, like a young animal.

Ahaax's face was as still as rock. He was standing again, but this time he didn't seem to care if anyone saw him. His eyes drilled down from his raised platform into the three of us. Gods, his eyes. Even at our distance, they were like two pools of black ink piercing through my heart. His gaze turned my blood to ice and rooted my feet to the ground. Just based on his expression, I would have no way of knowing what he was thinking. But something inside me knew. Something was *wrong*. Ahaax was *enraged*.

Calivar sputtered a few coughing-like sounds as he struggled to compose himself. "Wh- what are you waiting for?" he shouted at the crowd around us, shocking them out of their stupor. The furious captain pointed a crooked finger at us in the sand below. "Get them!"

The stands of people muttered among themselves. Then, a second later, a thunderous roar swept the entire arena. Across from us, a heavy, *very angry* man hopped over the rail surrounding the arena, over the moat of water, and onto the same sand we were on. He raised a fat fist. "For King Ahaax!" he shouted. Then another man jumped onto the sand beside him, and then another. Within seconds there were dozens of people in the arena, and they were all coming towards us.

Percival, Davit, and I rushed back to where we had entered the arena, but now the drawbridge was retracted. Our only exit was behind ten feet of water and however many feet of wood the heavy door created. Percival cursed, looking at his trapped hands futilely. We had come to the same conclusion. Something about the construction of these boxes prevented us from using our powers. We were effectively trapped.

Davit stepped in front of us, brandishing his weapon. In front of the rapidly approaching crowd of aggressors, the sword looked more like a toothpick. "I'm not gonna be able to do much with this for very long," my twin brother said, not letting himself turn his back on the crowd to face us. "Rose, do you think you could swallow these guys in sand or something?"

I shook my head quickly. It had crossed my mind as soon as we'd entered the arena, but there was a problem. "No, I can't manipulate sand. The grains are too big." The angry crowd couldn't have been more than fifty feet from us. We were quickly running out of options to survive this.

Davit's shoulders slumped. He turned, an expression of pure disbelief on his face. "What do you *mean* the grains are *too big*?!"

"Davit, get this box off of my hands," Percival said. His entire body was shaking.

"What? How?" Davit's voice was getting more frantic as the mob approached.

Our older brother looked incredibly frustrated. "*Use* your *sword* and *break* the *box*."

"Oh, okay, yeah." Davit took a deep breath and brought his weapon down hard on Percival's enclosed hands. The rusting metal of the box clanged, but it was still intact.

Percival nodded, tense. "Good, one more time."

The mob was right on top of us now. "Guys?" I alerted my brothers, frightened.

The closest brute to Percival was swinging his arm back, holding a piece of broken wood like a club. Davit brought his sword down on the box hard.

With an explosion of sparks and blue light, the restrictive metal box confining Percival's hands was blasted off on a bolt of pure blue lightning. The bolt went straight through the man who only a moment before had been poised to attack us. His body was gone in an instant; I couldn't even see what happened to it, everything was so bright. Percival was wrangling his own two arms with all of his might. He aimed the beam at the angry mob around us, blasting them back before they could even get close.

My senses were overstimulated. All I could see were flashes of blue light, all I could hear was buzzing, and all I could smell was burning hair. After what must have only been a few seconds, when all the threats to us in the arena were dealt with or had fled, Percival aimed his beam with great effort at the drawbridge. In an explosion of splinters and bits of metal, the door was destroyed (along with the surrounding wall) and there was a clear pathway out of the arena just on the other side of the moat of water. The beam of energy shooting from Percival's hands died down with a *spttz*, and he nearly doubled over, panting.

Davit put his hands on the top of his head, his mouth gaping from what he'd just witnessed. "Holy s…"

"Shut up," Percival breathed. He seemed exhausted. Far too tired to care about formality. "We need to get out of here."

I ran to my older brother. "Are you alright?" I asked, worried. I looked around the arena. We were surrounded by smoking piles of ash and clothes. The stands of onlookers were a chaos of fleeing masses. I looked up at the dais where the three men who'd captured us had been previously, and my heart sank like a stone. It was empty. They were all gone. *Ahaax* was gone.

Percival nodded, his breath steadying. He stood. "Davit, see if you can break these chains binding our wrists with that sword. Once Rose and I are free, we'll break yours too. Quick now. We don't have much time."

Davit nodded. "On it." With one swift motion and an elegant grace unlike my brother, Davit slashed the chain between Percival's wrists clean through. The new sword didn't even chip. Then Davit set about freeing my hands from their restraints in the same way, although this time he only needed to break the chains. It felt good to move my hands again; they were incredibly stiff.

"Okay, now get me out of these," Davit said to me. He handed me his sword, and immediately I almost dropped it to the ground. It was incredibly off balance. It felt like the tip was weighed with a heavy stone. The grip felt off in my hands. Just holding the sword felt almost unbearably strange in a way I couldn't describe. With great effort, I managed to raise the sword above my head and use its own weight to bring it down, cleanly severing Davit's chains.

"How do you use that thing?" I asked Davit, nearly panting from the exertion. It amazed me he was able to dispatch two hookclaws with what felt like a lunk of iron.

Davit looked confused as he took back his blade. "What do you mean?"

"You two, to me," Percival called. His back was turned as he looked at the blasted exit across from the moat. Davit and I quickly returned to our brother's side. "Both of you put your arms around my waist. Hold tight."

I did as I was told. Davit cracked open his mouth, about to make wise. Percival shot him a dark look, clearly done with his sense of humor. This caused Davit to quiet himself and wrap his arms around Percival's waist as well. Our older brother took a deep breath and placed one of his arms around each of us, and suddenly all three of us were lifted off the ground. An incredibly strong breeze blew through our hair as Percival carried us over the moat. We landed softly on the other side ten feet from where we began.

Davit's eyes widened as Percival let go of us. "You can fly?" he asked, stunned.

Percival looked behind us, towards the arena. His eyes narrowed ever so slightly in an expression that conveyed just a hint of surprise. "Yeah," he said with a nod. "I can fly. Come on."

Dark Omens

XXII

"In here, quick!" Percival dragged Davit and me into the first unlocked doorway he found as the sound of heavy footsteps approached. The room we entered was barely lit, a stark contrast from the hall we had just been running through. None of us made a sound as we listened to the patrol on the other side of the door. I didn't even breathe.

"Fan out!" a guard's harsh voice shouted. "Cover all the exits to the keep! They are three children! If they escape, it's your heads!" The thundering footsteps reached a crescendo and then slowly faded. The guards had run right past our door. It appeared we had escaped unnoticed, at least for the moment. But none of us eased at all.

Percival sighed. "That's not good," he said quietly. "They're posting at the exits."

My legs felt like jelly. "So does this mean that unless we find a different way out…"

Percival looked at me. He did his best to put on a strong face, but I could see right through it. "No. It will be alright." He paused in thought. Another breath. "Let's just see where we are, first."

With that, the three of us spread out and looked around the new room. It honestly wasn't that much. Just some tables with maps, a couple of bookshelves. It looked like someone's study.

I walked over to Davit, who was thumbing through random sheets of paper on a desk before him, looking like he was killing time more than anything. His ice-blue sword was lying on the table next to him. I looked down at the weapon.

Everything about it perplexed me. "How did you get that?" I asked, my curiosity getting the better of me.

Davit's eyes turned to the sword. "I honestly don't know," he told me frankly. "One second we were in danger, and all I could think about was that we needed some way out of it. On gut instinct, I called the water to me, and then I had the sword in my hands."

I furrowed my brow, even more confused. "But we can just manipulate our own elements. We can't turn them into other things."

Davit nodded along. "Yep. Good point. I'm thinking magic," he said dismissively. Clearly he was not as invested in the question of the mysterious sword as I was.

I turned away to check on Percival's progress and found him on the opposite side of the room. He was standing still, not doing anything besides looking at a weapon rack in front of him. But then I realized what he was looking at: a polished bronze spear with a slightly blackened tip. It was our father's, the weapon that Percival had lost in Bukarra. Percival cautiously grabbed the weapon, as if it would disintegrate at his mere touch. Behind me, Davit quietly put the papers he had down and looked at our brother with me. Percival was completely silent, but his expression said everything. The young king was wearing an look that I had not seen on him since he took the throne: deep, deep sadness. His eyes were closed, like he was lost in another world.

We let him stand there silently for a few more moments before we approached him. "Percival?" I said softly. "We should probably start looking for a different way out of here."

Percival's eyes opened. He scrunched his nose, like he always did when he was thinking. "This isn't an armory," he said.

Davit and I looked at each other. "Sorry?" I asked Percival.

Our older brother looked at both of us. "This room. It's not an armory. The only weapons in here are my spear and this." Percival grabbed a short sword from the same weapon rack he'd retrieved his spear from. The small sword was made of a metal colored deep red, but other than that it didn't appear all that special. Percival tensed. "If I had to guess, I'd say we are in Ahaax's study." He looked at the two weapons he was holding. "And these are the things he values most."

My and Davit's eyes both widened. "Oh great," my twin said, panicked. "So we escaped Ahaax only to walk right back into his bedroom. That's really great."

Percival ignored him. Judging by his face, he was still thinking. He walked right past both me and Davit, to the other end of the room.

"Hey, you know, that strong silent thing only works when we aren't in mortal danger," Davit said to him, turning.

Percival was staring intently at a bookshelf in front of him. Suddenly, he pointed at it fiercely. "The air," he said. "Something is different."

Neither Davit nor I knew what Percival meant, and we both reacted in different ways. I furrowed my brow again, completely confused. Davit waved his arms around and made noises like a fish out of water. "Come on!" he said.

In one quick motion, Percival brushed his spear-holding hand through the air. The bookshelf opposite us was promptly pushed over by a strong air current. Behind where the shelf had been was now an open entrance to what looked like a tunnel going deeper underground. I couldn't see past a few feet of light that was made by a torch situated in the new doorway. Percival laughed softly to himself. "I knew it," he said under his breath.

The three of us approached the entryway, knowing it was our best chance at escaping our prison alive. "I can't say

I'm thrilled with this idea," Davit said, crossing his arms. "Not big on entering The Tunnel of Dark Death."

"Well, you can go back into the arena. *That's* certain death, if you want," Percival remarked.

Davit looked at our brother. "Oh? You're funny now? That's great."

Despite talking, the three of us still stood outside of the dark opening in the stone wall. It was as if we all subconsciously knew not to go into the darkness. "What do you think is down there?" I asked quietly. It was unnerving. But I couldn't say why. This was objectively less danger than we had been in just minutes before, but why did it feel so wrong?

"I don't know," Percival said. He sighed. "But we know what's back there." I knew he was right. We really didn't have any choice. Percival looked down at me. He wasn't wearing any particular expression, but in that moment I was comforted. It felt nice to have my older brother there with me.

Percival held out his hand, which was holding the red sword. "Take this," he said.

I was surprised. "You want me to have a weapon?" I asked. I remembered how committed Percival had been to making sure we didn't even have a knife on the trip to Bukarra. He would never have given me a *sword*.

"You'll need it," was all that he said. Suddenly the situation was real for me. I was no longer a child. Percival was handing me a weapon, and now I was fighting a war. In my sweaty palms, I took the sword. It was heavier than I'd expected, but it was much more balanced than Davit's weapon. This weight felt good, like it would give power behind any swing.

Percival took the torch off the wall. "Whatever happens, stay close to me, okay?" He looked at both me and Davit. We nodded. Our older brother sighed one last time.

"Then let's go." And the three of us walked deeper into the cold stone passageway.

The tunnel took us down a spiral staircase carved from rock. Aside from the torch Percival had grabbed, there was completely no light, and there was no ventilation either. It felt as if we were walking deeper and deeper into a tomb.

After what felt like an eternity in silence but was probably only a few minutes, the three of us exited the stairs into a large hollow cave. The entire room was easily ten degrees colder than where we had come from. There were tunnels carved from stone marked at various points along both sides of the cave walls, twisting and turning towards unknown locations. Other than that, though, the cavern was completely bare. It looked like a good mix between a castle and a cave.

The three of us stepped into the cavern, our footsteps echoing off the cold stone walls. Before we could even walk a dozen feet, however, we heard a familiar voice that sent chills down my spine.

"Siege tunnels are a very effective way of escaping unnoticed." Ahaax appeared from around the corner of one of the stone tunnels. He was wearing a smug grin. "Most of the time." Instantly my senses went into overdrive. My head started buzzing ferociously hard, and combined with the low light it was almost difficult to see. In a flash, Percival raised his spear. Davit and I stood in shock, our weapons hanging uselessly at our sides.

Ahaax unsheathed his great sword from its position on his back, approaching us at a stroll. At his command, fire went down the black weapon, lighting up our surroundings. "My men are stationed at every entrance to the keep," Ahaax went on. "But somehow... I knew you three would find yourselves down here."

"Davit, Rose," Percival began, low. "Go. Find us a way out of here. I will deal with him." He was shielding both of us from Ahaax with his body, tracking the warlord's movements with each step.

Davit snapped out of his shock. He raised his sword. "What? No! You told us to stay by your side! We all have weapons now. We can take him!"

Ahaax smirked, still walking towards us. "Brave words, but can you back them up with action?"

Davit nearly charged in that moment, only just held back by Percival. "Come on, you wanna find out!" he said through gritted teeth. Ahaax only chuckled.

I felt sick to my stomach. We had two options: stay and fight with Percival, or leave him to fight Ahaax alone, but hopefully find a way all three of us could escape. The latter was our only real hope of getting out of here alive, but we would be abandoning our brother to our worst enemy.

"Davit," Percival said sharply under his breath, not taking his eyes off Ahaax. "I need you on this."

Davit stopped for a moment. "But…"

With one last step, Ahaax pulled his arm out from behind him and threw a ball of fire at the three of us. Without missing a beat, Percival swung his spear in the air. A great gust of wind diverted the fireball into a nearby wall. I could feel the heat against my cheek as the ball exploded.

Percival, assisted by the wind, lunged at Ahaax. Each clash of the two's weapons sent a shower of sparks in all directions. Percival looked back at us in a second's pause. "Go!" he pleaded.

In that instant I made up my mind. Steeling all my courage, I grabbed Davit with my free hand and began running towards one of the tunnels carved into the rock wall. Davit protested, but he ran along too. Behind me I could hear the zapping of electricity and the *fwoosh* of flames as the two men fought. The sounds of the fight only motivated me to run faster, turning through the tunnel, desperate to find any way to freedom. I was disoriented. As we ran, it felt like the buzzing in my head grew louder and louder; I just had to do my best to ignore it. Percival had dropped our torch in the fight, and I could barely see, but that didn't matter. Nothing mattered but escape.

Soon, Davit and I were out of breath and had to stop running. The sounds of the battle were now soft behind us. We had emerged into a large cavern similar to the one we had come from. However, this cave was so large, I couldn't see where it ended in the low light. I could only tell our surroundings by the sound of our steps echoing off the walls and the slight cool sensation of fresh air brushing on my cheek. *Air!* I thought. *A way out.*

Davit and I were still doubled over, panting. I had mostly regained my breath. My biggest problem now was my head. The aching buzz it had been before had turned into what felt like someone bashing a hammer on the inside of my skull. I needed to find a way out of these tunnels, but with my head the way it was, I could barely concentrate. It was making me angry. *What is this!*

A brittle breeze scraped through the cavern. Suddenly, the intense banging was not the only sound in my head. There was something else. Something that wasn't me. It sounded like bones scraping together, like metal could breathe. The sounds crashed off and through each other continuously until they were no longer just sounds. It was a voice in my head.

Ahaax, is that you? It was like death whispering in my ear. Davit and I both stood straight as arrows. We weren't alone.

The cold voice laughed. It was a terrible sound. Like the dying breath of a wounded animal. *No, not Ahaax. We haven't been introduced, little ones.* Something in the back of the cave shifted. It sounded like tons of rocks sliding off each other. Towards the far end of the cave, a single stalagmite glowed a dull magenta. Then another, larger rock next to it began to glow as well. One after another, the stalagmites glowed in a dull magenta, forming a perfect, unnatural line. And then I saw: they weren't rocks at all. They were spines. Massive spines.

"Rose," Davit managed a barely audible whisper right next to me. "What is this thing?"

I had registered my brother's voice, but I was unable to do anything else. In an ironic sense of humor, in that moment my mind was trapped in a council meeting months ago. One that warned us of a threat we didn't believe could be real. Every joint in my body was frozen as my breathing sped up. *No*, I thought. *No no no no.*

Another sickening laugh. *Yes*, the voice rasped in our heads. The shadows at the back of the cave shifted, only for me to realize that they weren't shadows. It was a single body. *I am the Rot that gnaws at the tree of life*, the voice whispered in our ears. Across the cave, a single giant wing unfurled from the ground, and then another. In front of us, it appeared as if the very ground rose. The cave cracked and groaned. Behind the two wings, a giant barb like that of a scorpion rose on a massive, spined tail. *I am what gives you the meaning of fear.* Horrified, I could do nothing but follow the trail of glowing spines with my eyes down from the tail, across the body that had to be at least twice the size of Redwood's, and finally ending in a massive obsidian head. On the great black head of the largest dragon that might have ever existed opened an eye the color of blood. The only detail that I could make out in that deep pool of red was a single slit pupil of magenta running down the middle. The head rose, and as the Elder Dragon in front of us moved, the very ground shook. *I am Venerus, and I am free once more.*

I could barely process what I was seeing. An Elder Dragon. In front of me. And it was real. Venerus was so large,

I couldn't even see Their entire body as it went back into the cave. The Elder looked down at me and Davit with those red eyes, each probably the size of us. I couldn't tell, but it looked like Venerus was smiling. Something about that stare… I was petrified, completely frozen in place. There was only one thought in my head: that as I watched the massive dragon in front of me open Their jaw lined with row upon row of magenta teeth, I was seconds away from death.

The very air in the cavern began to feel different as Venerus made a low, inhaling sound. The back of the Elder's throat glowed a bright magenta.

Before I realized what had happened, I was already a dozen feet away, running towards the door to the tunnel we had come through. Davit had grabbed my hand and was running the both of us through the dark. An intense crackling completely filled my ears, and I could see magenta light behind us. Neither one of us was prepared to stop running for any reason. The crackling was replaced by a much worse, much angrier *roar*. The entire cave system shook as we ran. We were being chased.

The two of us ran faster than we ever had in our lives. My lungs began to burn, but I didn't care. As we ran, we saw flashes of light in front of us as well. This light was different from the magenta behind us. It was hues of red, orange, and blue. As we ran farther, we heard Percival and Ahaax, still engaged in combat, louder and louder.

Davit and I burst into the large cavern we had originally entered, stopping only long enough to scan our surroundings. Across from us on the other side of the cave, Ahaax had a foot on Percival's chest, pinning him to the ground. Ahaax's sword was only inches away from Percival's gritted face, and the only thing preventing it from swinging down was Percival's spear blocking it.

As soon as Davit and I ran into the chamber, Percival's eyes flicked toward us. The tension on his face was replaced with panic, but only for a second. Percival returned his attention to the man attacking him and, in one clean move, delivered a swift kick to the man's shin, rolled out from beneath his foot, and threw both of his hands toward him, using the wind to send Ahaax flying into a nearby cave wall. The warlord fell down, dazed.

Davit and I didn't even stop running, going to our brother. Percival grabbed his spear and looked at us. "What are you two do—"

The tunnel we had entered through exploded in a blast of fragmented stone. Venerus' massive head just barely managed to fit through the larger opening. When Percival saw the dragon, his eyes went wide as saucers.

Davit didn't miss a beat, grabbing Percival's arm with his other hand as we passed. "Run run run run run," my twin brother was saying over and over again. Percival in hand, the three of us ran into the closest tunnel opening. I didn't think about where the tunnel would lead; I only knew we had to get out of there. The entire time we ran, Venerus' deafening roars followed closely behind. I didn't know if Venerus could even fit into the tunnel, but I didn't dare look behind to see.

We kept running. It felt like we would never stop until Percival shouted, "There, ahead!" In front of us the tunnel began to light up. Not dramatically, but it was just enough to tell the difference. Little pinpricks of light appeared in my vision. *Stars!* It was a way outside!

The three of us kept running, and soon I could feel the cool night air brushing my face. Finally, we ran outside the stone tunnel onto what felt like soft dirt. We were out! I didn't know how long it had been since we were in the arena, but it was still night, and there was a full moon high in the sky.

We exited the tunnel on the outskirts of what looked like a canyon. We were standing on just a small ledge, but in front of us was a stone bridge leading across a deep chasm. Percival took both my and Davit's hands. "Come on!" he said. "Just over the bridge! Keep going!"

We continued across the bridge. When we were about halfway over, my spirits were dashed. On the other side of the bridge at the gate, a dozen or more of Ahaax's men appeared, each one holding a sword, spear, or some other weapon. The three of us skidded to a stop.

"That's enough!" a voice shouted from behind us. We all turned to see Ahaax walking from the tunnel, albeit limping. Other than the limp, though, he didn't look too hurt from Percival's fight, and with this still flaming sword in his hand, he *did* look much angrier. As the soldiers on one side of the bridge and Ahaax on the other closed in, the familiar feeling of being sick to my stomach returned. *We were so close!* I thought, heartbroken.

Ahaax approached us slowly. "I could have given you so much," he spat at us. "I could have given you peace. I could have given you *answers*! I could have told you what you really are."

Percival stood taller. "I know what *you* are Ahaax." I don't know how he managed to do it, but despite everything in that moment, Percival managed to speak stronger than I had ever heard him, brushing off the warlord's comment. "Nothing but a murderous usurper. And you will lose."

Ahaax glared. He took his flaming sword in both hands. "I give you justice, of the *true* king." Then, I felt a familiar presence return to my head. Not like the evil violence of Venerus, but a friendly and kind voice. This was a friend, a friend who wanted me to know one thing.

Found you, he told me.

I heard a faint roar off to my right. In the distance were three shapes flying towards us. Birds? No... too big. I suddenly realized. It was Redwood and the other dragons! They were here! Somehow they had tracked us from Bukarra!

As a few seconds passed, the three dragons came into clearer view. Each was soaring through the canyon towards us, even Redwood, who hated flying. My heart lit up. We were going to get out of this! I turned to Davit. "We need to jump," I whispered.

Davit snapped his head towards me. "Off the bridge? Are you crazy?"

Percival, who had been speaking to Ahaax, glanced back at me. In one look I told him everything I needed. *Whether you feel Apolion's presence or not, please, trust me.* Ever so slightly my brother nodded.

Out of nowhere my head started hammering again. A second later, the side of the cliff face the three of us and Ahaax had emerged from exploded. Magenta lightning flashed out, and Venerus roared another mighty sound that shook the earth. The Elder Dragon looked around in the new night air They had emerged in, finally landing on the bridge above Them. Their eyes narrowed when they saw us.

Without a word, Percival grabbed me and Davit and ran towards the side of the bridge, with Davit screaming "Wait!" the entire time. As I closed my eyes tight, we jumped off the side into the canyon below. I thought I was going to throw up with the mix of adrenaline and feeling my insides and hair being pulled up around me. I heard screaming, a good deal of it being my own. After a few seconds, we landed on a solid surface, but one that had much more give than hard ground would. I opened my eyes and saw that Percival, Davit, and I were all on Redwood's back, flying through the canyon.

I couldn't help it; I started laughing and crying all at once. I put myself face down on my dragon's back and spread my arms out in the largest hug I could manage. "My sweet boy came back to me!" I cried.

Percival hunched next to me, getting close to the dragon's head. "Get us out of here, Redwood. Get us far from here." He stood to full height and whistled at the other two dragons following us, telling them to stick in close.

Behind me I thought I could hear the sound of Ahaax furiously shouting, but I couldn't be sure because of the wind, and I was unwilling to look behind us for fear the monster Venerus would be there I kept my eyes closed tight. I was shaking, although I knew it wasn't from the cold air. I didn't know what emotions I was feeling at that moment. Happiness? Terror? Probably those and more.

That was how we flew for the rest of that night, the three of us on Redwood's back. We didn't even dare touch the ground until we were on the other side of the Black Mountains. Our trip to the royal palace was similarly tense. We knew we had been gone for longer than we planned, so all three of us wanted to return faster than we had come. We managed to make the trip back in only four days, the whole time never stopping in a settlement except for food and sleeping on the backs of the dragons at night.

It was just sunrise when we returned to the palace. The morning air was alive with the sound of songbirds. The courtyard was abuzz with activity when we landed: everyone in the palace was wondering where the king had gone. Scouts could see the dragons for miles before we entered the city, so when our dragons landed in the courtyard, everyone knew to expect us.

I dismounted Redwood slowly, unsure. I still didn't know what I was feeling. The entire past week had been a blur. I had barely gotten sleep any of the nights. Each time I closed my eyes, I heard Venerus' awful roar. I took a few steps and caught sight of Davit next to me. Surprisingly, his face was also flat. He hadn't made any jokes the entire way back.

The doors to the palace on the other side of the yard swung open, and Pevincy came running out. I had never seen our guardian look as ragged as he did then. Judging based on sight, he did not get much sleep either.

"Your Grace!" the old guard cried as he ran up to the three of us. He looked at each of us individually, first Percival, then Davit, and then me. He looked at a loss for words, rotating his head to each of us as he spoke. "Are you... what happened to you children?"

At first we were all silent. I supposed we were trying to find the words for what we had just been through. The more I thought, the more I couldn't think what to say.

Then, to my side came a slight sniffle. I turned and saw Davit brushing his nose with his sleeve, his eyes starting to well. Just like that, I felt everything I'd experienced the past week come back to me at once. The sandsnake, the ruins of Bukarra, getting captured, the arena, Ahaax... and Venerus. *Gods*, I thought. *Venerus is free. They're really free.* I began crying too. I couldn't help it. Not just crying, I began to weep. Davit, when he saw this, broke down as well.

Pevincy, looking concerned, scooped the two of us into a warm embrace. It felt nice. For the first time in a week I felt safe again. My body shook as I sobbed. Percival approached quietly behind us, wrapping his arms around us as well. He wasn't crying, but he had clearly been impacted by what we had just been through. He looked up at Pevincy and spoke softly. "Assemble the council."

Percival

Confrontation

XXIII

As we walked through the palace's marble halls, I felt a pang of guilt for my two siblings walking along absently behind me. The worst of their tears had passed outside, but as we walked both Davit and Rose would occasionally sniffle. The past week had to have been the worst of their lives. I had carefully been watching them as we flew back, looking for how they were dealing with what we had been through. What I saw frightened me. I could probably count the words each of them said on the entire way back with two hands. Davit had stopped cracking jokes, and Rose had stopped talking much at all.

It's begun, a dark thought crept into my head. *They will never be the same again.* I pushed the thought aside forcefully. Fear of war destroying my siblings was why I did everything I could to prevent them from seeing it since the outbreak. I wouldn't let them go through what I had as king. They would recover from this. They were strong.

Due to skills in administration that I could only hope to one day have, Pevincy made sure my council was all in the chambers by the time the four of us arrived. The lords were all in their seats, talking ferociously amongst themselves. Any conversation that had been going on between them, however, died immediately upon our entry, if not out of respect, then out of a morbid curiosity. Each lord stood, their eyes glued to me as the four of us walked to our chairs at the head of the table.

I was about to take my seat on my throne when I realized: there were still only three chairs for four of us. I remembered Davit standing for the entirety of the last council meeting. I found my brother standing quietly nearby, looking at the council uncomfortably. I gestured for him. "Come, Davit. Sit in my seat."

Davit looked sheepish, an expression unusual for him. "I'm fine, Percival, really," he said quietly.

I ushered him into the throne, my hand light on his shoulder. "Sit," I said. The matter was settled. Davit acquiesced and took a seat, Rose to his right and Pevincy to his left. The rest of the lords returned to their chairs. All of the eyes in the room turned to me, standing between my siblings.

The silence was like a physical barrier, separating me and my siblings from everyone else. What we were about to say would change their lives. Would change the world. At last, Pevincy reached out. "Your Grace," he started. "What happened to you three while you were gone?"

It took me a moment to find the words. I decided to start from the beginning. I told the council of our arrival in the ruins of Bukarra, how there was nothing left of the city but ash and debris. This was met with uneasy murmurs by the lords. Most of them.

"You were too late," Lord Carrington remarked gruffly in what was hard to distinguish between a question and a statement. The eyes of the rest of the room fell on the bald lord. He elaborated, "You were too late to stop Ahaax from destroying the city."

A dull throbbing materialized behind my eyes as I had to deal with my most antagonistic lord. I shook my head and told them what Ahaax had told us. "No, there was never a chance for Bukarra. By the time we had received the intelligence of Ahaax's movement in the region, it was likely already destroyed. Intelligence, by the way"—I looked at Pevincy—"that was fabricated. This spy of ours goes deeper than we thought."

Pevincy furrowed his brow. "Troubling," the old guard said, rubbing his chin. "If this spy is not only leaking our movements to the enemy but fabricating reports of enemy presence, the havoc they could wreak on our forces would be devastating. Just by raising a pen."

I nodded grimly. "I am making finding this traitor your top priority. Use the Circle. Investigate leads. Find them, Pevincy."

The guard nodded. "It will be done, my lord."

Carrington crossed his arms on the other side of the table. "I've never been that sure of our *traitor* problem." He looked around to the other lords of the table, making his case. "Where's the proof? How can we be sure that this isn't the work of a young king in over his head, and his *stooge* picking up after him?" He pointed his chin at Pevincy across from him. My head knight narrowed his eyes in response.

I glared at Carrington, doing my best to let that be the extent of my expression. *Don't let them see you slip*, I thought. *Act like a king.* "Proof?" I asked the lord. I couldn't help but scoff. "Ahaax admitted it to us himself."

At this, a surprised silence swept the room. Carrington furrowed his brow. Lady Aemelia, who I could tell by her vacant expression was only half-listening to the prior conversation, widened her eyes at me. The Lords Finnian and Florian each hiccupped once, one after the other, and the skeletal Lord Alaric nearly dropped his jaw to the floor. Clearly none of them were expecting that. I wondered if I should have been so blunt.

"Oh, children," Pevincy said softly. He wore a worried look. Out of all the lords seated at the table, he was likely the only one to care about *us* during our abduction.

I picked up where I left off, telling the lords how Ahaax and his Magus ally, Abominus, had appeared in the ruins. How the entire settlement was destroyed just to capture the three of us. The ultimatum: my life for peace. My siblings' refusal, and the arena where we were to be put to death.

Lord Finnian interjected at this point, scratching his blond head. "I just don't understand. How can a rebel like Ahaax have such a large fortress?"

Lord Florian nodded next to his brother. "Yes. It hasn't even been a year, after all."

A drawn-out wail came from the mouth of Lord Alaric. "Isn't it obvious?" he lamented at the two lords.

I looked at Pevincy. He looked back at me, and I nodded, confirming his suspicions. I turned back to the rest of the lords. "Lord Alaric alludes to where I believe Ahaax to have been stationed these past months," I said. I ran through the facts. "An arena like that. Sophisticated stonework architecture throughout the complex. Miles of underground siege tunnels? Based on everything I saw while we were his prisoners, I believe Ahaax to be hiding in the Last Palace."

Worried mutterings went up around the table. Pevincy shook his head, frowning. "Nothing is sacred," he said softly.

"A place of blood and death," Alaric confirmed in a raspy whisper. "Only evil lives there."

"That's not all," I said. I was looking down at my hand on the table. I had begun to lean, since I had been standing for the duration of the meeting. It was a hand that didn't look like mine. It looked older.

I could no longer avoid saying what I had been dreading. As I tried to find the words, I felt a lump in my throat. Even then, terror gripped me. I couldn't say it another way. "Venerus is back."

The room was abuzz with voices. Each lord was trying to ask every question they had at once, many of them the same. When they didn't get their answer first, the lords began to shout at one another. The headache I had been fighting intensified. "Please, quiet down," I said to the bickering nobles. It did no good. I didn't know if they even heard me. The only lord who wasn't shouting was Pevincy. He was occupied holding Rose's hand in his. He had risen from his seat and was now kneeling between my two siblings. They were having a soft conversation I didn't have the concentration to focus on.

I massaged my eyes, hoping to alleviate some of the pain. *What are they doing?* I thought hopelessly. *They're fighting each other like children. They have no way of facing our enemy. Our real enemy.* It was all too much. I needed quiet. "Silence!" I shouted. I didn't control myself well enough, and the shout sent a wave of sound through the room, throwing loose paper everywhere.

Fortunately, everyone was looking at me again. I told them of me and my siblings' encounter with the Elder in the catacombs of Ahaax's palace. I described everything about the dragon we had seen. There could be no mistaking the identity. "It doesn't matter what you have to say, or what you believe," I began. I looked into the eyes of each of the six lords around the table. They needed to understand. "Venerus is back. They *are* real, and for whatever reason They have allied themselves with Ahaax. This is no longer just a war, like one the kingdom has faced in its thousands of years. This is a conflict for our existence." The lump in my throat grew larger, and I had to stop myself. My hands were gripping the edge of the counsel table as I remembered the Elder Dragon's magenta stare. I began again, almost pleading. "I need all of you behind me. Behind this crown. Only with the realm united can it even hope to withstand this coming storm. Now is not a time for our petty squabbles. If we don't stand united, we will *all* fall."

I searched each lord's face, looking for a sign that my desperate speech swayed anyone. It did not appear so. Lord Carrington scowled at me. "This is ridiculous!" he huffed angrily.

A pit formed in my stomach. "My lord, please," I tried to calm him.

Carrington stood, his face reddening from fury. "He refuses to rule, and now he mocks our intelligence!" The lord jabbed a finger at me from across the room. "The Wicked Elder will never, *can never* return. You don't know what you saw. You…"

"They spoke to us." It was Rose. All eyes turned to my sister in her chair, including my own. It was the first full sentence Rose had said in two days. Her voice was quiet and distant.

Carrington huffed. "What was that, child?" he asked, more frustrated than hostile.

Rose looked pale. She turned her gaze to Pevincy by her side, who took her hand in his reassuringly and nodded. Rose began again. "In those underground tunnels… Venerus spoke to my brother and me." She paused again. It was clear she was struggling just to recount her story. "It was a terrible thing. Like claws digging into my mind, forcing its way around until it wasn't just myself anymore." Tears welled in my sister's eyes. "Nothing else could do that."

I felt deep sadness looking at Rose. I had only seen Venerus briefly after my fight with Ahaax. They never spoke to me. In a rare feeling, I *couldn't* understand what she was going through at that moment. It made me frustrated that I couldn't help.

Lord Carrington breathed heavily through his nose, his arms crossed. He was looking at Rose. Even *he* didn't seem to want to scream at a crying girl, but he was still unconvinced. "This is absurd," he said, and with that began towards the doors of the council chambers.

"My lord, please wait," I called, raising a hand, but it did little good.

Lady Aemelia rose from her chair as well. I knew I couldn't stop her either. "He chides *us* for failing to rule, meanwhile he spends his days making up fantasies." She laughed airily to herself as she left the chambers.

Lords Finnian and Florian exchanged awkward glances. Together, as with everything else, the two rose. "We're going to go with them," Lord Florian said to me.

Lord Finnian nodded. "All the best, Your Grace." The two sibling lords left the chambers, with the small frame of Lord Alaric moaning softly in constant defeat behind them.

As the door to the council chambers closed for the final time with a hard *thud*, I let out a sigh of failure. Ultimately, however, I couldn't be surprised at the council's response to Venerus' return. I had been trying to deny it myself the entire week back to the palace, but I didn't have the luxury of not running the entire kingdom.

When I turned towards my throne at the head of the table, I was met by the sight of Pevincy with an arm around Davit and Rose's shoulders, counseling them. "You're still here?" I asked, defeated, to the sole remaining lord.

"Come Final Night, Your Grace," Pevincy confirmed. I could always rely on him.

"You believe what I say?"

The old knight nodded. "I do," he said, troubled. "Unfortunately."

I sighed again, rubbing my eyes. The headache had begun to abate, but that was still the least of my problems. I turned to my siblings. "You two should go get some rest. Thank you for coming here."

Neither Rose nor Davit put up a fight. They simply received one last hug from Pevincy and shuffled out of the chambers without another word. I tried to convince myself it was because they were eager to sleep in their own beds once again. *But will they be able to rest?*

As I stood looking at the door after my siblings left, Pevincy spoke from behind me. "You should get some rest too, my lord."

The pit inside me grew larger, but this felt different. Not out of dread. This felt hopeless. "How can I?" I asked, turning to face my mentor. "Knowing what I now know?"

Pevincy nodded in understanding. "Knowledge is often a curse," he agreed. "But," he countered. "It is our strongest tool when we know how to use it."

Usually a talk from Pevincy would help me get my thoughts in order, but not this time. *How can anyone face this threat?* I wondered. I didn't think there was anything that could still my mind.

My head guard, sensing my troubles, smiled softly in his fatherly way. "A sleepless king is no good to anyone, Your Grace," he said. "The sun will rise tomorrow."

I took in his expression and knew he was right. For the time being, there was nothing that could be done. Ahaax, despite how powerful I knew he now was, was still a continent away. Still, I couldn't rest without knowing I was doing everything in my power. "You'll begin an enhanced search for the traitor immediately?" I asked Pevincy.

The knight nodded. "Immediately, Your Grace." He smirked slightly. I could tell he knew what I was going to ask before I said it.

I let out one last exhale, sure in the fact that my Justiciar would run the realm well while I slept. "Well, I won't keep you then," I said.

"Good day, my king," Pevincy responded, as it was still technically the morning we landed. *Gods,* I thought as I exited the council chambers. *That meeting felt like an eternity. It couldn't have been more than twenty minutes.* My eyelids felt like lead curtains. The lack of sleep from the past week was catching up to me now that I didn't have any pressing duties. The idea of once again lying in my bed was the first pleasant thought I'd had in a while.

On the other side of the wooden door, I was surprised to be greeted by the sight of Bryce. My old friend wrapped his arms around me as soon as he saw me. "You're alright," he said, relieved. It was a quick, tight embrace. Then Bryce stepped away and looked me up and down. "When you were gone for longer than was arranged without any word, we here all began to fear the worst."

My friend's worry comforted me. It felt nice to have a personal relationship within the palace that wasn't always about me being king. I made a slight, tired shrug. I didn't want to tell Bryce that everything I had seen in the week I had been gone led me to believe that a fear of the worst was, in fact, perfectly warranted. "Well," I said with almost a slight laugh, "we're all alive." The lack of sleep really was catching up to me.

Bryce smiled at my stiff humor. "Can I walk with you?"

"Always." With that, the two of us began towards my chambers. The grand design of the royal palace was so expansive that even the walk from the council chambers to my own personal room took several minutes. As we walked, the orange morning sun was shining rays through windows carved out of marble. The palace was coming alive. As I looked into the lush green courtyard below while we walked, I was able to see dozens of bodies, from scholars to servants, milling about preparing for their duties. While looking at all the people below, I couldn't help but realize that they were all relying on me.

"You're troubled," Bryce raised the topic as we walked. We passed a pair of two low-ranking nobles who looked about our age. They curtsied as I walked by.

I nodded politely back at the young women. "Sometimes it's hard to choose just *one* thing that troubles me," I lamented once we were out of earshot.

"Try," Bryce encouraged. He would be there when I was upset.

I sighed. It was still too recent for me to comfortably think about Venerus again, so I decided to focus on more earthly matters, saying, "Alright, we have a spy among our ranks."

Bryce raised his eyebrows. "A spy?" he whispered, surprised. "I mean, of course I had suspected, but I never would have thought someone would actually…"

I nodded. "Pevincy was the one who discovered it. You were likely going to find out soon."

Bryce furrowed his brow, troubled. "Well," he began. "Are there any leads?"

Shaking my head, I sighed, admitting defeat. "No. I've ordered Pevincy to redouble and expand his efforts, but even then I honestly don't know where to start." It was the truth. The idea that someone would willingly betray the kingdom to Ahaax shook me to my core. It threw my entire concept of who I could trust into question.

After a few seconds, I realized Bryce had gone silent. Turning, I saw that he had stopped walking a few steps back. His face was scrunched, deep in thought. "What is it?" I asked, pausing.

"It's just…" Bryce began. He walked back up to me so that we were even once again. We resumed walking as Bryce continued, "Every council meeting of yours I have been to these past months, there's always one person above the rest who objects to your ideas, always one person preventing anything from getting done, directly challenging you."

My palms turned sweaty as the realization of who Bryce was speaking of dawned. "Carrington," I said, mouth dry.

Bryce pursed his lips in grim acknowledgement. "Think about it, Percival. A traitor would have to have easy access to both crown and military orders. They would need to be within your circle. Every time Carrington resists moving his troops, it directly benefits Ahaax."

I had to stop walking. I suddenly felt sick to my stomach, leaning against a marble railing. I began running through the past eight months in my head. Everything Bryce was saying was true. It was always Carrington rallying the lords against me, convincing them not to organize their levies. Even in the meeting that had just concluded, it was Carrington who doubted the existence of a traitor at all. "I…" I began, my tongue feeling heavy. I looked at Bryce. "What would you have me do?"

Bryce cocked his head slightly. "Isn't it obvious?" he remarked. "Imprison him. He is a threat to the realm."

Then it felt like someone had poured a cup of ice-cold water over my head. The calculated efficiency in my friend's voice as he suggested imprisoning a member of my council sent a shiver down my spine. "What?" I almost gasped, taken aback. "But there's no direct evidence against him."

Bryce shook his head lightly. "A king doesn't *need* evidence, Percival. A king needs to rule."

My gut felt like it was weighed down by a stone sinking in a lake. I narrowed my eyes uneasily. "At what cost?" I asked. I picked myself up from my leaning position, ever so slightly tensing at where this conversation was going. "That sounds almost like your father."

Bryce's face darkened almost imperceptibly. He hid it well. His father was always a sore subject. "My father was a flawed man," he began.

"Your father tried to murder mine while he was the king's head knight."

"I never supported that," Bryce said, tensing. The two of us were silent for a moment. There was suddenly strain between us. Bryce continued, "But my father knew about honor. That's what his time in the Circle taught him. And more than that, it taught him that a king needs to *lead*."

"Bryce," I said, unnerved. I began walking again. Bryce's father served in the Circle of the Crown for King Oriond before my father. The Circle under my grandfather had a justifiably deserved reputation as the king's personal enforcement arm. My father had changed things. Bryce's father disagreed with that.

"Percival, that council was chosen specifically to handicap you," Bryce implored. "Every day they prevent you from ruling is a day Ahaax can call a victory." He sped up and stopped walking in front of me, forcing me to stop as well. He continued earnestly, "You have the chance to be a great king. The greatest king this land has ever known. But *you* need to rule. *You*." He poked a finger softly at my chest, not in an unkind way.

I looked into my friend's brown eyes filled with passion. I was uneasy. Everything he said was making sense, yet there was still a part of my mind that felt wrong. What he was saying, to directly defy my regency council, ignored thousands of years of established tradition. I glanced off to our side, noticing a large oak door engraved with golden bands. "These are my chambers," I said, deliberately changing the topic.

Bryce sighed. He knew the conversation was over. "You know where I'll be," he said, with a hint of something almost like disappointment in his voice. "Just think about what I said? For the realm."

I looked at him straight again, then nodded. It was the best I could give him. The entire conversation left me feeling deeply off. With a soft clap on my arm, Bryce left me at my chamber's door, walking farther down the palace hall. As I watched my friend walk off, about to enter my bedroom for the first time since I had been Ahaax's prisoner, sleep was once again far from my mind.

A Moment of Calm Between the Storms

XXIV

The day after we returned, the sun was high in the sky when I sat next to the shallow creek in the forest. My eyes were closed, and I took in the scenery of my natural environment: the soft bubbling of the creek and the sweet smell of summer green blowing through the air. I breathed out a long exhale. My shoulder muscles were just barely starting to lose their tension.

Despite my worries, almost as soon as I touched my bed, I was able to sleep through the entire day and night. Panic gripped my heart when Pevincy told me this as I woke, but my Justiciar reassured me that he had all palace matters under control. He had organized more patrols around the city to catch the traitor, but otherwise no pressing matters needed my attention immediately. Calmed, I figured the kingdom would be fine if I extended my absence just a bit longer. There was one last person I needed to reunite with.

I could tell she was approaching before I could see her. Her footsteps rustled the ground—lightly, much quieter than the average person, but I could pick even the smallest sounds out of the air from distances the average listener couldn't think of. Plus, ever since I was able to feel that hollow passageway behind the bookshelf in Ahaax's chambers, I had been honing my ability to 'see' objects around me by how they displaced the air. It was evident that *someone* was approaching.

Quickly after I sensed the invisible signs, Delilah appeared behind some branches on a path, walking towards me. Somehow, she was more beautiful than I remembered. She was wearing a matching blouse and pants the same color as her raven hair, with a green hunter's cloak wrapped around her shoulders. Her amber eyes still held their passionate glow. I couldn't help but smile as she approached. I felt a pang in my heart, surprised. I hadn't realized just how much I missed her.

I doubted Delilah felt the same way. She walked briskly towards me, glaring. I was too dazed from seeing her to realize there was only one possible target for her anger. "What's this s'posed t' be?" She thrust a paper at me. Her accent always came out when she was upset.

Just by a glance at the paper, I could tell I had written it. *Meet at our spot* was all that was written in black ink. Delilah huffed, crossing her arms. "This s'posed t' be charmin'?"

A knot formed in my stomach as I quickly realized my charming plan to reunite with Delilah was, in her eyes, not charming, and no longer going to plan. "I…" I tried to begin, blindsided.

Delilah rolled her eyes, flailing her arms as she spoke. "You drop off the face o' the earth fer tree weeks an' come back an' nothin's happened?" She scoffed, returning her arms to their crossed position, but this time her face looked more hurt than anything. "I thought I meant more ten that to you."

I was momentarily at a loss for words. When it was explained like that, my plan was obviously childish *and* selfish. Yes, I had been captured and that was out of my control, but more than that, I didn't even say goodbye to her before we left for Bukarra, something I *could* have done. I got so wrapped up in my kingly duties. I had no other choice, really, but I couldn't expect Delilah to understand, especially with what she didn't know. I didn't even think to consider it from Delilah's perspective, and as a result I'd hurt her. I felt terrible. "Delilah, I'm so sorry," I said from my heart. "I've never had a relationship like… this outside of the city before. My duties called, and I…" I didn't want to finish the sentence. *And I decided they were more important than you.* It made me feel awful.

Delilah looked at me with her large eyes. Her face softened slightly as she sighed. "Look, I know we come from two separate…" She paused, trying to find the words. "Walks o' life. I understand you have responsibilities I don't. But you're not the only one here. You gotta tell people if you're gonna vanish. Otherwise they start t' worry." Delilah rocked her body, slightly uncomfortable at her own vulnerability. She got through it and flashed me a warm, reassuring smile. "You don't need t' live that palace life when you're with me. You can be yourself, Percy."

Another pang went through me, this time of guilt, at the irony of her statement. Delilah really cared about me. It was clear the first genuine relationship I'd made outside of the court was real to her as well. But I was still carrying the sense of being weighed down. After all, how could I ever really be myself around her as 'Percy'?

Delilah nudged my shoulder playfully, wanting to get through the emotions. "Don't let it 'appen again, alright?" She took on a mock deeper voice to convey her meaning.

I smiled, remembering why I'd missed her presence so much. "Yes, my lady."

Delilah smirked and brushed past my shoulder. "So, what *duties* drag you away for almost a month?" she asked nonchalantly, sitting by the side of the creek. She picked up a flat rock in her hand and threw it into the water with a solid *plunk*.

"Oh," I began, sitting beside her. I quickly made up an excuse that wouldn't cause her to worry. "Just a royal trip."

Delilah snorted. "Wow," she laughed. "You could have at least lied and made up something interesting." She smiled roguishly at me.

I laughed uneasily, looking at the water. "Yeah." I cursed myself internally as I fueled yet another lie.

It was a pleasant day as songbirds sang in the air. A cool breeze blew through the trees to alleviate some of the midday heat. Delilah continued, cocking her head. "Royal trip, huh? Was the king there?"

The hair on the back of my neck stood at the mention of the word *king*. I looked over at the girl seated next to me. I decided to play along, raising an eyebrow. "Yeah, actually. He was there. Why? Do you like the king?"

Delilah nudged my arm playfully with hers again. "I do, a little. What's wrong with that?" she defended herself. Shrugging, she went on. "I don't know. He's our age, without his parents, and suddenly he has to run a kingdom and fight a war?" Delilah sighed, her long hair falling over her shoulders. "All I know is it takes a lot to go through that and still carry on day after day."

I analyzed Delilah's features. I wasn't expecting her to be so genuine. Somewhere deep inside me, I felt a flush of warmth at what she truly thought of the king. But I couldn't show it then. I tried to look as nonchalant as I could. This caught Delilah's eye. "Why? Do you not like King Percival, Percy?" she asked smugly.

I couldn't help but let out a laugh. "I…" I began. I leaned back on my hands. "It's complicated."

Delilah was smiling. "I think he'll be a great king," she said, as if confirming it to herself. She leaned back as well, placing her hand softly on top of mine. "Just give him time."

As I sat there, looking at the face of one of the strongest, most beautiful, kindest, and most understanding people I knew, I couldn't find the words to express how I felt in that moment.

"What?" Delilah asked, scrunching her nose.

Luckily I was able to form a sentence. I wanted to do something that would show her how much she meant to me. "Let me take you somewhere," I said.

She cocked her head. "Okay, where?"

"It's my favorite place since my childhood," I began. I had been thinking of taking Delilah there for a while. After I was captured by Ahaax, I knew it was what I wanted to do if I escaped him alive. "My father would take me there. But you can only go at night; otherwise it's not special."

Delilah chuckled, shaking her head slightly. "Alright, Percy, I'll let you take me t' a mysterious place only after dark. But don't think that I do this for everyone who asks."

I smiled warmly. "It'll be worth it," I confirmed. All I could think about then was how lucky I had been to stumble upon the lone hunter girl that night in the woods those months ago.

"Are you doing anything else today?" Delilah asked over the sound of the lightly bubbling creek. There was a air in her voice that hinted at what she wanted the answer to be. Shifting closer to me, she rested her head on my shoulder.

"No," I said, resting my head on hers. "Nothing."

Davit

I Was Wrong About You

XXV

The smell of sea breeze was on my nose as I stood knee-deep in the ocean. The orange horizon was dotted with various boats, likely fishermen or traders headed towards the capital. This was the first time I'd returned to my hidden little alcove along the beach since we had been captured by Ahaax. Honestly, it was the first thing I'd done at all since we'd gotten back. When Percival's council meeting ended, I was so emotionally shot and sleep-deprived that I went to my bed and slept through that entire day, and most of the current one. It was now evening.

Actually, I thought, cocking my head to the side. *This isn't the only thing I've done. I did have a meal of spiced sausages in the dining hall before coming here.* I nodded, satisfied that the last two days hadn't been a *total* waste of time. The spiced sausages *were* very good.

A strong wave washed up to my waist, and I snapped out of my food-induced daydreaming, coming back to the present. It was strange. It had only been a few weeks since I had been to my secret spot, yet something felt different about it that I couldn't place. The white sand beach felt almost smaller somehow.

As I scanned the beach, my eyes landed on Cerulia, who was dozing peacefully in the late-day sun with her legs resting in the air. She was lying on what looked like a bed of branches she had piled together for that specific purpose. I thought back to another time I had been on this beach. The day Percival flew here to get me. The day I hatched Cerulia's egg. That was only three months ago. I let out a laugh of disbelief. *Longest three months of my life.* It felt like I had experienced a lifetime in the same span.

Cerulia's legs were running softly and disconnected from each other in the air. She must have been dreaming. I smiled. Despite now being multiple times the size, she would do the same thing when she was younger. *Stop it.* I forced myself to look away, into the water. *Resist the cuteness.*

Ever since I saw through Cerulia's eyes in Ahaax's palace, it had been exponentially harder to avoid her, both emotionally and physically. Her thoughts were almost interwoven with mine whenever I was near her. Everything she felt, so did I, and as a result that made *me* feel like a neglectful jerk. Plus, that 'seeing through the eyes' trick went both ways, and Cerulia seemed to know my location at all times.

I sighed. It was a form of torture. I almost *wanted* to start to bond with the little blue dragon, but I still knew I shouldn't. If anything, I realized my time as a prisoner only cemented this fact. I saw Ahaax. Not only had I seen him, I'd been face to face with him. I *pulled a knife on him.* And he was still alive, and the war was still going on. It was my failure on the day of my father's murder tenfold. This time I didn't have the excuse of having no preparation. And I still failed to avenge him. I doubted I would ever deserve his final gift to me. I groaned, letting the weight of my head pull it down. *I came here to avoid my problems,* I thought. *Some job I'm doing.*

I cracked my neck, mentally changing topics and hyping myself up for what I was about to do. *Okay, focus.* I held my hand out in front of me. I did my best to recreate the scene of Ahaax's arena the best I could in my head. *Sword. Sword.* Sure, I had dropped the strange sword in the caves when I grabbed Rose to run from Venerus, but hey. I figured it magically appeared to me once, it could magically appear to me again. My gut tightened as I summoned a stream of ocean water into my outstretched hand.

Not only did my arm get soaked, but so did my face, as the spout of water I'd called came towards me with slightly more energy than I had intended. I spat out the salt water, wiping off my face with my hand, still without a sword. I could feel Cerulia rouse from the noise behind me. I turned towards my dragon, who had her head raised. "Not a word," I said sternly, pointing. I was confident the tone of my voice would persuade the nonverbal dragon to not say anything, purely with the hope of appeasing me.

I turned towards the open ocean. I huffed, cross with the behavior of the water. Taking a deep breath, I closed my eyes. *I did this before.* I scrunched my brow, thinking harder. *How did I do this before?*

I held out my hand once again. On the back of my eyelids, the scene of the arena came into clearer picture. The snarling hookclaw was pacing in front of me. I remembered how I'd felt at that moment. Frightened. But not for me. I was afraid for Rose and Percival behind me. I didn't care if I died, but I wouldn't let anything happen to them.

I opened my eyes. My gut tugged again. A concentrated stream of water burst from beneath my hand, coiling into my palm. It split into dozens of razor-thin strands, threading upward in unison. The blue strands shimmered in the evening light like ice, but they weren't cold. They twisted and wove together, tightening, hardening. In seconds, the same sword took shape: the same translucent, blue-edged blade I had held in the arena.

I breathed out, eyes wide. *That worked!?* Straightening, I adjusted my grip on the new sword with both hands. *Yeah, of course that worked.* Looking at the weapon, I couldn't help but smile like an idiot. Just holding the blade made me feel strong. It was heavy, but balanced, forged with the perfect combination to strike fast and hard. The pommel fit perfectly for me to hold with two hands. The entire sword felt made for me. Yeah, I had plenty of questions about how I actually got the thing out of nowhere, but really, it didn't matter. For the first time ever, I was holding a sword and felt *right*.

Grinning, I hunched slightly lower, raising the sword into an attack stance I had observed the knights use during practice. I began going through the set of moves I had practiced on that beach dozens of times before. Only this time, I was doing the moves correctly. I was gliding through the air and the water, seemingly slowed by neither. The blue sword was slicing through the air with no resistance. Every swing and swipe I performed was so fast I *should* have been sent tumbling from the speed, but somehow I was able to stay on my feet, using my motion from my last attack to propel me into my next one. *I'm on fire!* With a final spin, I executed an attack that would have severed the hand of my enemy flawlessly. Panting, standing waist-deep in the ocean, I may have looked like a moron, but I felt like I was on top of the world.

I stood once I was done sparring with air. I looked at the sword in my hands in astonishment. *Magic sword* was rushing through my head over and over. It couldn't be stopped. *Magic sword!* Just holding the weapon made me feel energized, like I could take on an army.

I turned the sword around in my hands. The metal was polished so well I could see my reflection clearly. In fact, I wasn't alone. There was a woman standing behind me. She had dark skin and sad eyes.

I let out a surprised shout, spinning on my heel. Since I was still in the water, this caused me to turn around and fall on my butt. I didn't care though. I raised my sword high from the ground, ready to defend myself from whoever had managed to sneak up on me. But no one was there. No one was near me in the water, and as far as I could see, no one was anywhere else on the beach. Even Cerulia was still fast asleep, curled in her branches.

Thoroughly spooked, I quickly stood from the water. Looking all around seemed to confirm it. I was alone on the beach. Shaking my head, I tried to calm my startled nerves. *I'm seeing things. I must be.* I looked back at the blade. Sure enough, it was only me in the polished metal. Something else caught my eye, though. A gold engraving on the blade, close to the hilt.

"*Ísilor?*" I said aloud. I could only assume that it was a name, but other than that I didn't know what it meant. *Weird,* I thought. *Why would a magic sword already have a name?*

The sun was beginning to dip below the horizon, turning the sky a nice shade of dark orange. I knew I had to leave now if I wanted to be back at the palace before dark, especially walking the wooded path home. Leaving then was just fine with me. The hair on the back of my neck was still standing up. Despite not being able to find anyone else on the beach, I couldn't shake the feeling that I was being watched.

Still holding *Ísilor,* I wanted to try something. I concentrated on the sword leaving my hand, returning to where it came from. Sure enough, the sharp blue metal of the blade began to *drip.* Slowly at first, then all at once my magical blade turned from a solid to liquid. A couple of gallons of water that used to be my sword fell into the ocean with a splash. "Huh," I said, amused. "Cool."

Cerulia stirred from her sleep as I walked onto the shore. Noticing me approach, the small dragon leapt up from her bed. She danced around excitedly. "Don't get any ideas," I said, pointing a finger at her as I walked by. "I'm walking home."

The dragon slumped at the news. She huffed. *Suit yourself,* it said. Leaning down on her haunches, Cerulia jumped into the air, taking flight and quickly climbing high into the sky. I looked up from my stationary position on the edge of the beach before the forest. It felt hard not to be a little jealous at how fast my dragon could travel. But I was doing this to myself, so who could I complain to? With a final sigh, I turned and began my walk home through the woods.

The night air was warm. The forest was alive with the sound of birds and buzzing bugs. As usual, Cerulia was flying directly above me the entire time. If I wasn't going to fly with her, she was going to make sure she didn't leave me alone. It was the kind of careful guardianship I respected in a three-month old. As much as I protested, I was beginning to enjoy her presence. I just wouldn't let her get closer. So long as she followed me *in the sky*, I decided I was fine with it.

As I was walking, I heard a weird sound off to my side. It sounded sort of like a quacking tuff, but more drawn out. Furrowing my brow, I stopped walking, trying to get a better sense of the noise. Then, it revealed itself for me.

A small, gray animal about the size of a flura wandered out of the green brush. It was probably only as tall as my waist, if that, but it was built heavyset, with four stocky legs. It had gray, pebble-like skin broken up with patches of both a scraggly, moss-colored fur and a darker, hard and spiky substance like a rock. The creature made the same squeaking sound I had heard before. It was obviously a lost little rockbear cub.

The cub looked up at me with frightened eyes in a long head. It bleated again, warily. It was admittedly very cute. "Aww, what's wrong, little guy?" I said, slowly stretching out my arm to see if I could get it to know my scent. I wanted to convey that I wasn't a threat. The cub approached slightly, cautiously. I craned my head. "Say, bud. Where's your…"

All at once I realized that the air had gone dead quiet. The bugs had stopped making any noises. There wasn't even a breeze. Suddenly, there was an intense buzzing concentrated in the back of my head. It was like clanging bells, so sudden and intense I turned around, as if the source were external.

Charging towards me was a rockbear about three times the size of the cub I'd just seen, and significantly angrier. *Found mama.*

Relying on pure instinct, I rolled out of the path of the charging animal. I'd cleared a collision with the ferocious mama bear who would have torn me to shreds just by the skin of my teeth. The adult rockbear stood between me and her cub, standing on her hind legs and roaring wildly. I scrambled away as quickly as I could on all fours through the dirt. My back to a tree, eyes glued to the bear only a dozen feet from me, I stood. Thinking quickly, I reached for my sword at my waist. Only for my hand to grab nothing.

A wave of panic shot through me. I looked down at my waist. There was no sword *there.* Of course there wasn't. *That's right,* I remembered with my usual ironic timing. *You didn't bring a sword. You got your sword from the water. Nice going with that decision!* I kicked the tree out of stupid blind rage, screaming a curse at my consistent luck.

Mama bear roared again. I stopped uselessly kicking plants and returned to the real threat. She was back on all fours, and her body was tensed. The angry bear jumped on the ground in front of her a few times, pacing. The symbols were easy to recognize: she was about to charge. And I was unarmed.

I extended my arms out in front of me, trying to calm the bear down while I backed away slowly. My efforts didn't do anything. The angry mother bear charged towards me. I brought in my arms close, shielding myself. I held my breath for the inevitable.

There was a blue blur accompanied by a *thump* and a swift gust of wind. Cerulia had dove in from the sky and landed between me and the bear. The unexpected arrival of a dragon caused the charging animal to halt abruptly, rearing back on its hind legs once again. The mama bear gave a threatening bellow. Cerulia didn't miss a second. She stood on her back legs as well, using her tail to balance herself. My dragon extended her wings as far as they would go, casting a shadow in what little daylight remained. Bringing her head back, Cerulia let out one long, consistent roar that shook my bones. The blue dragon mock-charged the bear multiple times, each time making the formerly aggressive animal look more and more unsure. Finally, the mother bear let out a final, uneasy growl. She looked back at her cub, standing behind her, frightened, and the two fled quickly into the woods.

Cerulia stared at the spot where the bears had been after they were gone for a few seconds more, growling. Then her head turned back towards me, her body loosening. She flicked her tail.

I stood with my back against the tree and my mouth hanging open. So much had just happened in so few seconds, my mind was still processing it all. Cerulia walked up to me lazily, making a soft humming sound. "You... saved me," I said to the dragon, my brow wrinkled. The surprise was evident in my voice.

Cerulia cocked her head at me, her big eyes catching the evening light. She sat down and looked at me expectantly, like she was waiting for me to figure something out. "You saved me," I said, remembering all the past times. "Here. With Ahaax." Despite me constantly pushing her away, Cerulia would always come back to me when I needed. "And I've been so terrible to you."

The little blue dragon who had been by my side since the day she hatched brushed her head along my arm so that my palm was resting between her eyes. "I'm so sorry," I whispered as I truly saw through my dragon's eyes for the first time. From then on, our minds were one. My thoughts were mixed with hers, and hers with mine. I was looking through my own eyes, but I could also see through *hers*. I saw my own stunned, freckled face as I was speaking.

I'd failed my father on the day of his death. I still wasn't the man I needed to be to win this war, but that didn't matter to Cerulia; none of my failures did. Even at my lowest point, Cerulia never left my side. She would be with me through it all, no matter what. And from then on, I'd be with her. "I was wrong about you."

Cerulia repositioned herself. Standing horizontally to me, she angled her body downwards so I would be able to easily position myself on her back. Flashes of the sky from above the clouds appeared within my mind: memories from Cerulia. She wanted to go flying. Still, I was uneasy at the thought. Yeah, I had managed to fly with Cerulia to Bukarra, but that entire trip was awful. I'd felt like I was about to fall off the entire way, and the last time I flew with Cerulia back home, I *did* fall off.

"Are you sure?" I asked, raising a nervous eyebrow.

Cerulia hunched lower, wagging her tail. A sense of calm returned to me at her glance. She wanted me to trust her. I breathed out, steeling myself. *Trust her.*

"You'll catch me if I fall again, right?" I asked, looking for confirmation as I positioned myself on the point of her back where her neck met her body. She didn't have her saddle, but weirdly enough it didn't seem to make that big of a difference.

Cerulia made a low chortling sound. *Yes. I'll try*, the noise said.

"Ah ha ha," I laughed dryly at the joke. *That was a joke, right?* Slowly extending her wings, Cerulia jumped into the sky once again, now with me on her back.

It's a weird feeling, your guts flying *up* within you. Even though I had flown on a dragon before, I still wasn't expecting just *how weird* it felt. In a split second I had come to the conclusion that Rose was in fact lying when she told me it was something you get used to. I had my eyes closed as we flew higher and higher. Sure, my sister was the only one with a fear of heights, but that didn't mean I *liked* them. I clung to Cerulia for dear life. Each slight bump in the air made me feel like I was about to go flying in the bad way.

You need to open your eyes, Cerulia was thinking. *This won't work if you don't trust me.*

With the wind blowing past my ears, it was almost too difficult to concentrate. *Trust her*, I told myself. I needed to let go of my fear. We hit a rough bump in the air, and my body momentarily rose up from Cerulia's. *Just my fear!* I thought, panicked as I tightened my grip onto the dragon.

The whipping wind was reaching a fever pitch. The edges of my limbs were beginning to go numb from just how hard I was holding on. I knew I was about to fall off if I didn't make a change. I needed to open my eyes. To trust Cerulia that it would be alright. *On three*, I told myself. *One… Two…*

I opened my eyes, and suddenly it was like *I* was the one flying. It was like they were my own wings, like *I* was the one controlling the movements in the air. More than that, it felt like I had been flying my entire life! It felt more natural than walking! I brought my body close to Cerulia's as she tucked in her wings. The two of us began an upside-down nosedive straight for the green treeline below. The wind brought tears to my eyes. We were going so fast that I had to think about how I breathed with the rush of air into my lungs. Yet I couldn't stop smiling.

Cerulia pulled out of the dive just feet away from the treetops, the air rushing behind us blowing through the trees. I pumped an exhilarated fist in the air and lowered back down. *What's next?* I thought, craving more. Cerulia picked up speed, and pretty soon we were back out over the ocean, the water rising in white foam in our wake.

I leaned ever so slightly to the side and stretched out my hand, skimming the water. It felt like a lot of small, sharp pebbles were hitting my hand at once. It wasn't actually that pleasant of a feeling. Bringing my hand back in, I laughed, if not out of comfort, then out of accomplishment.

Cerulia began climbing into the air again. Higher and higher. Soon, we were above the clouds. *Hold on* was the message my dragon wanted to give me. Cerulia brought us higher with one last flap of her wings, and then she let her body go limp. In a split second, I had wondered if my overenthusiastic hubris had gotten the better of me. The weird feeling of my floating organs returned as the two of us slowed and then rapidly sped up in a controlled freefall.

Cerulia angled her body so that it was pointing straight down and we were going as fast as we could. The air was beginning to feel like a physical barrier against my grinning face. The ocean below us was getting closer by the second. As I strengthened my grip around Cerulia, I let out a long, enthusiastic "WOOO!" Only looking back on it afterwards did I realize that despite the water getting closer and closer, there wasn't a second where I thought Cerulia would let us hit it.

My little blue dragon shot out her wings and propelled us just above the surface of the water at amazing speeds. The fishing boats were hauling in their catch for the day. The two of us flew between several small ships, probably giving their passengers a surprise. I waved to a couple of fishers standing on the deck of one, the wind making my hair flop all over my face.

He won't see this coming, Cerulia thought as we flew.

I was too busy laughing from sheer joy. I barely realized anything. "See what?" I asked.

Without any warning, Cerulia submerged us both just under the surface of the water. It was a blunt shock to my senses. What was weird, though, was that the water didn't slow us down at all. We were going as fast as we were flying. After only a second, Cerulia brought us both back flying above the surface. I sputtered out salt water. "Hey!" I shouted in surprise, caught off guard by my dragon's idea of a prank. I was pretty sure I saw Cerulia grin as she spun in a complete circle, managing to only dunk *me* in the ocean this time.

"Ha ha," I said flatly, wiping water off my face. In the corner of my eye, something caught my attention. It was a series of large rock pillars that rose from the ocean. Cerulia turned her head in the same direction. I knew we were thinking the same thing.

With an excited roar, Cerulia angled us in the direction of the rocks. We had flown well without any obstacles, but how would we do with things in our way? It was a question that would be answered quickly as we approached the pillars. We closed the distance in a matter of seconds. Cerulia tucked in her wings and rolled to the right to avoid colliding with a rock. She rolled left to avoid the same right after.

As we navigated the closely packed rock pillars, Cerulia's flying skills were impressive, but I was amazed at how *I* hadn't thrown up despite being flung around on her back. The last pillar ahead of us was a tall, skinny spire with an opening the shape of an *O* in its center. My dragon and I both sized it up in a split second. Cerulia was confident she would be able to pull off the maneuver, and with my adrenaline pumping I was feeling lucky.

Flying right towards the stone pillar, Cerulia tucked in both of her wings so they completely folded into her body. As we flew through the jagged rock opening, there was so little clearance I could feel the rush of wind from the hard stone just inches above my head. Once we were safely clear from the rock, Cerulia outstretched her wings again and kept flying. I leaned on my back, punching my fists into the air and screaming in triumph over and over. The whole trick was probably less than a second. But it felt exhilarating.

We flew like that for a little bit longer, gliding in the sunset's light. I don't remember exactly how long we were out. I just remember that I spent the rest of that flight realizing I had made the best friend of my life in a single evening.

Where Did This Thing Come From?
XXVI

The sun had just set below the horizon by the time the palace was back within eyesight, casting a dark purple shade over the night sky. Cerulia was gliding in the cool air low above the water. The Didah and Denebola falls each steadily increased their roars as we flew in closer. Torchlight from the city cast a steady orange glow above the cliffs, but at this time of day the gigantic cave opening between the two waterfalls was similarly glowing warmly. However, this glow wasn't from torches. At least, not most of it. As Cerulia and I flew towards the chasm-sized opening, the air rang with multiple simultaneous clinking and clangings, each off beat from the rest but in a consistent rhythm. The temperature of the air had noticeably risen as well. By the time Cerulia flew into the cave, the air had to be twenty degrees hotter than the outside night. We had entered the Royal Forge.

The Forge had been constructed within the extensive cave that had formed underneath the two rivers around Lungala. Most of the furnaces within the Forge were powered by one of the falls on either side of the city. The cave was so large, Cerulia was able to fly into the entrance without any fear of hitting a wall. There was practically no change from flying outside. And the Forge spanned every inch of that same cavern. It really was a sight to behold. I had been down there a few times before, but I had never seen it from the air all at once. At its full capacity, the Royal Forge could probably supply an entire army on its own, but for decades it had been running at only a fraction of its potential, supplying only the king's men and city guard. Still, just that was enough to employ hundreds of smiths from the city, and it kept the Forge alive as a city of metal and fire day and night.

Luckily I had a general sense of where I was going so I didn't get lost within the sprawling cavern, which I knew was something that could very much happen. The Forge was constructed in such a way that it was divided into six separate stone platforms that each rose higher towards the back of the cave based on what was being produced. The highest platform at the end was where the overseers typically operated. That was where I directed Cerulia.

My dragon's relatively small size made it pretty easy to land in a clearing on the top platform. The sudden appearance of a dragon on the work floor, however small, did cause some surprised shouts from the smiths, though (and one angry curse from the worker closest to us who dropped his blade in shock). As I dismounted Cerulia, I smiled around at everyone awkwardly, waving apologetically on behalf of my dragon who, unfortunately, had no hands. "Hi." I smiled. "Sorry." I was mostly met with unamused faces of highly skilled smiths who quickly picked up wherever they'd left off.

I turned back to Cerulia, whose eyes were glowing trying to follow everything that was happening around her all at once. "That was fun. We should do it again sometime, what do you say?" I rubbed her snout playfully. It was nice to finally get to have fun with her. "Stay here, yeah? Try not to get in any of these nice people's way. I'll be right back." My dragon nodded in acknowledgement. With that, she immediately began to wander curiously around the forge. I sighed, my shoulders dropping. I knew she understood what I asked. She just didn't care.

As Cerulia followed a rolling vat of molten steel, I watched on fruitlessly. Not wanting to get bogged down in what would soon be *someone else's* problem, I turned and began to search for who I was looking for. Even though it was now after dark, I was pretty confident he would be there. He was the Grand Smith after all. Sure enough, I found him not long after I started looking. Frankly, he was hard to miss. I raised a hand. "Isidore!" I called above the noise of the forge.

About twenty feet from me on the stone platform, a large, equal mix of muscles and man was facing away from me, seated on a stool, hammering at something I couldn't see. At my voice, the man cocked his head. He stood, doubling his already substantial height seated, and turned around.

Grand Smith Isidore was the tallest person in the room in every room he had ever been in. The dark-skinned man easily stood a head and a half taller than everyone around him. He was wearing a beige apron and undershirt that clearly showed off forearms that were bigger than my head. The Grand Smith was known for producing the finest metalwork in all the realm, both weapons and anything else that could be thought of, and Isidore, in his time in the role, hadn't disappointed anyone.

Isidore smiled wide as he saw me. "Prince Davit!" the head smith said in a booming baritone. "It's been too long!" He extended his arms as though he were about to hug me but frowned as I approached. "Why are you soaking wet?"

I stopped just short of him. He was right. I was still dripping from Cerulia's plunges in the ocean, despite the heat of the forge. "Oh, right," I said, looking down at myself. "I flew here." Judging by the response on his face, this answer only confused Isidore more. "Actually, this is kind of why I've come."

Flicking my fingers slightly, I pulled all the water that was clinging to me from my skin and out of my clothes. In all, it managed to form a sphere about the size of a watermelon between me and Isidore. Judging based on eyeball measurements, I determined there was just enough water there for what I needed. As I moved my hands, the sphere of water stretched thinner and thinner, slowly taking on a translucent blue shade until what had been a sphere of water was now the sword Ísilor held in my hand.

Isidore's eyes widened. "Hmm," he said in controlled surprise. "That's interesting."

"Tell me about it!" I said, smiling. I furrowed my brow, realizing my word choice. "Actually yeah. Can you tell me about this thing? I figured you were probably the most knowledgeable about this."

Isidore rubbed his chin with a large hand. His eyes scanned my blade up and down, analyzing every detail. He held out an open palm. "May I?" he asked.

"Of course," I said, handing him the sword. In the Grand Smith's hands, Ísilor looked like a toothpick. Despite the difference in size, though, as soon as the weapon went from my hand into Isidore's, the large man's arm was seemingly pulled to the ground.

Isidore grunted in a mix of surprise and exertion. "Well, to begin, it's off balance."

I laughed at his humor. "Yeah, so I hear." I remembered what Rose had said immediately after she had used the same sword to sever our chains in the Last Palace. She wondered how I could use something so unwieldy to kill two hookclaws. "Here's the thing." I took Ísilor back from the smith. I was able to pick up the blade from its position with the tip seemingly glued to the ground. It still felt *natural* holding it. With a little flourish, I was able to flip the sword in the air, catching its handle in the palm of my hand. "I can use it just fine."

The Grand Smith placed his hands on his hips at my trick. "Hmm. This *is* interesting," Isidore mused. "I've seen you with a blade before. There must be *some* sort of magic involved here."

"I like to think of it as skill."

"No, that's not it. Say, by the hilt there, what's that say?"

I looked down at the golden inscription on the blade, brushing off the attack on my pride for the sake of my own survival. "Yeah, I noticed that. *Ísilor*. Have you heard of it? It's not Lungalean."

"No, it's not," Isidore agreed. "It's Kavalish, the old language of my people. In fact, it shares a root with my name."

"Really?" I cocked my head. I did my best to sound invested, but I honestly wasn't that interested in a lexicology lesson in the middle of the night. Still, I knew it would be rude to outright ignore the smith whose help I had asked for.

Isidore didn't seem to notice. He nodded. Looking down at the blade in my hands, he continued. "*Ísilor*. It means *Swift Strike* in the native tongue."

"Swift Strike," I said with reverence. The name held power. As soon as I said it I felt like I could stand taller. I tightened my grip on the weapon. "Is there anything else you can tell me?"

The muscular smith crossed his arms. "The legend is that it belonged to a great leader of the clan. This was a thousand years ago or more, a relic of the Shattered Age, before the kingdom reached up north." Isidore waved his hand, brushing through the ages of history. He continued. "They say this leader created the magical sword Ísilor to secure and defend her people, providing them with everything they needed. She lived well into old age, serving her people for decades."

"Really?" I asked. I looked down at the blade, then back at Isidore. "Do you think it's really magic?"

He raised an eyebrow. "Considering you can pull the sword from water? I would say that maybe there's *some* truth behind it."

I nodded. "Fair enough. But did the stories ever say what this leader did with the sword? Any reason why I would have it?"

Isidore shook his head. I could tell his lack of specific knowledge about a weapon frustrated him as much or more than me in that situation. "Sorry. No one ever talks about after the hero dies. They only capture the moments of glory."

My shoulders slumped just a hair. "Poignant stuff," I quipped.

"I'm sorry, Prince Davit." Isidore sighed. "I wish I could tell you more."

I brushed him off. "Hey, don't apologize. You told me some really useful things." I hoped my reassurance sounded sincere enough to convince him. I wished I came away with more, but I really did appreciate his help. "I'll probably be going now. Goodnight, Isidore." With a feeling like taking a deep breath after holding it in, I let Ísilor turn back into water in my hand and fall to the stone floor.

Strangely, I had a difficult time falling asleep that night. I lay awake in my bed, staring at my dark ceiling, my thoughts racing. I couldn't stop thinking about all I had learned about my magical sword. Every question Isidore had answered opened up ten more undiscovered ones. Eventually I did drift off to sleep, but I wouldn't say it was any more restful.

I dreamt that I was standing alone in a plain field enshrouded by a gray fog. The landscape was completely featureless. As far as I could see, I was completely alone. But I *felt* like someone was watching me. I was holding Ísilor in my hands, hunched low, turning in a constant circle so I could check all my angles.

Then, footsteps. Somewhere hidden off in the fog. But they were approaching me. Tensing, I brought Ísilor up, ready to swing, only for an unseen force to pull the sword from my hands. In less than a second, the sword flew off and was swallowed by the fog.

My arms slumped to my side. *Seriously?* I thought. *I can't even win in a dream?* A realization dawned on me. *Wait, how do I know this is a dream?*

From the gray smoke the silhouette of a person appeared. A woman stepped out of the clouds, and she was holding Ísilor. She looked to be about thirty years old. Her skin was black and fair, and she was about half a head shorter than me. Strikingly black hair was tightly braided behind her head and stretched nearly to her waist. She wore an elegant collection of flowing, dark blue robes that clung closely to her body. The most noticeable thing about her, though, were her eyes. They were a stark blue, like ice. The color was so distinct I could easily pick them out through the distance and the fog. Everything about the woman gave off an air of power marked with beauty.

The mysterious woman walked closer to me until she was only steps away. She didn't look outright hostile. She was wearing a gloomy expression. It was a mix of sadness and distance, like her body was there with me, but her mind was somewhere else. It was looking at her pointed face that I realized I was looking at the same woman I had seen in Ísilor's reflection on the beach.

The woman began in a cold voice sounding near yet far away. "How young you still are. You still use what has been given to you like a child's plaything." Her voice echoed throughout the strange, foggy space.

Blindsided, I pointed a finger at myself, to clarify this woman was in fact speaking to me. *Of course she's speaking to you, you moron. You're the only two here.* The fact quickly became evident. So too did the fact that what this woman first said to me really seemed like an insult. I mentally reframed how this conversation was about to go. "Hi! You must be…"

"I am Orianna," the woman said with a refined voice, her posture held high. She held out Ísilor in front of her, blade pointed towards what would have been the sky. "I am the one who forged this weapon."

I snapped fingers on both of my hands. The way this Orianna started off the conversation made me want to be snarky, so I wasn't going to make talking easy for her. "Great! Can you explain..." I looked around the scene, waving my arms through the fog. "Any of this?"

Orianna's face remained flat. "In order to understand your present, you must begin to understand the past," she said obscurely. Before I could respond with a quippy remark at just how meaningless that statement was, Orianna closed the distance between us in a few quick steps. She pressed the thumb of her free hand against my forehead firmly, and suddenly the entire environment around us shifted. Gray fog was replaced with white snow blanketing rolling hills. I could see the sun low on the horizon with a glimmering halo of light hanging around it.

I looked all around myself, spinning so hard I nearly fell over. Orianna was standing next to me, unfazed by the scene change. She was looking ahead of us. I tried to blurt out a question in what I hoped would be comprehensible language, but she held up a finger, silencing me. I followed her gaze, looking at what had her attention.

Some distance away from us, two kids of roughly the same teenage years were walking in the snow. They were frozen mid-stride. I realized that in this strange landscape, time was frozen for everyone but Orianna and myself.

The mysterious woman standing next to me finally spoke again. "Centuries ago, before the kingdom of your forefathers stretched to these lands, two children discovered something Man never should have known." The scene around the two of us changed in rapid succession. I saw the two teenagers on a sheet of ice, then the two of them falling down below into a dark, frozen cave system. Orianna continued as the scene shifted again, "The Heart of Magic." The two teenagers stood with their backs to us. They were looking at a strange object suspended high in the cave in front of them. It looked like a monstrous, large magenta sphere, made out of equal parts mechanics and flesh. Despite the frozen time, the unnatural object still seemed to pulse a threatening glow. Just looking at the thing made me feel uneasy.

Orianna continued. "The Heart told the children that it was grateful to them for freeing it, and in return it would grant them each one thing in all of creation that they asked for. The children, inseparable since birth, both wished for the same thing. They wanted something that would protect their home and their loved ones from those who would do them harm. The Heart, seeing their differences, obliged. To the girl, the Heart bestowed a sword imbued with its own magical energy that would see her always strike swift and true. *Ísilor.* To the boy, the Heart gave a staff imbued with its own raw power. *Magarak. Chain Breaker.*" The scene shifted once again to each teenager holding their respective item, casting a distinct magenta glow over the entire scene. The uncanny magenta orb had faded in the background, eventually disappearing altogether as the glow of the objects increased.

With a blur of color, the environment once again went through a complete change. I was standing in the middle of a snowy village. "To each child, the Heart gave its own magic," Orianna resumed. "Time went on, and they each sought to use their newfound power to improve their world." I could see the girl from before holding Ísilor. It was now clear that the girl holding the sword was a younger version of Orianna. She was surrounded by the people of the village as she touched the tip of the sword to the snowy ground. Upon contact, the blade lit up magenta, and the snow began to melt, replaced with blooming flowers. "One through healing." The scene changed rapidly. I saw the younger Orianna using Ísilor to defend the village from raiders, to fell forests with a single strike. I saw her gain a following of villagers on her own merit. "But the other only through pain."

I turned. The scene took on a red, menacing air. I was surrounded by soldiers clad in black. There were thousands of them, each lined up in neat, even rows. I looked on as they all saluted a man standing on a cliff face above them. It was the boy who created *Magarak*, now an angry man at the head of an army. He raised his staff in front of him, towards a foreign village: the first object in his campaign of retribution. The scene changed. The man was in the burning village. He raised his staff, preparing to strike a cowering family.

"I had to stop him," the voice of the older Orianna said next to me. Scene change. I saw her younger self fly in at the last moment, protecting the family by blocking Magarak with Ísilor. Sparks exploded from the two weapons just touching each other. Scene change. Younger Orianna lunged at her former friend, sword outstretched. Scene change. Magarak's user, completely enveloped in a magenta cloud, his eyes glowing a flat magenta hue, used his magic-imbued staff to throw a mountain at younger Orianna, who, in a similar magic cloud with magic eyes, sliced the mountain in midair, completely eviscerating it. Scene change. More and more clashes between the two god-like Magi.

Finally, there was one last flash of pure white light. The younger Orianna was left as the sole survivor, collapsed in a barren field, sobbing. "When he was too far gone"—it was her older self—"I used everything I had to destroy what remained of the physical soul of the person I was closest to." The younger Orianna screamed a horrible cry of pain.

Elements of the scene slowly shifted. We were standing in a wooden throne room. I could see Orianna, this time older than the one standing next to me, seated in her regal chair, her crown positioned on her gray head. She was speaking to what appeared to be a party of travelers. The small man who looked like their leader was at the front of the group, near Orianna. He was holding Magarak. "Part of him remains," the current Orianna next to me said, almost longingly. "Only within the vessel." The travelers shifted. I was able to see a woman holding something else. *Ísilor.* The group of travelers made their way out of the throne room as the old Orianna looked on in silence. "As do I," my Orianna concluded. The ever-shifting scene around us faded away for the last time, and our surroundings took the gray, cloudy form they had when I'd first appeared. My vision was directed at Ísilor, now within *my* hand despite not starting out that way. Somehow, I could *feel* a part of Orianna within the blade.

"My vessel has been waiting ever since," Orianna said, looking at me observing the sword with a slightly condescending glare. "When I sent Ísilor off in my late years, it remained waiting. Waiting for the land to fall into crisis once more."

So many thoughts were going through my head. At some point, I think it was around halfway through, I had reached the point where I had so many questions that I stopped forming coherent thoughts. I was just operating from how certain words in my head made me feel. And I felt confused! Nothing was making sense.

I stood glued to the ground, helplessly looking at Ísilor. There was one thing I needed to know above all else. I raised my vision to meet Orianna's gaze. "Why me?" I mustered the courage to ask. I couldn't stop now. "Why give this power to *me?* Why not give it to my brother? He's the king! I couldn't even save my own father." I spat out the line. I didn't think I could ever live down the shame of Ahaax using the truth against me as a weapon.

Orianna looked at me. For the first time, her face seemed to soften. Not a lot, but enough. "There are countless futures, each constantly interacting with each other, always on a knife edge." I slumped my shoulders, feeling almost hopeless if she thought she was helping me with riddles. The strange warrior out of time continued to me. "You will come to learn the role you play in time, *Davit*."

I shot up straight in my bed, my heart pounding. Sweat was dripping from my brow. Breathing hard, I looked around, taking in my surroundings. I was in my bed, in my chambers, with no one else around me. After a few deep breaths, I was able to slowly lie back down, gradually calming. After all that, I couldn't help but have one last question.

When did she ever hear my name?

Rose

Injustice

XXVII

Rays of sunlight pleasantly warmed my face as I stood in Lungala's central square. A little sparrow was similarly basking in the warmth, resting in its nest atop a nearby building. I simply stood there in the sun, looking at the small bird from the ground absently. I wasn't quite sure how long I was standing there before I realized what was happening. I hoped it was at least less than ten seconds. *You're doing it again*, I scolded myself.

Blinking repeatedly, I shook myself out of my daydream, taking my eyes off the little songbird. The square was abuzz around me with people of every shape and size. Merchants lined the edge of the market, shouting prices and handling goods. Children were running in and out between the legs of adults in multiple different games. It was business as usual in the city square: alive and bustling.

I sighed softly. In the week since we had returned, I had been staring off into random space more and more. I couldn't really explain it (I had full awareness) or control it (I could start dazing off as soon as I stopped speaking). Most of the time it was only for a few seconds, but it occurred multiple times a day, and I was beginning to notice more and more. I forced myself to begin walking around to take my mind to different matters.

Beginning to feel cramped up within the palace, I wanted to go down into the city to distract myself from everything that we had been through. I would forever enjoy interacting with the citizens of the kingdom outside of the royal court, reveling in their stories and authentic experiences.

Like always, my trio of palace guard friends accompanied me as well. All three of them were off doing something close within the square. Killian was admiring a sword at a nearby vendor, Jules was arm-wrestling a burly man at a pop-up tavern, and Archie was seated on a barrel in a circle with a bunch of shifty-looking strangers, likely losing something valuable in a game of chance. As I looked at all of my friends, I *actually smiled*. I was beginning to feel like myself again, from before... what happened. With all of these people around, I felt *safe* again.

A little boy rushed past me, giggling. I watched as he ran, smiling. He was at the head of a group of children his age that closed on his trail. The boy was flapping his arms like a bird as he ran, and so were all the kids behind him. They must have been playing a game with dragons. The little boy in the lead ran about a dozen feet ahead of me, turning back around. With a giggle, he cried at the children, "I'm Elder Venerus! *Rawr!*"

My entire body seized. In that moment it felt like I was back in those black caves. *Venerus*. The young boy roared again, and in my ears I heard the skull-splitting sound produced by the horrible Elder Dragon. I felt the sickly cold chill of Their voice on the back of my spine. The child stretched out his arms. In my mind's eye I remembered Venereus' gigantic wings, so large that I couldn't see where they ended. The other children were swarming around the boy, and he was playfully swatting back at them with his outstretched arms. The mental image of Venerus's head flashed back into my mind. They had just broken through the tunnel, into the main chamber where Percival was fighting. They snapped at the stone around them, trying to get free. Trying to get at us. My breathing was picking up. I couldn't move. I knew I was about to lose my balance.

"Princess?" The word sounded distant and muffled. My chest tightened, and I could hear my heart in my ears.

"Princess? What's wrong?" the same voice said again. It was Killian. He had appeared next to me. I tried to answer him, but I couldn't. When I tried to speak, no sound came out. I felt like I was about to faint.

Before I knew it, Killian and I were moving through the crowds of people in the square. My friend had taken my hand in his, leading me quickly through the masses. We slipped between two market stalls, the overwhelming buzz of constant noise still lingering in my ears. Then stone walls of a shaded alley rose around us. Finally, we broke into a small clearing behind some buildings situated next to the river, although I was too disoriented to even try to guess which one.

"Breathe, Princess. Just breathe," Killian said to me calmly, his voice slowly coming back into clearer focus. "That's it."

I pressed my back against the building and slowly fell to a seated position, doing my best to follow Kil's advice. On instinct, I dug my fingers as deep as I could into the soil on the ground. The moist dirt and grass were refreshingly solid. I could feel my body slowly gaining strength from the earth as my hand was buried. Slowly, my breathing returned to its original pace, and the pressure on my chest began to fade. I thumped my head on the wall of the building behind me, back in the present. That had never happened before. I had never been so panicked I couldn't move or speak. And it was all because of a *child playing*. I closed my eyes tight, ashamed of the entire thing. I was stronger than that, wasn't I?

"Thank you, Kil," I said between breaths of air. I was embarrassed to be seen in that state just by my friend. I didn't want to imagine what would have happened if Killian didn't bring me to a less public place. I opened my eyes again for the first time in minutes. The river was flowing swiftly towards the falls a few feet in front of us. Across the water, there was a long line of people coming both into and out of the city, queuing at the large stone gates.

Killian sat beside me. He wore a concerned expression, accented by its usual kindness. "You've been through hard times, haven't you, Princess?"

I kept my gaze ahead at the water, not daring to look at my friend. I felt a lump form within my throat. My friends knew I had been captured, but I hadn't told them anything else about my experience. Each time I thought about giving words to what happened, I was brought back into the nightmare. Just knowing that Venerus was out in the world somewhere colored my perception. Even things I had found joy in once before, like exploring the town square, had been changed. Corrupted. A thin line of tears welled at the bottom of my eyes.

Killian's hand landed softly on my shoulder. "Shh, there now. It's alright." The warmth in the guard captain's voice did some work to help thaw my nerves. "You have people here for you, Rose. You're not alone."

My lip quivered as I turned to face the red-haired young man next to me at last. His words of support meant a great deal to me, more than I could have said in that moment without outright sobbing. "I…" I didn't get far before I had to stop myself, feeling another swell of emotion. Without speaking, I rested my head on Killian's shoulder. I physically couldn't begin to say what was troubling me, but his presence by my side was a comfort in itself. He wrapped an arm behind me in a hug, saying nothing.

We sat there together in silence for a few moments longer, gathering our thoughts. The river flowed ahead with a consistent *fwoosh*. Killian laughed to himself. Turning to me, he asked, "Do you think Archibald will have gambled away his clothes by the time we get back?" I laughed at the thought. Kil grinned. "I'm serious! One time before, the old fool managed to gamble away the bedding for every bunk in our entire barracks! Although… he *did* manage to win it all back later that day, plus all the cookware in the kitchens, somehow. But, wouldn't you know it," Killian said with a chuckle, "he lost it all again trying to secure himself a free helping of dessert for a month."

By the end of his story, I was laughing so much that I was snorting through my nose. My face hurt from how wide I was smiling. Soon, the attack I'd had was behind me. There was still a lingering sense of dread in the back of my mind, but speaking with Killian, I was able to function as I normally did. "Thank you, Kil." It felt like a weight had been lifted off my shoulders.

The charming captain looked at me. "Anytime, Princess." He smiled.

In the distance arose the sound of people angrily shouting. I furrowed my brow, looking around Killian to try to see if I could get a clearer visual. It sounded like it was coming from one of the gates. "What do you think's going on over there?" I asked, suddenly intrigued.

Killian was likewise curious. "I'm not sure."

"We should go check it out." I stood. Any doubt in my mind from before had been replaced by an equal mix of interest and concern at the clashing voices down the way. Someone could be in danger. With my powers, I was obligated to help. Before Killian could object, I was already making my way through the alleys, heading towards the shouts.

The voices were indeed coming from one set of the city gates. Two massive stone towers with a lattice of heavy steel between them. Dark green ivy crawled down from the towers like sprawling green fingers. I took note of this in the back of my mind. Usually, as was now, the steel gate was raised high so that throngs of people could enter the city freely. Although, as was now, so many people often needed to conduct business in the city that there was usually considerable traffic on the outside.

There was a relatively small courtyard just beyond the entrance of the gate where people could disperse once within the city. This stone clearing was where Killian and I emerged from the alley. A fair number of people were milling about, completing their daily responsibilities, but compared to the central square we had been in previously, the area was practically depopulated. As Kil and I investigated further, two polar opposite figures appeared behind us.

"What'd we miss?" Archie whispered to his captain. His voice carried the hushed, shrill tone that I immediately knew meant he didn't want me to hear and realize the two had been gone. Even though they were behind me, I could *feel* Jules roll her eyes at her sibling's poor attempt at a coverup. Luckily for the portly guardsman, my attention was focused elsewhere at the moment. I'd found the source of the shouting.

Each city gate was always stationed with at least six guards: a pair atop each tower and two on the ground stationed by the gate itself. It was the two guardsmen on the ground who were responsible for the noise. The guards, clad in their amber-colored armor and helmets, were standing imposingly over a small, skeletal man. Something about this didn't feel right. As I approached, the harsh voices of the guards began to take on clearer words.

"How many times do we have to tell you this?" the guard to the right of the man said angrily.

"Leave, *now*," the guard to his left spat. "Or we will make you leave."

The small man flinched at the threat. "Please, I'll give you all I have," he begged. "We were in Belora. We didn't have time to get supplies. My daughter needs medicine. If I could just get..."

The guard on the right shoved the man, hard. The frail father fell backwards, nearly tumbling over. "That's it," the guard raged. The two closed in on him.

I'd had enough. My face was red with anger. "Leave him alone!" I shouted at both of the guards, walking swiftly forward. Killian tried to get me to stay with a quick call. I didn't care. I kept walking.

The two guards stopped their approach, turning towards me. The father had just enough time to take a few frightened steps back. One of the guards sighed. "Great," the other guard said to his partner. "Another one."

I walked within feet of the guards. Their treatment of that poor man made me livid. I wasn't even thinking. "What would make you think it is okay for you to treat someone this way? Have you no honor?"

The guard on my left grunted hotly. "Listen, *girl*, the regency council has prohibited anyone fleeing the east from entering the city. It's that simple."

The guard on my right chuffed in agreement. He leaned closer to me. "What makes you think *you* can talk to *us* like that, eh?"

My blood was boiling. I collapsed my open hand into a fist by my side, feeling something loosening within my gut. In a flash, a vine of ivy shot down from the top of the gate tower. The vine wrapped around one of the guard's helmets, quickly yanking it off with such force it hit the stone ground and bounced away.

The newly revealed guard's face wore an expression that was an equal mix of confusion and embarrassment. He didn't look that old, about the same age as Killian. He had boyish hair that flopped over his eyes. Just then I thought, *What gives this person the idea he can push around someone twice his age?*

The still-helmeted guard stammered a little. "Princess Roserené?" he asked, not believing the heir to the throne would make an unannounced visit to a simple gate check. The young boy guard in front of me looked at his partner, then whipped his gaze back around in disbelief. He too quickly knelt.

I scowled at the two men. They had learned humility too late. "I will speak to you however I like." I had to hold myself back from spitting at them. "Not because of my blood. But because you are dogs. You are beneath me." I pointed a finger at the accosted father who was still standing nearby, looking at me with wide eyes. "You are beneath this man. He does not deserve your contempt or fear. I have seen things that rightly deserve both. Things you would never wish to imagine." This was the first time I had spoken of what had happened at the Last Palace out loud. But these two men were acting just so absurd to me. "This is a fellow man! He deserves your compassion, by the gods!" I breathed out, trying to regain some semblance of control over my speech. Turning my gaze back to the father, I softened. "Go, retrieve what you need for your family, by the grace of the Crown Princess."

The small man's eyes immediately welled with tears. He clasped his hands together in front of him. "Oh, bless you, Princess," he said. He took my hands in his. "Divines and Elders both! Bless you!" I smiled as I watched the father stumble deeper into the city, clearly out of his element.

Behind me, a man cleared his throat. "Erm, Princess Roserené?" It was one of the gate guards. The one with his helmet still on. "May we rise?"

I spun, anger reignited. "No," I said, my emotions getting the better of me. "You stay there and think for a while." Leaving the two guards to their fates, I turned and began walking away from the gate, back into the depths of the city. My stomach still burned with fire. I had to make this right.

"Princess?" Killian inquired after me. My three friends had been huddled together, watching my conversation with the guards, ready to step in if needed. "Where are you going?"

"To speak with the king!" I shot back at him, not even turning.

Appeal to the Heart

XXVIII

I'd found Percival where I knew he was going to be. The large wooden door to the council chambers was too heavy for me to throw open with one hand, but I still managed to get it to swing all the way on its hinges with an angry shove. The council had not been in session since Percival told them the story of Venerus; they had refused to come back. Now the king was situated around the carved table of Lungalea with his highest-ranking generals, looking at various different papers.

I stormed into the chambers. "A complete ban on entering the city?" I slammed my hands on the table, glaring into my brother's eyes. Royal tradition would have been appalled by my behavior. But I was appalled too. "They are your own people, Percival! They're being treated like animals!"

All the eyes of the generals in the room shifted from me to my brother. The young king returned their gazes awkwardly, surprised. The crown he was wearing fell slightly lower on his head. Percival returned my look fiercely, trying to hide his frustration from the generals. "Excuse me for a moment," he told the aged faces around him. Standing, Percival gave me a look that let me know how displeased he was. I was so frustrated I didn't care. At least I had his attention.

I followed Percival into the hall. There were people walking about to and fro within the palace, but the halls were so wide a pair could have a conversation fairly privately. Once the door to the chambers had closed again, Percival began, irritated. "Rose…"

"This is absurd," I fumed. I was pacing, not knowing any other way to burn off my anger. "How could you let this happen?" I snapped at my brother.

"It was an order of the council, passed while we were imprisoned," Percival explained. "Pevincy tried to resist, but he couldn't do it by himself."

I shook my head in disbelief. I was really beginning to hate the entitled lords of the regency council. Still, that couldn't have been everything. "You're the king," I reminded my brother. He needed to start acting like it, for the good of his own people.

Percival looked at me, suddenly on unstable footing. "Please don't ask me to go against the council, Rose," he said warily.

I scoffed. "What good would it do?" I motioned to the doors to the council chambers. "You've already gone back to playing general. It's like you don't even care about the people."

My brother glared, hurt at the insinuation. "Of course I care about them. I think about every single…" Percival stopped himself, hearing the rising emotion within his voice. He rubbed his eyes, clearly frustrated. "After everything we had gone through, I had hoped you would finally understand," he said quietly, almost to himself.

"Understand what?" I responded bitterly. I crossed my arms.

"That we are in a war, Rose." Percival looked me. There was a dreadful finality to his voice. "You now understand better than most the real enemy we face. I'm focused on war more than anything because I *have* to be. If I don't, there won't be anything else."

My brother's tone shook me slightly. The terrible glow of Venerus' eyes reappeared in my mind. For the first time, my fury was replaced with another emotion: fear. The air felt colder.

Percival noticed the shift in my stature. "I'm sorry." His voice was softer. I knew he didn't intend to frighten me. With another sigh, Percival began again. "I *do* think about my people, Rose. Night and day. But you've seen this city yourself. The entire island is covered. There's just no room."

I shrugged. This whole problem seemed to have an obvious solution. "Then why don't we just expand the city off the island?"

Hands on his hips, Percival shook his head. "It's not that simple. The council would never approve of expansion. The city's been on this island for over one thousand years; the tradition is deeply ingrained. Besides, using their own funds for eastern refugees?" Percival scoffed sadly at the idea. "They would never go for it."

He didn't seem opposed to the idea. I pushed him. "Percival, that council is *awful.*"

My brother looked at me. "Yes," he said matter-of-factly, as if I had just pointed out that the sky is blue.

"But *you* aren't," I reinforced. "Your heart is so big. I saw it when we were captured. But that council crushes that heart." Percival and I often fought about his rulership, but I never doubted him as my brother. "The best kings have the biggest hearts. It's what makes them look after their people, not just *rule* them. Listen to your heart, Percival. Council be damned."

I could tell my older brother was thinking about what I'd said. His ocean-blue eyes were moving in the rapid, slight way that showed his thoughts. Finally, he sighed again, closing his eyes. "I'm sorry, Rose. But I just can't take my attention away from the war right now."

I was so close, I could feel it. "I'll do it," I practically blurted.

Percival cocked an eyebrow. "You'll do it?" the young king asked skeptically.

"Sure I will." I had to think quickly on my feet. *What was I getting myself into?* "Assign someone to watch over me if you want. But I can oversee construction of the city outside the island." *What was I doing?* I nodded, throwing off the voice in my head. My *gut* told me this was right. "I'll make a house for every person outside of those gates."

"I don't know," Percival began, unsure. He rubbed his chin. "You're still quite young."

I furrowed my brow, determined. "Didn't you say you wished I'd grown from our recent experiences?" I asked, throwing my brother's words back at him. "*This* is my growth. I'm not just a little child anymore. Let me prove it. You can manage the war, and I can see to it that all those people outside will have homes."

A concentrated look appeared across Percival's face as he looked down at me. "That..." he began slowly, unsure. "That is actually a good point," he conceded. My brother breathed out through his nose. He nodded slightly, confirming his decision. "I will see what can be done," he said to me.

My spirit swelled. I wore the biggest smile I could remember as I wrapped my arms around Percival. "Thank you!" I cried repeatedly. I was practically buzzing. Already, ideas for planning the city expansion were running through my head. I had occasionally been given duties to perform around the palace, but nothing ever this big. My mind was on fire, but one thought was above all: that those people outside were finally going to get the help they needed. I hugged my arms around Percival tightly. "This is what you get when you listen to your heart!" I said, happily and excitedly tapping his chest.

Percival couldn't help but smile. "Alright, you're welcome," he responded, almost bashfully. I could feel my brother try to pull away lightly.

I held onto him a few moments longer. I couldn't help it. It felt nice, like how our relationship was before our father's death. With one last squeeze, I let the king out of his hug. I stepped back. Still smiling, I did my best to restrain my excited energy, looking as refined as a Crown Princess should.

My brother put a hand on the door to the council chambers. He turned back to face me, a slight grin on his face. "I'll speak with you later," he said.

Smiling from ear to ear, I nodded. Only after Percival had reentered his meeting and the door had closed with a hard thud did I let my excitement reemerge. I began jumping up and down like a giddy little girl. It was unbecoming of a princess, but who cared? For the first time in my life I was going to be able to help so many people. I ran off down the palace halls in search of my three friends, eager to share the great news.

Percival

The Astronomer's Watchtower

XXIX

"You wanted to take me to a tower in the middle of nowhere?" Delilah asked. She sized up the structure in front of us. To be fair to her, lit by silver moonlight, it didn't look like an ideal destination from the outside.

The Astronomer's Watchtower had been built on the outskirts of the woods surrounding Lungala centuries before. A massive telescope the size of a large room sat atop an intimidatingly large, round pillar of stone. The identity of its creator had been lost to history, but for generations after they became a memory, the tower attracted scholars from across the realm. Masterful lens craft and intricate metalwork combined so that the watchtower offered a glimpse into every Celestial Realm in the night sky. The height of the monumental construction combined with the door it opened to the untapped heavens made it my favorite place in Lungalea.

However, in recent years, the tower had fallen into disrepair. When we were children, my mother and father would take us on clear nights to learn about the stars. After my mother's death, though, my father's attention turned elsewhere. Fewer and fewer minds flocked to the observatory as maintenance became infrequent. By the time I came to the throne, I hadn't visited the tower in years, nor had anyone else. The outside showed patches of missing stone and bare struts.

"It's not just *any* tower," I informed Delilah, taking her hand as she walked through the entryway. There were no light sources within the watchtower, but that didn't impact us all that much. The observatory had a domed ceiling made of glass. On nights with a full moon, like tonight, there was enough light that Delilah and I could see our surroundings unaided.

The inside base of the tower was littered with wooden boxes and scattered science equipment. Moth-eaten sheets lay across the wooden floor haphazardly. Delilah sucked in the air through her teeth. "Well, Percy, I won't say that I was expectin' *more...*"

I laughed softly. Shaking my head, I pointed upwards. "Follow me." A marble staircase that spiraled all the way up the length of the tower began to the room's side. Delilah close behind me, the two of us began to ascend.

"You're sure no patrols will be by here?" Delilah asked as we rose. She looked over the stair railing, down the considerable distance we had already climbed. "On my last trip inta the city with Da, there seemed to be more of them than usual. They seemed to be looking real hard for something."

Knowing what Delilah was referencing, I began reassuringly, "Don't worry, I know who's patrolling where and when. Even if the man they assigned out here *does* come by, he's a friend of mine." Pevincy had increased city guard patrols both within and just outside of Lungala in his revitalized search to find the traitor in my court. My Justiciar had insisted on covering even beyond the city gates, believing the traitor could be leaving the town limits to relay information. The section containing the Astronomer's Watchtower was patrolled by Bryce. I had arranged for it. Subtly, of course, so as not to arouse any suspicion. Yes, it wouldn't be ideal if Bryce *did* catch us, as I would have much explaining to do for both my friends, but I was confident he would keep the relationship secret if I asked. Even then, no patrol was supposed to be out this far for hours. Delilah and I had our privacy.

Delilah shrugged. "You're the one with the information." She put faith into my answer.

Quietly, the two of us climbed the rest of the way, our heads craned up to see the stars through the glass ceiling. The stairs ended in a wide, flat, circular room mostly devoid of any internal decoration. The only notable artificial feature was a stand situated in the side of the room outfitted with cranks and levers of various sizes. The room, however, was far from boring, as the domed roof was completely filled with stars, so much that it appeared to give off its own faint glow. The full moon was high in the night sky, shining down on the two of us. Copper bands interspersed with glass lenses of varying sizes intertwined with each other, creating a fine web of metal built into the ceiling.

"Wow." Delilah put her hands on her hips, looking upward. "*This* is better."

I couldn't help but grin. "*This* is nothing," I said, walking over to the stand with the levers. There was a thick layer of dust coating the entire console, accumulated from years of disuse. I blew out a long breath, but the dust still clung to the handles, so I summoned a small local air current to make my gust more forceful. With a fresh cloud of dirt hanging in the air, the console was operable once again. Doing my best to remember how the operations worked from when I was a boy, I began turning various levers.

With a metallic clunking, the bands of the telescope holding the lenses in place began to move around the glass ceiling. Slowly at first, then picking up momentum as I turned the crank. The entire telescope was one big mechanism built into the room, the operational components connected to tracks that wound around the boundary. The lenses moved around the ceiling, crossing and overlapping with each other. Finally, the correct positioning of lenses had lined up, pointed at the moon.

The heavenly body appeared ten times larger within the circular lens on the ceiling. Intricate veins of gold created a fine lattice spanning the pale moon's surface. Every detail was enhanced, sharpened. It had been so long since I had been in the observatory, I had forgotten what effect the great telescope had. Looking at the serene moon, I was struck with the same awe I had as a child. It was as if I could *touch* it.

I only had a faint sense of what Delilah was thinking. Her amber eyes sparkled in the reflected light of the ceiling. She raised her hands to cover her mouth. "Gods above," she said, breathless. Smiling at her wonder, I walked from the telescope console to the center of the open room where she was standing.

"There's more," I said softly. Again, the bands on the ceiling began to move and shift. The clunking returned. Delilah looked at me, confused. "The whole system is on a timer," I explained, lying. In reality, I was using the wind to move the gears of the telescope into position so that I could still be next to her.

The lenses on the ceiling began to overlap, one on top of another. Soon, there was a different object within the round sight. A pinkish-yellow orb took up the entire lens. Bands of red clouds floated in silent harmony along the surface of the Celestial Realm. White lights interspersed with purple flashes danced across the sphere at its top and bottom.

Delilah recognized the Celestial body on sight. "Rayanna," she gasped. Her hands drifted down to her heart as if to still her breathing. Tears of overwhelming emotion welled at the edges of her eyes. I knew I had made the right decision bringing her to the tower, though, because she was wearing the largest smile I'd ever seen. Delilah's eyes glanced down to me, back up to Rayanna, back down to me. "Percival, this…" she attempted, but she didn't get far before covering her mouth again. I was heartened. For the first time since I'd met her, the huntress girl was speechless. All I had to do was show her the stars.

As Delilah simply stood there in the pink and purple light, she was the most beautiful person I had ever seen. Her shining hair rolled off the back of her shoulders with her head craned up. Her sharp facial features accented her expressions with shadow, and like lanterns her amber eyes seemed to light up the darkness. Gathering all my courage, I wrapped my arm around her waist, pulling her closer. She glowed with a soft smile. I wanted to kiss her more badly than I had wanted anything ever before. As I leaned in, something stopped me, a voice in my head. *If you do this, everything from here on will be a lie.*

I stopped just short of Delilah's lips, cursing myself. I knew the voice was right. I wanted to pursue my relationship with Delilah, but I couldn't keep lying to her, for either of our sakes. The time for me to make a decision had come: tell her, or end it here.

Delilah noticed the pained look on my face. "Percy?" she asked, lightly concerned. "What is it?"

Just then I felt like I was torn between two words. Two conflicting aspects of myself were clashing within me: King Percival, who must always put duty before everything else, and Percy, the boy who wanted to live a normal life. I sighed in defeat. It was time. "Delilah, I'm not…"

The signs were almost imperceptible. The air at the base of the tower was disturbed three distinct times. What sounded like a light breeze shifting through the stones soon became clearer. My ears picked out the sound floating faintly up to us: whispers. We were no longer alone there. *That shouldn't be*, I thought. The patrol wasn't due out here for hours yet, and that was just Bryce. Yet as the air shifted around below, I was now certain. There were three people in the tower with us.

"Percy, what's wrong?" Delilah asked, nervous. My silence from before couldn't have helped her ease, but I must have let slip on my face that there was now a new problem.

Silently, I brought a finger up to my lips, looking at Delilah. *Quiet*, the expression said. I pointed to the base of the tower. Slowly, I crept down the spiral staircase, investigating the noise. Delilah followed closely. We both shrank low behind the railing, hiding from any figures we might encounter.

As we descended, the voices became distinguishable, and the intruding figures came into sight on the tower's wooden lower floor. There were indeed three: two gruff, armored men stood facing us, while a third, smaller figure spoke to them. The third figure had their back turned to the staircase, so I had no way of distinguishing any features about them other than that they were wearing a dark cloak. Delilah and I quickly ducked when we saw the men, luckily managing to avoid detection. The three sounded engrossed in their own conversation.

"... a big gamble letting them escape," one of the gruff men was saying. He looked like a soldier; there was a large scar over his left eye. The man continued in a harsh voice, "He could have ended the war there and then."

"I never agreed to that," the cloaked figure countered. The voice sounded younger, and there was something familiar to it. "I gave you Percival and his siblings on the sole condition that they remained unharmed. A public execution wasn't in the plan."

My blood turned to ice as the realization dawned at once. The traitor to my kingdom was standing *right in front of me*. If I could only find out their identity without revealing myself. A spy would likely flee if confronted.

"Plans change, kid," the second, muscular man retorted. He had half a head of flowing black hair, and the other half of his skull was completely shaved. "Now, are you going to tell us what we came all this way for?"

The cloaked figure sighed, almost reluctantly. "Everything went exactly according to plan. Percival completely discredited himself with talk of Venerus. The council won't even see him now. He's completely isolated. The attack on Barra can happen without any forces intervening."

The man with the scared eye grunted, unconvinced. "You seem awful confident in the boy's situation for someone in your position."

"I know how he thinks," the hidden figure responded. His voice had a tinge of annoyance at the man's slight. "I'm his best friend."

I stood at once, not even aware of my movement. "Bryce?" My mouth hung open. *I'm his best friend.* The figure turned, cloak falling from his head.

My oldest friend stood there looking back at me. Bryce looked exactly as he had when I'd last seen him, just earlier that day. His recognizable dual swords were attached at his hip. His black hair hung low over his scarred eye. My friend didn't look any different, only he was now standing next to two of Ahaax's men. "Percival..." Bryce stammered.

The two men behind my friend chuckled. "Well, look at what we have here," the man with the half-shaved head remarked.

I was reeling. None of this was making sense. My head was buzzing ferociously as I tried to steady myself. "It was you?" I asked Bryce, trying to find the words. I stumbled from the staircase towards the center of the room. Towards Bryce. Surely this was just a misunderstanding. He would never betray the kingdom. "What...?"

"Percy?" It was Delilah. She rose on the stairs, her voice uneasy. "Who are these people?" She looked over Bryce and the two rebels at the door. With sudden horror, I realized I had inadvertently brought Delilah into the hands of two enemy soldiers.

Bryce glared at Delilah. "Percy?" he asked, confused. He looked back at me. I could see the thoughts running through his head. Finally, in a low, almost detached voice, he began, "This is where you've been? Every time you've neglected your duties as king these past months..." Bryce couldn't seem to believe what he was saying. "You've been running around playing pretend with *some girl?*"

Delilah's face turned pale. "King?" was all that she said, weakly. I turned to face her, my gut dropping like a stone. Watery eyes looked back at me like I was a complete stranger.

"You want to know why I did this, Percival?" Bryce continued, anger rising in his voice. He pointed at Delilah. "That's why! Because I couldn't stand to see the kingdom fall into the same trap it has for decades! My father served a crown that ruled decisively, that wasn't held back by noble politics. And when he tried to return the king to the ways of ruling, that crown killed him."

I was frightened to my core. Every word Bryce said revealed that this wasn't just some misunderstanding. My best friend had been betraying me deliberately for months. *Please stop*, I wanted to plead with him, to salvage something of who he'd once been.

Bryce looked at me, his eyes filled with a betrayal of their own. "I thought you would be different," he said with something almost resembling *hurt* in his voice. "But you haven't ruled for a single day since you took the throne."

The two enemy soldiers were starting to look bored. "Well, this is all very emotional," the one with the scarred eye began. "But I think you two will be coming with us now."

The half-shaved man chuckled darkly in agreement. "A routine message run, and we brought back the kingling… and a pretty girl." He grinned a half-toothed smile at Delilah. "Lord Ahaax will surely reward us for this."

The two men approached, stopping only short of Bryce. The dark-haired boy's jaw clenched, as if he were hesitating. My best friend looked at me, green eyes filled with anger. Finally, "Take them," he ordered. The words hit me like a physical punch in the gut. I struggled to move, my feet frozen to the floor.

The man with the half-shaved head approached Delilah on the stairs. "Come here, girl," he said, sickly, reaching out an arm.

"Get away from me!" Delilah shrieked. In a flash, she jabbed the man's nose with a punch, backing farther up the stairs.

The attacking man staggered. He put a hand to his face; when he pulled it away, it was covered in fresh blood. "You bitch!" he shouted in pain. Pulling a knife from its sheath at his waist, the shaved man resumed his advance.

At the sight of the blade, I reacted on pure instinct. *Delilah*, I thought, panicked. I snapped out of my paralysis. My arm rose, blue arcs of lightning running up and down its length. A concentrated bolt of pure energy shot forth from my palm, striking the man with the knife on his side. The force of the blast sent the man through the wall of the tower. When the dust cleared seconds later, there was a gaping hole six feet wide where stone had been moments before. The man was nowhere to be seen.

Bryce and the surviving soldier flinched, both tensing. They each turned their eyes to me. Bryce unsheathed both of his swords, and the scarred man took off a long blade that had been resting on his back. At that moment, I didn't care about either of them, though.

Delilah was panting heavily beside the gap in the stone wall. Her eyes were wide with shock. She looked in disbelief at the opening, then turned towards me. She was wearing a mix of emotions and adrenaline. Her mouth opened and closed a few times, unable to find words. Then, without another thought, she turned and jumped through the new stone opening, running into the night.

I threw up a hand after her. "Delilah, wait!" I cried.

"Don't let her escape," Bryce commanded his ally. The scarred soldier grunted in acknowledgement and began to chase Delilah into the darkness through the hole.

"Wait!" I lunged after the man but was caught in midair by another body colliding into me.

I was thrown to the wooden ground, pinned by a foot standing on my chest. Bryce lowered his two swords to my head. "I'm sorry, Percival," he said, looking down to meet my eyes. His voice was strained but sincere.

Like that mattered. From that moment on I saw Bryce for the traitor he was. Someone whom my father had treated as a third son, whom he had taken in *after* the boy's father tried to murder him! My family had given Bryce a home, food, and training for half of his life. And he had gone and spat on that legacy. He spat on the memory of my father, spat on our friendship. And now, he was preventing me from helping the woman I loved.

"*You,*" I growled at the man who had once been my closest friend. My body was literally shaking with all the energy building up inside it. All I had to do was touch Bryce's chest with my open palm and his body went flying across the base of the tower. I sprang to my feet. For a moment I was tempted to lunge after Bryce, to inflict on him *my* pain. But I turned my head back towards the stone opening in the wall I had created. I needed to get to Delilah.

Channeling the winds, I leapt into the air, flying through the jagged hole. It was a warm night. Once outside of the tower, I flew higher to get a better view of my surroundings. Luckily the full moon had clearly illuminated the scene. Delilah was running in a full-blown sprint away from the tower towards the woods. The scarred man with the blade was frighteningly close behind her and appeared to be gaining.

I directed the winds to propel me towards the two of them at top speed. Flying low to the ground, I was able to grab the hem of the man's shirt in my hands, lifting him up with me. "Get away from her!" It was a booming voice that wasn't my own. Holding the man by the collar in front of me, I didn't care where I was flying. I just needed to make sure Delilah was out of harm's way. With the air rushing past my ears, I felt the man's body impact a solid surface in front of me, but I was able to keep flying like nothing happened. A second later, we flew through another, equally hard wall of rock. Turning back around once we were clear, I could see that we had just flown straight through the Astronomer's Watchtower.

I drifted back to the ground, dropping the scarred soldier's limp body. My entire body felt numb. I was panting hard, unable to stop. Then I heard a twig snap from behind me. *Another attacker.* With a guttural shout, I spun on my heel, my fist cocked back, arcing with lightning.

Delilah's small frame jumped back from me, terrified. I would never forget the look on her face. It was worse than anger or confusion. It was raw *fear*, and she was looking directly at me. Tears spilled from the huntress' eyes. She stammered, "*What* are you?" Turning, Delilah ran as fast as she could into the dark forest.

I extended a hand after her. "Delilah, wait!" I breathed, pleading. I paused. Something about my hand caught my eye. Turning my wrist around, I saw my palm. It was shaking and stained with red. I brought my arm in and looked down at my other hand. They were both red. I gasped in startled shock. *What had I done?* I had killed two men without even *thinking* while doing it. It was just a reaction. In my nine months of war, taking a life had never been a simple response. The way Delilah had looked at me—like I was a *monster. Was she wrong?*

Heavy breathing sounded in the tower doorway behind me. Without turning, I could feel Bryce lean against the entry by the displacement of the air. "This is what happens,

Percival," he breathed through gritted teeth, "when kings refuse to rule."

The fire inside me roared back to life. *One last problem,* a voice in my head spat bitterly. I clenched my bloodstained fists. In a flash, I spun and launched myself at Bryce, blue lightning shooting off from me in all directions. He couldn't possibly have reacted in the time I closed the distance between us. I grabbed Bryce's throat in my outstretched hand, flying us both upwards inside the Astronomer's tower. Any doubt in my mind about my previous actions was gone just seeing my enemy's face. *I can kill one more,* I thought, my vision pure red. *So long as it's him.*

Bryce slashed at me with one of his swords as we ascended. The blade cut through the surface of my cheek, causing me to drop my foe in surprise. My old friend tumbled through the air as he fell down the tower. I wasn't going to let him go, flying through the air and grabbing his shirt. I delivered a swift, electrically charged punch to his gut. Bryce gave me a swift kick in return. Charging a blast of lighting from my arm, I sought to deal a final blow, but Bryce avoided the bolt by dodging at the last moment. The missed beam of energy exploded upon impact with the wooden floor. At the bottom of the tower, a fire broke out, likely triggered by the wooden floor and loose sheets.

The two of us traded equal blows as we fought. I would climb in the air higher and higher, and Bryce would pull me down, using the momentum to make himself rise. The fire at the base of the tower had grown rapidly, soon engulfing more than half the structure. With a strong punch to the eye, Bryce knocked me off balance just enough to where we both were nearly engulfed by the rising inferno. Smelling singed hairs, I was enraged by the near miss. I choked Bryce's throat in my hand, gripping as tight as I could. My old friend swung one of his swords back, aimed at my head. At that second, a rumble shook the entire structure of the tower. The air superheated. In split-second dread, I guessed the flames must have reached the tower's ancient, stored reserves of lamp oil. A searing fireball explosion shot throughout the structure. Bryce and I were both caught in the blast, each of us sent crashing through the glass roof of the ancient telescope into the warm night sky.

I came back to consciousness a few moments later, a searing pain shooting through my left leg. My eyes opened groggily. Every sensation I had was one of pain, from dull aching to intense burning. I was lying surrounded by stone ruins, the only light from scattered flames burning through the grass. The Astronomer's Watchtower, or what was left of it. Nothing more than a circle of stone five feet high remained where the magnificent observatory once stood. I thumped my head on the damp ground, feeling like I could weep. My favorite place, gone.

Mustering what little strength I had left, I tried to stand. Pain so sharp my vision turned black was the only response I received. Buckling, I immediately fell to the ground. I looked down. My left leg was lying under a piece of stone debris up to the knee. I tried to pull myself backwards in an attempt to get my leg free, but I was met with a similarly painful result.

I sucked in the air through my teeth, trying to absorb the pain as best I could. I looked around. Standing a few feet to my right, looking at me solemnly, was Bryce. He was holding one of his swords in each hand by his waist.

My instincts took over again. I raised my fist at the traitor, willing lighting to flow through me once more. A few sparks fizzled from the tip of my hand, but nothing else. I gasped, completely exhausted. Trying to pull myself free again, I came to the sickening realization that I was trapped. Bryce watched my efforts in silence. I glared at him indignantly. "Go ahead, *traitor*," I spat. "Kill me. Just do it then."

Bryce took a moment before responding. I couldn't tell what was going through his head, but at the moment his face made me so sick I didn't care to even try. Then, the young man sheathed both of his swords. "I never wanted to hurt you, Percival," he had the nerve to say. "But the old ways are dead. We can't be buried with them." With that, Bryce turned and silently walked out of my line of sight.

Furious, I tugged at my leg again, ignoring the pain. I had to get free. Had to get Bryce. He needed to see *justice*. I desperately shot an open palm towards the piece of stone on my leg, doing everything in my power to channel a force of wind that would blow off the debris and free me. This was similarly useless, and the exertion caused my vision to go dark.

Frantic, I whistled loudly through my teeth. "Apolion!" I shouted at the top of my lungs. "To me!" It was a long shot. I knew he couldn't get there in time. Whenever I was with Delilah, I ordered my dragon to stay miles away. I didn't know for sure if he even knew I was in trouble until I called him. "Apolion!" I shouted again desperately, deep into the fiery night.

Nothing Left

XXX

Not a single voice spoke in the council chambers. The revelation of the traitor's true identity hung in the air like a noxious cloud. I was breathing though my nose hard, both from rage and pain. My knee had swollen badly from the injury I'd sustained. The pain was manageable as I was sitting on my throne, but I needed a crutch in order to walk. Apolion had managed to free me from the ruins of the Watchtower, and we'd flown back to the palace immediately, already having wasted enough time. The first thing I did when I touched foot on the palace grounds was order the city guard to scour every road, every back alley for that traitor. I didn't even bother trying to convene my council, instead summoning the only people I thought I could still trust.

"Bryce?" Rose said softly across the table from me. She and Davit were both still in their pajamas. My sister shook her head, distraught at the idea that someone so close to us personally could be working for the enemy. *Could be* the enemy.

"I should have known," I spat out, hating myself. It was the truth. My blindness and sentimentality put the entire kingdom at risk for a length of time that was still unknown. I did the one thing kings weren't supposed to do. I gave in to my emotions.

"No, my king," Pevincy objected by my side. He looked at me fiercely. "Bryce was my steward in my care. His treachery falls upon *my* shoulders." I could tell the betrayal of his pupil hurt Pevincy deeply, but the elder statesman was able to mask his emotions well.

I swatted aside the attempt to placate me. "Your steward, Pevincy," I acknowledged. "But he was my *friend.*" The word tasted like bile in my mouth. I didn't even know how much of it was the truth. Did Bryce ever even care about me? Regardless, nothing could make up for my failing to see him for who he really was.

The room fell silent once again. We were all deeply shaken, unsure where to go. Rose was the one who ended up giving voice to this uncertainty. "So, what now?"

It was an intimidating question. One I didn't have an answer to. There were so many things I needed to be doing at once, but at that moment I felt like I was the most powerless man in the kingdom. I dropped my head, defeated and without a response.

"Is there anything you learned from your encounter, my lord?" Pevincy asked, probing. "Anything at all that could give us insight into the enemy's plans?"

I didn't have to try hard to think back to the confrontation with Bryce. It had never ventured far from my mind. Thinking of our fight only threatened to swell the barely restrained anger within me, but something he'd said to the two soldiers before he knew I was there returned to my mind. "Barra," I remembered. It was like a spark had reignited in my head. I looked at the other three faces around the table. "He said they were going to attack Barra." I had recounted the conversation I had overheard before our battle. The news of an oncoming attack on the largest city within the Golden Desert darkened everyone's faces. Mostly.

"That's great!" Davit exclaimed, exuberant. Every pair of eyes turned to my younger brother. I glared, not in the mood for his humor. "Well, I mean, not about the attack *exactly*," Davit clarified. "But doesn't anyone else see the opportunity here?" He glanced around at our faces. No one did. *What could he possibly be getting at?*

Davit continued. "Think about it. Ahaax is going to attack Barra either way. You're Ahaax. You're winning the war. You're on a roll. Suddenly, you capture the three royal children! *Great!*" He clapped his hands for emphasis. "But then they manage to escape. That's not great. For a rebel leader, that's catastrophic, and threatens the stability of your entire uprising. So you need to do something that will restore faith in your leadership. Hell, I'd bet those goons who were here to get information from Bryce probably weren't even specifically for planning an attack. In your story, Percival, Bryce said the real plan was to convince the council that you couldn't rule. *That's* how Ahaax salvaged our escape. He used it to destabilize your leadership. Even *if* Bryce manages to sneak past the guards, he doesn't have a griff or any other way of travel besides foot. He won't get back to Ahaax for a month at least. All of this is to say, regarding attacking Barra, Ahaax had already made up his mind." Davit crossed his hands over his chest. He wore a satisfied expression.

All of us looked on in stunned silence at my brother. Somehow, he had managed to make perfect sense based on excellent military deduction. My brother, who until a few weeks prior couldn't hold a sword properly. "Alright," I began, skeptical. "What is your point?"

Davit's eyes widened, like he couldn't believe the rest of us couldn't see what he was getting at. "My point is, for the first time in this entire war, *we* now know where Ahaax is going to hit next. *And* we know he'll probably do it in a few weeks. That gives us just enough time to evacuate the city and plan a counterattack for *him* to fall into!" Davit's eyes were practically glowing. "Don't you see? For once, *we* have the advantage!"

I furrowed my brow, concentrating. After everything we had been through, Davit was finally starting to make some sense. I glanced at Pevincy to see if what I was hearing was true.

The elder knight rubbed his chin. "He's right," Pevincy concluded. He turned his gaze to me. "The council lords would never lend their troops now, but if you muster portions of the palace and city guards, Your Grace…" My Justiciar nodded. "Combined with a summons from the city of Barra itself? We could have twice the numbers of Ahaax, judging from what you relayed from your time in the Last Palace."

"Then it will be an even fight," I said darkly. "Let us not forget, Ahaax wields the power of an Elder Dragon."

A chill fell over the room. "All the better to plan ahead," Davit chipped in.

I gazed at my brother. It was hard not to feel a little proud at the contributions he had made. "How did you get such an understanding of logistics?" I asked, slightly humbled.

Davit shrugged absently. "I don't know. You kept me locked in my room for six months. I couldn't use a sword, but I could read." He crossed his arms again, slightly bitter. "*A lot.*"

A plan had started to form in my mind. I began doing the internal calculations of troop movements and supply lines, already running through the elements of the defense of Barra. I leapt at the opportunity to try to focus on another topic besides Bryce, even if it was still consistently clawing at the back of my mind. Thinking of his face continued to stoke the fire of rage in my heart.

"Alright." I cut off my internal thought process before I could go further. I turned to Pevincy. "See it done."

. . .

Later, as night slowly turned to morning, I stood in my chambers, watching the rising sun from my balcony. I couldn't sleep. My body was still constantly aching, my leg throbbing. And every time I closed my eyes, I saw either Bryce or Delilah's face. I clenched a fist at my side, leaning on my crutch.

"Is that *all* you have to tell me?" I asked through teeth gritted from annoyance and pain. I turned away from the sunrise. Pevincy and two city guard captains had assembled in a line before me. "That you *haven't* found him?"

"We're sorry, m'lord," the portlier of the two captains said. "We've searched everywhere. It's possible he's already fled…"

"Search harder!" I said loudly, losing my patience. I approached the two captains, getting close to them. "I don't care if you have to look behind every door in the city. Do it! I want that traitor brought to me in chains!" The two captains shrank back, rooted to the ground. What were they doing wasting time standing there? "Go!"

The captains quickly filed out of my chambers with a "Yes, m'lord," each. Breathing heavily, I watched my door close with a profound sense of frustration. Bryce couldn't have fled the city yet. They just weren't looking hard enough. They would find him.

I noticed a figure in the corner of my eye. "I'm not in the mood for one of your lessons, Pevincy," I sighed in exasperation. I had realized I may have been forceful with the guards, but they needed it.

"I'm not here for a lesson," Pevincy said softly. His graying whiskers shone lightly in the dim morning rays. He leaned backwards, propping his hands on my dresser. "I just thought you may want to talk."

I rolled my eyes. The old guard was dangerously close to overstaying even his welcome. "No. If you haven't noticed, I'm very busy."

"You haven't been sleeping," Pevincy mused, sounding like a parent correcting a child who didn't know any better.

I snapped. "Well, what would you have me do?" I almost shouted at him, turning. The hand not using my crutch dropped to my side in exasperation. "Honestly, Pevincy? What would you have of me? I'm damned when I'm the king. I'm damned for trying to escape the crown!" I huffed, storming across the room. My eyes fell onto my dresser on the far side, where resting was my royal crown. I clenched my fists at my side. I hated that crown. It symbolized every chain that bound me. I wanted nothing more than to unleash a pure, concentrated blast of lightning onto it, melting it into a bubbling puddle. And yet if I did, I would lose one of the last things that connected me to my father. My fingernails dug into my palms.

"I'm fighting a war with only palace troops at my disposal. None of the lords on the council designed to help me come of age are actually interested in me ruling…" My voice rose. Everything I was feeling was becoming too much to control. Anger found its way into my voice. Anger at the world.

Anger at myself. "I am the most powerful king in the history of this entire land," I lamented, "yet I cannot even fight back against a murderous tyrant."

Then a thought entered my head. I laughed grimly to myself. "Perhaps I *should* become my enemy." I thought back to my fight with Bryce. His father served a crown unrestrained by tradition or morals. A crown Ahaax would have returned. And Ahaax was currently winning the war. "Perhaps I *should* become like Oriond, or Ahaax even? Perhaps the king *should* have his own gang of violent enforcers? Perhaps he *should* imprison his own lords without cause? Perhaps…"

"He should search behind every door in the city to find one traitor who's already fled?" Pevincy completed for me.

I scowled at the old guard. Pevincy went on. "You could do all those things, Percival. You're correct. You are already stronger than any king who has come before you. You could unleash your fury on the people of your kingdom with the justification of fighting Ahaax. You could become a god. But you won't do those things, because it's not who you are."

I huffed morbidly. "I don't even know who I am anymore."

Pevincy nodded. "Aye, I know." He continued. "The conflict you're describing is one within yourself. I've known you since you were a babe, boy. Do you think I haven't seen you struggle with your duties since coming to the crown?" He stood from his leaning position on the drawer, approaching me. "You're torn between two selves. The king. And Percival. Duty, and heart."

I shook my head. "A king should be separated from his emotions." I recited the foremost lesson I had been taught many times. "My father instilled that within me."

Pevincy sighed. "Your father was a *great* man," he said firmly. "I will regret until my final day that it was he who left this world before me." The wizened man in front of me paused, as if debating what to say to himself. "But even Arturus was wracked with doubt all throughout his rule."

My eyes widened. "What?" My father had always appeared as resolute as a statue when he sat upon the throne. How could he have doubted himself?

"Arturus was well aware of the restrictions two thousand years of history had put on the crown," Pevincy continued. "He had seen the kingdom change around him, and how the crown had failed to keep up. His entire reign was a constant struggle within himself. The question haunted him: respect the crown, or honor the people?" Pevincy shook his head sadly, remembering a good friend. "He was wiser than I could ever hope to be. He always wanted to go further. To expand what it meant to *be king*. Even until the very end."

I was taken aback. To know even my father struggled with the weight of the crown... I wondered how he would have thought in my situation. I was wracked by a pang of sadness when I couldn't ask him. Would he have listened to his council? Or would he have done what was right for the good of the realm? "But..." I began. A lump was threatening to rise in the back of my throat. I did everything I could to prevent its advance. "Every time I have tried to be something... *other* than the king it ended badly for everyone involved." Delilah's horrified face flashed back into my memory.

Pevincy looked at me sadly, his hands clasped together at the waist. "I'm sorry, Percival," he said in a soft, sympathetic voice. "That isn't an ill that can be cured by ruling."

Tears swelled in my eyes. It was an almost alien feeling. I nodded, not expecting an answer that would make up for losing the two people closest to me. "It's just..." Everything reached a breaking point. The lump in the back of my throat caught my voice as tears fell from my eyes. I thought of Bryce's face, but not during our fight. From before. When I called him friend. He was smiling. "Why did it have to be him?"

The tears came forth all at once. Pevincy brought me in swiftly for a silent embrace. The man I had come to know as a second father held me so tight I thought he would never let go. I shook as the sobs wracked my body, deep wails coming from within. I don't remember how long we both stood there in my chambers, but neither of us said a word. I only cried endlessly in a mix of anger and heartbreak at a cruel world, and Pevincy held me the entire time.

Davit

Come Final Night

XXXI

Rose and I ran together through the palace halls. Morning rays of sunlight shone through the windows, interspersed evenly by the rock of the walls. It had only been two days since we'd found out Bryce was the traitor. Everything within that time had happened so fast. Almost immediately, Percival mobilized half of the palace and city guards, preparing to begin the march for Barra. I had thought everything was going to plan, though, until Rose knocked ferociously on my door early that morning, waking me up. She was nearly frantic. Percival was leaving without us.

The two of us ran as fast as we could from our wing of the palace. As my lungs began to hurt from the pace, it was one of many times I cursed the palace for being so damn large. Luckily, our journey was a straight path. We knew where Percival would be. It was where he went whenever he left the palace.

My sister and I each threw open a door to the palace courtyard, panting hard. Percival was adjusting the saddle on a nearly flight-ready Apolion, surrounded by Pevincy and the rest of the green-armored knights of the King's Circle. The heads of the knights turned to us at the booming sound of the doors opening. Percival didn't turn. He continued adjusting his dragon's saddle, back to us.

"Percival, wait!" Rose shouted breathlessly.

"After everything, you're still just gonna leave us behind?" Anger dominated my voice between heavy pants. I put my hands on my knees, catching my breath. The palace really *was* too large. "What's this supposed to be, anyway?"

Percival sighed. He said something I couldn't pick up to his knights. The five helmeted soldiers aside from Pevincy approached us as Rose and I got closer. Percival turned. His face was flat, not really portraying any distinct expression. He looked like his old self. "This is *war*." My brother looked at both me and Rose like we were children.

That was it? I thought, incensed. "So what? It was war fighting in the arena! It was war when we were running from an honest Elder Dragon! Gods above!" My arms flopped to my sides.

"We're coming with you," Rose said, softer but just as determined. She looked into my brother's eyes sympathetically. "Let us be by your side, Percival."

The young king's face hardened. "No." He turned away, conflicted. There was something about his voice just then. A crack. Percival sighed again, continuing. "I've lost enough of those I hold close to me. I won't lose you two as well." He turned to the head of the King's Circle. "Pevincy, monitor these two closely until I return."

"What?" I protested.

"Percival!" Rose cried.

Pevincy's face looked pained. "My lord…" he began.

Percival shot him a stern look. "I command you, Pevincy." His mind had been made up. "As your king."

The old guard captain sighed, defeated. "Your will be done, my lord." With a glance at the Circle, an armored man and woman took both Rose and me by the arms, leading us firmly but not painfully back to the palace doors.

"Percival, let us help you!" Rose called to our brother as the distance between us grew. She pulled against the armored woman holding her wrist.

I was similarly struggling uselessly. "He has an Elder Dragon, Percival!" I shouted, trying to at least reason with my brother. "You need us!"

It didn't do any good. My sister and I watched helplessly as Percival gave a few final orders to Pevincy, climbed onto Apolion's saddle, and launched them into the golden morning sky. As the large dragon quickly became the size of a bird on the horizon, I was filled with a deep dread. The knights brought us into the palace, and the massive wooden doors closed once more.

They put me and Rose in a random sitting room situated in a tower in the royal wing of the palace. Our guards walked us into the room, then briskly departed, closing and locking the wooden door behind them with a heavy *clank*.

"Damn it!" I slammed my fist against the door, cursing both the guards and Percival for his stubbornness. I pulled hard against the handle for no real reason. I knew even if I was able to somehow get through the iron lock, there were two palace guards stationed right outside.

Rose was pacing. She rubbed her chin. "We need to think of a way out of here," she thought out loud. "We need to get to Percival."

I propped a leg against the wall for better leverage, pulling back with all my might. *What else was I supposed to do?* "Really?" I called out the obviousness of my sister's statement through strained teeth. I pulled again. No luck. "How?"

Rose thought deeply, her brow wrinkled. "Perhaps we could convince the guards to let us out somehow?"

My hands slipped off the door handle from exertion. I would have completely fallen backwards on my butt if I didn't regain my balance, swinging my arms around frantically. Back on two feet, I sighed. Getting through that door was hopeless. "What are we gonna say?" I turned my gaze to Rose. "'Help! My guts are melting, the cure is across the kingdom!'?"

Rose scowled. "This is serious, Davit," she said, cross. Turning away from me, she went back to her thinking. I walked through the room, crossing my arms out of frustration. *There had to be some way out of here!* I just needed to think outside of the...

A window on the far side of the room caught my eye. I was struck with a terrifyingly brilliant idea. Walking over from my point in the room, I was able to look through the glass panes, downwards from our position in the tower. The royal palace had originally been constructed with even blocks of marble, but throughout its thousand-year history, some of those blocks had eroded to become jagged and edged. Combined with the occasional windowsill and buttress... I grinned at my own genius. We were probably one hundred feet up in the tower. But we just might be able to climb down.

I turned to my sister, still thinking hard across the room. *Time to make the hard sell*, I thought. "Rose, I know you don't like heights..."

She looked at me uneasily. She already knew what came next. She knew me. Her face turned slightly paler. "Please, don't say..."

"But..."

The climb down from the tower was tense, even for me. If it wasn't a life-or-death situation to save my brother, I don't think I would do the experience again. The foot and handholds we had available were incredibly narrow and jagged. While actual constructed elements on the palace walls like windowsills *did* help, whatever relief I got was limited, since they were usually carved and rounded with no edge to grasp.

As bad as the climb down was for me, I knew it was *much* worse for Rose, who I had to spend the better part of five minutes just convincing to climb out of the window. My sister was practically frozen above me, clinging desperately to the marble wall. I would shout up the occasional encouragement to keep her going, but when my foot or hand would slip at just the slightest wrong position, I sometimes found it hard to be supportive.

Somehow, I eventually got low enough on the wall where I could jump to the ground. I misjudged my height and fell a little harder than I meant to, but I was just grateful to be back on solid ground *alive*. When Rose caught up with me, she stayed crouched low on the ground for several moments, her eyes closed, muttering prayers of thanks.

"That's alright," I said, standing awkwardly. "Let it all out."

Rose breathed hard. "Sometimes I really hate you, Davit," she moaned.

"Everyone does," I said reassuringly, patting her back. "Come on. To the courtyard."

In a stroke of astounding luck, there were only two people in the courtyard that early in the morning: two palace guards. Unfortunately, they were standing in front of what Rose and I desperately needed: our dragons.

Cerulia and Redwood were both in their adjoining stables carved into the courtyard rock wall. Each of them looked similarly anxious: stamping their feet, unable to sit still. The two dragons both tried leaving their dugout wall, but one guard each was stationed just outside the entryway, using a dulled wooden spear they would point at the dragons every time they tried to sneak out. (More Cerulia sneaking than Redwood. My sister's colossal dragon was so large he would walk towards the guard and get poked in the nose.)

The treatment of the dragons made me angry. Only *I* could poke Cerulia when she was being annoying. I started towards the two guards, but Rose held my arm. I looked back at her, confused. She pointed in front of us.

Pevincy was walking swiftly out of the palace doors, looking similarly upset. "What do you two think you're doing?" he boomed at the guards, making them both shrink back as if the dragons were now their second worry.

"The king's orders, m'lord," a guard skinnier than a branch replied, startled. "'Keep the dragons calm!'"

Pevincy brushed them aside. "You're not calming them, you're scaring them!"

"*We're* scaring *them*?" the second guard peeped out.

The head guard huffed angrily. "Go!" he commanded. The two palace guards ran off quickly, holding their poking sticks. With the speed and eagerness they left with, they were probably glad just to get away from the dragons.

Pevincy walked up to the winged creatures calmly. Each dragon looked at him with analytical eyes, observing every detail in a way they hadn't with the two guards. "I apologize for them," the elder soldier said to them both softly. Pevincy looked at Cerulia and Redwood unlike how most people in the palace did. He didn't look at the dragons with fear or with a detached awe—more like how you see an old friend.

Redwood and Cerulia each lifted their heads. Pevincy turned to see what had gotten their attention. Rose and I were approaching our mentor cautiously, unsure. Ultimately, he was still an agent of the king. We didn't want to do anything to Pevincy, but we both wordlessly held the same understanding: nothing would stop us from getting to Percival, not even the man who was like our second father, no matter his orders.

"I would deeply regret it, Pevincy," Rose trembled. She brought a hand up in front of her. "But I can have you waist-deep in this ground in a single second." Her voice faltered. Would we really have to go against *him*?

Pevincy looked at us with caring eyes. He wore a soft smile. He laughed lightly to himself, like he was pleasantly surprised. Then he looked back at us. "Go to him."

Rose dropped her hand. The muscles in my body untensed. "Really?" I asked the old knight, arms falling to my sides. "Just like that?"

Pevincy held his kind smile. He nodded. "I have taught Percival all I can in what it means to be king," he told us with a sigh. As he looked at Rose and then myself, I could see a faint glimmer of pride in the guard's eyes. "You two must teach him what it means to be *human*." He shook his head, sure in his way. "If the king sees fit to punish my actions on his return, so be it."

Rose and I looked at each other, then back at Pevincy. We both smiled. The old guard took a step closer. All three of us took the others up in an embrace. Pevincy hugged us firmly. "Come back to me," the knight ordered. He looked down at my sister and me. "All three of you."

Rose smiled up at him, looking determined. "We will," she said.

"Promise," I chipped in.

With one last squeeze, Pevincy stepped aside and let the two of us saddle up our dragons. It was actually the first time I had saddled Cerulia since I had bonded with her. It was much easier now that I wasn't trying to self-sabotage. Knowing we were already behind on time, Rose and I promptly took to the skies on our respective dragons.

Flying high, it wasn't hard to spot what we were looking for. "There!" Rose cried over the air, pointing. Her finger was directed at what looked like a layered line of ants leaving the city. Percival's army.

I took up Cerulia's reins. "Come on!" I said to my sister.

"Davit, wait!" Rose held me back. I paused before I could fly Cerulia down to the army below. Rose continued. "We should follow them. Wait until they're at Barra. That way Percival can't just send us back."

Having not even thought of that, I nodded in agreement. "Smart!" I shouted over the wind to my sister.

So, for the next two weeks, we trailed Percival and his army as it marched across the kingdom, always flying just out of sight. Supplying ourselves for the duration of the trip was relatively straightforward. You're a lot more believable when you say you're the prince and princess when you have two dragons standing behind you. Townsfolk across our travels recognized us instantly, asking how they could help. They even offered us rooms in inns on the nights the army was camped near a town. Discreetly, obviously.

Finally, after fifteen grueling days of marching at top speed, the king's army had arrived in Barra just after the sun had set. Admittedly, being the largest settlement in the Golden Desert wasn't that big of an achievement, but you wouldn't realize that by looking at the city. Barra was a giant patchwork of orange adobe buildings stretching for miles across the sand. Lights within the city at night lit the desert for as far as the eye could see. The Great Lake Oressor ran horizontally to the east, making Barra feel coastal despite its being hundreds of miles inland. The lake was fueled in part by a river that ran around the city to its north. A great dam stood halfway between the town and the lake, diverting some of the river water for the people.

As we flew over the city, the streets were eerily deserted. *Already evacuated*, I realized. The only signs of activity in the sprawling desert metropolis were concentrated around the city center, where Percival's army had set up camp. Riders on the backs of griffs ran in and out of various city blocks, relaying messages between the chain of command. Baggage trains and multiple tents of varying sizes had been set up in a large pavilion below. One tent of emerald fabric laced with gold thread stood out. If Percival was to be anywhere down there, it was likely in there. There was also the slight hint of the golden figure of Apolion sleeping just behind the same tent.

The soldiers on the ground quickly scattered to make way for our landing, largely due to Redwood. Confused voices arose as Rose and I dismounted. Apolion raised his large head drowsily, cocking it when he saw us. Cerulia and Redwood both walked over to their dragon companion, nuzzling him upon arrival. Rose and I turned toward the emerald tent. Without further delay, we walked through the half-open flaps.

Percival was indeed in the tent. He was seated at the head of a small wooden table draped with maps of the city, flanked by a couple of his generals. My brother looked up at our arrival, eyes widening when he saw the two of us greeting him.

"Surprise!" I feigned happiness, arms crossed. "Don't get too excited now. We wouldn't want to chase you across the continent again."

Percival stared at us in stunned silence. He couldn't seem to comprehend what he was seeing. After a few moments processing the scene, he let out a strained, "Leave us." No one in the room moved, neither me and Rose or the two generals beside Percival. I think both of us thought the king could have been referring to the other. My brother turned his gaze to the two wizened warriors beside him. "Now," he said forcefully. The pair of generals quickly shuffled around the table and out of the tent, not wanting to draw the king's fury.

Our older brother turned his gaze towards Rose and me. His face morphed into one of equal parts confusion and anger. "How did you two...?" he began, exasperated. He thumped a fist lightly into the wooden table. "Damn Pevincy," he cursed. Percival began moving towards the two of us. "Ahaax's army will be here within the day. There isn't much time..."

Rose and I both took steps back as he approached. Our sister raised a scolding finger. "Don't you dare send us away again," she warned. Percival stopped, hesitating.

"Let us help you," I appealed to my brother. "We know what we're up against."

"No you don't!" Percival snapped, shouting. The young king caught himself. He paused, face softening. "Davit," he said with a defeated sigh. His eyes were closed, but not out of frustration. He looked pained. "In the last nine months of war, do you know how many men I have killed?"

It was an odd question, one I wasn't expecting. Before the last few weeks, Percival had rarely ever spoken of the war with me. I would have never expected him to be so blunt. I had no idea what to say. High? Low? "I…"

"Thirty-three," my brother confirmed for me. His voice was distant. He didn't say it like it was something to be proud of. "I remember every face." Percival paused. He looked at me with a level of consideration I had never seen from him before. He continued, "I do not regret my actions, because they were taken in defense of my home and my family. But killing should *never* be just a reaction, something you go charging off to do. It… changes you—in little ways or large may depend, but once you take a life…" Percival looked at me and Rose, his eyes as deep as oceans. "You are forever changed.

"I kept you away from the war for so long because I'm terrified of what it will mean for you both. I saw how you changed after we returned from Ahaax's imprisonment. We were lucky to escape that encounter alive and as relatively unharmed as we were. I…" Percival choked on his voice, pausing with emotion. Clearing his throat, he went on. "I failed to stop that. But I wouldn't fail again. I *won't* lose you both."

My body felt strange, my hands sweaty. Percival's look had shaken me. Hearing my brother, who I had grown up with, talk about killing was an uncanny feeling. He wasn't even sixteen years old, yet he was speaking like a veteran back from campaign. His voice was laced with regret, not at what he had done, but at what could have been. It made me reconsider my goals. For the past nine months, I had *dreamt* of killing Ahaax with my own hands. It was only just, after all. But looking at Percival after he spoke, I wondered how I would feel if I had gotten what I wanted.

"Percival." It was Rose. She began next to me, her voice caring and sincere. "The only way you could ever *lose us* is if you keep pushing us away. Whatever may happen in this coming battle: win, lose, rise or fall, we do it *together*." She placed two clasped hands over her heart. "Since you came to the throne, you have been too busy being king; you haven't been *Percival*. We all lost our father when this war began, but Davit and I?" Rose motioned to me and herself. "We lost a brother too." Percival's face fell. His eyes turned to both of us, looking deeper than our faces. Rose began again. "But these last few weeks? In these life-or-death scenarios, you were *him* again! Come what may, I say truthfully, I would rather die beside my brother Percival than see him be consumed by the king. We're by your side, come Final Night."

Percival's gaze drifted to the table absently, lost in thought. "When all is dark," he whispered the end of the saying. The king turned his attention to me. "Do..." He looked for the words. "Does she speak for you as well?"

I was equally impressed by my sister's moving words. Turning my shocked expression from her to my brother, I wiped the look from my face. "I mean, she said it better, and with less cursing." I shrugged. "But the message was mostly there."

"I..." Percival began. He looked at the table, arms propped against it. "I see now." Like he was doing calculations in his head. He brought his gaze back up to my sister and me. His voice took on a stronger, surer tone. "I have failed you both. As a king. As a brother. I'm sorry."

We both closed in around our brother. "Oh, *shut up*, Percival." I brushed him off as Rose and I both embraced him.

"Just don't ever leave us again," Rose said, tightening her grip.

Percival laughed softly. "Never," he promised.

And maybe get a sense of humor, I thought, but decided not to ruin the moment and be happy with the more emotionally present King Percival.

Standing there in our embrace for a few moments longer, even I had to admit it felt nice. It felt like I was with my two siblings again before all the violence and conflict of the last nine months. It was really nice.

"Well, if you two *insist* on staying here," Percival began, unwrapping us from his grip. Our brother turned his attention back to the wooden table in front of us. "I suppose I could enlist you to help prepare. There is a question that has been confounding all my best minds: what to do about Elder Venerus? Despite our numerical advantage, we don't have any way of countering an Elder Dragon besides the three dragons of our own." Percival sighed, looking at both my sister and me curiously.

Rose was looking on in an uneasy silence. Something Percival had said must have caused her to drift off somewhere. I, however, was wearing a devious grin.

"Actually," I began. It was an idea I had been mulling over in the two weeks of our journey. I knew a confrontation with Venerus was unavoidable, so I knew we needed a way to even the field. My mind combed through all the books I had read on desert warfare, but then the idea struck me like a child with a match. I remembered our last time in the Golden Desert. Looking at both my siblings, I said, "I have a really, really, *really* crazy idea."

The Battle of Barra

XXXII

The approaching army appeared as a line on the horizon under the midday sun. The desert heat was scorching as it rose off the golden sand. My siblings and I were standing together in a line, just in front of a formation of royal palace guards numbering about five hundred in total. We were situated on a sandy plane, the city of Barra to our left, the waves of Oressor on the right. Trenches hastily dug out around us spanned our line of sight, reaching towards the city. Rose and I had both been fitted for armor within the army camp the night before. My sister had managed to secure a sleek set of black light plate armor, while all I had acquired was a silver and emerald brigandine. Sure, I was protected, but I didn't feel *nearly* as fashionable.

Percival watched the enemy army approach between me and Rose with a looking glass. My brother was clad in his gilded royal armor, enough to keep him protected, but not too much so he couldn't be agile. Just then, a soldier on griffback rode up to us. He reined in his mount. "Your Grace, the warriors of Barra are in position," he said to Percival.

The king nodded, still gazing through the spyglass. "And the boltcasters?"

"Primed and calibrated, my lord," the soldier confirmed.

Percival lowered the handheld telescope, looking at the royal guardsman on the griff. "Good man," he said, sending him back to the gathered soldiers behind us. Our brother sighed, uneasy. "There's still no sign of Venerus." We each looked up at the clear blue sky. There were hardly even any clouds. "I don't like it," Percival continued.

I was similarly nervous at what I couldn't see. There was a consistent dread in my gut, like I was steadily approaching a terrible outcome. I looked down at my waist. Where a sword in its sheath would usually hang was a silver canteen of water with a flip-off lid. I had been practicing summoning Ísilor the night before, and I had become pretty reliable in my time. Cerulia was only a few hundred feet away back in the city. With my sword and dragon, I felt unstoppable, but still, the doubt nagged. I couldn't help but feel like all the planning in the world couldn't match an Elder Dragon's might.

The approaching army had advanced until they were a couple hundred feet from our soldiers. As they came into view, I could see the majority of Ahaax's army was made up of lightly armored foot soldiers. Tactically, they weren't that large of a threat, but they made up for it by wearing an intimidating snarl on seemingly every face. Towards the back of the formation were a series of large, heavily reinforced, rattling cages. I gulped as the beasts within became clearer: at least two dozen pacing hookclaws, and next to them, what I instantly recognized with a shiver as the wrinkly claws that had grabbed at me in Ahaax's keep. *Mournwings*: large, humanoid batlike things with skin like leather that lurked in the southern mountains.

Then, the enemy stopped. Only a single figure continued walking towards us. The three of us standing in a line recognized him instantly, even if we couldn't see his face directly. "It appears they'd like to parlay," Percival observed, nodding in the man's direction.

"It's a trap," I cautioned my brother. He wanted to lure us away from our men.

"Most likely," Percival agreed. He looked at me confidently. "But we have a few traps of our own, don't we?" I saw what I thought was a glimmer of pride in my brother's eye when he mentioned my battle planning. His look filled me with resolve. The three of us walked forwards.

Ahaax stopped ten feet from us. He looked unchanged from when I'd last seen him a month before. The warlord was wearing the durable yet light red and black armor he had worn on the day he murdered our father, and on the day he captured us. His large black sword extended from its sheath on his back. He wore a confident, almost bored expression. A look that made him appear as if he were in total control. The pompous expression ignited a blaze within me.

Ahaax looked around the three of us at our mass of troops. His eyes widened slowly in mock surprise. "It appears my informant has been discovered," he mused flatly, as if he were just now seeing the army for the first time. The false king turned to my brother. "I *do* apologize for that," he said without a hint of sympathy in his voice. Only malice.

Percival glared. "Rest assured, he will see justice the same as you," he said in a commanding tone. A swift breeze blew through the air from behind us. My brother went on, "Your forces are outnumbered. I will give you only one chance, Ahaax. Surrender."

The warlord glared at the king. "Surender? Why would I possibly do that?" His voice carried a dulled anger. "You three at least are now aware of the power I *truly* possess. You realize how outmatched you truly are. Your *offer* is an insult." Ahaax shook his head. Black eyes turned to each of us. I felt a mix of anger and fear as two holes drilled through me. "I did not expect you three to be here, but the gods have seen fit to grant me this boon. You will never have my surrender. And *I*, children, *make no such offer.*"

I could feel all the moisture being pulled from my skin into the air. The familiar buzzing returned to my head, concentrated directly upwards. The blue sky filled with black clouds within seconds. Streaks of lightning shot in all downward directions at once. And the lighting was red. "Incoming!" Percival shouted to our soldiers behind us.

The next few seconds were a single, rushed blur. The titanic, dark shadow of the Elder Dragon Venerus broke through the black storm clouds. With a scream that shook the ground, the Elder launched a stream of magenta electricity from Their gaping maw through the assembled soldiers behind us. *Man shall once again know fear!* Venerus' unforgettable, bone-chilling voice forced its way into our heads. Most of the guards had managed to leap to safety into a nearby trench, but some unfortunate men were too slow to escape the bolt. Ahaax lunged at Percival with his fiery blade. My brother deflected the attack with his spear, beginning a duel as the three of us rushed back to our troops. Ahaax's army charged through the plain towards our men with a bellowing roar. They would clear the difference to the first line of trenches in only a matter of seconds. The forces of the kingdom braced themselves for the assault.

The two armies clashed with a thundering *crunch* of wood and metal. I ran through the first line of guardsmen. I couldn't stay to fight yet. Everything had to go exactly to plan. As I ran to get a clearer position, I pushed aside the thought that the plan itself was only half assembled and fundamentally crazy. Nothing else mattered. Adrenaline was pumping through me. I completely lost track of Rose, Percival, and even Ahaax.

Venerus made a swooping turn in the sky in front of me, preparing to make another pass at the soldiers on the ground. I came skidding to a halt in the sand. My attention lowered towards the edge of the city, towards a line of four wooden constructions that looked like large crossbows on rotating stands. *Boltcasters.* I whistled as hard as I could through my teeth: alerting the caster crews of their rapidly approaching duty. *That's one*, I counted off in my head. Venerus roared another monstrous sound as They swooped in low over the city. Clanking into position, the boltcasters lined up their shots and fired.

The Elder Dragon opened Their mouth, but before another catastrophic bolt of lightning could come forth, two weighted steel nets wrapped around each of Their giant wings. With a surprised screech, Venerus spun through the air, crashing hard into a soldier-less patch of sand adjacent to the battle, forming a large, deep crater. A massive cloud of dust shot into the air as a result.

I couldn't celebrate being the first person in history to get an Elder Dragon shot down, though. I knew it wasn't the end. Not by a long shot. I whistled strong through my teeth once again. *And that's two.*

With a mighty roar each, our three dragons flew into the air from their hidden position within the city—the element of surprise no longer needed. In a flash, the dragons were above the battle. Cerulia quickly landed on the sand next to me, growling into the crater. Redwood and Apolion were both hovering over the Elder Dragon still struggling in Their nets. Simultaneously, my siblings' dragons unleashed an onslaught of elemental breath into the crater: Redwood smokey fire, Apolion lighting colored brilliant blue. I had to cover my eyes, the light the attacks created was so intense.

The two hovering dragons continued their blasts uninterrupted for multiple straight seconds. I was beginning to think that we might have gotten lucky for once: that no living thing could survive an assault like that. Suddenly, Venerus' enraged head shot up from the crater, snapping at the two dragons attacking Them, causing them to fly backwards in retreat. Cerulia and I jumped back from the crater's edge as Venerus clawed out with their wingtips, not looking any weaker, but definitely looking angrier.

Venerus turned Their gaze down from the air to me and my dragon. Their blood-red eyes were filled with fire. A pit miles deep formed within my gut for two reasons. The first was because an enraged Elder Dragon was looking directly at me. The second was because I knew I now had to resort to the *really* crazy plan… and hope it went for the bigger target. *Come on*, I told my terrified self, *hold*. It felt like an eternity, but it couldn't have been more than a single second before the giant head of the Elder lunged straight for me, jaws wide.

Reacting on the buzzing instinct within me, I was able to throw myself backwards just in time, managing to send Venerus' head into nothing but the sand. The impact sent a resounding *thud* throughout the ground. *Excellent*, I thought, almost subconsciously.

Cerulia chirped in alarm from the other side of Venerus' head. She made eye contact with me, and the thought was instantly communicated. The little blue dragon pounced on the sand around her, and then she began to jump quickly and repeatedly. The impacts were definitely smaller than the Elder Dragon's, but they resonated throughout the sand all the same. "Atta girl!" I encouraged my dragon for following the plan.

Venerus brought Their head up from the sand, Their teeth barred. Again, the Elder snapped jaws larger than my body into the ground where I had been just moments before. Another resounding *thud*. I could feel the displaced air blow through my hair as I landed backwards in the sand, scrambling. Venerus brought Their head back again. *Come on*, I thought, unsure if I could avoid a third attack. *The battle. Cerulia. Venerus! Surely those have to get something's attention.*

In that moment, it was as if my thoughts were answered by the gods themselves. A resounding *boom* shook the sand behind me. Turning, I saw mounds and mounds of dust flying into the air. Something was rapidly approaching from beneath the ground. I frantically jumped out of the oncoming beast's path.

A second later, the sandy ground exploded in a cloud of dust. A massive dunewyrm the color of clay launched itself into the air. Venerus didn't have time to respond to what was happening before the wyrm, at least twice the size of the one that had attacked us before, wrapped itself around the stunned Elder. Venerus shot out lightning, but the wyrm's hardened skin seemed to be resisting the worst effects.

I pumped my fists up and down from pure adrenaline watching the two colossal beasts clash, my dragon next to me. The plan worked! It *actually* worked! The dunewyrm constricted around the thrashing Elder, emitting a guttural cry. The sand beneath me began to sink as the wyrm burrowed underground, attempting to drag what would be its prey along with it. Rapidly shifting my attention to make sure I was not included with the two, Cerulia and I scrambled out of the expanding crater. As we reached the edge and turned around, I saw Venerus' struggling head attempt and fail to resist the wyrm, the extent of the Elder's body slipping beneath the sand.

The crater was hauntingly quiet. I stood there for a moment in stunned silence, panting ferociously. The sounds of battle and clashing soldiers were behind me, but they were faint in my ears. I couldn't shake the feeling. Despite it all, *it still felt too easy*.

Suddenly, an explosion of sand and lightning sent Cerulia and me flying backwards. I don't know how far I flew, but I landed face down on hard sand, ears ringing. My dragon quickly recovered, running to my side. With her assistance, I staggered to my feet, everything in pain.

The large, obsidian-black head of Venerus was looking down at me. The Elder Dragon was shaking, either from anger or exertion I couldn't say. *Plan failed*, I thought with dread. Even worse, I had no more plans remaining.

Looking down at me with pure rage, the colossal dragon *spoke*. Not in my head. "**Sarfoss ke Veneer sha...**" the Elder Dragon growled with a sound that physically shook my entire body. I had no idea what it meant, but as Venerus craned

Their head, the back of Their throat lighting up with magenta crackles, I wondered, did it really matter?

The Elder was interrupted for a second time when a bolt of pure blue lightning hit Them on the side of Their head, resulting in a moderate explosion. They roared in frustration. Percival, on the back of Apolion, flew into my line of sight. My brother pointed his bronze spear at the Elder Dragon, shooting another blue missile of electric energy. "To me, monster!" my brother shouted, his voice carried by the wind.

Venerus turned away from me on the ground. *Insolent....!* the familiar skeletal voice cursed in my head. Slowly, the Elder Dragon unfolded Their two giant wings, black as night. The air generated by Venerus taking to the sky felt like the wind during a storm. Dazed, I stood watching as Percival and Apolion rose higher and higher into the air, zapping with lightning the massive dragon right behind them.

I couldn't stand there for long. The sounds of shouting behind me quickly redirected my attention. I turned, getting a sense of the battlefield. Our forces had gradually fallen back into a wide *V* formation towards the city as they resisted the advancing enemy army. Palace and city guards blocked and slashed at both man and beast alike. Hookclaws and mournwings scattered the field sparsely, picking off the occasional soldier where they could.

The epic fight between dragons had drawn a good deal of attention to where I was standing. As I turned from the crater back towards the battle, four of the enemy soldiers were running towards me, all looking equally large and angry. I reacted on pure instinct. My thumb flipped open the lid to the canteen at my waist, and I drew the water from within. Ísilor's blue blade was in my hand a second later. Clashing with the enemy soldiers, it was almost like my hands gripping the sword were moving on their own. I blocked a strike from the first man to get to me, parried his next one, and delivered a clean slash across his chest. The man fell to the ground and didn't get back up. I stood there for a split second, looking at the body. Something felt different then.

I couldn't reflect on my actions for more than an instant as a second approaching soldier swung his weapon at me. I slid under his attack with grace I had never before possessed. Turning, I slashed again, dispatching another foe. I made my way deeper into the battle, through each enemy. Ísilor's magical steel was a blue blur around me. I deflected every attack, parried every other strike. Soon, I had a moment's reprieve, my immediate surroundings cleared of hostile soldiers. I looked down breathlessly at the weapon I held in both hands. *Orianna?* I thought of the Magus who had appeared to me in my dream.

Swiftly, I brought my head back up to check on the wider battle. The kingdom's *V* had grown deeper. Our troops were beginning to stretch into Barra itself. Ahaax's men pushed their advance further, greedily. The rebel soldiers shouted as they beat on the palace guard. I grinned. *It was time.* I unclipped a second object from the belt around my waist: a bronze warhorn carved in the shape of a dragon's head. I took the horn, blowing with all my might.

At the call, the sand behind the enemy army exploded in a thousand individual bursts. At once, a wave of Barran soldiers launched themselves from the ground, charging the foe from behind, unified by a single thunderous war cry. Half of Ahaax's army quickly turned. The aggressive shouts soon transformed into ones of panic and confusion as they became surrounded by our men. I grinned madly at the successful trap.

A group of three burly enemy soldiers had seen me blow the war horn. They all paused, angered. "Get him!" one of them shouted. All together the three men rushed towards me. I brought up Ísilor, feeling like I could conquer whatever the world could throw at me.

In a blur, my blue dragon had flown from above my field of vision and landed directly on the middle soldier. He cried out but was quickly cut short. Cerulia spun faster than I would have thought possible, snarling ferociously at one soldier and sending the other sprawling with her tail. With another tackle, the single remaining soldier was quickly no longer an issue. Cerulia pounced on her target one last time and circled back to me, cocking her head. My eyes widened. "Wow," I gasped at the ferocity of my dragon. "Don't get on your bad side."

A ferocious roar distinct from the Elder Dragon's sounded from across the battlefield. Cerulia and I both turned. Redwood arose from a group of kingdom soldiers, flying up higher and higher towards Percival and Apolion and Venerus. The Elder was viciously chasing after my brother and his dragon. Both dragon and rider would shoot their energy attacks at the monster, but it seemed to do little good. Percival needed help badly.

I turned to my little blue dragon. "Go to him," I told Cerulia. She looked at me reluctantly, her large eyes capturing the afternoon sun. I felt a pang of pain shoot through me, realizing I didn't want to send her away. I was conflicted; my brother needed all the help he could get, but I would be sending my little dragon to face an *Elder*. The irony was not lost on me that just a few months ago I would have done so happily.

I took Cerulia's head in my hands, resting my forehead on hers. Despite the ongoing battle, it felt like we were the only two in the world just then. "Go," I said softly, pained. "But come back to me," I demanded. My dragon leaned back on her haunches. She made a determined chirp. *Obviously.* With that, Cerulia launched into the sky, flying fast towards the thunderous battle above.

As I watched my dragon rise, I felt a hand grab my shoulder from behind. "You!" a voice shouted as I was pulled violently. Caught off guard, I tumbled onto my back. Ahaax swung his flaming sword towards me in a one-handed arc. On impulse, I brought up Ísilor, just barely casting off the attack. I rolled backwards, assisted by the seemingly magical reflexes my sword was giving me. Ahaax continued through gritted teeth, glaring at me with eyes that could kill. "*You* have been nothing but a debilitating *nuisance* to me since the day in the ruins!"

I stood, hunched in an attack stance. Here I was: with Ahaax, and a sword. Every emotion I'd felt in the past nine months swelled within me at once: anger, terror, sorrow. But one feeling rose above all else, strengthened by them all. *Determination*. Here he was, and I was going to *get him*. "Yeah," I said, low. "I have that effect on people."

The two of us charged. When we met in the center of the sandy plane, our blades clashed off each other in something that seemed as much a dance as it was a fight. Ahaax swung his orange blade to cut right through my midriff. I slid under, faster than he could anticipate. Delivering a swift kick to his shin, I knocked the warlord to his knees. Ahaax growled. He raised his free hand at me. A geyser of orange flames shot in my direction. I rolled out of the way, feeling the side of my face heat up uncomfortably quick.

Back on two feet, Ahaax pressed his attack relentlessly. I was taking more and more steps backwards, defending myself from his blade with mine. I was quicker than he was, but he was far stronger; I could tell with each blow. As he continued his assault, I wondered how much longer I could last against him. Ahaax raised his hand again and threw another fireball towards me. Panicked, I leapt out of the way… and landed in water.

I looked around, momentarily confused. On the ground, I was completely covered in water. *I was in Lake Oressor.* I smiled madly. Just from being in the water, I could feel my depleted energy return. My limbs felt lighter. I jumped to my feet. Ahaax growled at my rebound. He charged. Turning the tables, I flung my free hand at the oncoming warlord. A concentrated stream of lake water launched him twenty feet back, gasping and sputtering. I didn't let him catch a moment.

Launching myself upon a geyser of my own creation, I fell upon Ahaax with my blade. Left and right, up and down, I was breaking through his defenses. The warlord stumbled on his back foot in the shallow lake water, not expecting my second wind. I could tell by his face, *he was slipping.* I pushed my advance, harder and faster. *I could do this!*

Ahaax shoved back my blade fiercely with his own. "Enough!" he shouted. The strength of the shove was enough to momentarily stagger me, but not for long. Ahaax launched more fire at me. Spinning, I dodged and launched myself back to him. The warlord sidestepped my attack, grabbing my free arm. Before the panic of the moment could even set in, Ahaax delivered a swift jabbed strike to my face with the same hand in which he held his blade. My vision went dark as I heard a sickening *crack.*

As I staggered in a dazed pain, Ahaax held onto my arm tightly. I was thrown into the water, disoriented. Ísilor had fallen somewhere out of my hand into the lake. A second later, I felt a hard kick in my ribs. I coughed in shock and pain as I felt the bone break.

I felt around desperately in the water, trying to crawl away, looking for any help I could find around the battlefield. It had cleared substantially since I'd last observed it with detail. Our troops were surrounding the final troops of the enemy. I was able to see Rose for the first time since the battle began. She was fighting with her red sword against an enemy soldier, but it looked like she was managing to hold her own. I tried calling for my sister, but not even a whisper came out, and instead I felt a shooting pain throughout my chest.

Ahaax walked up to me slowly. I was in no state to fight back, crawling around blindly in the water. He could take all the time he wanted. I could feel the heat from his sword of fire on the side of my face. Ahaax began, "I will tear down the old order to create a new one, Davit. A better one, established on strength and the resolve of the will of those who *fight*." *Does he think I actually care about his speech?* The warlord turned his gaze to me. "And you would prevent that." His face was a mix of contempt and something almost resembling pity. Ahaax sighed, bringing his sword above his head. "Still… I *am* sorry for the way this had to end."

I was looking at my surroundings helplessly in the water. The three dragons and my brother were flying around so high above they looked like bugs clashing with a falcon that was Venerus. Rose was still fighting the soldier, but another had appeared as well. She was on the back foot, and there was a pacing hookclaw eyeing her nearby. Panic gripped me. I restarted my vigorous crawl through the wet sand, grasping for anything I could use to get out of this situation. Pain wracked my entire body, but I didn't care. Rose needed help. She needed *me*. Then, my hand landed on a familiar pommel. I groped around again, feeling the handle of Ísilor once again in my grip, half buried in the lakebed. The familiar energized feeling returned to me. My voice had a new strength. "I'm *not*."

Screaming at the top of my lungs, I put every measure of energy I had left into one last swing. Ignoring the pain, I turned, swinging upwards with Ísilor in both hands. I swung as hard as I could, giving it everything I had left. The blade made contact with Ahaax's flesh and continued, slicing clean through. The warlord screamed in surprise and pain, falling to his knees. His sword fell as well, still held in his severed hand five feet away.

I climbed as quickly as I could to my feet. My vision was going black in certain places, and I guessed I would be in extreme pain were it not for all the adrenaline in me at that moment. Staggered, I looked down at Ahaax kneeling in pain, clutching where his hand used to be. I held Ísilor in my grip. *I could kill him right here.* I looked back at Rose. Alarmingly, the hookclaw had closed half the distance since I'd seen it, circling my sister. She didn't have long. I had to make a decision.

With barely a second glance, I flung another hard spout of water at the incapacitated warlord, sending Ahaax stumbling deeper into the lake. *Rose*, I thought, my energy rapidly fleeting. *Nothing mattered but Rose.*

I did an equal mix of stumbling and running as I desperately approached my sister. She was fiercely holding off the two soldiers advancing on her, but it was only a matter of time before her defenses cracked. The hookclaw nearby still eyed her hungrily. With little warning, the large creature sprinted towards her. "Rose!" I did my best to shout. She couldn't even see it behind her.

Not thinking, I willed Ísilor to return to its liquid state in my hands. I launched the water as fast as I could at the hookclaw charging Rose. In midair, my blade reformed, plunging deep into the feral animal. Had I more sense at the moment, I would probably be shocked at this ability I had never before demonstrated, but now wasn't the time. I pulled my fully formed blade from the dead hookclaw and swung at the second soldier attacking Rose, slicing through his armor and sending him to the ground.

With a final *huff*, Rose's pierced the padded armor of the soldier she was facing with her blade. The man fell to the ground, unmoving. Rose looked at me, breathless. "Davit?" she asked.

I was panting just as hard. I tried to think of something to say to my sister, but just then a piercing whistle sounded across the battlefield. We both turned.

Ahaax had crawled his bloody way back onto the shore, breathing heavily. From nearby, two mournwings answered the warlord's call. The frightening creatures dropped the guardsmen they were prodding and flew to their summoner, taking one of his arms each in theirs. Struggling, the creatures managed to fly Ahaax some distance away from the lake, but his weight was too heavy, and he was dragged on the ground just as much as he flew. The mournwings dropped Ahaax by a harnessed griff, with one of his soldiers helping the wounded man.

"No," I wheezed, watching Ahaax escape. I made eye contact with him one final time. There was only one thing behind his black eyes as the rebel I had maimed fled from the battle: no annoyance, or pity, or even contempt. Ahaax looked at me with pure unfettered *hatred*. It was a look I returned.

I tried to run after the fleeing traitor, but I only managed to get one step. I lurched forward. My vision went completely black as my legs failed me. Completely exhausted from it all, the last thing I remembered as I hit the soft sand was my sister shouting my name next to me, sounding like she was miles away.

Rose

A Monster Among Men

XXXIII

"Davit!"

My brother collapsed limp into my arms. His weight caught me off guard. I was surprised at how suddenly weak I was, the exertion from the battle only just then catching up to me now that most of the enemy had been pacified. I hadn't realized just how tired I had truly become so quickly. From the moment Venerus first descended through the clouds up until that point had mostly been a blur. I had completely lost track of my siblings in the chaos, running purely on adrenaline, desperate for survival. All the while my head was incessantly buzzing, as it seemed to always do in the worst situations.

The weight of my brother brought us both to the rocky ground. He seemed completely unresponsive. Panic gripped my heart. I looked around my surroundings desperately for any assistance. Across the battlefield, Ahaax was fleeing from the city on griffback. The warlord was hunched over on his mount, a dark cloak draped over him. I didn't care. Ahaax could run and cower all he wanted; the battle was won. Davit needed my help. I looked frantically, calling for any nearby friendly aid. "Someone help, please!"

"Let me see him, Princess." It was a familiar voice. A tall muscular woman kneeled by my side, taking my brother gently in her hands. It was Julianna, I observed with shock. I blinked hard rapidly. Surprisingly, my friend from back home in Lungala was still tending to my brother. Julianna took off Davit's armor and placed an ear on his chest.

"Jules...?" I said, dazed. "What... How are you here?"

A mounted soldier rode steadily beside us with a shorter, much stouter fellow soldier on the steed's back. "We were a part of the guard regiment called up for service by the king," Killian said atop his griff. My captain friend looked down at me, a warm smile of reunion on his face. "Princess." He nodded respectfully.

"Can you believe it?" Archibald said as he slid off the animal's back. "Us! In combat once more!" The portly guard laughed happily. His attention turned towards a line of Ahaax's men, who were being rounded up as prisoners by our troops. "Hey! I saw that! Don't think I won't teach you a lesson just because the battle's over!" He walked fiercely over to the gathered soldiers.

Julianna was feeling points around Davit's body gently, assessing his condition. My brother's breathing had entered into a slow but steady rhythm. "A few broken bones, and plenty of scrapes, but he'll be alright, my lady," Jules said, looking at me. She nodded reassuringly. "I'll see he gets the help he needs."

A wave of relief washed over my body. I felt like I could cry. I had never even considered a life without my brother. I was overjoyed that I wouldn't have to yet. As I knelt there in the dirt surrounded by friends, a sense almost resembling calm had returned to me. The enemy had lain down their weapons. The fighting was over. I sheathed the red sword I had taken from the Last Palace at my waist. I had almost forgotten I'd been holding it that entire time.

A piercing screech filled the air. In a blue blur, Cerulia flew down from the sky. She positioned herself over Davit's body, tensing. The little dragon growled dangerously at each of my friends if they even tried to approach my brother. Jules instinctually flinched back; Killian had to reign in his startled griff.

"Easy girl, easy!" I said soothingly to the agitated dragon. I extended my hand, letting her recognize my smell. Ever so slightly, Cerulia's body came unwound, still standing over my unconscious brother. "We're going to get him help." Looking at me trustingly, the blue dragon acquiesced, letting Julianna call a few others over to begin treating Davit. Cerulia curled up beside my brother, watching the soldiers work carefully.

Cerulia's landing had brought my attention elsewhere. I looked upwards. Percival's cataclysmic battle with Venerus was still going on high in the sky. The effects of the battle had resulted in a series of large clouds forming around the combatants. The dragons would fly in and out of the clouds. Lightnings of blue and red clashed off each other, accentuated by the occasional column of flames from Redwood. Half of the time, shadows cast on the dark clouds were the only sign I could see of my brother and dragon still alive.

My gut tightened almost painfully watching the battle above the clouds. Venerus' might was unmatched, so I had sent Redwood up to assist my brother, but the Elder Dragon was still more than holding Their own fiercely. I felt completely helpless wanting to assist both my dragon and my brother, but I was stuck on the ground. The titanic shadow of the Elder flashed on a cloud, and the sky filled with a thundering roar. The fear within me deepened.

Just then, another mounted soldier rode up to us in a hurry, but unlike with Killian, I didn't recognize this woman. "My lady," the soldier began breathlessly. She looked panicked. "The general Calivar. The enemy is going to blow the city's dam!"

My eyes widened. "What?" I gasped. The dread within me magnified tenfold. Ahaax's final act would be to doom all of Barra. I couldn't let that happen.

My gaze turned to Killian. The mounted captain on griffback understood my look. He extended an arm to me. "Hurry, Princess," he said. I took Kil's arm and pulled myself onto the griff behind the captain, wrapping my arms around him for balance. Before we could leave, I looked at Archie and Julianna.

"Go!" Archie waved us on. His voice carried a tone like he couldn't believe we would stop to wait for the two of them. "We'll catch up with you!"

With that, Kil lashed his mount's reins, and the two of us began off down the plain. It wasn't as fast as flying on a dragon, but we were still moving quite quickly. Within a minute, we reached the edge of the slope where Barra's massive wooden dam loomed ahead. The structure stretched across the lake's narrowest point, a towering wall of reinforced timber and stone supports that held back the vast waters of Oressor. Below the dam, the ground dropped sharply into a sloping channel that descended toward the northern edge of the city, where the controlled runoff fed a wide river that split through Barra's lower districts. A scattering of weathered wooden buildings surrounded the cliffside near the dam to assist with its functions, with various desert vegetation like shrubs and flat cacti scattering the scene haphazardly. The sound of rushing water grew like thunder in my ears as we arrived.

A group of four of Ahaax's men were assembled at the edge of the dam led by Calivar. The belligerent general was barking orders like a dog to the three other men as we approached. Towards the dam, they were pushing a cart loaded to the brim with barrels filled with what I assumed was an explosive mixture. "Come on, you useless lumps!" the enemy captain shouted, standing in his night-black armor. "Faster!"

Killian skidded our griff to a halt when we were about fifty feet away from the enemy soldiers. The two of us quickly dismounted. Killian unsheathed a silver sword, and I readied my stolen blade. The buzzing in my head, dulled since the end of the battle, picked up once again, concentrated at the front of my head towards the four men.

Calivar turned as he heard us get down from the griff. His large battle axe was hanging at his side in one hand. "Well, if it isn't one of the little *rats*," he snarled, glaring at me.

The look of the rabid man threatened to send chills down my spine, but I held firm, tightening my short sword in my hand. "The battle is lost," I said with all the strength I could muster. My voice sounded surprisingly confident in my ears. "Surrender with honor." I knew there was almost no chance of the man in front of me doing that, but I still had to try.

"If you destroy this dam, you destroy all of Barra. The river flows around the city; everything will be wiped out!" Killian tried to rationalize with the captain.

Calivar glared at my friend. "Obviously," he sneered, morality completely absent from his mind. "If Lord Ahaax cannot have Barra, then *no one will*!" The snake-like man half-turned, calling out behind him, "Men, light it!"

The three soldiers in front of us stopped pushing the cart. One of them pulled out a knife and stone. They struck it, sending out a small spray of sparks but failing to catch on the fuse the man was kneeling beside.

I breathed in quickly. The distance between us was too great. There would be no way I could run to the three soldiers in time and prevent them from lighting the fuse to blow the dam. An animal-like terror took over. I noticed there was a large, multi-armed cactus standing just on the edge of the cliff face to the side of the three men. I jerked the arm that wasn't holding my sword. With a sensation that felt like pulling a weed from the ground, there was a slight resistance as I tugged my hand forcefully.

Suddenly, the six-foot-tall cactus flew out from the soil, its long roots exposed to the open air. There was a split-second shriek of panic, and then the cactus flew into two of the three soldiers, including the one with the lighter. The two men tumbled onto the ground a dozen feet away from the cart. They moved around slightly but soon stopped, groaning.

Calivar watched two thirds of his forces become immediately incapacitated with his mouth hanging open. The enemy captain turned to me, his eyes filled with fire. *"Rat!"* he shouted, raising his axe.

Eyes widening, I lifted my sword. The axe came down with such force that my weapon blocking it was swept aside. My wrist shot with a searing pain, bending unnaturally far back. With a hurt gasp, I rolled out of the way before the rest of the attack could go straight through me.

Across the field, the remaining soldier was picking up the flint and steel his companion had dropped. I gasped. Killian was hunched low, his sword ready to strike Calivar, who was still uncomfortably near me. "Stop him!" I shouted in panic to my friend, too quickly to elaborate in more detail. I rolled out of the way of another axed attack.

Killian glanced at the soldier striking the match. He turned back to me. With a split second's hesitation, my captain friend ran to the cart on the dam, his sword raised, and clashed with the remaining soldier.

I turned my attention back to my own fight just in time to avoid a third heavy attack. I scrambled to my feet. Backing away, I soon realized much of this fight with Calivar would be defined by me avoiding his blows entirely. He was far too strong for me to counter directly. If only I could somehow get through his defenses.

None of the fighting was made easier by the incessant banging in my head. The constant buzzing would intensify worse in whatever direction Calivar was about to land a blow. I was fighting a battle on two fronts, and it was quickly sapping my energy.

Rolling out of the way of another attack, I was panting heavily. My stamina was running out. I needed something I could defend myself with. In the corner of my eye I saw the perfect thing. I extended my free hand outwards. A large, wide-paddled cactus bent towards me at my influence. With a tightening in my gut, one of the large paddles flew off the plant and towards me through the air at high speeds. In the next second, the paddle was in my hand.

Calivar was standing about ten feet from me, a confused and angry look on his face. The captain charged me. Quickly, I summoned the roots from a nearby shrub above ground. I lashed the roots around my left arm, securing the paddle about two feet across to my forearm. Calivar swung his blade. I blocked with my cactus-shield. With a hearty *thunk*, the axe practically bounced right off. I delivered a swift kick to Calivar's gut, and he staggered. Jumping to my feet, I looked at my left arm, somewhat surprised. The impromptu shield was both light and fairly durable.

Calivar quickly regained his breath. With an animalistic grunt, he began another series of slashes and swings. I was able to block most of them with my new shield, but not without great effort. My buzzing head was reaching multiple crescendos. Each time Calivar would strike, the sensation would gradually pick up, peak, and then recede, only to quickly repeat the process anew with the next attack. All of this happened multiple times in each second, disorientating me. It was swing and *buzz*, swing and *buzz*.

Suddenly, a thought hit me: what if it was *buzz* then swing? The realization dawned: every time Calivar raised his arm, the buzzing peaked. Not after the attack or even during. Before. What if the buzzing was a warning: an alarm of an immediate danger? I tuned out all my thoughts in that moment, forcing myself to be driven purely on instinct. Everything next happened in a microsecond. Calivar reeled from the momentum of his last attack. He stepped backwards, almost imperceptibly so. The buzzing in my head picked up, concentrating in a spot right behind my left ear. I slid on the ground to the left. Calivar swung so hard that his own strength sent him off balance. I kicked the captain's leg in, sending him to the ground. With a hard thrust, I slammed the spiked side of my cactus-shield into Calivar's face.

The enemy soldier fell on his back. His free hand shot to his face and pulled away bloodied. He looked at me with his mouth agape, shocked. I was also shocked, my jaw hanging open. *Gods above*, I thought wondrously. *This whole time, my debilitating hindrance was actually my greatest strength.* Suddenly, I forgot all about my tiredness. I felt like a whole new person. For some reason, I was wearing a crazy grin.

For the first time, I pushed the attack on Calivar. As he got up, staggering, I slashed fast and repeatedly. The enemy captain took steps back, unsure, and I kept pushing him. I would get another split-second buzz somewhere within my head, make the appropriate dodge or block, and actually counterattack, not just sideswipe his weapon. I was thinking a mile a minute, but all my thoughts made sense, flowing together seamlessly like I was in a finely choreographed movement. Calivar stumbled back closer to the dam, onto hard, rocky ground. I used this to my advantage. Between my swipes, I began throwing rocks of various sizes into my foe, denting his plate armor.

Calivar stumbled backwards, breathing hard. In the moment of reprieve, I saw Killian in my field of view. He was still locked in combat with his enemy soldier. Then, with a move of equal parts strength and grace, he tricked his enemy into lunging, then sidestepped, cutting his enemy clean through the side. I breathed a small sigh of relief that my friend was no longer in danger. Although, based on the skill I'd just seen, I doubted he ever really was.

There was another angry grunt in front of me. Calivar was panting. His axe was held in both hands, ready to charge.

Screaming, the bloodthirsty man ran forward, directly for me. Feeling a heavy weight lift deep within me, I flung my free hand forward. A stone at least one hundred pounds flew through the air, striking Calivar directly on his breastplate. The captain launched through the air so hard he collided with the cart of explosive materials on the dam and broke right through them with a high-pressure explosion of fluid in all directions. My former foe was left groaning in the wooden rubble. In a single instant, both the enemy captain and his destructive plan were neutralized. I breathed another sigh of relief, putting my hands on my knees.

"Wow," a voice I instantly recognized said behind me, stunned. Turning, I was greeted with the sight of Archibald and Julianna, both panting. Archie brought up his hands in a mock defensive posture. "Whatever you say goes from now on, Princess," the balding guard remarked. "No problem."

I was breathing hard as well. Between the battle before and the fight I'd just had with Calivar, I was at my physical limit. Still, seeing all three of my friends from the palace in front of me could always bring a smile to my face.

Jules was looking around the scene: the two unconscious soldiers lying underneath a cactus, Calivar dazed in the wreckage of some noxious liquid. "I apologize, my lady," the female soldier said. "It looks like we got here too late to be of any real help."

Shaking my head, I was still wearing the same smile. "No, you're just in time," I said gladly. Looking at Julianna, another thought came to my head. "How is Davit?" I asked, concerned, remembering the state of my brother.

"Secure and stable, Princess," Jules said. Her face conveyed a confidence that instantly reassured me. "He's resting back in the city."

Killian walked up beside the three of us. "I suppose we should head back, then," the red-haired guard said. "There are still duties left to be done. We can send men back to collect these prisoners here..."

"*Idiots*..." It was a strained whisper behind us. All four of us turned. Calivar was propping himself up in the wooden debris. He was coated in a black, oil-like substance. His face grimaced from pain, teeth barred.

"What was that, traitor?" Killian asked the defeated captain, stepping forward. My friend raised his blade out of caution.

I could see Calivar roll his eyes. His arm moved down to his waist, pulling an object from his belt. It looked like a whistle. "You don't even see our strongest card," he spat. With that, Calivar put the whistle to his lips and blew. A shrill, unnervingly loud noise rose and carried across the entire battlefield. I looked on with a confused expression. *What was his aim?* Then I saw.

Back in the city, the ten or so remaining mournwings still harassing our soldiers stopped what they were doing. At the whistle's call, each freakish creature looked up and began flying higher into the sky, screaming out an awful call. As I watched them, I saw what the beasts were heading towards. At once, five mournwings each began swarming around Redwood and Apolion, still in the clouds. The batlike creatures surrounded our dragons, biting and slashing. Percival would fire his bolts at them, but seemingly each time, a mournwing would fly out of the way. The new onslaught was an unshakable distraction for my brother and the two dragons. They broke away from their conflict with Venerus, unable to maintain the fight on two fronts.

The Elder Dragon beat back Their wings. Then, with a roar that shook the earth, Venerus dove down towards the city below. Opening Their black maw, the Elder unleashed an uninterrupted beam of magenta energy onto our men. In an instant, dozens of my kingdom's soldiers disintegrated, caught up in the blast. My feet were rooted to the ground, blood cold as ice. Venerus flew low over the city, sending up a cloud of sand in Their wake. With instant terror, I realized They were rapidly flying towards us. "Take cover!" I shouted at my friends.

The four of us scattered into the small wooden buildings located close to the dam, all with Calivar laughing in a mix of delirium and madness behind us. I was panicking, not thinking about what I was doing. A primal terror ran through my veins. I vaulted into an open window of a single-roomed building just as I felt the ground shake like it had been struck with a god's hammer.

Trembling, I placed my back against the wall of the room and stopped all sound. I didn't even breathe. My eyes were clamped shut as tight as they could. I could feel tears forming within.

Petrified, I felt the deathly cold voice of Venerus sneak back into my head. *Your kind intrigues me, Sarfoss,* it said. The ground rumbled with each step the Elder took on Their winged claws. They were searching the buildings. *Where are you? You cannot hide from me, child.* The rumblings were getting steadily closer. There arose a subtle, deep pulsing, different from the Elder's footsteps. *Thoom... Thoomthoom,* repeated. With sickening dread, I realized I was hearing Venerus' pulse. I had to clamp a hand over my mouth to prevent any noise from escaping. *I hear your heart,* they said, closer. I could sense a large, imposing shadow filling the window. *I smell your fear.*

Suddenly, there was a shout from outside my window. "Over here, monster!" it called. I could feel Venerus' head turn away from my building. Turning as well, I looked out the window.

Killian was standing in the open, looking directly at the Elder Dragon. His arms were waving, and he was moving around frantically. "Over here!" my friend shouted again.

Venerus, who had been directly in front of the building I was in, approached Killian slowly, like They were *curious.*

"No, over here!" a separate voice from across the way called. Venerus and I both turned our heads again. It was Julianna, similarly in the open, similarly drawing attention to herself.

"Hey! Hey, over here!" Archibald shouted next to his sister.

With a feeling of intense nausea, I helplessly put together what my friends were doing: distracting Venereus... from me. I looked at each of my three friends from my position on my knees behind the window. *No!* I wanted to scream desperately. *Stop! Please stop! You don't know what you're doing!* But I couldn't shout; I couldn't even make a sound. And I couldn't look away. I was completely frozen.

Venerus approached the two sibling guards, close together. My two friends diverged, each trying to get the Elder's attention. In one movement, the dragon's head lunged forward. Black jaws closed around Archibald, and there was nothing left. Then, the Elder turned Themselves. Julianna was hit by the scorpion-like tail with a sickening *crunch.* Her limp body flew through the air, landing on the ground dozens of feet away, hard.

I watched in frozen horror. Tears streamed down my eyes. I couldn't feel my limbs. My chest hurt.

"To me, monster!" Killian cried again. He was still running, still waving his arms and shouting. *Stop,* I begged internally. *Please.* Not even a whisper escaped my parted lips. Venerus approached my last friend.

In the final moment, Killian's green eyes made contact with mine. He saw me, huddled a hundred feet away in my wooden building. *And he smiled at me.* The same way he had on that night many months ago when we snuck out of the palace. The same kind, unforgettable smile. The final moment felt like it spanned an eternity. And then, my friend Killian's body was completely enveloped within a beam of red lightning.

Then it was only me and Venerus. The Elder Dragon turned from the scorched patch of sand and earth They had left behind. Their eyes of blood directly pierced through me, hiding behind my wooden window frame. *There you are,* They breathed down my spine.

It felt like a blade had stabbed right through my heart. Venerus walked closer and closer to my building, but I couldn't move. *Archie, Jules… Killian,* I thought, my face completely soaked with a mixture of sweat and tears. All of my friends, gone in an instant. And it was because of me. Venerus brought Their terrible head back once more, the back of their throat beginning to glow. I witnessed it all unfold. *Move!* I screamed in my head. But I was stuck. I tried doing something, anything, and nothing happened.

At once, it was like a multi-ton boulder fell from the sky directly onto the Elder Dragon. A cloud of sand and dirt exploded into the air. There was a quick and vicious clash of roar and snarls from two titanic beasts. In the shadow of the dust cloud, I could see the silhouettes of two distinct dragons locked in a violent brawl.

When the dust cleared, Redwood was standing in front of my small wooden room. My dragon was unable to be stilled, pacing over and jumping ferociously on his patch of ground. His wings were extended all the way, making him appear as big as possible and blocking me from sight. Redwood reared back, bringing himself up onto two legs—something I had never seen my dragon do before—and roared an earsplitting battle cry at Venerus.

The Elder Dragon straightened Themselves, recovering from Redwood's unexpected bombardment. Still at least twice as large as my dragon, Venerus unfurled Their wings and let forth a bellow of their own.

Then, a concentrated bolt of pure blue lightning hit the Elder Dragon in the center of Their chest. A massive blast rose up, sending Venerus reeling backwards. The Elder roared ferociously at Their attacker, momentarily stunned.

Apolion swooped low and fast near the larger dragon on the ground. On his dragon's back, Percival unleashed another uncontained blast of lightning at Venerus from the tip of his spear, resulting in a similarly large explosion. The monstrous Elder Dragon roared in frustration, launching Themselves into the air after my brother once more, Their hunt for me seemingly forgotten.

As I watched my brother and his dragon climb higher and higher, chased by a monster I couldn't envision in my worst nightmares, my body regained some sense of feeling. I was able to throw myself onto the ground of that small, cold room. I could hear Redwood hum outside, concerned for me, but he was too large for even his head to get through the door. I couldn't pick myself off the ground to go comfort my dragon. The only movements my body made were from the sobs I was finally able to produce. *My friends are dead*, I realized. *My friends are dead.* My ears were ringing; I felt like I could vomit. *My friends are dead.*

I wailed a sound that became the loudest in the world.

Percival

A Clash above the Clouds

XXXIV

I brought my body low as close to Apolion as I could, reins in one hand, my father's spear in the other. The wind whipped past us as we rushed through the electrically charged air. The slightest bit of drag as we flew could slow us a fatal amount. Soaring ferociously atop my dragon, I only had one objective on my mind: be faster than the Elder Dragon behind me.

I was too busy fending off mournwing attacks to even realize Venerus had left our battle in the sky and had flown to the ground: towards Rose. I followed the Elder quickly as soon as I recognized something was wrong, but my progress was consistently hampered by the batlike creatures. Eventually, I had managed to fend them off and strike back at Venerus, but not before They had eviscerated Rose's group of palace guard friends. *I should have been faster.*

The Elder Dragon roared deafeningly loud behind us, snapping at Apolion's tail with their maw. The sound rattled my skull. I couldn't think about that now. I couldn't think about Rose or Davit or anything else besides my survival. I had to trust that my siblings were okay and push through, for their sakes as much as my own. Feeling a concentrated buzzing towards the back of my head, I tugged on Apolion's reins, willing my dragon to spin left. A split second later, Venerus' lightning blast shot through the air where we had just been.

"Well done, Apolion," I encouraged breathlessly. Despite my words, I could tell my dragon was getting tired; we both were. We had been flying since nearly the start of the battle and had continued after it had concluded, firing bolt after bolt at Venerus that entire time as well. In the back of my mind I knew I had already used my powers much more than I ever had at once before. I knew my effectiveness as a fighter would not last for much longer, and I was similarly aware of the limit of my dragon's ability to stay in the air and fight simultaneously. Either I found a way to end this fight soon on our terms, or Venerus would quickly be in an undeniable position to end it on Theirs.

Ahead of us high in the sky, a great dark cloud larger than all the ones surrounding it had been whipped up by my fight with the great Elder. Lightning, *natural* lighting in a solid white, flashed fast and repeatedly. It was my best chance. If I could use the natural energy within the cloud combined with my and Apolion's power, perhaps we could stand a chance at matching Venerus' might. There was another, darker part of my mind that knew I simply had no other alternative plans left.

I pulled back on Apolion's reins, flying us higher into the afternoon sky. Venerus roared again, chasing us closely behind. I turned in my dragon's saddle, pointing the tip of my spear at the Elder. A straight line of blue shot forth and hit Them on the side of Their great black maw. The explosion shook Venerus' head to the side, but They quickly recovered, bellowing even more violently. I cursed under my breath. It seemed that as I was getting weaker, They were only getting stronger, shrugging off my attacks. We continued our climb upwards to the storm clouds.

In front of us, there were two piercing screeches. I turned. The final two mournwings I had left unaccounted for swooped down on me fast. The terrible creatures slashed at my hair and skin with their claws. I tried my best to fend them off, but it wasn't easy with both of my hands full and simultaneously having to avoid Venerus' lightning strikes behind us.

One of the mournwings dove for me again. I lunged hard with the hand holding my spear. The tip of my weapon pierced through the winged creature, sending it limply spinning into me. The impact of the mournwing's body threatened to knock me off Apolion. My body lurched backwards. In my moment of reaction, I accidentally let go of my spear. "No!" I cried, but it was already too late. I could only watch helplessly as my father's bronze spear tumbled through the air into the cloud layer below. A pang of sadness gripped my gut, but I forced myself to turn forward. I couldn't focus on anything else right now. I had to fly with Apolion.

The second mournwing attacked, clawed hands outstretched. The thing stubbornly kept flying out of my grip as I swung my hand after it desperately. The creature slashed skin all over my body. Finally, I felt my fist close around the mournwing's skeletal leg. *Got you*, I thought. With great effort despite the wind, I threw the creature in front of me with an exerted shout. The air carried the tumbling animal into Apolion's jaws, which clamped down sharply, turning it into two separate pieces falling down to the ground behind us.

At last, my dragon flew into the gray, storming cloud high in the sky. I could feel all the hair on my arms and neck stand up as we flew into the supercharged air. Apolion had to brake left and right to avoid stray bolts of lightning the cloud generated. Just flying in the air, I could feel a current begin to charge within me. Small blue arcs of electricity began to fizzle off me involuntarily as I felt my energy begin to return and then exceed what it had been for most of my fight.

Venerus charged behind us, leaving a trail of water vapor in the air that followed Them. Apolion rolled out of the way at the last second, his wingtip nearly caught in the Elder's jaw. My dragon flew around in a wide half-circle, positioning Venerus now in front of us, hovering in the storm cloud.

Now is the time. I could feel more energy within me than I ever had before. I placed my free hand on Apolion's scaled hide. It was buzzing. I felt even stronger. My dragon was lending me his strength. I thanked him mentally, taking a deep breath. My gaze turned back to the colossal dragon ahead of us, roaring monstrously. Channeling the winds, I flew out of Apolion's saddle, getting to an appropriate distance in the sky before channeling all the energy I had. I could feel my stomach tighten painfully. Lighting completely filled the sky, shooting off of me and striking me directly, making contact with my breastplate. As the electricity ran through me, I was overcome by an alien feeling of boundless energy. My very fingertips were exploding sparks. It was too much for me to contain. Struggling from the exertion of it all, I turned towards Venerus in midair. Bringing my arm back, a bolt of pure plasma ten feet long materialized in my palm. *This was my last chance.* My teeth were gritted from everything between pain, pressure, and fear. I brought my arm forward to throw my bolt.

At that moment, the Elder Dragon shot forth a beam of sickly red lightning straight through my chest. My body arched backwards in an upside-down *U*. The pain was excruciating, I had never been through anything like it. Instantly my entire vision went a crimson red. In that second, it felt like time was frozen. Like I could feel every instant of my skin burning, melting, alone in an endless black void where I was the only inhabitant.

I knew that I was going to die then, or that I was already dying. It felt like my blood was on fire. Every tragedy from my life flashed through my head: my father's murder, the ruins of Bukarra, Bryce's betrayal. It all just felt so hopeless, pointless.

That's right, Venerus' voice dug into my skull as I writhed in the air. *Life is pain. You struggle endlessly, and how are you rewarded for your efforts?* The face of Delilah the last time I had seen her forced its way into my mind, her twisted expression and eyes full of tears. My actions had made me a monster for her to run from. Why should I even bother to continue trying?

Everyone leaves eventually. It is inevitable. As am I. I am life's cruelty made flesh. A reminder that you will die alone and in pain, as will those you love.

Those I love... It was my own voice in my head, faint and distant. I saw more memories. I was back in the palace courtyard after my siblings and I had returned from the Last Palace. Pevincy greeted us, embracing his three adopted children. I felt the warmth of the hug from my family. As I stood suspended in the sky above Barra caught in red lighting, I could feel my posture begin to straighten.

No! I thought defiantly. I remembered the night I'd stood in my chamber with Pevincy after Bryce's betrayal. How the weight of the world had come crashing down on me all at once, and my mentor was there without a word. Those who loved me had never left, they were *still* there. Rose and Davit were in the city below. *That's why I fought.* I could feel the power within me surge. The total burning pain had become a different sensation: power. The searing red behind my eyes began to gradually shift into a purer blue the color of sky. *For those I love.* I was next to Delilah, sitting next to the creek. I could smell her sweet raven hair as she rested her head on my shoulder. *And for those I may yet see again.*

The Elder Dragon Venerus was watching my revelation, hovering in the air with a curious unease. The being of evil couldn't comprehend what gave me strength. I only took a slight note of Their reaction. My senses were overloading. I couldn't even feel my body, just the energy flowing through it. "See my thoughts, monster," I said to the Elder in a staggered voice that boomed like thunder. "And for the first time know *fear,* for I am life persevering!" Unable to contain the energy within me any longer, I unleashed my power in a flash that shined like a star.

I heard a loud, monstrous shriek of pain. And I fell fast. The air blew my hair above my head; the wind was deafening in my ears. My eyes were open, but just barely. All I saw was a blur of muted colors. My entire body was intensely sore, and incredibly hot, despite the rushing wind. I was faintly aware that I was in freefall thousands of feet in the air, but I was too tired to pay it much attention. I just wanted to drift off to sleep. As my eyes slowly opened throughout my fall, I saw an amber-yellow blur quickly appear larger in my widening field of view. My heart skipped a beat. For a moment I thought I was looking into Delilalh's eyes.

With a worried cry, Apolion grabbed my falling body gently in one of his talons. The dragon quickly but softly slowed our descent just as we landed upon the ground. Had Apolion been a second later, he likely would have been too late to catch me. My dragon released me softly onto the sandy ground, nuzzling my dazed form with his snout.

It took me a few moments to process all that had happened. I rose to my feet shakily, using Apolion's head as an assistant. Somehow my whole body was both in pain yet also numb. My head still felt fuzzy. Analyzing my surroundings, I saw that Apolion had landed just outside of Barra. In front of me there was a gigantic cloud of dust and sand still hanging in the air from where Venerus had fallen from the sky. *Did I... I* thought, exhausted, looking at the cloud. *Did I do that?*

Lying a few feet away in the sand, a glimmering object caught my eye. I breathed in sharply as I recognized my father's spear. The weapon was submerged halfway in a sand dune, buried from the force of its fall. I limped over, not believing my eyes. Taking the bronze shaft of the spear in my hand, my vision was confirmed: it really was there. I made a sort of half gasp, half laugh. Tears welled at the edge of my eye. I thought I had lost it.

There was a sound of rushing feet and clanking armor behind me. I turned my head. Apolion growled, barring his teeth. The five knights of my Crown's Circle I had brought with me to Barra were running towards me rapidly. Despite their heavy green armor, my guards were able to close the distance remarkably quickly. All of them kneeled as they arrived. "Your Grace, you're unharmed," the knight at the head of the group breathed. "Thank the Divines."

I nodded to the armored men and women before me, bidding them rise. "Yes, my knights." I did the best I could to sound regal, but the exhaustion still seeped through my voice. "This battle has been won."

Before any of my external senses detected anything, I felt a familiar buzzing manifest towards the back of my head, concentrated behind me. My spine stiffened. I could feel *Their* presence. The knights in front of me flinched, unsheathing their blades. I took my spear in both hands and turned.

As the cloud of dust cleared, the Elder Venerus was left glaring at my dragon and me. Standing on the ground, They looked even larger than They had in the air just moments before. The terrible dragon's barbed tail swished through the air as They gazed at the group of us. I lowered myself slowly, getting into a battle posture once more. Exhausted as I was, if I had to continue this fight for the sake of my family and kingdom, so be it.

For what felt like an eternity, no one moved, neither human nor dragon. Venerus held the analytical gaze at me, Their blood-red stare attempting to pierce through my defenses. I firmed my resolve, shifting my spear in my grip. Finally, the Elder breathed out long. *Savor this victory, Sarfoss,* Their chilling voice whispered in my ear. They snarled. *Darkness has awoken. The night is coming.* Then, the Elder Dragon extended Their black leathery wings one final time and launched Themselves into the golden sky, flying towards the Black Mountains and becoming smaller and smaller on the horizon.

Not until the dragon was beyond eyesight did I or any of my knights loosen our tensed frames. The air was quiet. It felt strange. There were no sounds of conflict or violence. The battle truly was over. We had won. One of my emerald knights approached behind me. "Your Grace, we have secured the surrender of most of the rebel army with minimal casualties to our own troops. In addition, we have the enemy general Calivar in our custody."

I turned to face the guard addressing me. Barely registering what he had said, I put my hand on his arm, tired. "Where are my siblings?" I demanded.

The green knight looked at me through his helmet. He hesitated. "Prince Davit was injured, but he's stable and recovering," he began. "But, the Princess…"

As soon as the man told me what had truly happened, I was running towards the dam. My exhaustion was seemingly left behind with the group of guards I ran from without another word. I needed to find Rose.

I found her easily by the sight of Redwood curled up in a ball. My sister was in a small weathered room, weeping quietly to herself. I ran towards her, not bothering opening the door to the building and instead just vaulting through the open window. I scooped Rose's small frame reassuringly in my embrace. My sister thrashed violently at the contact. "No!" she screamed, trying to get away. "No!"

"Rose! It's me! It's your brother! It's your Percival!" I soothed my hysterical sister. I began petting the top of her head gently. Rose sniffled, calming. "You're safe now. It's all over."

My sister collapsed in my arms. *"Oh Percival,"* she wailed, sobbing into my chest. *"They're all dead. They're all dead."*

As I held Rose's shaking body in my embrace, I felt my blood turn ice-cold. With a horror dulled by the emotions of everything I had experienced that day, I realized my greatest fear had been realized. My sibling had seen war, and she would never be the same again.

A King of His Own

XXXV

Pevincy and I were the first ones in the council chambers, so we had the pleasure of watching each of the other five lords of the kingdom as they arrived. Each lord hid their true feelings upon seeing me differently. Lord Alaric commented on my good health and endurance after surviving Barra. Lords Finnian and Florian each complimented an aspect of the battle plan itself, insisting that they too had always wanted to bring the fight to Ahaax. The Lady Aemelia held a slightly bemused expression, looking at me as she entered. She complimented the royal garments I was wearing, and was I standing taller? It suited me. Finally, Lord Carrington entered last. The belligerent lord didn't say anything to me directly, but it was obvious he was deliberately avoiding my eye contact. With a curt nod in my general direction, the lord made his way into the room.

I watched as each lord found their chair and sat. They seemed so focused on themselves that they didn't even notice the five members of the Circle of the Crown standing a few feet behind each seat. Despite their pleasantries, each lord was betraying their nerves in small, almost imperceptible ways: a slight fidget, a glance. They had good reason to be on edge. They had ignored their king and his fears for months, and those fears had just been confirmed for the whole kingdom.

"I thank you all for coming so quickly," I began. My eyes drifted to each lord as I spoke. "It *has* been a while since we last met, hasn't it?" I let the silence hang in the air like a cloud. It had been just over a month since I had seen any of the lords in the room besides Pevincy. Not since they stormed out of the last meeting at the mention of Venerus. They didn't have that option now, and I wanted them to know it. I put on a similarly fake smile as the lords opposite me. "Regardless, this meeting will be short, as there is only one agenda item. As of now, I hereby dissolve this regency council and will reign as king in my own right. I thank you for your service to the crown, but it is no longer necessary. You may keep your titles and return to your lands. That is all."

Shockingly, the room did *not* burst into a chaotic scene of confused shouting. I don't believe that had ever happened before. Instead, each lord looked at me in silence. The five faces were different in their own ways, but they all were wearing an expression that was a mix of confusion and uncertain humor, as if I was just about to laugh at a bad joke and give them confirmation that it was okay for them to laugh too. I did not.

"Wh… What, Your Grace?" the faint, hollow voice of Lord Alaric whispered from his large chair.

I turned my attention to the man of bones. "This council is dismissed," I said, calm and in control. My gaze went around to the other lords. "Your service in my court is done."

"But… it's tradition!" Lady Aemelia cried nervously at her end of the table. "You can't just…"

"Listen, *boy,*" Carrington growled. The lord's eyes had fire in them, pointed directly at me. He stood abruptly, his fists clenched.

Instantly the swords of my five knights stationed around the table unsheathed in one synchronized motion. Each Circle knight positioned themselves towards the aggressive Carrington, ready to dispatch him instantly if he came too close to me. Looking to my side, I noticed even Pevincy had his blade at the ready. I grinned lightly. I could always count on him to be *my* lord.

Lord Carrington looked angrily at the knights, but he didn't move. With a huff, the lord barked, "What is this supposed to be, a threat?"

I furrowed my brow. Despite everything from this war, the man in front of me had learned nothing. "A threat?" I asked, clarifying for him. "No. This is not a threat. It is a display of a fraction of the power of the king of all Lungalea." I motioned my hand at my knights. Just as quickly as they had been brought up, they all brought down their weapons, and I began to walk around the table towards Carrington. "For the past nine months, our own infighting has been our biggest handicap. We have held power, but we have refused to use it." I paused, reflecting on my battle with the Elder Dragon above the clouds of Barra. "I have now met a power that we are practically hopeless against, and I will be held back no longer." I shook my head, firm in my resolve. I had finally approached Carrington on the other side of the table. The grown man was still half a head taller than me, but I was glaring into his eyes. "A person I once held dear recently told me that *kings need to rule.* In a certain way, I believe he was right. Do you have a problem with that, Lord Carrington?"

The lord's black eyes were staring back at me ferociously. His face was straining, like he was constantly on the verge of shouting, his nostrils flared. "The nobles of the kingdom will never go along with this," he growled through gritted teeth.

My eyes narrowed. "I just defeated an Elder Dragon. I believe the nobles will follow whatever I say." I emphasized every word. "I ask again, *do you have a problem with that, Lord Carrington?*"

After a tense moment, the furious lord's gaze lowered slowly. "No, King Percival."

I nodded, taking one step backwards. "Good," said the king. "Then you are all dismissed." No one moved for a few seconds more, likely from disbelief. When I remained firm in my stance, they began to understand how serious I was. Silently, the five lords slowly shuffled out of my chambers. No longer lords of the kingdom, they would go back to their own lands and return to being dukes and counts. The air was abuzz with a positive energy. The scales of power had just shifted measurably, and perhaps irreversibly. The first independent action of my reign was to go against thousands of years of tradition. Would this be a sign of things to come? Would it be necessary?

My thoughts were interrupted as the door to the chambers closed. Pevincy walked from his side of the room and put a hand on my shoulder, a smile on his grizzled face. "Well done, Your Grace. I'm proud of you." The guard's eyes turned to the heavy closed door. "But some may not take their loss of power and your ascending to rulership well. That move could have just made you some enemies."

I nodded. "Perhaps." None of the lords wanted to work with me before. They may have been out of my court and no longer direct obstacles, but I had a lingering feeling that at least one of the diminished nobles would try to make my life as difficult as he could. "But we will deal with those problems when they arise. Our kingdom has far greater concerns at the moment than a few discontented lords." I flashed Pevincy a smile and began to head out of the room. In all, I thought that was one of the most productive meetings I had ever had with my council.

"Your Grace?" Pevincy said behind me as I was about to leave the chambers. I turned. "It was me who let your siblings escape their surveillance and reach their dragons. I sent them to Barra."

I raised a single eyebrow. "Of course." Obviously it was Pevincy. Who else would it have been?

My Justiciar continued. "It was a direct violation of an order from the crown. Treason. I accept any punishment you see fit to inflict upon me." Pevincy bowed his head.

I had to try hard to stop myself from laughing. From his tone and facial expression, I could tell Pevincy genuinely meant he wanted repercussions for disobeying me. The thought was strange and alien. "Alright," I began in my kingly tone. "As consequence for betraying your lord, I require you stay by my side throughout my reign, continuing to provide me with the best counsel you see fit to give, to the best of your ability, for the rest of your days."

Pevincy's face softened into his familiar warm smile. "Thank you, Your Grace."

I returned the expression. Turning to leave, I made one last request. "Keep me human, Pevincy." I looked my mentor in the eyes. "Lest I become what we are fighting against."

The guard was silent for a moment but then responded with a short, "Of course, Percival." It may have just been the lighting, but there was a glimmer in his eyes, as if they were holding back tears. I turned and left the room.

It was a short walk to my next destination. Opening the door to the modest chambers, I was met with the sight of both of my siblings when I had only expected to find one. "Oh, you're both here."

Davit and Rose were both sitting upright on my brother's bed in his chambers. Rose was situated just behind Davit, resting on her knees. She was just finishing wrapping his chest with bandages as I entered. "This one is too embarrassed to let the palace healers tend to him," Rose said flatly, nodding to our brother. She smoothed the end of a bandage into place on his back shoulder.

Davit grimaced slightly at the pressure. "Hey, I'm a hero, and I don't think it's too bold of me to say so," he chimed in. "And a hero shouldn't have to worry about a pretty healer seeing his scrawny chest." His voice tapered off as he finished his sentence, his confidence fleeting.

I chuckled to myself. For the first time in weeks, the three of us were back at the palace and Davit was his usual humorous self. Things almost felt normal. I approached my siblings a few steps more. "How are you?" I inquired to Davit genuinely. My physicians had told me he had broken his nose and multiple ribs in his duel with Ahaax. *My younger brother fighting that man on his own, and* **winning**, I thought with pride combined with a small amount of disbelief.

Davit's nose was still slightly swollen, and his chest was red at the edges of his bandages, but he looked to be in his usual good spirits. My brother grinned up at me from his seat on the edge of his bed. "I'm ready to go, Percival. Send me back out there." He chuckled softly.

I smiled at the humor. "Don't worry, you will," I reassured him. "But for now you need your rest." There was a slight tug at my gut as I wondered if Davit knew just how quickly he would be returning to war. I wondered how long his enthusiasm would last.

Rose smoothed down the end of a final bandage. "All done," she said to Davit. Quickly and without another word, our sister gathered her things and headed for the chamber door. She flashed a polite smile at me as she passed, avoiding my eyes. The air around her was different.

I turned to watch our sister exit the room. I let out an uneasy sigh as soon as the door shut. "How is *she?*" I asked Davit, my eyes still looking at where Rose had been moments before.

My brother sighed as well. Shifting sounds behind me told me he was adjusting his position on his bed. "I don't know," Davit said frankly. I turned to face him. He went on. "That in itself is strange. We've always had a sense of where the other was for as long as I can remember. But for the last couple of weeks..." Davit shook his head. "Something is different about her, Percival. Something's changed."

The pulling in my gut got worse as my fears were confirmed. I had noticed Rose's change in behavior as well. I was hoping spending more time with Davit would help. It appeared I was mistaken. "She's strong," I said as reassuringly as I could.

Davit nodded. Then, "She told me what happened, you know." He brought his eyes up to me and shrugged. "Well, the broad aspects. I pieced together the rest." He sighed again, a troubled look on his face. What Rose had seen in Barra no one should ever have to see, let alone someone who had only lived thirteen summers. "Is *anyone* strong enough for that?"

Looking back at the door, I couldn't give my brother an honest answer. I remained silent, almost lost in my contemplations. After a few reflective moments, I changed the subject, turning my attention back to Davit. "You certainly showed *your* strength," I began. "My generals told me what happened. You *defeated* Ahaax, and when you had him at your mercy, you left him to save our sister."

Davit shifted uneasily in his bed. I could tell by his face that he had thought about that moment many times in the weeks since it had happened. Then he straightened, looking at me. "She needed help."

"I know," I said with a smile. "It was the right decision." I looked my brother up and down. I realized for the first time I was seeing him not as a boy, but as a young man. "In the past few months you have grown more than I would have once thought possible. I believe you are ready for the responsibilities that will now begin to quickly come your way." I paused. "I was wrong about you, Davit."

My brother's eyes widened into dinner plates. He rubbed the back of his neck, looking down, embarrassed, but also appreciative of the compliment. "Well," he said. "I had some good examples." We smiled at each other wordlessly. We were both just happy the other was there. Finally, I turned to leave the room. Right before I left, Davit asked one final question. "Percival?" he called. I turned in the doorway. He looked unsure. "Things really aren't ever going to be the same, will they?"

I looked at my brother. The question from someone his age felt like a punch in the gut. But I wasn't going to lie. "No. Never."

Davit mulled over my answer. I left his room.

I found Rose standing on one of the palace's balconies, overlooking the capital city accented by the orange setting sun. There was a dark gathering of storm clouds far off over the ocean, occasionally rumbling with cracks of white, but otherwise it was a pleasant night. Rose had her back to me, silently watching everything unfold below.

"I enjoy coming to places like these," I began to my sister, walking up beside her. "I feel it gives me a reprieve from my responsibilities as king. When I stand up here, able to see half of the city in one glance, the countless people walking in the streets, it makes me feel small. It is a nice feeling to be reminded of now and then." I stopped at my sister's side, leaning against the railing she had her hands propped against. Rose's face was concentrated on the city below. The expression she wore was difficult to read. Perhaps it was because there was no strong sign of any emotion at all. I was hoping what I had to say next would put a smile on that face. "The council has acquiesced. You shall have all the support you need to expand the city. You can give those people a home." I looked outside the city across the river, where the tent city of eastern refugees had been set up for months at this point. I felt a mix of joy and relief as I realized that with the dissolution of the council, helping those people could actually become a reality.

Rose's face remained unchanged, as if she hadn't even heard me. Something within me felt uneasy at her response, or lack of one. "Rose?" I asked as she kept looking ahead.

"That's good," Rose acknowledged lightly, distant. She was silent for a few moments more. I was about to begin speaking again when Rose continued, "I've been coming up here more often. Ever since…" She trailed off, not letting herself finish the sentence. *Ever since the battle.* "When I look at these people below," Rose continued, barely above a whisper. "Hundreds? Thousands? I wonder if any of them know just how fragile everything they see is. That in an instant, a force they would struggle to comprehend could come and erase everything they have ever known." Her eyes were locked ahead of her, refusing to meet my gaze.

The vague feeling of unease solidified within me as I spoke to my sister. Davit was correct: Rose *had* been changed by the battle. I recognized the same signs I had seen in some of the soldiers I had fought with during this war. I recognized some of the same signs I had once fought with myself. Rose had barely managed to escape death at Venerus' hands, but her mind was still in Barra. As best as my information knew, Ahaax's Elder Dragon ally was still off in the east, and for whatever reason They had not attacked Lungala for the extent of these past nine months of war, even before They had revealed Themselves. I had to trust that They would continue to stick to this pattern, knowing that it was our only real option for survival.

Still, the mark Venerus had left on Rose had been branded into the actions of my little sister in small ways. She had become quieter and had stopped smiling. She hadn't met my gaze since Barra, and I had a suspicion why. Rose had always put her duties above herself. She wouldn't hesitate to go back into war if her people needed it, but I would always have to be the one to send her there. It made me hate myself as I learned to balance my responsibilities as king and brother, but I knew for the good of the realm my siblings and I would have to go back east with our dragons if the kingdom had any chance of winning this war. Letting Rose and Davit fight in Barra was one of the hardest decisions I ever had to make, and I would have to make it again and again as long as this war lasted. I knew there was no other way around it: Rose was in this situation because of *me*, and I didn't know if I could ever forgive myself.

"Rose," I began, "about Barra..." It was my fault Rose had seen what she did. But I was going to be by her side whenever she needed me. I had seen the horrors of war more than I would have liked since its outbreak, and I had seen what they could do to people. The horrors of the battlefield would eat away at even the strongest soldiers on their own. I vowed I would not let that happen to my sister.

Rose grimaced suddenly. Her eyes closed, and her head tilted down towards the marble railing. She did her best to steady her breathing. "Not right now, Percival."

"After what you saw, no one would..."

"Please," Rose insisted, her eyes still clamped shut. "Not right now."

I looked my sister over. She *was* strong, it was true. To almost any outside observers, it would look like the princess was just in deep thought. But what I had seen of my sister broke my heart. I nodded softly. "Alright. Not right now." But I knew this subject would have to be addressed eventually. For the sake of everyone involved.

The two of us turned our gazes to the sunset on the horizon turning the evening clouds into the color of fire. A flock of gulls was gliding serenely between the fishing boats out in the harbor below. It was Rose who restarted the conversation this time. "I saw you die in Barra."

Her voice still held the distant, almost cold whisper-like quality she had taken on, but the material of what she had said caused me to look at her sharply, shocked. Rose had noticed my expression, continuing. "When Venerus hit you above the clouds, I watched as your body shriveled and writhed."

Rose looked straight ahead as she spoke. I could hear fear in her voice, like she was reliving the scene in her head. My body remembered the moment as well. When Venerus' lightning went through me, I had never been in more pain. I could feel my blood boil. It was still a mystery to me how I'd survived.

"But then the lightning began to change color," Rose continued. Her gaze turned to me. "From red to blue. Theirs, to yours."

My brow furrowed. "What do you mean?"

Rose looked at me intensely with a mix of fear and hope. "Percival," she said. "You took the power of an Elder and used it as your own." She shook her head. "That shouldn't be possible. *Ever.*"

The tips of my fingers turned faintly numb. I looked at my hands. What had happened after I was struck with the bolt was still a blur of blue and red inside my head. I didn't even remember feeling any part of my body, only the energy flowing within. And somehow I had survived a direct attack from an Elder Dragon. There was no other way to explain it. What Rose said she saw must have been true. I'd used Venerus' power against Them. *But how?* I thought, baffled. How could I possibly have harnessed the power of an Elder? I glanced back at Rose, who was clearly thinking along the same line.

I put a grin on my face. Regardless, I realized I didn't necessarily need to know *how* it had happened. But I did know something. "Do you know what this means?" I asked my sister.

Rose shook her head lightly. "What?"

"It means we can win this," I said, leaning in slightly, determined. "This can be the spark of hope we need to light the fire to win this war!"

My sister exhaled softly in disbelief. I could tell she was conflicted. She wanted to believe, but she had also seen the raw power of Venerus closer than anyone else had. "How?"

I took Rose's hand lightly in my own. "Together." I looked my sister in her blue eyes. "And I'm never going to leave."

There was a quick flash of white lightning in the storm clouds on the horizon. A few seconds later, the rumble of thunder met our ears. Rose looked out over the ocean. I felt her hand tighten around my own, seeking reassurance. Then she leaned closer to me, resting her head on my shoulder. I wrapped my arm around my sister in a gentle embrace as the two of us watched the golden sun sink lower.

My Name Is Percival

XXXVI

I watched from the shaded cover of the trees before stepping into the clearing. My heart was pounding. Despite confronting both my Counsel and siblings after the Battle of Barra, this was the event I had been dreading the most.

Delilah was working with her four younger siblings in the garden just outside their house. The family was in the middle of harvest. Delilah was on her knees in the dirt, filling baskets with various crops and calling orders to keep her siblings in line whenever they wandered. Her raven hair glowed in the evening light. I thumped my head against the tree I was hiding behind, sighing hard. *Don't let things end the way they did*, I told myself. *She deserves that much.* I didn't want things to end at all, but I knew this was how it had to be eventually. With a deep breath, I stepped into the clearing.

Delilah heard me coming before I was even halfway to the house. Standing, she brushed dirt off her knees and gestured her siblings inside the house for privacy. The kids noticed my approach as well, and there were a few objections, but none of them were willing to stand up to their big sister, and soon Delilah and I were the only two outside. Her arms were crossed by the time I reached her. Delilah's angular face was as motionless as a statue as she looked at me. I would have to speak first.

"You deserve to know who I am," I began.

"You're King Percival," Delilah cut me off. Her voice was flowing with a mix of anger and annoyance. "Your siblings are the crown princess and prince. Your father was the last king. You've been fighting a war throughout the entire kingdom, and I'm fairly certain you have a dragon somewhere nearby." Delilah put her hands on her hips, scowling at me. "It looks like I know you fairly well already. Unless there is anything else, *Your Majesty*?" She spat the last two words.

I was caught entirely by surprise. I had been expecting to have to explain myself to Delilah, but it appeared she had just explained everything for me. "No, that was basically everything," I said, my mouth practically hanging open embarrassingly. "You knew who I was?"

Delilah crossed her arms. "Please, Percival, I've known for a while." She rolled her eyes with a scoff. "A noble boy named Percy? Are you serious? Don't insult me any more than you already have."

I furrowed my brow, frustrated now myself. "Well, if you knew who I was the whole time, why didn't you say anything?"

"Because I didn't care!" Delilah threw her hands up, exasperated. "I didn't fall in love with the crown! I fell in love with you!" Delilah wiped a tear that had fallen from her eye. She turned partly away from me, hiding herself.

It felt like I had just been hit from a direction I wasn't expecting. *She loved me?*

Delilah continued with one slight sniffle. "But you still kept *lying* to me. Day after day, every time we saw each other. I thought you might have felt the same way about me. But you still couldn't even tell me the truth about yourself. It wasn't even up to you when I saw who you were that night. *The King.* Were you ever going to tell me?"

I felt numb. I had thought I'd frightened Delilah that night when she discovered my true identity, but the issue went much deeper than that. The past few months I had spent with Delilah were the only time when I felt like I could be my true self. I was using her to hide from my responsibilities as king, and in doing that I had not only brought her into direct danger with Bryce and Ahaax's men, but I had been breaking her trust every day I saw her for months.

"I'm sorry," I said softly, looking into Delilah's amber eyes. She was the person who I cared about the most. She was who I longed to see as soon as I opened my eyes in the morning. And our entire relationship was a lie. "For that night. For the lies. For everything." I breathed in deep. Suddenly, I found myself blinking back tears. It was an unfamiliar sensation, and it caught me off guard. "I understand if you never wish to see me again, and I will respect your desire." Hanging my head, I turned to leave, not bearing to stay another minute when I knew my relationship with the girl I loved had ended.

"No," Delilah said fiercely behind me. I faced her again. Tears were on the sides of her cheeks, but she looked more determined than I had ever seen her. "You're not leaving yet. You are going to stay and tell me why you did what you did. Why did you make me fall in love with you?"

I smiled in pain at the attitude that had attracted me to this huntress girl to begin with. Walking back towards Delilah,

I explained, "For my entire life, I had grown up under a set of rules that were not my own. I spent my childhood being raised to run a kingdom, not live a life of my own. But when I'm with you?" I laughed softly, remembering how I'd felt the first night I saw the woman in front of me now. How her hair sparkled in the moonlight. "I'm a boy again. You knew me without the burdens of the crown. You knew me as a human. Delilah, you helped me rediscover who I was, who I *want* to be." I took her calloused hands softly in my own, hesitantly, expecting her to pull away. She didn't. "You helped me rediscover how to laugh, how to smile... to love." I squeezed her hand, looking directly into her eyes, my face inches from hers. "Delilah, I love you."

Delilah looked back at me deeply. Her lips were parted slightly. She shook her head, backing away just a step, unsure. "Love is trust, Percival," she said. "I love you, and you love me... but you still lied. I don't care if no one in the kingdom knows about that love, but how can I love a man who I can't *know*?"

"Delilah, I am a fool," I almost blurted out. It was a general realization I had on my way over to Delilah's house, but one that only solidified as I tried to walk away from the girl in front of me. "I am constantly wielding whatever power I have to try to prevent the inevitable. I try to keep those I care about from war, even though I am the reason they end up in danger. For the past nine months I have allowed myself to be handicapped by lords who couldn't care at all about ruling themselves, and on top of all of that, I couldn't even be honest with you because I was terrified that once you knew who I was, I would just be the king again, and the most meaningful relationship I had ever managed on my own would be gone."

I sighed at the end of my speech. Delilah was still holding my hands in hers. I continued softly, stepping closer. "But I promise to you, no matter how foolish I may become, my love for you will always return me to sanity. I vow that there is no part of me that is not yours, from now come Final Night." Against my best efforts, a single tear fell from my eye down my cheek. I cursed myself internally, trying to prevent any more.

Delilah was looking up at me with a softened expression. Slowly, her hand rose to my cheek. Softly, as if it would crumble at the mere touch, she put her thumb to my cheek and wiped the tear away. "You *are* a fool, King Percy." She smiled, a tear of her own running down her face.

I returned her expression. "Forever in your service." The two of us leaned in simultaneously, and our lips touched in a kiss defined by love and passion. Delilah wrapped her arms around my waist. My entire body felt like it was buzzing, but I was in control of my own energy.

With barely any realization, the wind lifted the two of us into the air. Neither of us paid the change in altitude any attention. The only thought on my mind in that moment was my love for Delilah as our lips stayed connected. Together, we held each other tightly, never letting go as we rose higher and higher into the clear and golden sky.

Glossary

King Apolion "The Mighty": 2035-1988 BW (reign 2000-1988 BW); Apolion came to the throne during one of the kingdom's most dire hours, at the height of the Shattered Age. When the crown's territory was only the city of Sodon and the surrounding area, Apolion ascended to the throne and began a campaign to not only survive the turmoil, but to retake lost lands. Through force, diplomacy, and cunning, Apolion was immensely successful in this effort, and practically singlehandedly reversed the kingdom's decline. But his reign was cut short when he was murdered by an assassin's blade on the orders of a rival kingdom.

King Arturus III: 48-0 BW (reign 17-0 BW); Father of King Percival I and the royal twins Crown Princess Roserené and Prince Davit. Leader of the armies of Lungalea in the Eastern Uprising (19-17 BW). Arturus' reign was spent trying to rebuild trust between the crown and the citizens of Lungalea following the decades-long rule of his father, Oriond V. His murder by his long-thought dead brother, Ahaax, would send the kingdom into the first war within the royal family in hundreds of years.

King Bail IV "The Burnt": 1546-1513 BW (reign 1526-1513 BW); Scholars agree Bail IV was a young and reckless king. His reign was wholly unremarkable except for the story of his death. Having always been fascinated with the power of the dragons, Bail ordered his men to capture a dragon from the Home of the Elders and bring it to him. His failed attempt to ride the dragon resulted in his untimely (and unsurprising) demise, and created a tale of hubris still told to children to this day.

Bluffit: A small, delightfully fluffy animal native to Lungalea. Bluffits use their strong hind limbs to hop along the green fields of the continent in groups of five to ten, constantly aware of any nearby predators with their large ears and excellent hearing. Because of their small size and soft fur, Bluffits have historically made charming pets for Lungalean children.

Crysnake: A long, slithering predator native to Lungalea. Specimens range from one to six feet long. Crysnakes can be spotted by their glass-like armor, which can glimmer in the sunlight at certain angles

King Dalmar "The Depraved": 1056-1020 BW (reign 1030-1020 BW); Dalmar was the last ruler from Lungalea's Second Dark Age. In keeping with the practices of the royals during that age, King Dalmar practiced magic frequently. It was Dalmar who used cursed blood magic more than any other ruler before or since. Eventually Dalmar's sadistic ways were ended by his brother, Derwin, slaying the king in noble combat and taking the crown. As a result of the "Blood King's" actions, magic has been outlawed in the kingdom ever since.

Dragon: The dragon family can be split into six separate species: Wyrms (creatures with no limbs for flight or movement), Lindwyrms (creatures with two frontal limbs for movement and none for flight), Amphipteres (creatures with two limbs for flight and none for movement), Wyverns (creatures with two limbs for flight and two hind limbs for movement, assisted by their wings (The dragon Apolion and Elder Dragon Venerus belong to this group.)), Lesser Drakes (creatures with four limbs for movement and none for flight) and Greater Drakes (creatures with four limbs for movement and two limbs for flight (The dragons Redwood and Cerulia are both Greater Drakes))*.

*It is important to note that dragons are one of the most variable species found on Lungalea. The above attributes are the most common with each category, but there has been known to be aberrations (eight winged Drakes and front limbed Wyverns, for example). As such, in this account, and in common conversation, all of these different creatures can be referred to under the common name 'Dragon'.

Griff: A large land-dwelling creature with the head and talons of a hawk and the body and speed of a common horse. Where others around the world use horses to traverse land, the people of Lungalea use griffs. Ranging in colors from gray, brown, and black, wild herds of griffs range the emerald fields of Lungalea in numbers sometimes greater than one thousand.

The Last Palace: The second grand palace the royal family of Lungalea resided in throughout its history and the last residence before the settlement of Lungala. Occupied until the end of the Second Dark Age, the palace was abandoned because of the actions of King Dalmar "the Depraved," whose dark rituals had corrupted the very ground for miles around. From this story the palace gains its name, a fitting description as well as a grim reminder.

King Maggelle I "The Founder": 2790-2723 BW (reign 2746-2723 BW); The first ruler of what would become the Kingdom of Lungalea (for over one thousand years after the founding, the kingdom bore its founder's name as simply Maggelle's Kingdom). Maggelle led the expedition from the Republic of Anian that settled the shores of Lungalea. After the republic fell and the empire rose, Maggelle severed ties across the sea, and was crowned by the people in the year 2746.

Maggelle's leadership of the humans on Lungalea allowed for him to have a direct relationship and contact with the Elder Dragons, and for centuries after him every ruler of the kingdom would be able to commune with the Elders. The paragon of rulership, Maggelle's name would be an honor among kings for the entirety of the First Age, only falling out of favor with King Maggelle IX "The Cursed".

The Old Lands Across the Sea: The collective term for the lands to the east of Lungalea across the ocean, where the original settlers of the kingdom originated from. Knowledge of the Old Lands has waxed and waned throughout Lungalean history through periods of enlightenment and darkness to the point where very little of the composition of the lands is known by the Third Dark Age and no contact is maintained across the sea.

King Oriond V "The Old": 86-17 BW (reign 80-17 BW); Father of King Arturus III and Ahaax. Oriond's first decade on the throne was governed by his Regency Council after his mother, Queen Jesamine was carried away by an outbreak of Scarlet Pox. Originally, those around him saw much hope in Oriond that he would take steps to end the current dark age. He had clearly been in love with a noble girl for his entire childhood, and observers hoped for a joyful king. Tragically, Oriond's love was taken by the same illness as his mother around the time he ascended to the throne, and the king that rose from him grew cold and hard. Oriond V's reign was one marked by whispers of unrest, whispers which would be brutally put down at first notice. Curiously, shortly after the Eastern Uprising, Oriond vanished without a trace, never to be seen again.

Recency: It is tradition in Lugalea spanning thousands of years that a king or queen must be at least sixteen years of age in order to rule. If the ruler ascends to the throne prior to this age, the realm historically has been cooperatively governed between the ruler (as far as they are capable) and a council of six lords. Usually, the prior ruler has great sway in who sits on the council, but in the case of an unplanned death of the monarch (as in the regency of King Percival) a congress of lords is held after the death of the ruler to choose who among them the six should be. Once the ruler reaches sixteen years of age, the council is automatically dissolved.

The Shattered Age: 2339-1888 BW; Caused by the death of King Maggelle IX, who had no heirs, the Shattered Age was the second age in the history of the kingdom. This was a time of full-scale war between members of the royal family fighting for the crown. To this day, scholars debate who should be called king or queen during this time due to the hundreds of claimants over the centuries. During this turmoil, many territories would break away, declaring themselves entirely independent from the kingdom and eventually starting their own houses. Other names: The Years of One Hundred Kings; The First Lungalean Dark Age.

The Third Lungalean Dark Age: ~513 BW - Present; The current age of Lungalea. Characterized by the lack of quality rulers while at the same time increasing central power within the kingdom. While some kings and queens from this time deserve praise, many tended towards despotism. This age is also characterized by the lack and censorship of knowledge, only starting to be undone by the reforms of Arturus III. The name of the age is a subject of debate, as scholars have questioned if the lack of enlightenment within the kingdom truly constitutes a Dark Age on the scale of the Second Dark

Age or the Shattered Age. While there has been relatively little conflict compared to past ages, the poor quality of leaders, lack of communication with the wider world, and complete cessation of contact with the Elder Dragons lend the name some authority.

The Thousand Isles: Contrary to its name, estimates of the number of islands within this large archipelago range anywhere from the high tens to the middle hundreds of thousands. Located across the sea to the Southwest of Lungalea, the kingdom possesses knowledge of closer and many of the large islands and their kingdoms, but much of the territory still remains clouded in mystery.

www.ingramcontent.com/pod-product-compliance
Lightning Source LLC
Chambersburg PA
CBHW070733180626
46818CB00007B/2819